Rattlesnake Ridge

a novel by

Philip Simmons

Kathryn Field, literary custodian for
Philip Simmons
74 Taylor Road
Center Sandwich, NH 03227
603-284-6335

homefarm@worldpath.net

Wasteland Press
Louisville, KY USA
www.wastelandpress.com

Rattlesnake Ridge
by Philip Simmons

First Printing – October, 2004
ISBN: 1-932852-76-X

Printed in the U.S.A.

For the People and the Land that I loved

Chapter One

1

"Do I deserve him?" asked Lily Garnett.

Kathy avoided her eyes. "That man follows you like a puppy."

Lily palmed a new head of iceberg and whacked the stem side against the cutting board to pop it open. They were making up salads in the kitchen at DooHickey's.

"Too much niceness overwhelms me," Lily said. "Not sure I can live up to it."

This time Lily caught the cross look Kathy had been trying to keep hidden.

"You're embarrassed I'm even saying this," Lily said.

"We deserve every sweet thing in this world, you want my opinion," Kathy said. "And Kyle Cooper is more than just *nice.*"

Kathy had an eye for Kyle, and Lily knew it. Poor Kath. Lily didn't understand why men didn't stick to her. She envied Kathy's blonde curls, and the way her plump curves filled out her waitress's uniform. When Kathy walked, everything bounced. She always got the better tips.

"And besides," Kathy went on, "everybody knows women are the superior species."

"Who says?"

Kathy gave her a level stare. "Look who starts wars. Look who's in jail."

"Not Kyle," Lily said.

Kathy shrugged, her back to Lily now, headed for the door. Following, salads balanced on her left arm, Lily pushed back out into the heat, smoke, and noise of a better than average lunch crowd.

Lily Garnett had once been a fair basketball player. Taking after her father, she was a tall affair of bone and leverage, with a swinging grace that suggested quick slashing moves to the basket. She walked without wiggling and never wore makeup. When he hired her, Waldheim had wondered aloud whether she would be right for DooHickey's. With her plain, angular face, her straight brown hair simply clipped behind her head, her long farmwoman's stride, she could not help but mock her uniform, the black pseudo-dirndl with gathered waist and lace-fronted bodice meant to serve up offerings to the Black Forest God of Cleavage.

DooHickey's was still basically a burger and beer joint even though Waldheim, in a bid for more tourist traffic, had dressed it up with brass and ferns and brought in a chef who added quiche to the menu. It drew mainly locals and ski bums, plus a few real estate agents with prospects they thought might go in for the local color. An electrostatic air filter crackled on the ceiling, doing little to clear the air of smoke, and less to rid the place of general end-of-the-season funk.

"Lily," said Tubbs, sitting on a stool at the end of the bar. She was on her way back from delivering the salads. "I want to go snorkeling in your panties." He smiled good-naturedly, as though

2

commenting on the weather, which in a way he was.

"I'm not wearing any," Lily said. She snatched up an empty glass and moved on. There were only a few people who seemed real to her anymore, and these she had known her whole life. Lately—sometimes she thought it was ever since Nevada—it seemed that she just couldn't connect. Even Kathy, sweet as she was, would be quietly forgotten once one of them quit and they went their separate ways. She wondered at this defect in her character, this inability to take seriously anyone not born in Shaftesbury, New Hampshire, the small town twenty miles south of here where her family had lived forever. Thirty-five years old, Lily was what New Hampshire people called "land poor." Her family had owned nearly all of Rattlesnake Ridge, and had owned it for over a century, yet Lily bagged groceries, cleaned houses, even beat out the local high school kids for babysitting. Waitressing was a step up. For the past year she had chosen to live in a sort of exile here in North Ridgeway, a town built around skiing, factory outlet stores, and their associated hedonisms. It had been a good change at first, but by now, late March, winter had gone on too long. Kyle, who did carpentry in Shaftesbury, may well have followed her around like a puppy at first, but now he seemed tired of the long drive up to see her, tired of waiting for her to decide what to do with her life. Maybe just plain tired of *her.* She stood still for a moment, something she rarely let herself do, and looked down the length of the room, seeing the tables of laminated rock maple coated in thick polyurethane, actually sawed-up hunks of the defunct Twilight Candlepin Bowling Lanes, seeing the moose head, several deer racks, and improbable trophy fish that cluttered one wall, all of them gotten mail-order, seeing the people lining the bar, clumped around tables, settled over food and drink—people somehow comfortable with the ordinary business of getting on with things. She would forget them all as easily as she would lose the three orders in her head once she took the next three.

"Throw a rope to a drowning man," Tubbs said as she passed him this time. "Drown," she said.

Back in the kitchen, she told Kathy, "My energy today, feel like I'm wading through mud." Once she would have called it an imbalance in her aura.

"You need some sun, babe," Kathy said. "Up the radiation content. We should go to Florida, soon as the season's over."

"Kyle would never go."

"Who's asking him?"

"I should be eating more vitamins," Lily said, "or seaweed."

"Ten percent of the sunlight enters directly through the skull," Kathy said.

It was during the afternoon lull that Howard showed up. Her brother lived vaguely in the West—,at the Center, mostly, and sometimes in Denver and who knows where else. He surfaced in New Hampshire every six months or so, surprising Lily always with his ability to be casually menacing. Kathy waved her over, anxious. "Go ahead and take your break. He's in the parking lot."

But then Kathy pulled her sleeve, twinkling. "He didn't say anything too outright insane right away. Sure I don't want to meet him?"

Lily groaned and pushed through the door to the kitchen, through the steam and stink, past the surly Hungarian cook doing prep for that night, and out onto the loading dock. Her brother, in full lotus, was sitting on the hood of his ancient BMW, face tilted

4

up to take the sun.

"Great rays here," he said, when he heard her steps. "I think you're on a nodal point, solar-wise. This parking lot. Fantastic."

"You managed to convince my friend you're not entirely insane," Lily said. She stepped off the loading dock into the lot and approached the BMW.

"You're asking a question do I want to get laid."

Lily stared. She had never known anyone so effortlessly insulting as her brother.

"The answer is yes," Howard said.

"Howard—" But the words stuck. She had much of her day ahead of her still—troubles to consider, hours of numbing work— but here was her brother in the middle of it like a stalled truck.

"Get to the point, is what you're saying. Just like Dad. Miss Businesslike."

Lily waved off the reference: Howard was always trying to get her to join some conspiracy of feeling against their father. It was a game she didn't want to play.

"I'm working, that's all," she said.

"I want to see my little sis. It's good to see you, Lil."

Howard removed his sunglasses and pulled out of the lotus, letting his feet dangle down against the front bumper.

"Oh, Howard," Lily sighed. Then she laughed suddenly. "It really sucks seeing you."

"Sweet," Howard said. He pushed himself off the car and stood straight, then leaned back against it. He was tall and thin, his blonde hair now sparse at the crown. He wore a down vest and jeans, but it was all too crisp and clean, Lily thought. A condescending attempt to look like the local he had managed to

5

avoid becoming. Howard had been sent away to prep school, and then a fancy college, which he never finished.

"I put in the fax machine you wanted," Howard said.

"I didn't want it," Lily said. "It was your idea."

"Maintenance guy let me in. You're all set."

"I've got no need—"

"You're on the cutting edge," Howard said. "This is 1989. The age of possibility."

"You want me to thank you," Lily said.

"Expressing appreciation of others is one of the ten habits of successful people."

"Who said I wanted to be a success?" Lily said. "I'm busy, Howard."

"Let's do business, then," Howard said. "Two items. First, mother. I told you it might be bad, and it is. Cancer. For real, this time. She wants to see you."

Lily waited until she could take a full breath. Their mother, Constance Thompson Garnett, lived at the Center for the Study of the Cosmic Order, a religious commune in eastern Nevada, where Lily herself had lived for several years, until her disaster there ten years ago. She had not seen her mother since.

"What do you mean, 'this time'?" she asked. "Have there been others?"

"As it turns out, who knows," Howard said. "The potentials are always there. A matter of the right lines of force converging."

"Why should I go?" Lily knew she was asking the question of herself. "She asked for you, Lil." Howard's voice softened. "She sent me." He sounded as if he knew he had scored a point.

"What do the doctors—I assume she's seen a real doctor?"

6

"Took her to Salt Lake. Do Mormons count? Virile oncologists, deep-chested nurses, everyone in white robes. Electronics, lab work, pathology, computer printouts. She hated it. Breast cancer. I could fax you copies of all that stuff." When Lily thought of cancer, she had always thought of finding an ant mound in the backyard: you kick your toe into the spongy ground and find a hidden frenzy, a dark turmoil of replication branching into the unseen earth.

"Has it spread?"

"They don't think so. Not yet."

"What else did you want to see me about?" she asked.

"You'll come?"

"I'll think about it."

"Terrific, Lil. Pleased, I really am. Item two: I want to let you in on some of the things I'm doing."

Lily groaned, walked away, walked back. "No, Howard."

"Lily, I'm your brother, and you'll listen to me."

Lily was amazed that Howard continued to want to involve her in his schemes.

"Another deal of the century?" she asked.

"You're more or less on target," Howard said.

"You don't need me," Lily said.

"If you're not in on it, it doesn't count somehow," Howard said. "Like the old days."

Lily knew he meant it. It was endearing, really, and a little sad, how he clung to her still. And she had to admit she still felt a big sister's urge to look out for him.

"You want to show your sister your slimy pet snake," Lily said.

"Not slimy at all, as you well know. Dry and cool. Hold them at the throat, pleasant how they wrap around your forearm."

Lily couldn't hold back a laugh. "Howard, is it possible that you're a stranger person than I am?"

Howard laughed warmly. "We please each other."

"The sick part is, you're right."

Howard now drew himself up, serious. "Lily, I have to tell you, there are certain things have been set in motion, some of them with consequences for both of us."

"There will be people getting in touch with me," Lily said.

"More or less. Not people, as such."

"Please," Lily said. "Not this Fax Man crap."

"He's an electromagnetic presence," Howard said. "Part of the global consciousness."

"Didn't you tell me you had met him?"

"I was in a room once and he was strongly rumored to be there."

"In corporeal form?"

"As far as that goes, yes. It's like the wave-particle duality. For certain purposes it's convenient to think of him as occupying a body."

"Spare me."

"Your negativity only weighs you down, Lil. Be light. All I can say for now is that certain information will be coming your way. Certain energies are enfolding into configured systems. Structure and function. All you have to do is pounce. Balance your checkbook. Be ready."

Lily turned to go, striding firmly back toward the loading dock. She would have liked to believe that her brother was enough of an incompetent to be harmless, but experience had proved otherwise. There had been money borrowed and never repaid, a car borrowed and destroyed. For a while now he had had some vague involvement in real estate out west, the latest in a series of largely imaginary careers. It was never clear, from Howard's telling, whether he had actually done a thing or merely thought about doing it, talked about it to so many people that the imagined deed had taken on a palpable life.

She heard Howard call out behind her: "Patience is not a Garnett virtue."

"Neither is communication," Lily said, turning. She looked at her brother across ten yards of asphalt scummed with dumpster spillage, fragrant now in the year's first warm sun. "You want me to listen, you're going to have to tell me what this deal is about."

Howard grinned and crossed his arms tightly over his chest.

"I relent," he said. "I'll tell you."

Lily stood with hands on hips, seeing for the first time her brother's nervousness, his smile tight across his teeth.

"It's about the land," Howard said.

Lily waited, sure now that she was looking at the clean-shaven face of doom.

"It's an evolving concept," Howard said. "But Mom wants to develop."

"I don't believe you," Lily said, though she could easily believe him.

The Garnett family holdings swept up from the shore of Abenaki Lake to the crest of Rattlesnake Ridge, nearly three thousand acres in all. And Garnetts didn't sell. They didn't develop. All of her life Lily had accepted these facts as what went

9

without saying, part of what it meant to be who she was: the descendant of men and women who had muscled a town out of the wilderness in the time of King George III, people hard-bitten and shrewd (her mother's people, Thompsons, had come over from Maine in the 1830s and had all been lawyers) who had lost everything and then bought it back and held on while those around them failed and died and moved away.

But at her parents' divorce several years ago the land had been divided, with a sizable chunk going to Lily's mother (who had inherited the Thompson legal talent) and a hundred acres apiece going to Lily and Howard. The unthinkable had become possible.

"Mom is dying, Lil. She's learning to surrender control."

"To you? That's even harder to believe."

Howard's jaw tightened, and for a moment she saw her little brother again, fists balled, face flushed, victim of some childhood taunt.

"You find it difficult to take me seriously, I know. As a man of substance. All you have to do is talk to her."

"I'm not sure there's much point," Lily said.

Howard was taunting her back, knowing that Lily had refused all of his previous offers to mediate between her and their mother. The events of ten years ago—Johnny Ray's murder and the awful aftermath—had opened a breach, and her mother's further retreat into mysticism had widened it. More recently, when Constance sold the Thompson farm out from under Lily, the break had been complete. "Ask yourself this," Howard said. "What are you building? Where are you headed with this?" His palms-up gesture took it all in: her silly uniform, the loading dock, the salt-stained cars in the lot. It was a question her father might ask.

"Nowhere," Lily said, smiling weakly. "I'm just trying to 'Be Here, Now.'" She was thinking of her father now, knowing that this was just the sort of response to infuriate him. Forrest Garnett, after all, had a Ph.D. and had spent most of his life finding ways to avoid living in Shaftesbury—lately he had been living in St. Louis, where he did consulting work. Years ago, Lily had refused his offer to send her to college, and he had never really forgiven her for it.

Howard spoke carefully now: "I'm working with Lawrence Mongerson."

Lily shook her head. The name recalled little: bright eyes, a blonde beard?

"From the Center?" she asked.

"Your friend and mine," Howard said.

Mongerson: the echo of a voice, a hungry presence. Had he been attracted to her? Was he the one always hanging around? Lily shook off the memory, as she had shaken off all memories of that place for years now.

"Just tell me what I have to do to stop you," she said.

Howard smiled, showed her the palms of his hands. "No details yet," he said. "Stay tuned."

Lily was moving again. She went up the concrete steps of the loading dock before turning at the door.

"Don't get Kyle caught up in your schemes."

Howard raised an eyebrow, doing his imitation, she knew, of a genteel detective they had watched as kids on one of those TV shows from England.

"And of what use, madam, could he possibly be to me?"

After Howard's visit Lily had to sit for ten minutes in the women's room, breathing through what in her Nevada days she

11

would have called her heart chakra, until she was steady enough to balance a tray. It was going to be a long night.

Later on, the bartender had the music up loud to make the place seem more crowded than it was. The ski patrol guys were playing foosball, with another eight or ten onlookers cheering viciously at every goal. Lily, taking a breather by the kitchen door, didn't want to look over there, at the four players hunched over the table, wrists and elbows jerking, but she could not escape, even above the booming of the music, the repeated thwack of the ball being struck by the feet of tiny plastic men. Their fierce attention frightened her. It was the sort of group energy that could, with a slight shift of focus, hoist a woman onto a pool table and pin her there, like they did to that woman down in Fall River.

Were women better?

And then the thought returned to her, the one that had embarrassed Kathy earlier: "Why would Kyle put up with me?"

"Lily," said Tubbs. "What I want to know is, do you sweat?"

"Die, Tubbs," Lily said.

"This is a waitress talking."

"Pay your tab," Lily said. "Then die."

"Someone who relies on tips."

The foosball crowd roared for a goal.

"Slowly, painfully, and alone," Lily said.

Kyle Cooper climbed the stairs of Lily's apartment building, his boots shunk-shunking up the bare concrete steps, his heavy hand slapping the metal rail with a dull thwang. He would ask her tonight, no matter what. There were not many men tall enough to suit her. He was strong and good natured. He had no credit card debt. He believed in the Golden Mean. She had told him he had great buns.

Kyle heaved his way through the fire door into the hallway, where the taped seams of sheetrock walls showed through the one coat of paint, the fluorescent lights made him look paler than he was, and under the thin carpet the plywood flooring trampolined beneath his weight. The whole building was designed to last exactly nineteen years before crumpling like wet cardboard. He always felt vaguely criminal just coming in here. It was the kind of place you saw on the TV news: the reporter pointing to a bloodstain and then getting some neighbor to say, "We thought he was such a normal person." Kyle had seen people move in and out. Every few months a different version of the same bleary-eyed, chain-smoking woman in sweat pants would haul boxes out of a rust-eaten car and then a few months later lug the same boxes out to the car and drive off to do it all over again someplace else. Or that professor down the hall, what's-his-name Bernie, with his twenty-year-old VW squareback with the Greenpeace and Vote McGovern bumper stickers, his futon, his baseball card collection. Taught courses about witch doctors, Lily said. Offered to put her in some kind of trance. Or that skinny guy who moved in downstairs with nothing but two televisions, three rifles, and a case of beer. When he left he owed rent and had pissed on the rug. Lily deserved better than this.

Kyle, a carpenter, was not poor, but planned to do better. He owned a scuffed-up rabbit hutch of a house in the Shaftesbury village center, but had recently bought eight acres in the part of town known as Upper Corner, where he hoped someday to build something halfway decent, something post-and-beamish, the oak-floored cherry-trimmed center-chimneyed south-facing salt box of his dreams. And Lily Garnett was the woman he wanted to do this with.

The hallway seemed scaled for humans slightly smaller than Kyle. It made him walk with shoulders rolled in and forward even more than usual, a gait that he had always hoped would make him less imposing. In tight hallways like this, Kyle couldn't help fearing that some poor birdlike woman, small and alone, would back out of her apartment door, twist the key in her lock, turn to look over nervously hunched shoulders and, seeing him, scream. It had happened to him more than once, and above all the other more complex embarrassments and hurts he had ever suffered, he feared most this instinctive quailing, this stark moment in which a fellow human being saw his shape and recognized, at some cellular level, the hulked menace of a predator. The fear of such moments made him shy in the ways that big men often are: he kept close to walls, spoke softly, avoided strangers' eyes, left one or two empty urinals between himself and the next man in the men's room, never spoke to a woman unless she had spoken first. And all this, he knew, only made him appear more furtive and criminal. He admired, in the way one might admire what other species do—the razzle-dazzle monkeys perform in trees, say, or the bright arc of a dolphin's leap—he admired those men who arrived at each scene of their lives like movie stars at a debut, springing from the limo tuxedoed and tanned, one arm clutching a bejeweled fiancée, the other raised to the admiring throng, striding up the red carpet in the floodlights as though toward grace itself, toward the final glittering hoo-hah of destiny.

Still, he was steady and sincere. He knew all the square dance moves: balance and swing, ladies' chain, grand right and left. When he and Lily were kids, they both had made the eccentric choice of George as their favorite Beatle. He had had to know, once and for god-dammed all, just where they stood.

She would not be home until late that night. He had her spare key. There was too much play in the dead bolt, and the frame was flimsy. One kick and the whole thing shatters. Kyle thought for an instant of going down to his truck for his tools, but screw it, that was the maintenance guy's job. Kyle had seen him around—wet-look hair, ropey forearms, jailhouse tattoos—and had already asked him twice to get on it, each time getting a shrug, a smirk, a nod. Screw it.

Kyle pushed into Lily's apartment and flinched at the cold inside. Below freezing out, and she had forgotten to close a window, unusual for her. Or was this the start of some new attitude? He snapped on the light, moved quickly across the room to shut the window, but was pulled up by a new presence on the kitchen table: a fax machine, plugged in, green light lit. What was Lily doing with a fax machine? He moved over to the window and shut it tight.

Only a couple of Kyle's wealthiest clients—guys who couldn't

15

stand not working every minute—had fax machines in their houses. Kyle rubbed his face, then stood blinking, trying to bring the green light into focus. He had worked hard that day. All he had wanted was to shower, eat something, snooze until Lily got home, then ask her to be his wife. Simple as that. But now, this. Timing was everything, right?

Kyle had just started to remove his shirt when the phone rang. Does a fax machine ring? He fumbled amid the mess of magazines on the coffee table, hoping, unreasonably, that it might be Lily. She never called from work.

"That you, Kyle?"

Kyle recognized the voice of Shaftesbury's one police officer.

"Adam." Adam and Kyle had known each other since childhood.

"Listen. Have Lily call me. It's important."

"You want her to call, you better tell me what it is."

"You her secretary?"

"I think I'm doing you a favor."

"Somebody's done surveying work on Rattlesnake Ridge. Howard's land, I think. Her mother's too. Bud Grisham was back there and saw it. Thought she ought to know."

Kyle sucked in his breath, thinking: Howard's making his move.

"I'll tell her," he said evenly. "But why am I hearing about this from an officer of the law?"

"Now, Kyle, I'm not sure I could tell you that."

It had always been hard for Kyle to take Adam's law enforcement career seriously. He wasn't sure Adam did himself. Adam had an office adjacent to the fire station, but much of the

16

time his cruiser could be seen parked at his own house, where he and his wife, Marilyn, managed the affairs of three hundred chickens, a half-dozen Herefords, and two wise-aleck sons. Adam kept a radio and scanner in his kitchen, and was available if anybody needed help. Shaftesbury was a town of eight hundred year-round residents plus a couple thousand summer people. It had one blinking light and one general store, which was owned by Adam's brother. No one seemed to expect Adam to treat police work as a full-time job.

"You don't know or you just aren't telling?" Kyle asked.

"Why don't you leave that to me," Adam said. "But you can bet that Bud wants this checked out. So does Orville Rogers."

For different reasons, Kyle could have said. Bud Grisham, in addition to being a selectman and therefore Adam's boss, was the town's biggest real estate broker and developer. Everyone knew he had been eager to sink his talons into Rattlesnake Ridge for years. Bud's fellow selectman, Orville Rogers, was the anti-development head of the planning board, and Bud's nemesis.

"You seen Howard?" Adam said. "Got to ask him some questions."

Kyle glanced at the fax machine across the room. Could it be Howard who had put it there?

"I didn't even know that Howard was around," he said.

"Don't worry, I'll track him down," said Adam. I ought to talk to Lily's mother, too."

"Good luck," Kyle said. "She's still living on that commune. Talks to the angels. Lily hasn't heard from her in years."

Kyle listened to Adam's breathing. He knew Adam wanted to talk, despite also wanting to sound like the professional cop.

17

"Jeez, Louise," Adam said. "I hate to see this happen."

The Garnetts' property on Rattlesnake Ridge abutted the national forest. Local people had for so long hiked its trails, fished its streams, and hunted the deer and black bear that lived in its woods, that they thought of Rattlesnake Ridge as public domain, and rightfully theirs. They were wrong. The land represented the largest privately held undeveloped property this far south in New England. What was more, it included most of the remaining undeveloped shoreline on Abenaki Lake, an eight-mile-long stretch of emerald clear water in the heart of the state's tourist region.

"I don't want to see Lily's face when she hears about it," Kyle said.

After Kyle hung up he stared at the phone, and once more tried to rub the fatigue from his face. Adam Townsend. In high school Kyle would ride in the back seat of a Chevy that seemed the size of a barn, choking down gulps from the pint of whisky Adam and his friends would pass back from the front seat. Sometimes Kyle felt that they were all still kids, just pretending to be grown-ups. Doing a pretty bad job of it.

But then Kyle looked down at his hands, the skin there thickened and rough, one thumbnail split. Not kids any longer. A day with the nail gun had left his right hand tingly, unable to make a fist. Kyle fumbled with the buttons on his shirt, thinking, as he did too often, of arthritis and old age. Good work for a young man, in the open air. But how much farther toward forty would he want to go framing houses in the cold? A few years ago he had tried to move indoors, doing cabinets, setting up his own shop in a rented barn. But the end-of-the-eighties slowdown had pulled him outdoors again, blasting nails into studs with the air gun, or pounding them home with the twenty-ounce hammer. Nobody was buying custom cabinets now.

Later, in the shower, the apartment having warmed some, he twisted the Massage-O-Matic shower head until it shot fine needles into his neck, so sharp they numbed the skin. He hugged his shoulders and felt the hot water sluice down his chest.

Would she marry him? He had no crippling deformities. He had no ex-wives. He drank in moderation. They both liked anything with Robert DeNiro in it. And yet the question wearied him. He had already asked her to marry him three times.

He was pretty sure she liked his body. This involved liking a lot of hair. Hair sprouted exuberantly from the tops of his toes, armored his shins like greaves. A thick midline rope rose from his pubic hair to the mat that covered his belly and chest. As he passed thirty the mat had spread over his shoulders, where now he wore the tufted epaulets of some savage foreign legion. Shirtless he was a curiosity to young children at the beach. Had he not shaved, sometimes twice a day, the hair would have swept up over his Adam's apple, scaled the chin, stormed the face and crowded his eyes. His eyebrows bushed out from his forehead and swooped off to the sides like on the *Thor* comic book version of Norse gods. She found him crushingly handsome. She nestled in the thatch on his chest like a burrowing animal. He was quiet and neat. He did not run up large phone bills. They liked their Chinese food spicy. She liked to take the full weight of his body on hers.

Much as he hated himself for even thinking about it, he knew that whoever married Lily Garnett would be marrying Rattlesnake Ridge. Not sure the land was worth the trouble. But had the land been Kyle's, he would already be living on it. He even knew the spot: a place Lily and Howard called "the clearing," a meadow on a level shelf just beneath the last ascent to the ridgetop. As a home site, his own eight acres couldn't hold a candle to it. The clearing was on Lily's land—or what had been her land since her parents' divorce. There was a good spring for water if you couldn't drill into the ledge, and you could clear for a stunning view of Abenaki Lake. But Lily couldn't seem to bear the idea of touching the clearing, though she talked often enough about wanting to live there. Kyle and Lily had even fooled around up there once, marking out with sticks where the house should go.

Kyle crouched down—he had to in order to tilt his face up into the shower's spray. As though trying to drive all thoughts of land from his mind, he let the hot water beat his brow It was not land Kyle wanted, but Lily: her swinging limbs, her faceted beauty, her sweetly sorrowing soul. Showered and changed, Kyle came out of the bedroom to see the green eye of the fax machine. And now there was a red one, too, flashing. Flipping on the light, Kyle saw that paper had curled out of the top of the machine. A message.

> Facsimile for Lily Garnett
> From: Center for the Study of the Cosmic Order
> Basin and Range Biosphere, Nevada
> Dear Lily,
> Forgive the expedient of this mechanism. Or don't bother: one must move beyond the need for forgiveness. I have resolved, recently, to stop waiting for eternal life. We are living in eternity already, right now.
> In the sixties today, cold at night. The sky is blue, plain blue.

Love,
Your mother

Kyle tore the paper from the machine and carried it across the room to the sofa, where he sank heavily in, staring at these words fresh from creaking, twittering space, thinking: this ruined it, for sure. He could not ask her tonight.

At the end of the night, having dished out barrels of beer nuts, hauled tubs of empties and trays of fresh ones, served her last Dooburger with fries and her last baked potato with cream cheese and artificial bacon bits, zapped her last plate of nachos in the microwave, having swabbed and upended the chairs on the table tops so the kitchen boys could vacuum, Lily was finally out of there, past the reeking dumpster into the blue mercury vapor light of the parking lot, scuffing the unmentionable scum from the bottom of her shoes, so that she appeared to be trying to ski cross-country across the asphalt to the battered Subaru station wagon waiting ugly and familiar at the far edge of the lot.

"Night," called Kathy, from her car door, too tired even to wave.

"Night," Lily said, not caring whether she had made herself heard. The lanky dishwasher boy sat in his break chair on the loading dock, smoking, watching the women get into their cars. Probably rubbing up a hard-on beneath his filthy apron, Lily thought. The kind of boy who would do it with sheep.

She drove through the deserted center of North Ridgeway, then turned off Route 35 toward the mountain. Her building was part of a new development called Village Square, consisting of shops arranged around an arid space complete with fountain (dry now) and bandstand gazebo (silent), with apartments on the second floors. Conceived at the start of the 1980s real estate boom, the place had a theatrical feel, like the set for a ghost town in the year 2020. The shops had never filled, because few shoppers wanted to drive in this far off the main strip. The walkways were done in brick that had already heaved with the first March thaw. Lily got her apartment cheap because the management was desperate. Most of the units on her floor were vacant; the owners had set lights in them on timers.

Kyle hated Village Square for its tacky design and cheap construction, but Lily herself loved it. It was the only brand new place she had ever lived: clean sheetrock walls, shiny hinges on the doors, an exhaust fan over the stove, lights you could flick on with a switch instead of staggering into a dark room like the Mummy swiping the air for the pull string. Since her mother sold the Thompson farm, Lily had rented places in Shaftesbury: trailers, spare rooms in stuffy attics, moldy cabins, once a hayloft in a barn. This was the first time in her life she had lived in a place that was all straight lines and right angles, where the upper sashes on the double hung windows hadn't been painted shut for a hundred years.

But she could also appreciate Kyle's feelings about the place. It was so tacky and new that it seemed barely real. Looking through his eyes, she could imagine one day stepping into her apartment and forward into white space, an absolute void. If she screamed, no one would hear.

Except Bernie, the shaman down the hall. Funky Bernie. "Bald as a baby's ass by the time I was thirty-five," he told her. Said he'd like to take her on a shamanic journey sometime. She had to admit that his hairlessness intrigued her.

She pulled into the nearly empty lot and parked next to Kyle's truck. He would be asleep on the couch. They had been going out for two years, and the man still would not get into her bed without being explicitly invited. A grown man who would turn off the light before undressing, less out of modesty than from a quaint sense of politeness. Strong as a horse, though. And she needed him there tonight. What gnawed at her, the rat in the grain bin in the back storeroom of her mind, was that he might not be there some night. Strong, faithful Kyle. To imagine him leaving her was to imagine a complete reversal of his character, yet it was exactly the sort of thing she did too often: see the devil peering through an angel's mask.

"All our repressed thoughts, fears, feelings," Ananda had written, "what psychoanalysts call the unconscious, all this manifests as radiation." Maybe, Lily thought. All that stuff had made sense to her once. She had spent her first three years at the Center listening to the tapes of Ananda's lectures from the '50s, practicing yoga and meditation, tuning herself to the Mind Plane. Nowadays she still found herself breathing an occasional "Om" to steady her nerves, but she couldn't work up the enthusiasm for anything more rigorous. If she took karate, and enjoyed it, it was not for the spiritual angle but because she liked to punch and yell.

When Lily pushed open her apartment door, the light from the hall was enough for her to sense Kyle's slumbering mass on the sofa, and in the same moment to register, in the instant before she flipped on the light, a green light gleaming at her from across the room, together with a smell: that odor of electrically charged air — was it ozone? In the dark she now approached the fax machine. She leaned forward, sniffing, hands held back as though it would bite.

Kyle stirred on the sofa. "It was already here when I got in tonight," he said. "You didn't see them do it?" Lily asked.

24

"Who's them?"

"I don't know, I just figure Howard couldn't manage on his own."

"He come see you?" Kyle asked.

"Oh, shit-shit-shit." Lily walked a quick, tight circle in her kitchenette, eyes glancing about, finding only clutter: the morning's dishes, unread mail. "He's gone mental. Absolutely, this time."

Kyle sat up on the sofa, rubbing his face. "Who in your family hasn't."

"Shut up," she said. "You eat anything?"

"Can't remember. What is that thing, anyway. Some promotion?"

"A confusion of levels," Lily said. "My brother thinks enlightenment is a matter of getting the right hardware."

"Lily." Kyle sat with shoulders slumped, the unhappy bearer of bad news. "You better call Adam Townsend tomorrow."

"Tell me my dump sticker's expired," Lily said.

"Says there's been surveying done on Howard's land. Your mother's land, too. Lines have been flagged." Lily forced herself to take a breath, let it out. "We're remaining calm, right?" she said. She looked at Kyle, at his open and honest face. How long would he put up with her?

"No reason to get lathered," Kyle said. "Could be anything."

"Exactly the problem," Lily said. "Howard found me at work. Said Mom wanted to develop." Lily opened the refrigerator and stared into it, an activity that always gave her odd comfort, as though in the glow of that chilled space she could find whatever the day had torn from her grasp. "He also said they've confirmed the cancer."

"You think you should go out there?"

"No. I don't know. Let's not talk about it."

She extracted a yogurt and let the refrigerator door swing shut.

"They've already done the surveying?" she said.

"Yup. Adam said Bud Grisham wanted to get to the bottom of it. Orville Rogers, too." "Kyle. This has not been a good day."

"Come here," he said.

Lily sat down beside him, swung her legs up on the sofa and leaned back against him. She let him knead her shoulders, his strong hands feeling for the knots in tired muscles. When they first started going out, this delicate attention to anatomy had surprised her. Kyle seemed able to see, with his fingertips, the entire structure of muscle, cartilage, ligament, bone. She closed her eyes as he worked with his thumbs, up from the shoulder blades on either side of the spine. Lily moaned softly, and her shoulders dropped an inch.

"God," she said.

"Goddess," he said.

"What's Adam got to do with this?"

"I guess he's working for Bud," Kyle said. "Or who knows, maybe Orville's sniffing around for some way he can stick his thumb in there, slow things up. They could be jerking Adam around every which way."

Bud Grisham had spent the last forty years buying up old farms, splitting them into smaller parcels, selling some to summer people up from Massachusetts, keeping some for himself. In this way he had come to own land throughout Shaftesbury, nearly seven thousand acres, in all. The only man who could match him was Lily's father, and he had never sold anything except timber cut

26

from the land. Orville Rogers had started the town's planning board mainly to bumfoozle Bud's development schemes.

"Bud Grisham always tells me he'll buy that land if I ever need to sell it."

"You're not selling, are you?" Kyle asked.

Lily would have turned her head and given him a dirty look, but she wanted to let him keep his hands on her back. "What does Bud want to do with it?" Kyle asked.

"Bud's an ass and always has been," Lily said.

"Probably put in condos."

"Illusions of grandeur."

"Cut ski trails, put in a lodge" Kyle said.

Lily put her hands over her ears, and said loudly: "It's just woods, anybody can see that."

"An RV park with roadside snack bar and a gift shop that sells those balsam-needle pillows and rubber tomahawks."

"Eeee!" Lily turned to put a hand over Kyle's mouth, but he twisted out of reach.

"A marina on the lake, with an airport runway and a cable car to a ridgetop conference center."

Lily was nearly shouting, trying to drown him out: "It's mosquito infested, hardscrabble, swamp maple and hemlock—"

"And it's yours," Kyle said.

"And it's mine."

They were suddenly quiet.

"And you're a Garnett."

"Known for stubbornness," Lily said.

Kyle reached around and cupped her breasts in his hands.

"It's three in the morning," Lily said.

27

"Night time is the right time."

Lily twisted away, out of his grasp. She looked at Kyle wildly.

"That fax machine. It's not yours?" she said. "I mean I know it's not yours, but somehow I was hoping it was."

"Howard left a window open."

"He's been here. The jerk came into my apartment!"

"To give you a fax machine. You've been reverse-burgled."

"Can I call the police?"

"On your own brother? If it will make you feel better, I'll kick his butt for you."

"No you won't, Kyle. You never do."

They both stared at the fax machine.

"Has it, you know, transmitted anything?" Lily asked.

Kyle picked up the fax, which he had folded and placed in a back pants pocket. "I wasn't sure I should show you," he said. "On top of everything else."

Lily scanned the words hurriedly, then again more slowly.

And now Kyle Cooper, arms aching from the work of a long day, with another due to begin in four hours, could only look at this woman whose inward gaze seemed to glide darkly away from him. He watched her lips form one silent and astonished syllable:

"Mom."

Kyle thought: they begin life as their mother's daughters, and they're bound to end that way, too.

He would ask her to marry him. Tomorrow.

Lily woke late the next morning knowing that before she ate breakfast, before anything, she would drive down to Shaftesbury to check on the land. Kyle had already left for work, and Lily was on her way out the door when the phone rang. It was Adam Townsend.

"I've already heard," Lily said. "I'm coming down."

"Good, I'll meet you."

"Were you invited?"

"Do I have to be?" Adam said. "I'll be at the Weed homestead."

An hour later, Lily drove in through Lakeside Farm, where her Uncle Clarence and Aunt Sylvia lived. The 200-acre farm, which occupied the eastern end of the Garnett land, included the entrance to the Old High Road, the only access to the property. The ridge ran east to west, with the national forest starting at the ridgeline and going north from there, and the Garnetts owning the whole southern slope, right down to the lake. Leaving Lakeside Farm, the Old High Road passed through her father's land first, then Lily's, then Howard's, dead-ending at Constance's land at its westernmost end.

Lily drove past Uncle Clarence's barn and parked at the gate where the Old High Road began. Adam's cruiser was already there, along with Orville Rogers's rust-eaten Jeep. Stepping out of her car, standing once more on the land, with the forest's cool winter breath on her face, she felt calm and sure, no matter who or what was waiting to meet her. With an old sense of relief she could never quite name, Lily slipped past the gate, down the hill, and into the woods.

Rattlesnake Ridge had no rattlesnakes, and the Old High Road was actually quite low. Whereas crops had failed in Shaftesbury's stubborn soil, fear and fantasy had always thrived, and were recorded in its place names. The early settler startled by a milk snake wanted to believe this wilderness even more perilous than it actually was. The builders of the "Old High Road," Weeds, Beans, and Foggs among them, wanted to believe that the road's gentle upward course from the shore of Abenaki Lake along the bottom of this narrow valley reached some grander end than the swamp where the road in fact dwindled to a path and sank. After a hundred years of striving, the owners of a dozen farms along its length had abandoned them and given them back to forest. Only the stone walls lining both sides marked the road's former importance. Now it was used mostly by skiers and snowmobilers in winter, hikers and berry-pickers in summer, and every few years Lily's father hired one of his poorer cousins to bring a logging truck and skidder in for timber.

Legends clung to Rattlesnake Ridge, however, and even more firmly lodged in the local mind than the idea of rattlesnakes was the story that grizzly bear bones could be found there. Lily's grandfather claimed to have heard it in his youth from an old Indian trapper who said the bones were there if you knew where to look. Lily had done a report on it once in high school. Grizzly bones, she learned, had been found in Canada as far east as Labrador. The story may have been a shred of Indian ancestral memory from the time when grizzlies really did roam these woods, a millennium or more ago. Now it was nothing more than a good story for scaring children around a campfire. One of the reasons Lily could be so at home in these woods was that even the biggest local black bears, unlike the far more dangerous grizzlies, would run at the sight of her.

Lily crunched through snow that was ankle deep and crusty beneath the recent dusting that had thrown a fresh white coverlet over the litter of needles, twigs, and late winter grit. This was only March, two months before you would see any new green. Deeper in the woods, you would still punch through drifts to your knees. It was maple sugaring time, freezing nights and warmer days, and the old road's median humped high with the heave and thaw. Pebbles pushed to the surface, and in the mossy patches where the sun struck through the forest, the pebbles were pocketed by air where ice had melted away around them. It had warmed overnight, and with the temperature in the low forties, the snow glistened, slick and stained with mud where it had been trampled in recent days. The surveyors had been in here, and Bud and Adam and Orville and more, too, from the looks of it.

The road crossed and re-crossed a small stream that in summer light was brown and golden, but now was at most a gray trickle bubbling beneath a flume of ice. In the 1940s, in a fit of improving spirit, Lily's father and grandfather had laid in some new metal culverts, but these had all filled in or washed out, and the road was now slashed through by the stream so that Lily stepped gingerly across ice or jumped where the ice looked thin. The old culverts from the road's founding were granite slabs set on stones to sluice the water beneath, and some of these remained. Great hemlocks followed the course of the stream bed, their shallow roots drawn to the damper earth. For Lily, walking on the land had

31

always been a form of thought, and today she found herself thinking again about all that her return to Shaftesbury ten years ago had marked the end of. Just out of high school in the summer of 1971, Lily had skipped out on her father's plans to send her to college, and instead had driven her Volvo station wagon to the West Coast. When she looked back, it was hard to believe she had ever had the nerve to do such a thing. She had been driving since she was 15, had an athlete's confidence, and could handle cars, trucks, and tractors with equal skill. But to strike out across the country, sleeping in rest stops and campgrounds on a foam pad in the back of her car with the doors locked—you could blame it on the '60s, even though in Shaftesbury the '60s was mainly something you watched on TV. Better to call it youthful stupidity. She had been seeking, she supposed, some species of the Sublime not available in New England, and reaching the Pacific, she thought she had found it. At first she did little but walk the beaches drunk on sun and light and air, staggered by the brimming weight of blue, rocked by the heave and curl and crash of waves, startled by shorebirds. She smoked pot and marveled at God's colors: seaweed's sudden green, the raw white of a bleached shell, a crab's pale pink.

Lily remembered stopping at a seaside fish place near Malibu, talking with her father on the outdoor pay phone at the edge of the gravel parking lot. Cars with surfboards on their roofs, ferociously tanned people eating fried fish on paper plates at redwood picnic tables, seawind whipping the salt grass, hurling road dust, in the distance the thump of surf. Falling on everything was a plenitude of California sun that would have seemed to her father (the hill-shadowed, leaf-shaded, Calvinist New Englander) a kind of indecency, exposing all the world's filth to light and air, but which to Lily descended as a form of grace she had never imagined. Raised on guarded joys and complicated weather, Lily eventually came to understand those vacant and endless and too-ready California smiles as expressing the only kind of selfhood possible under such simple skies: open, exfoliated, laid bare. It was a state she doubted she could ever attain.

"You sleep in that car?" Her father's voice slid down the wires from a hollow old room in the Thompson farmhouse. "In the open?"

"It has curtains," Lily said. "I made them. Calico."

"You could have a decent dormitory bed."

"I might as well be in a convent."

"That, too, can be arranged."

"I need some time to find the real Lily, Dad."

"When you do, tell her I said hello."

Then she met a guy named Johnny Ray Bushman on the Santa Monica Pier, and he brought her to a Grateful Dead concert in San Francisco, and soon she sold her car and moved into Johnny's van, traveling up and down the coast from Mendocino to L.A. while Johnny sold dope to his many acquaintances.

She remembered Johnny Ray cross-legged in the back of the van, after midnight, counting cash by candlelight on a wrinkled paisley bedspread. He wore a sleeveless T-shirt, muscles rippling in his long, graceful arms. Lily lounged on a foam mattress, propped on one elbow. They were parked behind a friend's apartment in Santa Cruz, having spent the evening making the rounds, Johnny's purple and pink van rolling through the streets from one party to the next like the doper's version of the ice cream truck, blowing

33

Grateful Dead out the windows. Lily learned that for all his hip ways, his hustler's charm, even his understated macho swagger, he was at bottom a polite, middle-class kid born John Raymond Bushman and raised in the better suburbs of Chicago, with a few semesters of college credits and every intention, so he said, of going back to finish the degree.

"What will you study?" Lily asked.

"Botany," he told her. "Plant science. Work on better strains of marijuana. By the time they legalize it, bingo. I'm there. I'm positioned."

"My dad wants me to learn Greek and Latin," she told him.

He looked at her thoughtfully, the skin of his face golden in candlelight.

"Could be useful," he said. "*Alma mater. Ipso facto.*"

"Dead people speak Latin," Lily said. "And priests."

"Cogito ergo sum."

"How do you do it?" Lily asked, seeing then in his playful expression all that seemed denied to her own cramped and needful self.

"What?"

"Have such *fun* with everything?"

For it *was* fun, those days. Until he started going away for days at a time to "business meetings" with people he would never identify or describe to her. Lily, sensing danger, pleaded that they split the coast and find something better, something cleaner (and by this time she must have been thinking, without knowing she was thinking it, about the granite knobs and wind-stunted spruce of Rattlesnake Ridge). He agreed, but not before scoring one last big deal, the sort of deal, apparently, that required that the people he saw at his business meetings not be able to find him. Not knowing that it was already too late, Lily thought they had reached safety when they traveled to eastern Nevada and found their way to the Center.

The Center for the Study of the Cosmic Order was housed in a collection of dusty wooden farm buildings and battered house trailers nestled at the foot of Small's Peak. This was the wide open basin and range country of sagebrush and dust, a land of jackrabbits and coyotes and rattlesnakes and antelope, a few cattle and fewer people. The commune had been founded in the 1950s by Henry Crandall, the son of a Methodist minister from Kansas. Crandall had studied through the '30s and '40s with an Indian yogi who gave Crandall the name "Ananda," Sanskrit for "bliss." Ananda eventually moved with his own disciples to Nevada, where he died in 1970, before Lily got there. A couple dozen of his students still carried on with his teachings, a blend of Christian and Hindu mysticism with cross-references to modern psychology, quantum physics, and the semantic theory of Count Alfred Korzybski. Ananda had been charismatic and a genuine mystic, and as far as Lily could gather, he had also been a decent and straightforward man. His remaining students included a former schoolteacher from Chicago, a California poet, a man who used to train dolphins and killer whales, ex–ranch hands and short order cooks, carpenters and reformed thieves, waitresses and a former symphony conductor, housewives whose kids had grown, retired widowers who had arrived by Winnebago and never left. They grew their own food, raised livestock, and held down jobs in the local community, their more esoteric spiritual practices brought firmly to earth by the business of slaughtering chickens and shelling

35

peas.

"Did you ever feel, growing up, that you were destined for greatness?" Johnny Ray had once asked Lily.

They walked in the evening's first cool, the sun gone behind the Baker Range at their backs, walking away from the farm down the gravel road sloping gently toward alfalfa fields that were fenced against sagebrush in the broad valley bottom.

"It wasn't a phrase we used," Lily said.

"In my family," Johnny said, "it went without saying. Of course, for my father, greatness meant heading domestic sales for a pharmaceutical company."

Lily thought then of Rattlesnake Ridge, of her entire patrimony of swamp and ledge, wooded acres threaded with stone walls, so many feet of Abenaki shoreline.

"For me," she said, "it just meant holding on to what you have, trying not to shrink."

"What is it for you, now?" he asked.

"This," Lily said, turning to hold him, pulling his hips against hers. "And this," she said, pointing to their two hearts. "And this," she said, drawing an imaginary line from the top of her head to the heavens.

"Yes," he said. "Yes. Me, too."

What would later hurt Lily the most was to think of how in those last few years at the Center Johnny Ray really had changed, how the swagger had been refined out of him, how the sweetness rose in him like cream, how they had both started behaving like grown-ups, how in the end she was convinced that he had been saved. After five years, during which time her mother came and settled in there, too, Lily felt it was safe to get pregnant. Three months later, she got a call from the coroner in Ely, asking her to look at a man with a tag on his toe and say his name.

Lily chunked her feet hard into the snow, took in a sharp breath of cold March air, weary now of the memory. She stared hard at the big sugar maples along the stone wall—she had always thought of them as fat ladies—and wrenched her soul back into place, this place, her place. She tried to imagine this land 130 years ago: the fields cleared from wall to wall, a few cattle and sheep grazing among the stumps and rocks, standing hay in that field, corn in the next, a landscape created in the image of an England left behind a hundred years earlier and remembered only in the blood. But Lily's attention would not hold, and she found herself seizing on one more memory, hoping perhaps foolishly that it would blot out the others.

It had been one of the last good times, and it always came to her with a smell: the sweet and acrid spice of burning sage, mingled with dust suspended in dry heat. They drove overland in the truck, she and the man who liked to hear his entire name read out to him like a guitar riff: Johnny Ray Bushman. They picked their way up a dry wash and then found the canyon road, little more than two wheel ruts sometimes gone entirely under sage, sage that was gray green and then white with the sun's glare, that scraped beneath the floorboards and got snagged and burned on the exhaust manifold, the fumes filling the cab. She wondered how the fumes might affect the baby, then just two months in her belly. Three miles in, after a hairpin ascent up the side of the sun-bleached canyon to the ridge, they emerged parched and blinking into an ocean of air stretching eighty miles into blue haze. The road then followed the ridge up to where it met the shoulder of Lion's Peak, and there a

37

spring fluoresced from the hillside, the still pool blanketed with bright green algae and fringed with grass and muck amid all that dry gray and brown. There was an abandoned trailer there, small and bean-shaped, its sides battered and blackened by fire. Lily climbed out of the truck, with the smoke of burning sage still rising from beneath it, and shook her head to clear it of sage and sun and dust. Johnny had a blanket and a knapsack and led her to the shade beside the trailer, where they sipped water from a plastic jug and ate apricots picked that morning in the Center's orchard. When Lily felt the last tremors from the truck ride leave her body, and a light breeze lifted the hair on her arm, she raised her sundress up over her hips and lay back, pulling him toward her.

To her surprise, being pregnant had made sex easier for Lily, and she found herself wanting it more, maybe just wanting the reassurance of his body, his weight, his fullness inside her, the salt of his skin, his breath in her ear. Wanting him never to go away. These days she often came before he did, and when she did, as now, liked to roll on top of him and ride his hips, lifting herself up on her arms to watch his back arch, his throat pulse, his eyelids flutter. Until she could not help but arch her own back and raise her head and find herself poised for one sure moment at the ridge's crest before lifting her wings to take the air, rising up on a gust, and up again, and up, and up, and up, and then she was gone into the gray and dull green of sage, into the ocher and sienna of those canyons and farther, to where the land flattens and the river widens and meanders toward some distant green before its silt muddies a blue bay.

Normally the turnoff for the Weed homestead was visible only to the practiced eye. Like many of the old roads lacing these woods, it was thoroughly grown over, appearing as two wheel ruts separated by a humped median. Now a single set of footprints marked the way. A dozen yards in along the turnoff, the first thing that would have greeted any visitor coming in from the road was the tiny graveyard, with its low enclosure of lichen-mottled stones. A white wooden sign, placed there by Orville Rogers a few years back during his grave census project, said Weed Cemetery.

Up the slope two dozen yards was the cellar hole where the house had once stood. She had come to this place many times as a girl, not knowing that it would one day be hers, but as any child will to a haunted place. She had sifted the mound of pulverized brick in the center, where the chimney had stood, and found porcelain shards with hints of blue pattern set off against the clean white of the broken edge, bits of blue glass, and once, a thimble, which her mother had accepted with grim thanks.

And now, standing stiff-backed on what had been the doorstep of that ill-fated house was a man Lily Garnett did not particularly want to see: Adam Townsend.

Five years ago, just before the intermission at an amateur performance of *Oklahoma* in the Grange Hall, she had walked over the creaking floor to the coatroom, hoping to sneak out unnoticed. Rustling among the coats for her parka, she felt him move in behind her. Coffee, after shave, sweat. A whisper: help you find something? His trousers rubbed against her backside. A finger grazed her jaw. Whisper: my pretty Lily. She gave him an elbow in the gut, surprised at how soft he was there. It was hard to hurt a man with a paunch like that, but she staggered him back a step and pushed past him out the door. Five years ago like yesterday. They had hardly spoken since.

He took a few steps down the slope to meet her as she marched up. Barrel-chested and broad-backed, Adam Townsend looked every bit the lumberman he would still be had not his knees given out on him and Bud Grisham gotten him the police job. Though he was not yet forty, his gimpy knees added an exaggerated dip to his step, and an old problem with his back made him appear always on the verge of turning to speak to someone over his left shoulder. He walked with arms hanging slightly out from his body, backs of the wrists forward, a man accustomed to heavy lifting. He was bare-headed, without gloves, his heavy coat unzipped.

Seeing him come toward her, Lily squeezed her fists tight in her coat pockets. This was her land. One wrong move and she would punch him in the throat.

"You wanted to talk to me," Lily said.

"I hope you don't mind," Adam said.

"I'll tell you in a few minutes."

Lily was surprised to see that Adam was nervous. He couldn't quite meet her eye. Lily moved past him, walking up the last few yards to the granite doorstep of the old Weed place. She stood on the doorstep and looked down at him.

"Where's Orville?" Lily asked. "I saw his Jeep."

"Must be further in, where they're doing the work," Adam said. "He didn't tell me he'd be in here."

"Why did you ask me to meet you here instead of where they're working?" Howard's land, where the surveying was being done, didn't start for another several hundred yards up the road. Lily was eager to have a look.

Adam gave a shy smile. "Just like this spot," he said. This part of the property had been in Adam's family once. He and the

40

Weeds were related. "Sentimental, I guess."

He walked up to stand beside her on the doorstep. They stood with the cellar hole behind them and looked down through the lines of maples, which were black against the snow, and the paler beeches in tight gray skin clinging to their tawny leaves, down the gentle slope to where you could make out the low wall of the burial ground.

Lily sighed, felt her shoulders relax. She couldn't help but feel better out here.

"I like it too," she said. "Sad, though."

Lily could just make out the two familiar old graves, the stones cracked and tipping, the inscriptions weathered, barely legible, lichen on them like mold. They had set them within sight of the door. The two stones were for Sarah and Lucas Weed, aged one and four years, dead three weeks apart in that hard winter of 1850. Within sight of the house they had chopped two holes in the frozen earth and laid their children in. Adam's great-great-grandfather's brother's children. The next spring the family was gone, as were fifty others that year, lured west by railroads and stories of black topsoil yards deep in lands newly cleared of the Indian menace. Within sight of the door. Grief crazed, perhaps, or driven by some Puritanical urge for mortification, or just too damn cold that February to work any further from the house—though she figured the graves were dug first, the wall added later, after the thaw. Weeds.

"What's going on, Adam?"

Adam's laugh was short and too loud in the still woods. "That's what you're supposed to tell *me*."

"Like I'm supposed to know."

"You get any offers on this land?"

"What does it matter?" Lily said. "I'm not interested."

"You ever been approached by anybody from an outfit, the Mongerson Corporation?"

Lawrence Mongerson. Blond hair, bright eyes. So now he was a corporation. Lily realized she didn't feel like telling Adam all she knew.

"Why do I get the feeling that you're out of line here?" Lily asked.

"Let me judge that."

"Has there been some crime committed?" Adam dug at the ground with the toe of his boot.

"I hope not," he said quietly. "We just want to check things out, is all."

"We?" Lily said. "You mean Bud Grisham. You're here scouting real estate."

Adam looked at her levelly now, a slight flush coming to his face.

"There's a lot of people in this town would want to be sure things were handled right here," Adam said.

"Including you," Lily said.

"Have to admit," Adam said, "I take a personal interest."

Lily stalked down the slope toward the graveyard, heels chunking in the hard snow. Adam waited a moment, then followed after, thinking: the barest touch. Of this much he was guilty. The downy hairs on her nape. He could have nibbled her ear.

Adam's footsteps behind her sounded halting, almost delicate. Maybe he was trying to be polite, now, she thought, trying to keep down the jangling of all those cop things he insisted, ridiculously, on wearing out here in the woods: nightstick, keys, cuffs, gun, who knows whatelse. Her elbow sinking into his gut, which looked like those giant bladder balls they used to play games with in gym. No end to his softness, no way in to the hard place where she could hurt him.

Lily passed through the gap in the enclosure and stood in the center of the graveyard, which was no more than fifteen feet on a side. Adam remained outside; they stood with the low stone wall between them.

"You hear from your mom at all?" he asked. "At the holidays, maybe?"

"They have different holidays where she is," Lily said, looking down, without seeing, at the two old gravestones. She was thinking about the fax she had gotten last night, and about her mother's health. None of it was Adam's business.

"She's taken a different path, for sure," he said. "You know I always liked her, though. A different kind of woman. I can respect that."

"Not your type," Lily said.

Adam snorted a laugh. "No, not my type. Her own type all by herself."

Lily shuffled her feet in the snow. She hadn't worn her warmest boots.

"Are we done now?"

"I thought I knew you, Lily. You were always a nice enough girl. Ever since you came back from that—your little escapade out there—" Adam faltered. He knew what had happened to her out west. Everyone in town did. "You don't have to be so hard."

"Nice doesn't pay the bills," Lily said.

"I'm just saying you don't have to take such an attitude," he said.

"And you don't have to give me lessons in deportment."

Adam hung his head a moment. "Maybe I deserve that," he said quietly.

If this was a bid for sympathy, Lily wasn't selling.

"I'm going up the road," she said, stepping quickly out of the graveyard and down the path to the Old High Road. Adam followed, again a few steps behind. Lily didn't wait for him to catch up, but walked on at her own rapid pace. She was long-legged, and had developed in childhood the habit of extending her stride. Hiking, most people had trouble keeping up. It wasn't long before she knew she had him winded. She heard his breath behind her, the cop gear on his belt making a racket like he was walking in armor.

It was not until she saw the first orange flags that Adam tried again to speak.

"Lily. What I was. Going to. Say."

Double strips of orange surveyor's tape hung from a branch to mark the corner, with a metal pipe driven into the ground and spray painted day-glo.

"That time in the Grange," Adam said.

Lily stood at the corner and sighted up the boundary line between her and her brother's land, the line cleared of brush and running due north. Surveyors had hung strips of orange tape at intervals of thirty feet or so, the bright flags oddly festive in the dull winter woods. Lily charged up the line, boots sinking into deeper snow. She was aware of Adam behind her, that he was trying to say something, but she had other concerns now. The line ran up the hill, an obscenity, a challenge to her blood.

"I just wanted to say."

And then she saw him. "Jesus," Adam said behind her.

Green wool pants, plaid wool jacket. It was Orville Rogers.

"Jesus," said Lily. He lay face down, head uphill, showing them the lug soles of his boots. One arm folded awkwardly beneath his chest. Lily was about to bend down, thinking heart attack, thinking stroke, when Adam said "Don't." Orville's glasses lay beside him in the snow., his hunter's cap was on sideways, his face in the snow was fishbelly white. He had fallen and then not moved.

"Let me," Adam said, pushing past her now, his bulk suddenly efficient, the things on his belt suddenly *tools*, necessary as the hammer and tape measure, screwdriver and nails that Kyle strapped on every day.

"Let me check," Adam said, and somehow it had taken both of them that long to see the wine-spill on the snow, the sticky stain drying in the rough-napped wool in the center of his back, and the glistening hole at the base of his skull.

"Jesus," Adam said, already reaching for his radio. "Jesus H. Christ."

From the second story they were framing, Kyle looked down on the yard with its neat stacks of plywood and two-by stock under lumber tarps. Off to one side lay a tangle of warped reject studs from a bad shipment, and a pile of unusable scrap, and beyond that, at the edges of the work site, the mounds of earth covered with dirty snow heaped along the ragged fringe of trees. Order and disorder held in precarious balance, the way they were on any job. Part of the pleasure of building was to work the raw edge of that line, the sawdust blown free in the wind, the sawn board in your hand. Seeing Howard's BMW scoot up the rough drive, he knew the scales had just tipped toward chaos. Howard hailed him from the window of the car, so that Kyle had to leave off nailing in that window header and climb down to put his hand in Howard's bony but surprisingly strong grip.

Howard was out of the car by then. In open-necked dress shirt, clean down vest, and jeans, he stood smiling by the side of the venerable 2002, always in Kyle's eyes the excessively cheerful, confident college man.

"Positively elemental," Howard said. He waved a hand to include the yard, the men perched and banging on the skeleton of a house. "Dirt, rocks, wood, nails. Positively chthonic. You could build planets."

"We use synthetics now," Kyle said.

Howard had the annoying habit of smiling as though whatever nonsense you had just spoken was exactly what he wanted to hear.

"I know," he said. "Plastics, microporous membranes, polymer resins, photoduplicated woodgrain. Fantastic. The world is becoming all Mind."

"You still in Nevada?"

"I'm here and there. We're all mobile, uplink and down. Flexible grid. Fax Man is everywhere these days. It's liberating, really, not having to think about physical location. Big projects in the works, money-wise. Major impact. Things you can see and feel. We're global now."

Howard had never been exactly balanced. Kyle had been best friends with him in grade school and junior high, but then Howard had left for Exeter and then Williams, drifting in and out of school, studying Asian religions, music, painting, finally leaving without a degree. With all his advantages and fancy schooling, Howard had made a career out of explaining his life.

"Sorry to hear about your mom."

Howard gave a nod of thanks. "How's Lily, mood-wise?"

"Not sure you want to know."

"She's too touchy, Kyle."

"Why didn't you tell her you had already started surveying?"

Howard's face lost its focus, as though he were waiting to hear instructions through an earpiece. "I may have forgotten to mention it," he said weakly.

"You expected us not to know?" Kyle said.

"Have to admit," Howard said, recovering. "The small town factor. Working out west you forget. Wide open spaces and all that. Dense auric fields here, incredible."

"We talk," Kyle said. "We carry tin cans attached with string."

"Yes," Howard said, smiling, nodding again. "The web of

47

communal life. Outstanding."

Kyle gave Howard a long look. As always when he had not seen Howard for months, he couldn't help but thicken Howard's hair, make him the small and lithe golden boy he had been, balancing on a tree limb, swinging on a rope, then pitching into the emerald waters of Abenaki Lake, rising sleek as an otter, eyes bright, spitting a shining arc. He had trouble fitting this image to the faded figure before him, a man who somehow did not quite fill his own shape, smudged around the edges like someone recovering from a long illness.

"How long are you back for?" Kyle asked.

Howard laughed at this joke they had between them. It was the question always posed to the scattered sons and daughters of Shaftesbury. You might have been away skinning polar bears, ruining the economy of a small Third World country, in jail for bigamy. But all the local mind cared to know was whether you had come back to stay.

"I refuse to regard you as a provincial," Howard said.

"Why fight it?" Kyle said.

Kyle's parents, though not natives, had come to Shaftesbury when Kyle was a toddler; both were schoolteachers and college educated. But after finishing at Abenaki High, Kyle had done two years at UNH and then come home to work in the trades.

"Mr. Carpenter," Howard said. "Is there much work?" Howard pretended to be looking over the house they were working on.

Not especially caring for Howard's tone, Kyle didn't bother answering. To him at this moment the half-finished frame rising above them seemed stunningly beautiful, the stud walls golden and delicate as lace, portioning out blue sky. He felt lucky, and eager to be balanced once more high in the light and air, a hammer in his hand. "You're busy, I see," Howard said. Then he jumped back in his car and cranked the engine, his movements angular and quirky as a puppet's.

"Oh, and Kyle?" Howard poked his head out of the window and spoke over the engine noise. "Like, the real point to my seeing you? Mongerson. Don't miss him. A friend of mine, bought Jackson Island, wants to build a house. Fantastic opportunity. Keep your answering machine in good working order."

He was off before Kyle could ask for an explanation. Jumpy, Kyle thought. Even considering that business about the land, he seemed more revved than usual. Cocaine? Kyle watched Howard's car pull away down the rough dirt drive, thinking: No, it's just Howard.

Once sure she was out of sight, Lily slowed her pace, crying freely now. It did not come in sobs but in a steady leaking of tears, so that she kept her head up, watching in fascination, in some separate part of her mind, the blurring of black tree limbs etched against the pale sky, like ink lines bleeding into wet paper. With an effort of will, she relaxed her fists in her coat pockets. Now drained of adrenaline, Lily could almost consider curling up at the base of some tree, on a south-facing hummock where the snow had burned off and left dark green moss papered over with dry leaves. She would pull her knees toward her chest and sleep in a decades-long enchantment. A child's fantasy, she knew. But what was this land if not some quality of mind beyond reason, all figment and fancy, hoary chimera and sweet illusion, a way of inventing a world? What Adam Townsend and the others could not understand was that none of this, the depredations of surveyors hacking sight lines, leaving their bright orange flags, even the horrible dream logic of Orville Rogers' body thrown down as a sort of boundary marker, none of it surprised her. She had not asked for this land, and now it was giving her answers for which she didn't know the questions. Her brother had told her things had been set in motion. It seemed that poor Orville had gotten in the way. But something was missing here. She knew that her brother could be callous, unscrupulous, even cruel. But she had to believe he would stop short of murder.

The way now was muddy, the snow slick where it had been trampled, ruts churned by the parade of four-wheel drive vehicles that had passed this way. They had arrived with sirens and lights as if to scare off bogeymen: Pinkham County Sheriff down from Ridgeway, state police major crimes unit up from Concord, and that muscle-bound Lieutenant Campo from Troop N. Men bright-eyed with adrenaline trying hard not to show their excitement, their glee, even. Like this made their decade. Shaftesbury's first homicide, or so they seemed to be calling it. Poor Orville: childless, the last of his line. Rogerses from Shaftesbury had fought in the Revolutionary War. In the 1830s there had been over forty Rogers households in East Shaftesbury. They were known to shout from one homestead to the next, relaying messages over miles.

Campo had taken Lily aside for questioning, writing her answers on a small pad he produced from his belt, concentrating as he wrote like a schoolkid practicing his letters. Campo: bullet head, a linebacker's build. He had come into DooHickey's, liked his burgers tough as hockey pucks. Gave her a long roadside lecture once after stopping her for speeding. Dragging it out. She figured any chance he could get to stand with a woman's head around waist level.

Before long Bud Grisham, all six feet, eight inches of him, came striding up, voice booming, bald head gleaming above the proceedings like a mountaintop observatory. He looked bad, though, ashen. His rival dead there in the snow. State cops hauled him off to the side, getting his take on things.

They strung that yellow tape everywhere, and some guy counting footprints was yelling for everybody to keep away. No use: they had already swarmed that body as if it were a fumble on a football field, drawn by the glamour of the freshly dead. What good did they think they could do? Some shaved-necked kid measured the thickness of trees. A man took pictures with a Nikon, crouching for the best angles, a comic book rolled up in his back pocket. The county coroner got down on his knees and felt Orville's head, wiping at the wound with a rag. Orville Rogers's face squinched tight as if to say leave me alone. A half-dozen men worked over the area with rakes. What good did they think?

Orville Rogers was a man Lily had known not well, but well enough, familiar as a kind of weather. He had taught her Sunday school class one year. A pinched but kindly face, steel-rimmed spectacles, hair gone white at the temples. He raised rotweilers, built elaborate bird houses, sang tenor in town musicals. Now he lay in gritty late-winter snow while men wrote numbers on clipboards. Somebody shoveled dirt into a sieve, scraping frozen chunks against a screen, building a cone of clean earth.

Tiptoeing to the edge of this scene came Uncle Clarence and Aunt Sylvia. They looked for a moment like children lost in the forest in a fairy tale who had come upon some awful enchantment, and their faded and rumpled clothing seemed out of place amid all those dark uniforms and sleek machines. Sylvia in her old wool coat and sensible boots, silver hair wrapped in a scarf, put an arm around Lily and held the scene in stern regard, disapproving aloud of the mess. She wanted to walk Lily out of there, but Lily didn't want to go, feeling somehow that she should wait until they removed Orville's body.

At last she realized that her waiting would do Orville no good, either. But she insisted on walking out alone, leaving Sylvia there with Clarence, leaving them all to their business. She made her way back the mile and a half through to her car with everyone still in there behind her, radios and voices filling the woods with a sort of tropical noise, all squawk and crackle and hoot.

Lily was glad to reach the end of the road: her feet were cold, and digging her keys out of her pants pocket, she realized how cold her hands had become, too. By the time she reached home, all she could think of was a shower and bed, and she wondered if she were coming down with a fever. She called in sick to work, stood beneath hot water until her skin felt like boiled rubber, then slid between her sheets into dreamless sleep. She woke knowing only that it was dark outside and that the phone was ringing by the bed.

"People in town have always said you had so much potential," Bud Grisham was saying. "You should look to your opportunities."

Lily held the receiver away from her ear. Bud often spoke as though shouting down hecklers.

"Next time you see them," Lily said, "tell the people 'thanks.'"

Bud Grisham was a man for whom total baldness had been a spectacular success. Even hearing him on the phone, it was hard not to picture him striding powerfully across a landscape he was destined to buy and sell at profit, his gleaming summit making him seem like Real Estate itself, a moving mountain. It seemed the only significant property in town he had never profited from was Rattlesnake Ridge.

"Terrible, of course. Terrible, terrible thing. People don't realize that Orville and I were friends, spite of everything. You know a man your whole life...." His voice trailed off. Coming from Bud, this was more sentiment than Lily could bear. Then, as if cheering himself up, he said: "They'll catch the one that did it."

"I'm not sure I find that comforting," Lily said.

53

"Depending on who it is, you mean."

"Not exactly," Lily said.

"You're a hard one to figure, Lily Garnett. Not much different from your father, I suppose. Confess I've never made head nor tails out of any of you people."

"Maybe being understood is less important than being left alone," she said.

"That's just it," Bud said, raising his voice another notch. "You think you can just sit on that land and the world won't move on around you. Now look at what's happened."

"Are you suggesting that I or my father had anything to do with what happened to Orville?"

"Now don't get ahead of yourself, Lily."

"You son of a bitch."

"You can choose to misunderstand me. I guess that's your right."

Lily listened to Bud breathe into the phone.

"Lily, there's a time to be pragmatic. You know I'd hate almost as much as you to see that property get into the wrong hands."

"And whose do you consider the right hands?" she said.

She could sense Bud pausing for effect.

"You know this fellow Mongerson has bought Jackson Island."

This brought Lily a slight shock. Jackson was an undeveloped island in Abenaki Lake, visible from her land. She had often canoed there for blueberries as a kid, and later, when she was a junior in high school, had lost her virginity there to Frank Creed, who wore leather and had his own motorboat.

54

"Howard says that you know him," Bud said.

"I don't," Lily said. "Hardly." Bright eyes. And now more: his hand on her belly, his voice in her ear.

"Lily, all I can say, I'm here to help. Should the situation change there, should you ever want to sell, that offer I made you still stands."

"I don't like you, Bud."

"I'm sorry. And if you ever need me, I'll forget you said that."

Lily sat upright, hugging her gooseflesh. The clock read 8:13. It was cold in the room. She wondered where Kyle was.

Mongerson. She remembered now. He had stopped her once, on the porch of the Big House as she was leaving dinner. It was after Johnny Ray's death, and she was alone, as she remembered herself being much of that time, despite others' efforts to comfort her. It was late summer dusk, and from the porch you could look east down the gentle slope of the yard past the pickup trucks parked by the barns, beyond the road and out into the flat of the valley, where irrigated alfalfa fields bloomed an unnatural green amid the sagebrush and dust stretching twenty miles to where the next range rose jagged against indigo sky. She remembered his look as he ascended the porch steps: frank, friendly, gentle. On the porch, they had stood for a moment to watch the swallows dive for insects out over the yard. Then he placed his hand on her belly.

"You should have this baby," he told her, close to her ear.

She stood feeling the warmth of his hand, caught for a long moment in the thrall of the possibility that his touch seemed to create, a warmth against the coming cool of evening.

After Johnny Ray's death the thickening in her belly, the swelling of her breasts seemed only further proof that her life had

55

spun out of control. She began to talk of an abortion, which angered her mother. Then came the horror of the miscarriage, and the debacle was complete. The next few months were mainly a blank, a black well. Lily could vaguely remember long fruitless talks with the police about Johnny Ray's murder. Most clearly she remembered feeling that her mother blamed her for losing the baby.

There were two women in her mother: the dour New Hampshire farm woman with her face set grim against hardship and happiness alike; and the new woman who had come out of hiding in recent years, impulsively loving, yet changeable, childish and needy, woozily mystical, always worrying the rosary beads she had reclaimed from her childhood Catholicism. She had been at the Center for three years by then, and had let her hair grow out, a thick mane still black except for a bold streak of white that began above the right forehead and tapered back like an arrow or a root. It was this streak of white that represented, to Lily the new mother emerging from the old.

But when Lily lost the baby, Constance had withdrawn into her old New Hampshire coldness even as she nursed Lily to health. Lily could remember her mother standing in the doorway of the small room to which Lily had moved after Johnny Ray's death. Sheets taut over the single bed, the wooden desk with its straight-backed chair. Bare walls. A single bulb in the ceiling. The crucifix on the wall above the bed, a gift from her mother. With her hair pulled severely back, her face pale and drawn, her body slack beneath a loose cotton dress, Lily had found her convent, after all

"You didn't want me to have it, anyway," she said.

"That's not true." Her mother's dark hair hung stiffly to her shoulders, the shock of white like a reproach. Hands folded carefully before her.

"You didn't want me to have his child."

Constance had never really trusted Johnny Ray.

"He didn't have anything to do with how I felt."

Lily's short laugh. "Exactly what I mean. You never even factored him in."

"There are more important things in this world than men."

"You can say that, now. You've had your children."

Her mother's set face and her solid stance bespoke a stoicism so thorough as to seem a form of smugness, making Lily want to throw herself against it, to hurt her somehow.

"Think of Mary, the Virgin," her mother said. "'Let it be done to me according to thy will.' You've got to hand yourself over."

"She got to keep *her* baby," Lily said.

"Yes," her mother said, retreating into the hallway. "But she lost him, later." She made the sign of the cross and then closed the door.

After a few months, feeling stronger, Lily had decided it was time to return to Shaftesbury. By then she and her mother were barely speaking. Lily dressed and brewed a pot of chamomile tea. She took it with her out of the kitchenette, putting as much distance as she could between herself and the fax machine that still squatted on the table. She curled into her one comfortable chair, a crackling wicker monster she had rescued from her mother, who had slated it for the dump. Settling into its cushions, she could feel that it was always summer and she was on the screen porch of the Thompson farmhouse, with its afternoon breezes and view of the Pequawket Mountains. She leaned her head against the chair back

57

and looked up at her dusty and neglected Swedish ivy in the window. It had burned and shed leaves on the floor. Rather than get up to water it, she stretched out her legs to rest her heels on the slippery mound of unread magazines that covered the wobbly coffee table. If the pile slumped to the right, it might knock that old teacup, perhaps still half full, to the floor. If she married Kyle, would she have to clean house? The idea of being someone's *wife* seemed absurd to her, like an archaic disease, quinsy or rickets. Even now, as much as she wanted him there, she resented the urge to forgo her tea and instead rise to the business of tidying the place up for when Kyle got home.

If this *was* a home. When she returned to Shaftesbury, it had been to the Thompson farm, the only real home she had ever known, where Lily, her mother, and her mother's father had all been raised. The place had been vacant since her mother had gone to Nevada, and Lily had set to work putting it in order. For four years she had painted and cleaned, kept the fields mowed and the stone walls clear of brush. Then the legal tussle of her parents' divorce began, and its finish allowed Lily's mother to do the unthinkable: sell the great rambling white clapboard house and its sagging barns, disused chicken coop, fields littered with rusting cultivators and hay rakes, sell all of it and two hundred acres of wooded land to Bud Grisham.

She couldn't afford to keep it, was all she said to Lily: in any discussion of money or property Constance reverted to her most Yankee and tight-lipped self. And Forrest Garnett, who lived in St. Louis by then, could have had no interest in keeping it. After all, he had shown little interest in living there with his wife during their marriage. So that Lily could do nothing but stand by bewildered at her mother's plans to sell off all the old furniture in a farm auction that even now, five years later, caused the local antique dealers to greet Lily with an awkward pity. Lily had attended the sale, and with most of the three hundred dollars that then constituted her total savings, managed to rescue one piece: the giant wicker chair in which she had spent her best and dreamiest girlhood hours.

Sitting in that chair now, she brought the cup to her lips and sipped delicately, easing the hot tea over her tongue. She understood, of course, that her mother had reasons beside money to sell the place. It housed too many unhappy memories. Within two years of her marriage, Constance had returned from Boston to the Thompson farm to care for her ailing mother, the two women alone in the old house with crumbling horsehair plaster and mice scrabbling in the walls, cold water hand-pumped at the sink and the two-hole privy leaning off the back of the el. Forrest stayed in Boston to continue his career, becoming from then on a weekend husband and father.

Constance, still young, married but childless and alone, had been consoled by her mother (so she had told Lily once, years later, at the Center): "He'll give you children, you'll see. He'll want someone to give all that land to."

He did give her children, those weekend visits proving to be enough for the purpose. But he stuck to his rigid schedule even after the children were born, so that throughout Lily's childhood her father appeared in her life with the regularity and inscrutability of a celestial body. He arrived each Friday night at nine o'clock and departed after Sunday dinner for the drive back south. For most of Lily and Howard's early childhood, this was somehow enough: they adored him. When he came for his annual two-week vacation in

August, he would take the whole family to the Garnett fishing camp on Abenaki Lake, where they had no electricity, cooked on a woodstove, and hand-pumped water from a well There Lily's mother labored to keep them alive while Forrest, when he wasn't sitting on the porch, staring at the lake with a drink in his hand, took Lily and Howard for hikes or fishing for sleepy late-summer bass or simply to poke around the property.

In her mind's eye they were always hunched over something—Lily, Howard, and her father—in the yard, bent over some tiny thing held in her father's hand, while from inside the house came the dull gong of a soup pot being set down on the stove, the sturdy whack-whack of a cleaver on the cutting board. Lily could see herself out there, brow furled with concentration, and Howard, poor Howard even more susceptible to their father's magic than she, openmouthed with awe. Her father would have picked up any small ordinary thing—an earthworm glistening as it stretched and writhed and shed dirt crumbs, a maple seed with its archangel's wings, ovoid deer dung—he would pick it up and display it against the clear blank of his palm.

It was perhaps his celestial distance itself, his quality of being almost always not there, and when he was there of being always about to leave, it was this that allowed him to do his magic. Whatever familiar unremarked piece of the universe he laid a hand on was held up suddenly aglow in all its wonder: look at this pellet, he would say, the fibers there like whiskers, that's cellulose from the grass it's eaten; look at the veins in the seed's wings, how when held to the light, they're thin enough to see through; see how the worm has parts, how this band is pink like a baby's foot, this band purple like your lips when you've swum too long. Look, he would say:

look. Just look.

Lily sipped her tea with her customary care. She had always been especially sensitive to heat and cold. As a girl she dropped ice cubes in soup, had trouble eating Popsicles.

But neither of her parents knew the range of Lily's sensitivities. One summer when she was ten years old, dangling her legs over the edge of this same chair, rhythmically kicking her heels, she learned to bring herself to a kind of awareness in which physical objects acquired a soft glow, were revealed as buzzing hives of light. For a few extraordinary weeks that summer she walked in a blue aura that needled her skin and made her hair stand on end. She was able, with the same trick of concentration that allows children to fly in dreams, to pass her hand through a chair, a tree, and once, through another's body, as though through a swarm of bees. She told this to no one, and soon after, she took ill and found that when her fever broke the light had gone. When puberty came the following year, she grew embarrassed by the memory of those discoveries, learned to distrust it, and finally lost it altogether. It was not until years later, when she traveled to the Center, that the memory returned to her with the dim ache of a lost dream.

In a way, her years at the Center had been an effort to understand what had happened to her during those three weeks in 1964. In one of his taped lectures, Ananda had dismissed such phenomena as "carnival tricks," distractions from the true work of enlightenment. Lily was both saddened and relieved to hear it. She spent the hours before dawn in meditation, fighting sleep and boredom and pain in her knees. She learned to bring the earth's cleansing energy up through her chakras, one by one. She learned to project a cone of white light from the crown of her head toward

61

the rest of the cosmos. Often she found her way to a deep, restful calm, less often to a state of ecstatic, eyeball-jiggling bliss, but she had been able to reproduce that state in which objects and other beings were revealed as buzzing hives of light.

The tea did its work, and Lily felt the light tremors of her body easing toward rest. Relaxed now, breathing deeply, she could even look at the green eye of the fax machine across the room without feeling a thrill of alarm. She felt the return of her fondness for her brother's follies. It was that residual affection, she knew, that all along had kept her from turning the machine off. Family are the people you allow to drive you crazy.

7

The next morning, Adam Townsend woke in the dim light
before dawn. He had always kept a farmer's hours because he liked
to be the first one up and out in the quiet, but this morning he lay
in bed longer than usual, clutching the scraps of a pleasant dream,
and also wary of waking too fully, sensing the nearness of some
memory it would be best to avoid. In the gray light the room held a
stillness he had always liked. Things that wearied him in stronger
light—the clutter atop the bureau, the heap of yesterday's clothes
on the floor, the closet door that sagged on its hinges and wouldn't
close—all now seemed softened, their edges not so sharply defined,
full of promise, even. Adam closed his eyes again, took his half-
erect penis in hand, and found those wisps of dream: tangled hair,
soft pale flesh, an invitation. The rest eluded him. He opened his
eyes. Marilyn lay on her side, facing away from him. Looking at
the dark tangle of her hair now wisped with gray, her solid trunk
rising with each breath, the majestic mound of her hip, Adam felt
that momentary and casual awe experienced by men whose wives
outweigh them. Glad of her bulk, her warm weight, anchored by
her flesh, he felt the urge now to nestle in behind her and return to
sleep. But as quickly as the urge came, it faded, for like a muscle
cramping the memory of Orville returned: face drained and
blotched, squinched tight as though expecting a blow.

That image had been with him since yesterday, and Adam was
surprised at how badly it had gotten to him. As if he didn't know
the look of the dead. Adam now sat up and rubbed his face. He
sat on the edge of the bed in his flannel pajamas, his feet cold on

the bare wood floor. Through the window he could see a three-acre field he had let go, now filling with juniper, birch, and poplar. As if he didn't know. Because even in Shaftesbury police work wasn't all traffic and beach parking and helping old Mrs. Grimsby find her car keys. He'd had his unattended deaths, his accidents, but it hadn't seemed to matter yesterday. Everyone had been there—Campo, Major Crimes up from Concord—and Adam had been pushed aside, let stand off to watch like some kid. Campo did his best to ignore him. No one cared that his ancestors had once owned that land, that he'd walked the whole area a hundred times. Or that he knew someone was going to have to track down Peregrine Weed.

Adam rose, scuffled his feet into worn slippers, pulled on a robe, visited the toilet, then made his way as quietly as he could down the creaking stairs to the kitchen. He turned up the volume on the scanner and listened to bursts of static as he made coffee. Like some kid. He knew there had been talk in town of getting somebody new, somebody with the computer skills, more training. A cop for the future. He knew Campo had said things about him. As if he didn't know his way around a dead man.

Police work was changing. He had flown to Las Vegas for seminars. It was all public relations now. Lots of meet and greet. The state had sent him a kit to take into the schools: he had to stand in front of a bunch of fidgety fifth graders and tell them the difference between amphetamines and barbiturates. LSD, cocaine, PCP. He burned a little marijuana so they'd know the smell. Should kids really be learning this stuff? He covered the basics okay: traffic violations and DWI's. He handled the paper work, made his court appearances. Twice a year he drove to a target range down at the academy and fired a few hundred rounds with his Smith and Wesson nine millimeter. But the town wanted him to do bicycle safety. He got flyers for courses, some of them sent by way of Orville Rogers, with titles circled in pencil. Ritualistic Crimes, Defensive Tactics, Hostage Negotiation. *Hostage Negotiation?* In Shaftesbury? It was Orville, in fact, who had wanted to send him down to Georgia for the Death Investigation course, and Adam hadn't wanted to go. Now here was Orville laid out on ice, as if to say OK, go ahead and investigate.

Poor Orville. Maybe it was just as well for Adam to have the whole thing taken off his hands. Maybe he was in over his head. But it was the presumption that rankled him. The presumption that he'd be of no use. As if he didn't know.

Adam heard the oil burner kick in and knew he should get the fire going in the stove. But it seemed that all he could do was watch coffee dribble into the pot and think of all those others. He had found them stinking in overheated trailers. Houses were too far apart here for anyone to notice the smell. Mailboxes were at the end of the road. He had found them with the sheets fused to their skin. Keeled over in kitchens. He had found Mrs. Cummings immobile at her kitchen table, buttering toast now swarmed over with earwigs. Marston Hughes in the garden, the hose still in his fist, puddling the lawn, then running a muddy stream down the steep dirt drive and out onto the blacktop until the residents thought maybe a new spring had opened up and called him to investigate before the road potholed. Alice Forster in her nightgown, sprawled among the mewling cats. Lou Sheffield rigid in the tub, for Godssakes, the radio having slipped into the water. Ned Butterworth when the tractor tipped and rolled on him,

65

crushing his pelvis, and he lay there cursing and then gasping his life out before they got it off of him. Sue Parmenter, peaceful enough among peonies, ants in and out of her mouth as though you're welcome, come on in. Big Betty Norris frozen hard in the woodshed, gripping a splitting maul. Ed Tilton in his drive, slumped over the wheel of his car, having just finished putting a new roof on his house at age eighty- two. Jim Lyman, rolled on his side toward the back of the sofa, the TV on behind him, the picture full of drizzle. Here people didn't call their relatives when they felt poorly. They preferred to be left alone and found alone, pridefully unembarrassed, their final stunned posture a sort of testament of their fidelity to themselves, to the unimpeachable fact of their own flesh.

But what he had not seen, what he had not wanted ever to see, was a man dead by the willing hand of another. He thought about that Weed homestead out there on Rattlesnake Ridge, fields given back to forest, two children left behind in their graves, a hole in the ground where a house had been. Orville Rogers shot down and left there as a token, a marker, a sign of things to come.

Adam Townsend held his first mug of coffee and looked out the kitchen window toward the barn. The day was gray and raw. All was still quiet upstairs, though the boys would have to be up for school soon. Adam's two boys were twelve and ten now. He knew he was raising them badly. He knew that life was as solid as wind, that fate could topple on you like a wall.

There was Lily Garnett to consider. She had been edgy yesterday, at the Weed place. Maybe it was just her family, everyone knew they didn't get along, her mother and brother up to something with the land. All that was bad enough. But something else had Lily wired, he thought, something back of all that. Then again maybe she was just tired. Waitress, late nights. All that land and poor as a rabbit.

And it was hard to know, really, just how much that night, that touch, was still there between them. He knew she hadn't forgotten it. But how to measure such a thing? A few mumbled words, the press of his flesh against her backside. Unclean thoughts. Of this he was guilty. God, Adam moaned, but she put the flame under his pot, even now. The way her nostrils flared, her eyes fired with gold. Adam Townsend had never made the attainment of perfect virtue a particular goal. He couldn't help himself, and really, why should he, feeling now a gentle nudging from below the waist. A fragment of dream: pale skin through tangled hair. He put his hand down there to see if there was anything worth pursuing. He had remained faithful to his wife, in deed if not in thought, for all of their twelve years together. She had borne him two sons. But as for the pleasures of the flesh, he was lucky if every other week, and then she would just roll on her back, open her legs and say "Go ahead." Like she was doing him a favor. What harm, then, if he eased his own burdens in his own way? One of his life's few consistent pleasures. He had thought by the time he reached forty his jets would have cooled, but it was still there, this need.

Adam set his coffee down, leaned back against the counter. It was still quiet upstairs.

And sometimes he had crossed the line. A touch, a mumble, he had done as much more than once. But it didn't even take that. He could live without that if he had to. It took remarkably little. A minute's talk with that bank teller in Wilton, a shared glance, not even that. The brain is the largest sexual organ, he had read in a woman's magazine once, in the grocery checkout line. And then the woman who checked his groceries, tumbling the melons, hoisting bananas onto the scale. A few years ago, he had realized, with a light shock, that it was no longer the supple teenage girls at the beach but their mothers he wanted, with their ample thighs and plumbed depths, dark hair tufting around the edges of the swimsuit where a younger woman would have shaved. It took very little. A young mother bending into a car, buckling a toddler in, then herself, the raised elbow when she turns the key in the ignition, handling the gearshift, then biting her lip as she looks over her shoulder to back up. All women in cars everywhere, ahead of you the thin rectangle of her face in the rear view mirror, the arched brows, or pulling up to pass you on the highway, and you give her that sidelong glance with its bitter cargo of impossible hopes before she steps on the gas. Or coming the other way, a glossy pout and sweeping shock of gold glimpsed through windshield glare before passing in a blur.

What harm does it do, then, to imagine one of these women nibbling your neck in a motel room on the edge of Manchester, say, and why not imagine the urgent language of zippers and buttons and hooks and clasps and then see yourself easing her down on the bed, where she arches back into the mattress and pulls you to her, wanting you, so that for one fleeting stretch of God's sweet time all the rough ways are made smooth, and you move through heat and breath and darkness to her choked cries of pleasure, to your own brief animal joy?

Dear Lord, what harm could be done?

Adam Townsend, braced against the counter in a cold kitchen whose linoleum floor has warped and lifted along the seams, squeezed the last shiver from his reverie, knowing, sadly, that with such unseemly glue did he hold the pieces of his life together.

Adam was in the office that afternoon when he got the call from his brother Tommy, up at the general store, saying that Peregrine Weed had just walked by there, waving his rifle in the middle of the street, yelling something about trespass and the sins of the fathers.

"Was he drinking?" Adam asked.

"Something about mercy and judgment."

"I'll be right over," Adam said, looking out the window for a sight of Weed.

"The dark night of the soul," Tommy was saying.

Adam had encountered Peregrine Weed before. A sad case. Born in Shaftesbury, descended from one of the town's first settlers, he had moved with his family to Connecticut, where he spent most of his childhood, and later to Concord, New Hampshire, where he spent a number of years in the state mental hospital. Somewhere along the way he picked up the idea that he was the rightful owner of most of Shaftesbury. He had appeared in town the previous May and spent the next summer, fall, and winter squatting in a shack on national forest land north of Rattlesnake Ridge. He seemed to spend most of his time walking the miles of forest, hills, fields, and swamps that he claimed as his own. Day or night, he could be found walking the center line of the town roads, sometimes cradling his rifle. Adam had warned him about carrying the firearm, but on the two occasions he had checked it, he had found it unloaded. He could have had the Forest Service guys run him out of his shack, but he hadn't had the heart. Adam had not thought him truly dangerous, and like most people in Shaftesbury, he had come to feel that if Weed was a freak and a nuisance, at least he was one of their own.

Adam put in a call to Campo at the state police, strapped on his belt, and then drove the three hundred yards to where he could see Peregrine on the granite step in front of the post office.

"Which is greater, the grace that's asked for or the grace that's not?"

Peregrine held forth to the three or four people who had happened to come there at that time for their mail.

"I say not, for that is the grace prevenient and bountiful, not pinched by the lips through prayer but gushing from the heart untapped, unbounded, immeasurable, immense. If you would know that grace, what would you do? Shut yourself up in a cell and mumble? Study the light through stained glass? Bind up your body and deny your senses? No, you must root yourself in the dirt, let your bowels be granite, your belly the sinews of beasts, your lungs the very air lashed by trees, your gorge the soaring hawk, your head the devouring sun."

Adam Townsend stood at a distance, arms folded, wondering when he should make his move.

Peregrine Weed was twenty-eight years old, six foot, six, and thin as a sapling, with a scraggly red beard and hair surging out from beneath a sort of Viking helmet he had fashioned using a cow's horns. His legs were clad in deerskin pants that were stained and dark with wear, and leather mukluks whose leggings rose almost to his bony knees. Small pouches on rawhide strings dangled against his chest, as did several necklaces made from clam and mussel shells, beads, and the beaks and claws of birds. He wore a leather vest outermost, and a rough wool shirt beneath that,

70

and receding layers of undergarments that were, judging by the smell, seldom removed.

"Why weary yourself with thought, fruitless riddles, the turning worm of the mind?"

Adam Townsend moved forward and stepped up beside Peregrine Weed. He looked hard into the young man's eyes, searching for the weakness he knew would be there. He found it, and something else, too, furtive and dark, like a bird darting into a bush. It was this other thing, quick and secret, that scared him and at the same time filled him with the sadness of capturing a wild thing.

"You think me an idiot," Peregrine said.

"No, I don't, Mr. Weed. Let me have the rifle, please."

The man's eyes gleamed, and his face glowed with something like pride. He handed Adam the rifle as if it were a diploma.

"I killed that man you call Orville Rogers."

"Did you, now? Would you mind putting your hands on that wall there?"

Adam patted the man down. The stench was powerful. He pitied the people up in Ridgeway who would have to undress him. All those clothes, and it seemed like there was nothing underneath. Like peeling a spoiled onion.

"He was on my land, he was planning to sell it off. You think I don't know. I've got the papers."

Adam got the cuffs on, then fumbled in his pocket for the card with the Miranda warning printed on it. He could hear Campo's siren approaching. He wanted to get this done himself.

"Townsend." Peregrine Weed grinned down at him now. "I knew your great-great-grandfather. Ran a sawmill up on Folsom

71

Creek. Married a French woman didn't have a tooth in her head. We're cousins, I think."

"On my mother's side," Adam said.

"Tell me one thing, Adam," Peregrine Weed said. "Do you believe that the land has a soul of its own, or that our own souls take root there and grow?"

8

He could show up in a tux, hand her flowers, ask her to step outside to watch an airplane write her name in the sky. Or on a mountain top, with a bottle of champagne sneaked in the backpack. Even drive her to Boston, drinks at the Copley, zoom up the elevators of the Hancock Tower, looking out over the skyline. But instead he was driving in his filthy woollies, grease-smeared and speckled with sawdust, driving the old truck fast because, my God, he was actually trying to fit this into a damn *schedule*, get there by 3:00, propose marriage by 3:15, allow twenty minutes for further discussion and excited sharing of the special moment, then back in the truck to meet this guy Mongerson and try to land this job that could be the biggest thing in years. What would she say? He hadn't even found a way to wash his hands.

He was not a half bad mandolin player, when he had time to practice. He did most of her car repairs. Of the team sports, they liked hockey best. They regarded Bobby Orr's career-ending knee injury as an event on par with the Tet Offensive. He loved her. Could this be a big deal?

He knew she'd be home, catching a nap before work. Wanting to wake her gently, he used his key, pushed the door open softly. No use: she had been asleep in her chair, and seeing her startle, wake in fright to his bulk darkening the door, he thought: she'll scream. At his very presence.

"It's me," he said, sorry to have to say it. "Kyle. Home early."

She looked at her watch, and he saw now that what had startled her was the thought that she had overslept and was late for work.

"I was running," she said. "Those trees again. But sometimes they're people, twisting and reaching. They speak some squeaky fast language, like Arabs breathing helium. And the light is so bright it hurts, I'm squinting and can barely make anything out."

Kyle sat down on the sofa, his palms on his knees, listening, waiting for her to finish. He knew that when she told him her dreams, it was important for him just to listen. He didn't have to comment.

"There's someone I have to get to, a child maybe, though sometimes it's a little animal, or a rock with a face."

"Will you marry me?" he asked.

Lily's face took on a far-off look, as though he had spoken a name she had not heard for many years, a relative about whose fate she had often wondered but never spoke. I'm sitting here filthy, Kyle thought. I could have shaved.

Lily cupped one hand to her ear.

"Will you marry me, is what I said."

"What I thought. You're looking at me across a pile of magazines and a tea cup definitely with mold growing in it by now and asking me to marry you. I'm stalling for time."

"Is this encouragement?" Kyle said.

"Were your eyes always so blue?" Lily asked.

"They're brown," Kyle said.

"Thank God."

"What does that mean? Entire seconds are passing."

"It means maybe," Lily said. "I need more information."

"I thought if I came home early I'd catch you before you went to work," Kyle said. "Say yes, and then I'm driving back down to see a guy about a job, and then I'll come to the bar tonight and we'll celebrate."

"While I'm working," Lily said. "How romantic."

"I'll leave an enormous tip," Kyle said. "What do you say?"

"Who's the job for?"

"Big house. This guy Mongerson. Nuts, I think. Wants to build on Jackson Island. He's asking for bids. He says he knows you." Kyle hesitated. "And Howard. From out West."

"There was someone out there by that name," Lily said evenly.

"He made out like you were old pals."

"Jackson Island. Do they allow that?"

"You've got the bucks, I guess they allow anything."

"Kyle. I want to say yes. I can feel myself definitely wanting this."

"What most people would do in that case is to say 'yes.'"

"No," Lily said.

"Does that mean no?"

"It means maybe. But not right now. There are some things, you know, I still have to deal with."

"We've talked about all that." This is what Kyle had most feared. He knew all about the Center, had heard as much about Johnny Ray Bushman as he could stand to listen to, knew she had been pregnant once and about the shooting and that she had had a miscarriage. Lots of women have miscarriages, he had told her. This is the past you're talking about. She agreed, yes, it was all in the past.

"I don't want to drag all that into a marriage," she said.

"So leave it," Kyle said.

75

"I can't. I mean I want to. For you, Kyle, I really want to be strong enough to do that."

He crouched forward, leaned across the coffee table, took her hands in his big hands.

"I want you to marry me, Lily."

Something buzzed from across the room. There were several sharp clicks, a hum. They watched as a sheet of paper scrolled out like a white tongue.

"Mom?" Lily said. She jumped up from her chair and pulled the paper out of the machine. A strained smile. "This isn't from you?"

"I don't know the number," Kyle said.

She handed him the sheet of paper, a message from beyond. It was in hand-printed block letters of the sort Kyle had learned to draw in eighth-grade drafting class:

I'M LOOKING FOR YOU, LILY GARNETT
FAX MAN

Chapter Two

1

Forrest Garnett was the kind of man you would see with his tie yanked loose in the airport lounge in late afternoon, sixtyish, gray-suited, spraddled and mussed, tippling scotch, comfortable with his vices. He would have gotten to the airport early to have time for some quiet anonymous drinking. If you had any knowledge of the type, you would recognize him as one of those men whose sensitivity to life's shocks had rendered him nearly mute on all matters of the heart. A man who bears his disappointments with a sort of furious calm. He's a shade over six feet, one inch and still trim, with the lank and confidence of the former athlete. He still plays tennis twice a week, and though he's given up the top spin serve after wrenching his back a few years ago, he still hits a wicked slice that curves hither and bounces yon, taking you all the way out of the court on the backhand side.

If you bumped into his chair, he would flash up at you the grin of the eighteen-year-old dreamboat he once was, eyes set just a bit too wide apart for you to suspect him of cunning, smooth brow, cheeks and chin still taut as the day he shipped out as a radar operator on the aircraft carrier U.S.S. *Saratoga*, headed for the invasion of Japan, eyebrows still arched with the insouciance of the man who returned two years later, the war won, the invasion unnecessary, his ship left behind to be painted orange and smithereened in an atomic bomb test off the Bikini Atoll. Jaunty, you would say of him, slouched in that swivel chair, twiddling a finger for one more.

He is one of those fathers who loves daughters and for whom sons are a continual disappointment, and who is so tormented by his feelings for both that he cannot bring himself to speak to either. A man glad of his imperfections. In him there still was something of the resourcefulness with which he returned home, married the sad-faced girl in the New Hampshire town he had always been from but in which he had hardly really lived, moved to Cambridge for graduate studies at MIT, and began the solitary life that would be his refuge and ruin. Now forty years later, his ex-wife learning Sanskrit in a religious commune in the West, his daughter struggling to jump-start a life that had stalled ten years ago in a sagebrush valley in Nevada, his son a high-tech con man orbiting in some outer space flim-flam of his own imagination, Forrest Garnett shook the ice in the bottom of his glass and wondered, as he had often done since seeing the bear, whether it was too late to live his life over again.

His most recent troubles had begun three months earlier, in late March, when he received a phone call from his son. Howard called every few months, apparently just to rattle Forrest with the latest developments in his messily improvised life. Sometimes Forrest chose not to answer the phone—he didn't own an answering machine and used an answering service for business calls—and that afternoon he would probably have let it ring if a daydream hadn't got his guard down. St. Louis had been surprised by sudden heat, the seasons lurching directly from winter to summer without interval. On the sagging back porch of his apartment, shaded poorly by a sweet gum tree still in bud, unseasonably damp in his undershirt and shorts, he sipped ice water as he read *Proceedings of the Antennas and Propagation Society*. When the phone rang, he had just finished an article that referred unexpectedly to the work of the late Dr. Li, whose equation for the interactions between multiple dipole antennas had come to Forrest's rescue at a crucial point in his doctoral research many years ago, when Forrest was a young man. This brought a flood of pleasant memories: leaving the lab bleary-eyed late at night, the gloom of the deserted quad, a dank wind off the Charles River, and the ineffectual street lamps creating that exquisite sense of loneliness he cultivated then, and which he relished to this day.

Forrest walked barefoot over dirty linoleum toward the ringing telephone.

"Father, how are you?"

Even after months, the call had come too soon.

"Who's this?"

"Do you have more than one son?"

"I don't have any that I know of. Where are you?"

"On the road."

Too soon. For the fact was, however much he loved his son, he still disliked him.

"And the purpose of your call?" he asked, knowing, regretting, and at the same time enjoying that he sounded like what he had in fact become: another sour old bastard who had lived alone too long.

"Like get to the point, is what you're saying. Which I can understand, coming from your perspective. You're thinking 'I've got this no 'count son in a BMW somewhere outside of Albuquerque who needs my help and decides to call from his car phone even though I haven't heard from him in months.'"

"More or less my sentiments," Forrest said. "I never approved of the prodigal son story. Seems to me his brothers had every right to object."

"I was never much on the Bible," Howard said.

"A good thing for someone who majored in religion," Forrest said.

"Eastern religions," Howard said. "But I didn't call to discuss unpleasant subjects."

"I have some trouble believing that."

"You give the cut direct, Dad. They can never take that away from you."

"And let no one ever accuse you of getting to the point."

"Which is why I'm calling. I'm beginning to see some things more clearly, Dad. Certain data points are beginning to coalesce into curves that might be described by continuous functions."

"You're trying to tell me you've learned calculus."

"Better than that. I'm starting to approximate a life out here."

"Which is the point of your call. I'm standing here sweating in a kitchen."

"I think I've found something I'm good at, Dad."

"You've gotten somebody pregnant."

"Real estate. I seem to have a knack. The Garnett touch."

"Garnetts are complete idiots in all practical affairs," Forrest said, and in saying it, realized that it was true.

"I'm headed east. There are tremendous possibilities there."

"They used to say that about the West."

"The East is the new frontier," Howard said. "Grid density. Information flux. Awesome traffic. Is there anything you want me to pass on to Lily?"

"Tell her not to speak to you."

Howard's thin nasal laugh had always seemed to Forrest deliberately effeminate.

"You haven't heard the news yet, have you."

Forrest steadied himself. "Not sure I care to."

"You should open yourself up to more frequencies, Dad. And get this: they found Orville Rogers' body on Lily's land. It's a homicide situation."

Forrest took a deep breath, feeling the world lurch toward an ugliness he had not quite been ready for. And before he could exhale, the adrenaline surge of a father's fear:

"Is Lily all right?"

"I suppose so," Howard said.

Forrest could almost hear his son thinking of the least reassuring thing to say next.

"She was under suspicion, of course, but now she's fine. It was the weirdo, the guy with the antlers? Weed. Absolutely a mental case."

Orville Rogers. Peregrine Weed. The Rogerses and Weedses had been there at the beginning, in the 1770s and '80s, along with the Garnetts. All the old families going to ruin.

"How do you know all this if you're in New Mexico?"

"Oops," Howard said. "I lied a little, before. I'm in New Hampshire, just outside of Concord, in fact."

"You shouldn't lie when you have no good reason."

"I'm writing that down, Dad. I have one of those little

81

notepads suction-cupped to the windshield."

"I despise everything they stand for."

"I'll try and remember that." And then, after a pause: "What are you thinking about, Dad?"

"About all the questions I want answered, but not by you." Forrest realized he would have to call Clarence.

"Dad."

"What."

"All the talk shows say that you're supposed to tell your father you love him, because otherwise he might die before you ever do it."

"Oh, Howard." Forrest sighed through lungs that suddenly felt stuffed with steel wool. "Don't believe everything you hear."

"I love you, Dad."

"I have no intention of dying anytime soon."

"For God's sake, Dad. For once without irony. I really do."

"Irony is a moral obligation," Forrest said, though more gently. A ripple of admiration passed through him: where had Howard's generation learned this naive bluntness in such matters?

"I really did just come here from Santa Fe," Howard said. "Adobe is a fantastic thing. Buildings like bread dough. The only state capital that looks edible."

"Howard?"

"Still here."

"I have the feeling there was another reason you called."

"I thought you'd never ask."

"You need money, don't you."

"Not as such. I need you to be open to possibility."

"Something I try to avoid," Forrest said.

"If a friend of mine named Mongerson calls, will you listen to him?"

"I'm not answering the phone."

Forrest returned to the throbbing heat of the afternoon to stare stupidly out the front window, contemplating the spectacular dimensions of his failure. How had he ended here? he wondered. For he couldn't help but think of these years in St. Louis, consulting for aerospace firms, as an ending. He had spent too much of his life trying to avoid living in Shaftesbury. And now here he was, staring out of a window at buildings peopled with strangers. The house opposite, like his, like all the houses on this street, was a heavy and graceless two-story brick structure, its deep porches supported by squat brick pillars, the roof shingles curling with damp, the wood trim gone spongy, so that the entire mass, from the limestone foundation to the badly tilting chimney seemed destined to crumble into the damp earth.

How could a man produce an unlikable son? An unhappy daughter?

He supposed he had never given them enough attention. He remembered summer weekends in Shaftesbury when the children were small, how he could sit on the porch of that Thompson farmhouse for hours, watching maples lift in the wind, thinking, in fact, of the dynamics of air as it flows through a forest like a river through weeds, while about him his children silently clamored for his notice, clutched at his trousers, the quivering O's of their mouths made dumb by whatever filter allowed him to hear only the wild rushing of trees drowning in wind.

He hadn't checked on the land in a couple of years. Maybe it was time.

Waiting for the call from Nevada, Adam decided to vacuum the house. It was something he had done on only two other occasions in his married life, both times when Marilyn had been in the hospital after the birth of their sons. He did it now perhaps simply because he couldn't stand idleness. He had come home for the afternoon, and with Marilyn out running errands and the boys off on their bicycles, the house was too quiet. But he knew, too, that the work was fed by nostalgia for the unreasonable and giddy optimism of those other times when he had vacuumed. He and Marilyn had not been intimate lately, and he vaguely hoped the cleaning might get her attention.

The call would be about Mongerson, and Marilyn didn't like it when he tied up the line with lengthy business calls. He'd claimed his inquiry into Mongerson was just routine police work. She said he ought to let the state police handle the whole thing, like Lieutenant Campo said. Stay clear of the whole murder business, she said. He had taken Peregrine Weed into custody, over two weeks ago now. Wasn't that enough? Plus which, she thought Adam was getting too deep into Bud Grisham's affairs. But it wasn't just that. Ever since Orville Rogers, Marilyn had been on edge. As if his having been there, having found the body and then stood in the company of those men as they lifted Orville from the ground, had tainted him somehow. Made him the sort of man she didn't care to associate with. The whole murder business. She wouldn't let him touch her.

Adam wondered about the dust. He found it on top of the

window and door casements, on the curved upper surfaces of curtain rods. With a forefinger he wiped away the thin crescent of dust on the top edge of a keyhole cover. But it was not this dust he wondered at so much as the finer sort, the dust that floated in rooms as part of the atmosphere, spangled in sunlight, invisibly gray in shadow, but ever present, he supposed. He had read once in *Reader's Digest* that dust was made of literally everything: mountaintops and bits of dead skin, cornfields and burnt motor oil, river mud and asphalt, leaf mold and the insides of stars.

But how did it get from there to here? What machine had ground the universe so fine?

Adam had been in Nevada twice: once for a seminar on police department administration, once for a session on child abuse and neglect. He had met a few people on the Las Vegas police force. When the computer checks turned up nothing on Mongerson, he had called them. There had been a few calls back and forth as Adam tried to find somebody out there who felt like helping him.

Maybe Marilyn was right. Maybe it wasn't strictly police business. A few days earlier, Adam had hung up the phone in the kitchen and turned to see that Marilyn had been standing there in the doorway, listening.

She said, "I know what you're doing."

It was mid-morning in early April, cloudy and cold, snow still in the woods beneath the hemlocks and sitting on the ground on the north sides of buildings, the withered drifts gritty and pocked. The light in the kitchen was flat, and Adam, who had not made a fire in the stove, kept the furnace set low, hoping the day would warm.

"There's been a man killed," Adam said.

85

"You've got the man that did it," Marilyn said. "So don't give me that."

"It's not so simple."

"Bud Grisham wants to go after the Garnett land. What's that got to do with you?"

"Maybe you should stay out of things you don't understand."

"He jerks your string, you dance."

Marilyn wore her flower-print housedress underneath a worn terry cloth robe of faded yellow, and Adam found his gaze resting below the ragged hem, where her calves descended to her feet through a region too bloated to be recognized as ankles, as though the thick part of her leg flowed directly into her slippers. Her skin was pale, with red blotches like the explosions of some inner temper, the boiling surface of a distant planet. Adam shuddered inwardly in the cold light of the kitchen, thinking, she's not getting any prettier, is she now? He hated himself for thinking it, knowing on some level that in cursing her he cursed all that was ugly and bloated and blotched in his own shabby self.

"Bud made a reasonable request. Nobody knows who this guy is."

"Bud won't give you no raise."

"Not what I'm looking for."

"What, then?"

"This is the Garnett land," Adam said, exasperated that he should have to spell it out. But Marilyn had been born over in Effingham, and she would never fully understand what Rattlesnake Ridge meant to this town. She had not hunted and camped on it, had not gathered blueberries along its ledges as a kid, had been too heavy, even when they were courting, to want to hike in and make furtive love among its groves. It didn't even matter all that much to her that Adam's great-grandfather had sold the Weed farm to Forrest Garnett's grandfather after the Civil War, giving the Garnetts the largest single chunk in a domain shrewdly patched together from abandoned and exhausted farms, and then held together through war and depression when other families failed. A certain glamour attached to Forrest Garnett, who had lived down in Massachusetts mostly and had a Ph.D., yet who managed still to be a presence in the town. When sighted, he was someone you pointed out to children and visitors, sort of a celebrity. Marilyn would never feel, as foolish as it was, the mixture of envy and respect and fear toward the Garnetts that Adam and most of the people of Shaftesbury felt, nor would she understand what for Adam went without saying: that whatever threatened Rattlesnake Ridge threatened the town itself.

He removed the grilles from the heating registers and vacuumed out clods of dust and hair and dead bugs. He unscrewed light bulbs and washed them gently in the sink. For this is what no one understood. Orville Rogers may have been a burr in Adam's blanket, but Adam, like everyone else in Shaftesbury, had counted on him to keep Bud in check. As much as he owed Bud his job, as much as Bud signed the paychecks, Adam now felt wary, exposed. People wanted to think he was doing Bud's work, fine. But he wanted to think that he was doing Shaftesbury's work, too.

Adam dusted things he had never looked twice at, never mind handled, lifting from the slotted shelves the antique china, from Marilyn's mother, featuring scenes from Europe—what was that, Paris? The Eiffel tower. London's Big Ben. The leaning tower of

Pisa. With stubby fingers he hefted Murano glass ducklings and Bavarian porcelain milkmaids, briefly fondling the enameled cream and sugar set they had never used, the pewter candlesticks in which their candles had never burned.

Maybe Marilyn was right. Maybe he was getting in over his head.

The phone's ringing found him on his hands and knees marveling at the ingenuity of the men who had designed the old Electrolux vacuum attachment, whose swivel head allowed him to flatten the nozzle's sucking surface against the floor even when pushing it way back beneath the sofa. He hoped Marilyn would come home in time to see him doing this.

"How's the chicken farmer?" It was Paul Mansard from Las Vegas. They had shared a pitcher of beer once. Mansard wore cowboy boots, told snakebite stories. A bit of an ass, but he was all Adam had.

"The hens are a' layin'," Adam said. "What do you have for me?"

"Now, what was that you wanted again?"

Adam counted to three. Mansard knew what he wanted. Made a game out of jerking Adam around.

"Mongerson."

"Oh, thass right. Mongerson. Zippo on that one, good buddy. But I thought of a gal who might have something on him." Mansard's voice pulled away, spoke to someone else in the room: "Who was that chick, works for the county? Oh, yeah." Back with Adam. "Lady's name is Ringer. I'll get you the number."

"And any more on the Bushman case?"

"Man, I tell you," Mansard said, annoyed and playing it up.

88

"Not like I don't got anything else to do around here."

"You don't have to feed chickens," Adam said.

"No, I don't. Reckon that's one advantage I have."

"Bushman," Adam said.

"Like I told you, lead investigator on that one retired a while back. So happens I called him, seeing as I don't have no chickens to feed. Got his widow. Guy dropped dead three years ago."

"You find the file?"

"It's a thin one, like I said. Definitely a back burner type of case around here. They never really developed a decent suspect."

"Could you send me what you have? And I got one more name for you: John Harrington."

"Oh, ho! Now there's an old scumbucket from way back. Where'd you pull that one from."

"NCIC."

"Hey, I didn't know you had computers up there in New Hamp-sheer."

"We've got indoor plumbing, too," Adam said. Actually, the computer had been sitting unused on the desk in Adam's office for a year. That week he had finally gotten Louise over at the selectmen's office to show him how to use it. He had scanned all the unsolved murder cases in Nevada during the seventies and eighties. Harrington's name had come up as a suspect in two of them. Both of the victims had been suspected of narcotics trafficking.

"Harrington," Mansard said. "Larceny, assault. Not a nice person. He was sort of a fad around here for a while. Tried to pin a couple murders on him but nothing ever panned out."

"You got a file on him?"

"Friggin' files here, probably buried in a closet. We've had a lot of turnover in secretarial."

"'Preciate it," Adam said.

"New Hamp-sheer," Mansard said. "You guys all live in log cabins, right?"

When Adam got off the phone with Mansard, he called Deputy Sheriff Cheryl Ringer, who did civil work in the County Sheriff's office. He asked Ringer if she had ever heard of Lawrence Mongerson.

"Hotshot developer? Served him a subpoena sometime last year."

"What for?"

"Think it was a water rights case. Claimant said he sold him some land didn't have the water Mongerson and his partners said it did? Typical bullshit."

"You say he has partners?"

"Oh, yeah, like heavy duty."

Adam tried to picture Cheryl Ringer: tight khaki shorts, blonde braids like Heidi. He could hear her chewing gum. God help him if he wasn't getting a hard-on.

"Mongerson I don't know, but some of these guys I had to serve, I'm happy to get home at night."

"Bad guys, Cheryl?" Using her first name, for godsakes. He couldn't help himself.

"Oh, not the old-fashioned kind, like those movies? Where they shoot each other in Italian restaurants? These guys are New Age. Like, Yuppies? Most of what they do is legal. Construction, real estate. But somehow the drugs still get moved, and every once in a while a body shows up?"

"I thought you did civil work, Cheryl."

"Christ, I used to date one of these guys? Like, w-e-e-e-i-r-d. Half the day doing yoga, weekend workshops on self-esteem? Wanted to Rolf me. They eat hay. Muck from the ocean floor. All that California stuff."

"You're not from California?" Adam asked, thinking: good Lord. Rolf me. He slid a hand in his pocket. Like a roll of quarters. Money in the bank.

"Heavens, no. Wisconsin!"

The kind of girl who woke up singing.

"How come Mansard didn't tell me any of this?"

"Ugh, Mansard. Are you kidding? He's a pig. He's prob'ly on the take."

"And they kill people, these bad guys?"

"Oh, heavens, I suppose so. They have to. Only it's all so clean now. They never leave their living rooms. If they wanted, you know, to do something like that? Like murder? They'd want to call an 800 number. They'd want to put it on their VISA."

"Cheryl, will you see if you can find anything about a Mr. John Harrington? He might have done some work for these people."

"See what I can do!"

Adam reached further into his pocket. Thank you, Cheryl. Oh, God, thank you.

After the phone call from Howard in late March, Forrest waited two weeks to call his cousin Clarence, and when he did, he walked two blocks to use the pay phone at the corner pizza parlor. It was a popular place, known for its interior. People ate at Formica-topped tables amid pagan and Christian detritus, a crowd of plaster Venuses and busts of eyeless Roman statesmen, cupids and nymphs and your better sort of birdbath statuary, all of it parti-colored in the light of stained glass windows snatched from churches that had been demolished after their white congregations fled to the suburbs. Calling home from here met Forrest's need for self-flagellation, for it was in such surroundings that he could make his feelings of loss most keen. The pizza, like all pizza in St. Louis, was inedible. On weekend nights the waiting line stretched out onto the sidewalk.

Forrest punched code into the keypad and waited to be connected across a thousand miles to the companion of his youth, who now, like Forrest, was in his mid-sixties and had developed the sort of deeply lined, handsome and homely face that had helped LBJ win the vote in poor rural districts. Clarence employed himself as handyman, brush cutter, hay mower, storyteller, and Quaint Rural Character. He wore the standard uniform of the New England farmer: dark green work shirt and trousers, suspenders, brown leather work boots, greasy seed cap. Tourists sometimes pulled off the road to photograph him atop his old red Ford tractor, cutting roadside brush with the sickle bar. He also served as unofficial caretaker of the Rattlesnake Ridge land from his vantage on Lakeside Farm, which had once belonged to William Garnett, Forrest and Clarence's grandfather.

"You haven't been answering your phone," Clarence said. "I guess you don't want to hear what I've got to tell you."

"I already heard about Orville. Howard told me."

"You believe that's the worst of it."

"It never is," Forrest said.

"There's been surveying done. Constance sold out to some developer."

Forrest took the kind of breath the navy taught him to breathe when trapped in a confined space.

"You're going to tell me that's not the worst of it, either," Forrest said.

"Sold to an outfit, the Mongerson Corporation," Clarence said. "Whose regional representative, it turns out, is your son Howard."

The next step in the navy procedure involved lying on one's back. The floor at Forrest's feet was dirty tile sprinkled with cigarette butts.

"Now they've bought two more adjacent parcels. Did it all without going through Bud."

At a nearby table a large man in a rugby shirt and khaki shorts angled a slice of pizza into his mouth. As his face registered the pain of hot cheese searing his palate, he saw Forrest watching him, and gave a small, embarrassed smile.

"Now, don't lunge to conclusions, Forrest. For one thing, they've got no way into any of that land without coming through yours."

"And Lily's. And yours," Forrest said.

"Which they can't do," Clarence said, "unless all Howard wants is a timber operation."

Clarence was referring to a restriction in Howard and Constance's deeds. Their right of way on the Old High Road remained only so long as the land stayed in "current use," a designation that reduced one's property tax to nil so long as the land was used only for farming or logging.

"We'll figure this thing out," Clarence said. "Howard's your son."

"And that," Forrest said, "really is the worst of it."

"I'm not sure such gloominess is called for." The voice belonged to Sylvia, and Forrest realized she had been listening all along.

Sylvia Garnett, the daughter of missionaries, was one of those spry sixty-year-olds a community can't live without. You would see her around town wearing a tennis visor and glasses on a string around her neck, tending the flowers in front of the post office, or seated at a card table on the sidewalk, selling raffle tickets to raise money for the day care center. She ran a Great Books reading group at the library, helped with local theater productions, delivered hot meals to elderly shut-ins. She tolerated her husband's more relaxed approach to life.

"How's Lily?" Forrest knew that Sylvia would know the question was for her.

"She's lost ten pounds, Forrest. Edgy. Like I haven't seen her since she came back that time." "Tell her I asked about her," Forrest said.

"Tell her yourself. You ever think of coming back here?"

Sylvia knew him like a sister, and like a sister knew precisely how to nettle him. Ever since his own sister, Margaret, had died, Forrest had let Sylvia take over that job.

"Lily's rattled," Sylvia said. "This thing with Orville, and now the land being sold."

"Peregrine Weed claims he owned that land," Clarence said. "That's why he shot Orville."

"One of the last Weeds left," Forrest said.

"Seemed happy enough, before this, living out there in the woods. There's no place in this world for a man like that now."

"Driven out by men like my son."

"Howard looks downright chipper, you want to know the truth. Thinks this land deal is his ticket."

"He discussed it with you? Without shame?"

"You know how he is. Talks big, but it's hard to pin him down about anything. And this guy Mongerson, I saw him, too."

"A nice young man," Sylvia said.

"Maybe," Clarence said, "but if I was hunting I wouldn't want him behind me."

"You're too mistrustful," Sylvia said.

"The guy's got Sylvia buttered because he promised money for the day care center. Says he's got the permits to build a house on Jackson Island, big place. Going to hire all the local carpenters, trying to get in good with the natives."

"At least he's polite," Sylvia said.

"I don't suppose you think there's anything I should do about all this," Forrest said.

"Talk to your children for once," Sylvia said.

"That presupposes I have something to say," Forrest said.

"What's the matter with men?" Sylvia asked.

"Hold the fort, Clarence," Forrest said.

"As long as the ammo holds out," Clarence said. "Then it's hand to hand."

If you saw him in that airport bar again, you would think: a man who thrives on contradictions, who drinks more than is advisable and runs four miles a day, and who has that special Protestant gift of being comfortable with sin, the between-the-stirrup-and-the-ground confidence that in the end he will fall into grace. And you might be pleased enough to serve an older man who for once looks good with a loosened tie, so that you don't mind so much when he stares gratefully at your legs. As you walk away, you feel his gaze on you like a kind of heat, but somehow he makes it kindly and all in good fun. He's the sort of man you would introduce your widowed mother to if you felt she needed to get out more.

And if he told you about the bear, he would somehow manage to make it charming, even glamorous. A boyish adventure. A tall tale that happened to be true.

After his talk with Clarence, Forrest's sleep grew restless, his dreams full of the Shaftesbury woods he'd seen little of in years: a column of gnats spiraling in a shaft of sunlight, the shimmer of light off of hemlock needles, an owl coughing in the forest, the chorus of spring peepers in their vernal pools. His bedroom grew crowded with raccoons, squirrels, crows, all familiars of his New Hampshire youth. One night a swallow bashed the four walls of his room before he let it escape from a window. A deer nudged his cheek with a wet nose. He woke one morning with slick pellets of rabbit dung under the bed.

He had to consider the possibility that he was going insane.

Instead, he decided to take these developments as simply one more irruption of the impossible into his life.

It had been over fifty years since the last one.

Forrest grew up with the impression that God lived exclusively in New Hampshire, but not necessarily in the pristine white church in the center of Shaftesbury, behind which lay the humped and moldering graves of generations of Garnetts. Though he had spent enough drowsy Sundays in that church, Forrest's true religion, if he had one, was the sort of casual paganism practiced by many boys who spend the most important part of their lives in the woods. By the age of ten he had hiked over most of the thousands of acres of Rattlesnake Ridge, knowing by feel the network of stone walls and logging roads represented today on U.S. Geological Survey maps as a fragmentary grid of ghostly lines. The woods inspired whole categories of feeling: the spiced and secretive darkness of hemlock and balsam forest, the happy exuberance of maple, birch, and oak with sunlight dappling bright green leaves, and perhaps best of all, the ethereal light of a beech glade, with its pale gray trunks and a dense, uniform shade that could make one feel as though immersed in water.

To such a boy enchantment becomes routine. There was one place he liked especially to visit, the site of an old sawmill, now collapsed into a pile of rotting boards, its presence marked chiefly by the sodden mound of orange sawdust some twelve feet high, around the edges of which grew raspberries and milkweed. In the midst of an upstart forest of dense white pine, the place came upon one suddenly, an opening into sunwarmed space, the warm smell of sawdust, the hum and bustle of insect life in the grass, katydids fluttering into light, a chipmunk, surprised, ducking under the

97

punky boards. It was the sort of place that elves have finished dancing in just before you got there. Milkweed pods like parrots on their stalks. Forrest didn't know when or exactly where, but buried in his memory he had a clear image of taking an unbroken pod in his hands and splitting the leathery husk between his thumbs to reveal the flat brown seeds with their white feather parachutes furled and packed like fish scales. He loosened them gently and blew them free, by layer and clump, finally picking the last reluctant few out of the pod to reveal the milkweed's papery center, its undermost undergarment, featherlike and of the most delicate pale yellow, in whose folds and crinkles the tips of the white seed parachutes had been tucked and held.

He could not remember now if it had been there, or at some other place, that he had heard the voice, but he remembered the sensation of turning. Perhaps it had been at Elm Hill swamp, where he had sometimes walked along the prickly rampart of the beaver dam, water bubbling through the spiky thatch beneath his feet to meander through the weedy reaches below, eventually to find its way to Abenaki Lake. Or at the old mill by Folsom Creek, its quarried granite watercourse still and full of dry leaves. But once he had heard it, he listened for it everywhere, and so he had come to remember the voice as being always with him during that summer, booming out at him at the moment he turned to walk away.

Though the first time it had not boomed, merely said his name, "Forrest," softly enough that the sound could have been the crunching of leaves as he turned to peer back through trees, not knowing if he was turning to find the source of the sound or if the sound had come after, or simultaneously with, the impulse to break off his contemplation—of sawdust, the gnawed spikes of beaverwork, the lichens mottling a granite wall—to turn and stomp off in another direction entirely. But loud enough, still, to freeze him in the act of turning, so that he remained there motionless and unbreathing as he would when hunting, waiting for his rustling prey to show. He stood with body twisted, weight on his left foot, still as a scared squirrel, for a minute, two, three; then, when he had convinced himself that he had heard no more than the rubbing of branches in the wind, and when he lifted his foot to take another step and complete the turn, the voice struck him down.

He had read in the Old Testament about men prostrating themselves before voices and visions, but this had always seemed to him something only shepherds did, men in robes and long beards who spent weeks in the company of sheep and rocks, eating sour cheese. Even old Mr. Mudgett, his Sunday school teacher, though he had once worn a shepherd's robes and carried a crooked staff in a church pageant, and though each week he stomped crookedly up the aisle between their desks and beat his fists at the air, even Mr. Mudgett could not be imagined lying pressed to the earth as the ten-year-old Forrest Garnett now was, beneath the anvil of his name pronounced from he knew not where, pressed until the breath was squeezed from his lungs and his tongue was coated with dirt, his eyes squinched tight and then, with a burning rush, his bowels letting go a warm flood. He felt not reverence, nor awe, nor fear, even, but the wordless humility that comes of being reduced to one's animal parts and made a small, quivering thing waiting for the final blow to fall. The blow did not come, and the weight lessened, and eventually Forrest found himself with eyes open, breathing calmly, watching an inchworm reach the end of a leaf and rear up, fingering air. He raised himself, removed his soiled clothes and washed in the pond, then buried his underwear. He sat on a stone in the sun and breathed. He felt tired, sullied and elated as though he had been in a fight and won.

He spent the rest of that summer turning, expecting voices, hearing none. Though for several weeks afterward, physical objects wore a special sheen: the light through the steam rising from his oatmeal, the glimmering surface of his spoon, the splash of light on poplar leaves tossed in the wind. And there were moments when certain words spoken by others—ordinary words such as marshmallow or butterfly—seemed to take on a flickering, visible presence, winging from the mouth as if swathed in flame. But he never heard the voice again, and could never bring himself to tell anyone—except for Constance, once—what had happened.

It was a few days before Adam found the time to go see Lily. Mud season was on them. Snowmelt charged down from the mountains, streams gushed, water pooled in fields and on lawns, swamps rose, and the town's dirt roads, seventy or eighty miles of them, turned to the consistency of baby shit. Out on Abenaki Lake the ice went punky and puddled, then vanished in an afternoon. Soon the moose would wander down from the hills in search of new green. Adam spent most of three days out with Harold Butterworth, the road agent, posting roads made impassable by mud. He spent the rest of his time on patrol, rescuing the likes of Mrs. Grimsby, stranded in a driveway that looked like a demolition derby pit, or calling in a wrecker for those tourists up from Virginia — don't know what they could have been thinking coming here at this time — their big old Buick having slipped down Coombs Road like a hog looking to wallow. All over town, boots were left in mudrooms, heavy with mud, and trousers left there, too, spattered to the knees. Adam's cows bellowing in mud, thick right up their flanks, the barnyard gone to soup. Before dinner those days, Adam walked half naked from the kitchen door to the bathroom to wash mud from his arms up to the elbows, clean mud from under his nails, swab it out of his ears, sneeze mud from his nose, rinse it from his hair, flush grit from his teeth. The taste of Shaftesbury in April.

So that by the time he got an afternoon free, he was glad to be driving for most of an hour on state roads: clear and dry, wide and well drained. These roads were about the only thing the state of

New Hampshire saw fit to spend money on, and that was only because they kept the tourists happy.

He was nervous, again, about seeing Lily. She was touchy about the land, about everything. Or maybe he was the one uncomfortable. Was it just him? Was it all men? Within eyeshot of even a most-of-the-way homely woman, on some level he was always thinking: when and where. Cheryl Ringer. Just her voice. For the past few days she'd been there as a kind of voltage: all he had to do was plug in. Of course maybe it was just the Vegas connection, her voice, coming from a town built on money and sex, one of a thousand that would have set him off. On his visits there, Adam had been amazed, shocked, really, at the brazenness of it all. Billboards at the airport advertising strip shows, my God, you haven't even gotten your luggage yet. Walking along the Strip from one casino to the next, in any halfway shadowy place along the sidewalk, he'd be approached by men handing him glossy brochures, and good Lord, there's Cindy or Dena or Roxy showing her be-all and end-all, saying, "Call me. I'll come to your room within 30 minutes!" Back in his hotel Adam had called once, and a woman's voice answered: firm, businesslike, like waiting for him to order pruning shears or a pair of slacks. Adam hung up, embarrassed. Turned on the porn flicks on the TV—$22.95 for twenty-four nonstop hours—and jerked himself sore.

Here he was, the small town boy in sin city. A cop at a cop convention. Cops were notorious, right? He had heard stories of men who liked to do it in uniform, paid women to tie them up and walk on their chests in spike heels. But it was all Adam could manage to go with a few of the guys to a tittie bar, pay the five buck cover, have his hand stamped in fluorescent ink by a bouncer fresh off the pro-wrestling circuit, push his way into the dim, pulsing place, music making the air hot and dense as broth. He bought a five-dollar bottle of beer from a woman wearing clothing Adam could have balled up in one fist, and took a stool by the edge of the stage, which was thrust chest-high down the center of the room. He had expected sad cases, he had expected make-up applied with a trowel, tired women hoofing the stage thinking about getting done, getting home, thinking of laundry and kids and that no good son-of-a-bitch boyfriend, if he comes back I'm going to tell him take his sorry ass out of here, I mean it this time. And he got all that, though he didn't know he was getting it, because what he hadn't expected was that, my God, these women could really dance! They had the arms of rock climbers and the calves of quarter-milers. They snapped off routines like gymnasts, could do things with a fire pole for which there ought to be judges holding up scorecards. Adam sipping his five-dollar beer and staring up into the hot lights as into some vision of bounty, not flinching, in fact hardly noticing when one of the girls, in an orange terry cloth bikini, sidled up and slid her arms around his gut, pressed the length of her body against his and cooed something in his ear about a lap dance. Which Adam realized then was where the big money was for these girls, seeing around the dim perimeter of the room bare-chested women undulating over the fully clothed bodies of men sprawled back in the cushioned seating. Twenty dollars, said Debbie. I'm the only redhead. Adam couldn't tell in the dim multicolored light. I've got freckles, see? Debbie turned and showed him freckles on her ass. Debbie, it turned out, was from Eau Claire, Wisconsin. (Wisconsin! Adam thinks now, almost two years later, driving north to see Lily Garnett. Like Cheryl Ringer.

103

Another reason he got such a charge. The thrill of the girl-next-door gone bad, for what was Wisconsin, dairy? Those maps of the U.S. when he was a kid, each state with a picture of its most important product, cars for Michigan, corn for Iowa, Florida oranges, Wisconsin has a dairy cow, state had a law you had to serve cheese with apple pie. And now here's a representative of this wholesome dairy state barefoot and g-stringed lifting one ass cheek to show off her freckles. God bless America!) Adam made small talk: Debbie lived in San Diego, worked two weeks on, two weeks off. Lived with her brother, no kids. A lap dance. How about it?

But Adam went Debbiless, for once again he couldn't get out of the way of his own small town self. And more than that, couldn't quite get over the thought that these women were here working a job. He could not, in the end, quite enter into the fantasy that he, Adam of Shaftesbury, was the culmination of the desire of Debbie from Eau Claire. Adam returned to watching the dancers strut to the pile-driving music, muscles like they'd get you between a rock and a hard place, thinking: enough already, time to get home.

But he remembered the moment when, as he was sipping his beer, something shifted, like music changing to a higher key, and it was as though he was no longer gazing upward in wonder and shame but looking down on himself and all the rest of them with something like forgiveness, something like compassion. For were they not beasts, after all? The men, and the women, too? And could not there be something simple and kindly, if not downright noble, in these gleaming torsos and sculpted thighs, in these women in the room's dim margins ministering to the needs of Ed

104

from Detroit, Ernest from Ohio, Julio up from L.A., men chained to their lusts like dancing bears to their iron balls, hurtling through space on a planet intent on grinding them into dust?

Adam Townsend, rushing up Route 35 toward North Ridgeway in a vehicle his employers had paid for with money collected from the good people of Shaftesbury, New Hampshire, slowed his speed, the tires slowing down to a less fevered hum, looked out at the trees rushing past, and behind them to the mottled shoulder of Mount Penacook, thinking: I've got to square things with Lily, things can't go on this way. And then thinking: Marilyn, Marilyn, Marilyn.

He got to DooHickey's before the dinner crowd. The place was quiet as a cave, and at the back of it he saw Lily stooped over an empty table. He moved quickly toward her, into darkness, glancing at the gleaming ranks of bottles behind the bar only long enough to wonder why he had lost his youthful interest in drinking. Maybe he should try again.

"Lily," he said. "Quiet as hell in here."

Lily screwed on the top of the salt shaker she had just finished filling, set it carefully next to the pepper, straightened the card advertising the drink specials, unbent herself to face him.

"You were hoping for an audience," she said.

"Actually not. Just you," Adam said, regretting right away how aggressive he sounded. Realizing, suddenly, how much he needed Lily just now. If he had worn a hat, he would be holding it in his hand.

Lily gave him an appraising look. Cool. Unsettling how, whenever he spoke to her, she always managed to be in charge.

"This way," she said, and led him back through the kitchen.

105

She told the other waitress to keep an eye on things out front, she'd be right back. And even now Adam was unable to help himself, thinking nice-looking piece, that other one. On the plump side but firm enough.

They stood on the concrete loading dock by the dumpster.

"Thing stinks, doesn't it?" Adam said.

"We won't be here long."

Adam saw already that this was going badly. Maybe he should have tried on her day off.

"We don't have to think of this as official," Adam said. "I'm just here to talk, really."

"What about," Lily said. "I'm working."

"You're always working," Adam said. "Aren't they paying you enough?"

"They pay me." She gave an impatient snort. "Look, Adam, I've got customers coming in."

"What do you have against me, Lily? Or is that a stupid question." This was not how he meant to begin, blundering again into that coatroom. There, among the whispering nylon jackets, the slightest pressure of her hip against his coiled flesh. In over his head. His lips nuzzling the downy hairs on her nape an instant before her sharp elbow found his gut. So that now, facing Lily, he had the feeling of cringing before a blow.

"Lily, that time in the Grange Hall, a few years ago, I think you know what I mean."

Lily stiffened, her nostrils flared, a horse about to back and rear.

"I treated you with a lack of respect," Adam said.

"Yes," Lily said, like burying an axe in a stump.

106

"I feel bad about that."

Lily blinked, stared, her hands balled into fists.

"Okay," she said. "I guess we can be grown-ups about it."

"Good." Adam offered a cautious smile. "That's good, Lily. You know I wish the best for you and your family."

"Okay," Lily said. "What do you need, Adam?" Like get on with it, but softer now, as though trying out, at least for the moment, the idea that they were on the same team.

"Has Bud called you again about the land? Made any more offers?"

"He's called," Lily said.

"Anybody else?"

"Just Lieutenant Campo."

"He called you about the case."

"Yes, seems like every day. What is it with you guys? Same questions over and over, like you're teaching English to foreigners."

"We're thorough," Adam said. He couldn't help liking her, sour as she was.

"When I take an order, I don't ask six times. I write it on a pad."

"Just once more, promise: you ever hear from a Lawrence Mongerson?"

"I don't know why you're even pursuing this. Christ, you've got Peregrine Weed, right?"

"Do you know Lawrence Mongerson?"

"The only thing I know is, he's a jerk, because he was supposed to talk to Kyle about building a house but then never showed up. No one's seen him."

"Since Orville."

"I guess." Lily looked away, uncomfortable.

"Look, Lily." He took a step closer, and was surprised to discover that she was as tall as he was. For years he had spoken to her as though looking down. You just assume, with women. But now he saw that, if anything, she edged him by half an inch. Eyes brown with flecks of green and gold.

"Bud Grisham told me way back last winter your father was going to develop Rattlesnake Ridge," Adam said quietly. "Why would he tell me that?"

Lily flinched when he mentioned her father.

"People like to start rumors," she said.

"But maybe you know more about your father's plans than I do," Adam said. He felt himself crowding her now.

"People are free to speculate about my father's plans. I think Bud was just dreaming."

"Your father hasn't said anything to you about it?"

Lily looked away, and Adam caught himself once again wanting to take pleasure in the flush of her cheeks, the slightest quiver in her lower lip.

"I guess that's not something we would talk about," Lily said.

"Lily, you ever hear Bud say anything about Orville? You know anything about being angry with him? More angry than usual?"

Lily gave a short laugh.

"You're really hoping Bud did it, aren't you?"

"I'm not exactly sure what to hope for, Lily."

They both stared out over the stained asphalt parking lot toward the ragged fringe of ash and poplar tipped with swelling buds.

108

"Hope for peace in your soul, Adam," Lily said softly.

The words sounded to Adam like they had been spoken from someplace high in the air. And despite their strangeness, despite wanting to laugh them off, he couldn't help but find them oddly stirring. He looked at the side of her face: high cheekbones made her look almost Indian. When the Garnetts first got here, there were still Indians around. There was something unsettled in that face, something that had hurt her deep.

"Lily, I wanted to warn you. This guy Mongerson. Let me know if you hear from him. He's got connections with some people out west who have been involved in criminal activity. I'd hate to see Howard get mixed up in anything."

Lily looked at him straight on, as though at a wall in a waiting room. "Thank you for the warning, Officer Townsend."

Adam Townsend drove home in the last light, thinking: there, he had done something now, advanced something, nudged chaos back a step, even if the mere sight of Lily still quickened his pulse, and even if in the whole Nevada business he was operating on the most ill-formed hunches, a swarm of possibilities with Lily at their center, the hard heart of it all. Lily. Life had notched her blade good. Adam let out a breath and thought: I'm getting too close to all this.

He rolled down the windows and let in the cooling air. The days were longer now, sunset creeping northward on the horizon toward the solstice, toward that time of year, still two months off, when the setting sun shone down his drive and lit up his back steps. Sometimes he and Marilyn would sit out there, even in the black flies, even with the mosquitoes massing at dusk, just to take in the long day, to feel they had once more won through to the year's first warmth after a winter that always took hold of you and squeezed, held you until you had rattled and gasped what seemed to be your last.

Marilyn. They had bought that farm early one summer after the birth of their first son. He remembered one afternoon, the baby sleeping upstairs, when Marilyn had taken his hand and led him out to the back porch, then skipped down the steps and away out into the yard, laughing, saying come on, come on. Marilyn, who even then was on the far side of two hundred and eighty pounds, so that these rare bursts of girlish prancing came as a sudden delight, and something of a spectacle, yet one that gladdened Adam's heart much as would—and honest, he meant this in the best possible way, a man who had kept cattle all his life—much as would the sight of cows frisking in the fields. And she *was* frisky that time, giving him the come-hither and then plumping down on the grass, lifting her dress up and off over head and lying back, good Lord, what words were there for this? The muchness of her, the mostness, her plenitude stretched out in sunlight on the stubbled backyard of a farm that was at least partway theirs, and on which they looked to raise children and chickens and cows and a mostway decent version of their own harried and needful selves, so that peeling off his clothes he felt like singing, getting down on his knees before her abundance; there should have been rising to his throat some hymn of praise to the amber-waves-of-grainishness of it all, as he dipped in his oar and pulled for home, thinking purple mountains' majesty, thinking this land is my land, this land is your land, pulling a good stroke until something seismic, some force of the very earth he had not yet known to be within his grasp, heaved him up and rolled him over, her flesh now cascading over him with the force of a Niagara, so that he found himself on his back looking up into the green light of maples newly leafed against the early summer sun and thinking: this is it, this is heaven, now, I have died and gone there, and all that he had worried about before then seemed so very small, squeezed out of the airless space between their two beating hearts, her flesh heaving and pounding like surf, washing him over with bounty, until he felt urged up out of himself, his very life fired up and out of him like wet sand through a cannon, gushing up and into her, his damp and vital tribute then settling into her oceans, drifting down like sediment, glittering blond and golden in the light's last reach before finding a dim repose, this last dust of himself bedded among her sands and silts, received calmly and without surprise into the bottommost floor of things.

Adam Townsend, now in the shadow of Mt. Penacook, whistling homeward on a dry road built by men of foresight and purpose, slapped his hand on the wheel and wondered: would such a time ever come again?

Toward the middle of April, the phone began to ring more often. But Forrest wasn't answering. He would have liked his refusal to answer to be some monkish ritual of self-purification. For wasn't this what his life had come down to: minor feats of self-discipline? But, as much as he didn't want to admit it, the fact was he was scared. Things seem bollixed beyond repair. He was never supposed to have been the one in this position. When he was growing up, he had been told that the land would go into a family trust, with his older brother Peter in charge. But then Pete had gotten himself killed in the war, and his sister Margaret died later of cancer. His father, made bitter and fatalistic by these losses, never followed through on the idea of a trust and simply handed it all over to Forrest, the youngest. And now he had bollixed it up. He had married that Thompson girl and then left her, and now everything had gone to ruin.

Soon the letters began to arrive.

April 15, 1989

Mr. Forrest Garnett
6092 Pershing
St. Louis, MO 63130

Dear Forrest,

You know what's happening on Rattlesnake Ridge, so here it is and no bull. Your son and this fellow Mongerson are planning on making a mess

112

up there, so you're looking at the value of your remaining properties taking a dive. I'm still interested enough that I'll offer you one thousand an acre for the whole lot. That's 1.6 million. I know you've got a lot more than money tied up there, but if you were ever going to get out from under that land, now's the time. If you wanted to keep the fishing camp, we could talk about that.

The Orville Rogers business is over. They've got that young Weed in for psychological evaluation. I suspect they'll just keep him locked up in the hospital. Sad for all concerned.

Let me know what you're thinking because things may move fast here.

Yours,

Bud

May 2, 1989

Dear Mr. Garnett,

I've replaced some windows at Lakeside Farm and am sending you the bill as you asked. Clarence wasn't happy about it, of course. Wanted to fix the old ones himself, but they were shot.

Work has been slow, but I hope to hear about a big job soon. A house on Jackson Island,

113

if you can believe that.

    Sincerely,

    Kyle Cooper

May 8, 1989

Dear Mr. Garnett,

I need to speak to you in regards to the homicide case here on Rattlesnake Ridge. There has been no answer to your phone. If I do not hear from you I may have to ask the assistance of the local authorities there in locating you. In terms of the homicide, Peregrine Weed has confessed. He is being held in the state hospital in Concord pending trial. But the Attorney General has not decided what to do with the case yet. I am not all easy about the situation. Particularly I would like to know more about what has been going on with that property leading up to Orville Rogers's death. I need to know the nature of any contacts you have had concerning that property with such persons as include Mr. Lawrence Mongerson, Orville Rogers, Bud Grisham, your son Howard, your daughter Lily, and with the former Mrs. Forrest Garnett. Or anybody else. The date, time, and what the conversation was about is necessary for my investigation.

Your cooperation in this matter is expected.
And appreciated.

Sincerely,

Adam Townsend

Shaftesbury Police Department

May 10, 1989

Forrest—

You will have learned by now that I have disposed of my Rattlesnake Ridge property. I trust you approve of my method.

Constance

p.s. I <u>am</u> dying. Probably sometime this year. Thought you might want to know.

p.p.s. In truth, I don't care whether you approve or not. But you already know that.

May 12, 1989

Dear Forrest Garnett,

I'm not sure what you have heard about me by now, from your son or from others, but I feel that it is time to represent myself to you directly.

You may not remember me from the Center for the Study of the Cosmic Order. I imagine you do not wish to think much about that time. I'll say

115

nothing more, only that I felt very deeply for your family's loss. Among the good things to come out of that time are my friendships with your son Howard, who has become a valued collaborator, and with your daughter Lily, for whom I have always had great affection.

My own process over the past ten years has been the unfolding of tremendous energy in the field of real estate development. I feel truly blessed to have been a part of this extraordinary period of growth in the 1980's.

I feel blessed, as well, to have been influenced by your son in the matter of our involvement in the property you know as Rattlesnake Ridge. As I'm sure he has told you, we are planning a residential development there on the property once held by Howard and his mother. I have waited this long to contact you because our plans for the project remain quite preliminary. While the possibilities for the property are truly tremendous, it has become clear to me that they would be even more so should the property now held by you and Lily be included in the project.

I know that this property has been in your family for a long time, and that you are not likely to be interested in overtures from me or anyone else. I have a great deal of respect and fondness for your family, and out of that respect I will take the liberty of making myself quite plain: I am in a position to offer you $1200 per acre for the 1600 acres you hold, for a total of $1.92 million. The offer is for cash.

I want you to know that by now my interest in Shaftesbury has become as much personal as financial. You may have heard that I have also purchased the property known as Jackson Island, which I hope will someday be the site of my personal residence. In hearing Howard and Lily speak of Shaftesbury, I had always known it to be an extraordinary place, and recently I have confirmed this first hand. In my brief visits there I have already developed a tremendous affection for the place and its people. So much history there! After many wandering years in search of a home, I now know in my heart that I have found one.

Business has kept me away from the area for some time, but soon I hope that my schedule will permit me to return. I am looking forward, particularly, to renewing my acquaintance with your lovely daughter Lily.

My offer may be unwelcome. It stands, nonetheless. Please know that as a prospective new neighbor, I am eager to help you, your family, and the town in any way that I can.

Yours sincerely,

Lawrence Samuel Mongerson III, President

The Mongerson Corporation

May 17, 1989

Dear Forrest,

You haven't responded to my last letter and no one seems to be answering your phone, so I'll try again. Nothing has moved on Rattlesnake Ridge. No proposals to the planning board, nothing. But I suspect things will happen soon. To get a head start, I've had Adam Townsend do some checking into this Mr. Mongerson's background and qualifications. You may be interested to know that his company has specialized in buying up land around highway interchanges and building those high density townhouse developments you see everywhere now. You wonder what he has in mind for Rattlesnake Ridge. You may also be interested to know that he has apparently worked with people in Nevada who are suspected of involvement with criminal activity in that area. We are waiting for more details on that.

One more thing. I've run some more numbers, and can increase my offer to $1250 per acre, or an even $2 million for the lot. Please think it over.

Bud

To Mr. Forrest Garnett:

Incarceration provides time for reflection.

As I have said to the Planning Board and the Officials of the Town, the range lines are the key. Few people know them, they are forgotten. Double walls running east to west mark the boundaries of the lots. Lot lines run north to south, 100 acres to each lot. People forget the range lines. The space between the walls is four rods, and this is a PUBLIC way. I could walk through some people's dining rooms and be in my rights. The two rod wide corridor running north south between lots is also PUBLIC space. If owners would CHECK THEIR LINES, and CHECK THE DEEDS, they would see the truth of my holdings. The walls are there, telling us.

I am not a bad man, though I have bad in me. What I did was done out of necessity, and is regretted. THERE IS MUCH THAT IS NECESSARY AND TO BE REGRETTED.

The tree drops its leaves but remains rooted, strong. Stores its sap. It knows that spring will come. They cannot kill me, they cannot bury me. You will find me again.

I am asking you, Mr. Forrest Garnett, to restore my lands to me.

Sincerely,
Peregrine Weed

May 28, 1989

Dear Dad,

I don't understand what's going on, only that
things are getting weird here. I need some help.
Will you please please please please please please
please come visit?
Love,
Lily

What astonished Forrest most of all—beside the mere fact of
the letters, addressed to a man used to getting little that wasn't bar-
coded or bulk rate—was the number of people who still thought
he could have some effect on events in this world. At times
Forrest thought that his passage through this life was like that of a
neutrino: that chargeless, nearly massless particle so shy of
interaction that its existence could hardly be confirmed. Neutrinos
were caught in pools of water buried inside mountains, trapped at
the end of whirling cyclotrons, fooled into momentary alliances
with more stable particles, their passage the stuff of rumor and
implication. From the point of view of a thing so small, the
universe was almost entirely empty space.

He stood in his damp, rented living room, holding the letter
from his daughter. He had not slept well for two months. He had

been unable to work, and he seemed to see, hear, taste, and smell the world around him as though his head were wrapped in gauze, enclosing him within the bubble of his own hot breath. He stared stupidly out of his favorite window, thinking that his career seemed to have had few concrete effects save these: the solution of certain problems involving phased-array microwave antennas; the botched stewardship of a large parcel of land on the shores of Abenaki Lake in the state of New Hampshire; and the fathering of two children, neither one of whom made him unreservedly glad.

Forrest's first major disappointment with his daughter had come eighteen years ago now, when she decided not to go to the college to which Forrest had already paid a deposit, and instead "split for the Coast," her generation's equivalent, to his mind, of running off with the circus. He could have accepted the uncleanliness, the disorder, the utter bra-lessness of her life then— this, after all, is what young women *did* in the 1970s. He might have lived with the sex and the drugs, might even have been able to stomach the bogus spiritual rhetoric with which these various hedonisms were hyped. All this, he might have reasoned, was just youthful spirit working itself out.

What he could not accept, of course, was the man. Forrest had met him once, and that was enough. He flew to Nevada to do it, saw at once that Johnny Ray Bushman, spindle-limbed and goateed like the devil himself, deserved all the great old epithets traditionally reserved by fathers for their daughters' despoilers: libertine, rake, scoundrel, blackguard, rogue. Events proved Forrest right: Bushman made Lily pregnant, refused to marry her, and then got himself killed under circumstances that suggested his life up to that point had not been entirely up to code.

121

Painful to see how sadness had settled on her since then. Years of nothing jobs, a life without plans, at least none she had ever told him about. He knew she was living in North Ridgeway now, but he didn't even have her phone number. She had lived in so many places these past years it was hard to keep up.

Forrest decided it was time to get into the woods. What he needed was a hike up Rattlesnake Ridge, but instead he drove his car, a twenty-year-old Ford station wagon with bald tires, through the city, across the river into Illinois, and upstream to the state park where he could hike to the top of the limestone bluffs overlooking the Mississippi River. With a half hour's steady plodding, he reached the observation platform and looked out across the mile-wide expanse of the Mississippi, a burnished steel sheet in the hazy sun. A tow pushed its clutch of barges upstream, moving no faster than a man can walk, churning the water behind it to muddy froth. Up in the distance another could be seen headed down. On the near side of the river lay the broad curve of a channel that the river had abandoned for the time being, and which was now a weedy swamp waiting for the time, a hundred or a thousand years from now, when the river would swing back this way.

Forrest remembered reaching the top of Rattlesnake Ridge with Lily once when she was six—or eight, or ten? From Lookout Rock one could gaze out over the shimmering miles of Abenaki Lake, and trace the intricate geometries of its islands and coves. One could see almost all of Shaftesbury, though to the unpracticed eye there was little to see. From that height the town's hills flattened, and its roads and houses disappeared into a nap of green, so that one could imagine a land without owners and boundaries, and suffer for a moment the sweet and fatal illusion of inexhaustible bounty.

"Every time I get up here, I feel I could just lift off and fly," he had announced, hoping to delight her with this childlike thought.

Lily looked at him sharply, for she was that way even then.

"No, you can't," she said. "You're a human being."

"But I have wings," he said, spreading his arms.

"Dad, you shouldn't be joking."

Forrest felt something of that deflation now, for even though he had once seen bald eagles soar from this same spot, he now felt weighted, sunk to the floor of the ancient inland sea from which the muddy river was a slow, clotted release.

Forrest turned his back on the view and struck off down the trail into the woods, moving through the heat as through hot broth. The sun reached its height, and the woods smelled as though drenched in liquor. A half mile in, he found a level spot in dappled shade amid a stand of mature oaks. As he unslung his knapsack and sat with his back against a tree, folding his legs stiffly beneath him, he remembered when Lily had tried to teach him about meditation. It must have been soon after her arrival in Nevada, when she had called him flush with excitement over her new discoveries.

"You've got to find the gap between your thoughts," she said. "Then widen it."

"Are you sure that's a good idea?"

More came back: the day he got that call, he must have just moved himself, to St. Louis. She had caught him in an unguarded moment, standing on the warped linoleum of his new kitchen, staring out the windows of the back porch at unfamiliar foliage. In a word or three, describe the foliage. They had both been caught up in the sense of new venture, charged with the boosterism of fresh starts and clean slates.

"You can reach through to your immortality," she told him.

"Should I cancel my life insurance?"

Lily giggled like a girl. "You sound happy, Dad."

"Hard to believe," Forrest said.

"Dad, I'm starting to believe it's possible to live a remarkable life."

"Me, too," he said.

It must have been about that time that he took off for a hiking trip in Alaska. It was the only time he had seen grizzly bears in the wild. There were none east of the Rockies, notwithstanding the old story about grizzlies being sighted on Rattlesnake Ridge. He donned hiking boots and shouldered a heavy pack as he had not done since he had been a young man, and set off with a woman twenty years younger than he—she had lived in the downstairs apartment, was practically a stranger—on a two week trip in Denali National Park. They crossed barren alluvial plains in sight of the looming white mass of Mt. McKinley, forded broad shallow streams gray with glacial silt, tented on the tundra, ate bags of gorp and reconstituted powdered food, had sex that Forrest remembered as being more arduous than it was worth, and learned in the course of two glorious weeks to despise one another thoroughly. Later, he told Clarence about the trip without mentioning the woman, but he imagined that Clarence guessed the truth. And he told how one day he had watched several grizzlies hunt ground squirrels a half mile away, on the opposite slope of a narrow valley. He told Clarence how the big animals shambled, loped, and leaped after their prey, their fur silver and blond and golden and brown, rippling in the sunlight. They made good sport of it, and for one hour, there in a high treeless place of grasses and salmonberry and blueberry and moss, rocks and snow and sky, Forrest had looked on at a world utterly indifferent to his own.

For that hour he forgot the trip's complications and dissatisfactions. Happiness had seemed possible. He had even been willing to believe that Lily's happiness had something to do with sitting pretzel-legged and emptying her mind of thoughts. Forrest's own legs had never been limber enough for him to sit comfortably on the ground for long. As for emptying his mind of thoughts, he could as effectively empty his lungs of air: after a minute's concerted squeezing, it all came rushing back in.

Forrest ate his lunch methodically: tuna sandwich, a box of raisins, an orange, and a candy bar, exactly what he would have eaten on the top of Rattlesnake Ridge fifty years ago. Afterwards he stretched out full length on the ground in hope of sleep.

Thoughts rushed in: that by now, late June, the black fly season would have passed in Shaftesbury, and the mosquitoes would be reaching their peak; that his son Howard had infuriated him by waiting until age ten to learn to ride a bicycle; that Lily's unhappiness really dated all the way back to puberty; that his union with Constance, when viewed as the sum of its consequences, had been a mistake of cosmic order; that all of this was his fault; that none of it was.

Forrest sighed, weary of thoughts he had been having too often lately. He had not meant to be one of those fathers who loomed over their children. His own father had been one of these, a tower of a man, handsome at sixty, still splitting four cords of firewood each year, defying his wife's orders, defying the doctors until, after three hundred nights of sleeping upright in a chair, he decided to lie down and die in his own bed at seventy-two. Though Forrest had not wanted to loom, he had perhaps taken his own looming presence as natural and right. He had crowded both Lily and Howard, and when he left, he had left them giddy and reeling. Or was he kidding himself? Maybe he hadn't mattered all that much.

Remembering Lily's advice to find the gap between his thoughts, Forrest closed his eyes and tried at least to summon thoughts he had not had recently: that the bark of birch saplings is a reddish bronze; that nuthatches feed upside down; that the song of the white-throated sparrow, rising up a plaintive third before fading out in a series of small gasps, a song he had heard only above three thousand feet in New Hampshire's White Mountains, was the most sorrowful, beautiful sound he knew; that beauty itself was banal; that the backs of his thighs itched; that midwestern forests smelled of putrefaction; that he wished he could sleep; that the moon shining though wet, bare branches laced together a circular reflection among the network of twigs; that he was growing drowsy; that the way his first dog, Spooky, had cocked his ears had always made him think of a friend of his mother's who later figured in his sexual fantasies; that he missed the smell of someone's skin other than his own, and thus enjoyed public transportation; that the production of sound out of a soprano's mouth might be described by Bessel functions; that the Berlin wall was being picked apart with kitchen utensils; that politics was the exquisite elaboration of human stupidity; that summary statements about the nature of politics were a juvenile indulgence; that he wished he could sleep; that he wished he could hug his son and daughter to his chest as he

126

had when they were young; that he wished his son and daughter would disappear from the face of the earth; that he regretted never having learned to tell a crocodile from an alligator; that he thought he had read that the difference between them was subtle but important, or subtle and not important, or that there really was no difference at all. At length, Forrest Garnett fell asleep. He had no dreams. The sun arched high across the sky. Within the circle whose diameter was defined, Leonardo-style, by the span of his arms, two hundred thirty-four earthworms mulched the soil. When he woke, Forrest saw an adult male grizzly, weighing approximately eight hundred pounds, hunched over not twenty feet away, grunting in an effort to defecate. His fur was dark brown, the great hump of muscle between his shoulder blades tense with effort. He did not look at Forrest until, with a final grunt, he released a shining black load, gleaming and sweet, steaming in the sunlight. Then he swung his blunt head toward Forrest to fix on him a stare of complete indifference. Forrest sat upright, feeling his own bowels quiver on the edge of release. The feeling came to him, as it had not since Alaska, of being part of the food chain. Then the bear turned, swinging its weight gently, shambled off through the trees, and was gone. Forrest was left clutching his knees, shaken, faint, and, he realized later, disappointed. He had wanted the bear to speak his name.

Not long afterward, Forrest found himself in the airport, his one bag and briefcase at his feet, a collection of letters loosely stacked on the table before him, held in place by a sweating glass, which glued the papers together with its sticky ring. He drew his pen from his shirt pocket, flipped to a fresh page on a narrow-ruled notepad, and set to work.

127

Dear Bud:

Anyone attempting to get me off that land will have to pry my cold, dead fingers from the last birch sapling, etc. At the very least you will have to reckon with Clarence and Lily.

As a taxpayer, I must object to your use of the town's police officer to do detective work on your competition.

Forrest

Dear Adam,

Concerning the recent unfortunate events on Rattlesnake Ridge, I have nothing to relate.

Best regards to you and your family,
Forrest Garnett

Dear Kyle:

Check enclosed. If those sills are rotted out, replace them. And again, don't let Clarence pay you a cent.

Be careful on Jackson Island.
Forrest Garnett

Dear Constance:

No, I do not approve. My condolences.
Regards,
Forrest

To Peregrine Weed:

I have great affection for your family. Your grandfather once took me deer hunting. We saw nothing, and froze.

Our deeds to the land on Rattlesnake Ridge are available for inspection at the Pinkham County Registrar's office.

I wish you well.

Sincerely,

Forrest Garnett

Dear Mr. Mongerson,

Your proposal is, of course, absurd. As for your settling in Shaftesbury, there is no law that I know of which would prevent it. I am sure that if given the opportunity I would treat you as any native treats the flatlander with money in his pockets: with suspicion and contempt masked by indifference. I will make no comment on your relationship with my son. As for my daughter whom you profess so much to admire: should your mere presence within the same zip code cause her the slightest twitch of discomfort, I will arrange to have the marrow removed from your bones and spread on toast.

Sincerely,

Forrest Garnett

Dearest Lily,

Beware, beware: there is blood in the water and the sharks are circling. (Forgive an old man's theatrics.) Will I come? Yes. A thousand times, yes.

Your father.

Chapter Three

1

Facsimile for Lily Garnett:

Dear Lily,

I assume Howard has told you that I'm
dying. That in itself is nothing extraordinary, life,
after all, being a terminal condition. My case
differs only in that metastatic breast cancer tends
to firm up one's schedule. I won't rehearse for
you all I have been through since the diagnosis last
fall; that would be laborious in the extreme, and
I'm not sure that you, who after all have been only
my sometime daughter these last years, would be
interested.

I am tired much of the time. Forgive me.

There are mornings when I discover that
shrewd and skillful men have worked all through
the night to replace my marrow with lead. To sit
upright is the work of an hour. There are
evenings when after meditation the lead has been
flushed away (I can actually see it, a gray mush

puddling at my feet), then replaced with golden light, my bones hollow and light as birds', the whole of me subtleized so that I am ready to rise through the roof, through plaster and lath and sheathing and tar and asphalt and on into the darkling sky.

But such moments are rare.

Your mother

Lily had come in late, and found Kathy already steamed in the kitchen, pushing a loop of damp hair up under the net Waldheim made them wear when they did prep work. They were doing salads, and Lily got right to it without a word: together they tumbled heads of iceberg beneath the cold water tap before chopping them into chunks, they sliced cucumbers into cool disks, cut tomatoes into firm, bland wedges, julienned peppers, then dumped handfuls into bowls with a drizzle of sprouts and a spoonful of croutons over the top of each.

"Sorry I'm late," Lily said, when she at last felt her body settle into the rhythm of the work. "I got a fax."

"You got more than that to apologize for, babe," Kathy said.

"Such as?"

"Where do men come from?" Kathy asked. "What planet, I wonder?"

"Did we have a bad date? Who? And why would I need to apologize?" "It was a truly weird person, though I can't say the date was bad, exactly. More like being kidnapped by aliens. Entertaining. *Men.* Are all their hormones different, or only some of them? I swear, it's like, you're talking to a guy and just waiting

132

for the beam of light to come down, and for him to say, 'I must return to my ship.'"

"Who?"

"Your brother."

Lily, slicing tomatoes, concentrated on keeping her fingertips away from the blade. "You went out with my brother. Without a chaperon."

"You didn't tell me he was dangerous," Kathy said.

"Was he?"

"No. Unfortunately."

"What did you do?"

"Dinner at the North Slope. Then we drove around like in high school. We didn't fool around, if that's what you want to know."

"I'm sure I don't," Lily said.

"At first I wanted to, but he didn't. Then he wanted to, but I didn't."

"So that was it?"

"Don't worry, big sister. He's really an okay guy."

"He talked about himself the whole time," Lily said.

"He's got a lot of ideas," Kathy said.

"That's the problem," Lily said.

"Believe me, babe," Kathy said, "I've been out with lots of guys who've got only *one* idea, and it doesn't exactly appeal to a girl's higher aspirations."

"And then there are the guys," Lily said, "who are just a little too good to believe. You keep waiting for them to screw up."

"Show me one, babe," Kathy said. "And I'll marry him."

"You can't," Lily said. "Because he's already asked *me*."

Kathy had turned away from Lily, lining up the finished salads on trays, then sliding the loaded trays carefully onto a rack one by one. In Kathy's movements Lily could see the firmness and precision beneath the feminine softness of her flesh. Kathy would make a good but demanding wife, Lily thought. No nonsense. But over the past six months Lily had come to see how the habit of loneliness rested just below the surface of Kathy's humor, giving the hard edge to her tone that some mistook for high spirits or even sexual desire. Kathy had had too many boyfriends for too many years for it to be just fun anymore. In recent weeks Lily had sensed, as she did now, that Kathy was losing patience with her complaints about Kyle.

"You've already got my opinion about *that*," Kathy said, still with her back turned.

"You think he's the patron saint of body hair," Lily said.

"Where I'm at now, babe, is any man who takes his shoes off before unbuckling his trousers is two rungs up the evolutionary ladder."

Kathy shoved the last tray onto the rack with a bit of extra force. She had trouble meeting Lily's eyes, and Lily, wishing she could just hold her then, put a hand on her arm.

"Poor Kath. We'll find you somebody."

"We didn't last night, I guess," Kathy said.

"Howard *didn't* try anything. I'll kill him."

"Just rest your soul, darlin'," Kathy said, taking off her hair net and tucking it in her apron. "He didn't try one blessed thing."

Facsimile for Lily Garnett:

Dear Lily,

What I meant to say is that I no longer want to be your sometime mother. Women of my generation were raised to believe that parents and children didn't have to say that they loved one another. It was supposed to go without saying.

I am yours always. In all things, yours.

Your mother

Kyle was running late. He had been up the night before writing bids for jobs he knew he wouldn't get. He had overslept that morning, and rushed to the post office to mail the bids, then to Tommy's store for coffee and a cellophaned pack of doughnuts, running too late to say even hello to Tommy, stuffing a doughnut in his mouth as pretext for not speaking to Adam, who was parked on a stool in the back, just waiting to take up somebody's time, then driving a little too fast on the dirt road out to the job site, losing it on a sharp curve and scratching his fender in the brush. The crew was harried; the clients would arrive that night for their first stay in their new house. Kyle spent the day working through the punch list, bending his big hands to small tasks: fastening knobs on the kitchen cabinets, adjusting the hinges on a screen door, screwing in light bulbs and switch plates, installing a medicine chest in a bathroom, oiling down the butcher block counters in the kitchen. With each task his mind was focused on the next two to follow. Lily had told him once that waitressing was like that. Pouring coffee, she'd be thinking that party's salads and then that man's check. A whole night keeping three balls in the air.

He would get there at nine, when the dinner rush was over but before the serious party crowd got going. He would wait for the right moment. He would be gentle but firm.

When he was younger, a kid fixing a bicycle, nailing together a rabbit hutch from scraps of lath, building a tree fort, matter had been his enemy. The stripped bolt, the split board, the nail that would not drive true. He had thought the act of building something to be purely one of bending the physical world to his will, overcoming not only matter's intransigence but the clumsiness of his hands, the inadequacy of his tools, his own stupidity. Now he understood that the tradesman's true antagonist was time. It was no longer a question of whether he could do a thing, but whether he could do faster what he had done a hundred times before. "Stop and think" had been his father's phrase. Kyle had heard it whispered behind his back as he bent over the workbench in the garage, shouted from the porch as he whacked boards together in the yard, hissed in anger when he blundered. Kyle sometimes thought that when his father's time came, he would whisper those words with his dying breath. Stop and think. But now, stopping cost money. And thinking, though there was plenty of it—endless measurement and calculation, juggling the A, B, and C's of a hundred sequenced tasks—thinking of this sort was sometimes difficult, sometimes numbing, but always something to be merely pushed through, ordinary as hammering a nail. Stop and think.

136

He would not raise his voice. He would be entirely reasonable. He would tell her that he loved her.

Finally they swept, hauled, raked, and heaved heaps of refuse into the beds of several pickup trucks for one last run to the dump. Out of there at just before five, Kyle passed Adam Townsend, who was in his truck, headed the other way with a load of manure. Driving fast. Was he running late, too? What was the matter with them all? This was supposed to be life in the country. It was the middle of June. Kyle couldn't remember the last time he'd had a meal sitting down.

Things would slow soon enough, if no new jobs came through. He had only little things lined up, a month's work, maybe. He could use the time to do some clearing on his own land in Upper Corner. But lately he had started to have doubts about it. Over the last three months they had finished straightening and widening a stretch of the state road about a mile from Kyle's property. They had cleared quite a bit in the process, and now on windless days Kyle could stand on the height of land where he thought to build his house and hear the trucks headed up to North Ridgeway and back. The wispy hum and groan spoke to Kyle as if from the edge of a dream, reminding him of every mistake he had ever made.

Had he been wrong to stay home, to work in the trades? He had friends who did film editing in California, computer programming in Texas. His own life seemed to lack imagination.

But now, cresting Monmouth Hill at sixty miles an hour with its sudden, heart-stopping view of Rattlesnake Ridge and the glittering reach of Abenaki Lake, Kyle had his daily confirmation that, yes, Shaftesbury was the one patch of earth on which he cared

137

to live, even if he could rarely slow down enough to enjoy it, even if his thumbnail was split and his feet ached, and even if his family hadn't lived here for two hundred years. Down the hill and onto the only long straightaway in town, Kyle stomped the accelerator, cranked the window open, and bellowed into the roaring wind.

A few minutes later, he skidded into the patch of gravel that served as a driveway for his house. Bungalow. Shack. Really a series of shacks tacked together, each one smaller than the next, all akilter, so that one moved room by room as though through the builder's own cramped sense of progress, each diminished and slanting space another sour gesture toward pinched possibility, toward a future tapering to its frugal end. Last and least was the bedroom, the ceiling barely over six feet and kneewalled so that Kyle bulked against the sloped ceilings. He had brought Lily here a few times, but she had felt suffocated and refused to return. Smaller than a mobile home, tucked on a wedge of land next to a cemetery, the whole place could and should have been bulldozed and in an afternoon made to look like it had never been.

The only thing worth saving was the furniture: some pieces were refinished antiques, but the best ones Kyle had made himself. The Shaker table of pale birch in the kitchen, graceful and spare, the clever cherry writing desk in the den, in the bedroom the maple chest with a Birdseye top. Kyle's furniture was too well made to be marketable. It met Kyle at the end of each day with a kind of reproach: it had the precision and finish that the rest of his life lacked.

Kyle tore off his filthy clothes and bent his body into the rusting shower stall. He was only thirty-two, with time enough to look around. But the number of eligible, never mind attractive or even tolerably companionable women supplied by the Shaftesbury gene pool was limited. If it wasn't going to be Lily, it had to be someone else pretty darn soon. A helpmeet for his yonder years. But not Lily? The idea made him clutch his shoulders, grit his teeth in the spritz of luke-warm water and wonder if he wasn't born for some other life. Doctor, lawyer, Indian chief.

After the shower he would shave once with his old blade, then a second time with a new one, change into clean jeans and maybe even a dress shirt. He would try that styling gel that Diane at the hair salon in Wilton was always insisting would change his life. He would trim the hair tufting out of his ears.

He wondered whether money was an issue. Lily always said it wasn't, and for the most part he believed her, but you never knew, with a woman, if there wasn't some tucked-away part of her holding out for something better. Doctor, lawyer.

Three months ago he was about to be rich. That guy Mongerson wanted a bid on a house of maybe five thousand square feet, he said. Premium grade, on an island to boot, you're looking at two hundred per square foot, a cold million. His share enough so that he could sell his land and build on something better, maybe that property Bud had listed over in east Shaftesbury: twenty-five acres, half pasture, with a small stream and a view of the Pequawket Mountains. The meeting was supposed to be at the town dock, so they could take a boat out to look at the site. Kyle had driven like a maniac to get there, fat numbers doing the rumba in his head. He pulled up to find no boat, nobody named Mongerson, and only the last person he really wanted to see just then. Howard. Leaned against his BMW, smiling and showing his empty hands. Mongerson was away on urgent business, Howard explained. Denver, maybe Fort Worth. Had been gone for a week. Couldn't say when he'd be back.

"How long have you been working with this guy?" Kyle had asked.

"Time is a limited concept," Howard said. "Let's just say years."

"Is he legitimate?"

"I know nothing of his parentage," Howard said. "But perhaps you mean finance-wise."

"I mean am I wasting my time," Kyle said.

"We're talking net worth without limits as we commonly understand them."

Kyle considered whether he could punch a dent in Howard's car without hurting his hand too much. He decided to laugh instead.

"Howard, why do I get this feeling that Mongerson is a creature of your imagination?"

"You give me too much credit, Kyle."

And that was the last Kyle or anyone else had heard of Mongerson, as far as Kyle knew. It had been a bad time: they had just found Orville Rogers killed on Rattlesnake Ridge, and Lily had been all out of sorts. She had told him she could not, or would not, marry him. Since then she had been achingly polite, trying too hard. Kyle had been churlish, given to small and secret fits of anger: he had snapped pens, stabbed a screwdriver through the drywall in the back of a closet, stomped on lightbulbs.

Lily had gotten a letter from her father saying he was coming to visit at the end of the month, and now Kyle was nervous about seeing him. It was never easy, under the best of circumstances, to speak to the father of the woman you're fucking out of wedlock. Even worse now, when he and Lily were so on edge. Kyle had taken to spending the night at Lily's less often. They made love rarely, with a weary deliberateness, their exertions lacking that willing suspension of disbelief on which love depends. "Where are we headed?" he had asked her once afterwards, strangely wakeful as their bodies cooled in the dark. In a whisper that was sad and on the edge of sleep, she had said, "Paradise."

"Where am *I* headed?" Kyle asked himself now, stepping from the shower to feel the air cool his skin. Not to riches and fame, apparently. He wondered how much that mattered with Forrest Garnett. Not much, perhaps. He knew that to a Garnett what mattered more was who your family was. And Kyle Cooper, though he had lived here thirty-one of his thirty-two years, was clearly an outsider. Forrest Garnett seemed to like him well enough, gave him some work at Lakeside Farm, but at bottom Kyle had always been made to feel that difference between them. It was nothing ever uttered in words, but it didn't have to be. Forrest's stance, the set of his jaw, his easy recourse to silence, all spoke well enough of generations in the churchyard and two thousand acres at his back, a sufficiency that sooner or later he would use against you.

The first item of clothing Kyle put on was his watch. Running late. If he got there soon enough, he might get a corner table. He would order tonic water and lime. He would speak in complete sentences. She would know that Kyle Cooper was nobody's fool.

141

3

Facsimile for Lily Garnett:

Dear Lily,

The first hot day of the season; the sun seemed to shoot straight to the zenith. An old lizard, I warm my bones. There's still mud on the mountain roads, the passes aren't yet clear. I'd like to get up to see the bristlecones one last time.

Your mother

She had been looking at him a full minute before she saw him, seated at the small table by the door. She had often wondered about this quality of vision: that the brain could ignore the facts presented to it, dissemble, play dumb with the data. How often had she spent harried minutes searching for something—a wooden spoon, say—only to find it right there, smugly solid, in the very bowl she was stirring? Ananda used to say that the human mind takes in only one tenth of one percent of all the stimuli available to it. That could be measured, she supposed, with the right instruments. She remembered her father explaining to her that, though they watched only one channel at a time, the television antenna was actually receiving *all the channels at once*. So what demon was it—and by now she was striding toward the table, whipping out her pad, all this reverie having passed in an instant—who switched the channels, who chose form from shadow, and only now allowed these patches of gray and brown and white to be assembled into the image of a customer, patiently awaiting service?

142

Much later she would think that perhaps it was the man himself. Perhaps she had not recognized him as a customer because he did not wish to be seen as one and had managed to control his emanations as though fronted by some PR man operating in regions beyond the visible.

He was smiling as she approached. He knew her.

"Lily."

"You're Mongerson."

"How *are* you?" he said. He seemed overjoyed, yet oddly made no move to rise, did not offer his hand. His pleasure at seeing her was all in his boyish face, full cheeks, clear blue eyes, while his body remained inert as a mannequin.

"Mongerson," Lily said.

He laughed. "Lawrence."

"No, you were Larry."

More laughter. Utterly delighted.

"Ah, Lily, so much has changed." He gestured toward the chair opposite, raised eyebrows. Could she sit?

Lily glanced around. No one in the place. "For a minute." Fearing a sudden appearance by Waldheim, fearing—who knew what?

"So," the man said, leaning forward now, tips of his fingers together to make a tent. "The hardworking waitress."

It was his hands she remembered. Swallows dipping over the yard. Already the evening's cool in the air. Dark alfalfa fields at the foot of the slope, beyond them the lighter expanse of sage already in shadow, stretching to where tawny mountains received the sun's last red glow. It was this man, Mongerson, who had placed his hand on her belly ten years ago and asked her to bear the child.

143

Since then he had lived in her mind as a creature of fable only, a voice from a dream, everything about him forgotten except for that moment on the creaking porch, those words, that touch. To see him now, in light tweed jacket, sharply creased chinos, white dress shirt, coiffed, shaven, all his pixels somehow tweaked up a notch, eyes atwinkle, was to feel that she had just traded in her black and white set for color.

"You," Lily said. "You're so— so. *Vivid.*"

"You do remember me, then."

"Hardly. I mean no. I mean, frankly, I try to forget as much of that as possible."

"You shouldn't forget the good. There was a lot that was good out there."

She did not remember these perfect teeth. She wondered what it would be like to touch this expensive skin. Slick, perhaps, like new vinyl.

Lily found herself wondering aloud: "Are you angel or devil?"

"These categories aren't helpful," Mongerson said.

"My Presbyterian blood," Lily said. "I believe in hell."

"Why?"

"Been there." Lily felt a slight flush. She had revealed too much.

"Ah, Lily." Mongerson reached his hands across the table, but she kept hers in her lap. "I've been looking for you."

The realization, sudden and sure, seemed at once so trivial and so monstrous that she didn't know whether to laugh or break his nose.

"You're Fax Man."

"At your service."

144

It was all Lily could do to keep from taking him by the lapels. She leaned forward, glaring, so that he sat back in his chair.

"Don't you dare take advantage of my brother."

He faced her without a quiver. "I don't know what you're assuming," he said blandly.

"That you'd have him make a fool of himself on your behalf."

"He's of legal age, and certainly capable of making a fool of himself on his own behalf. On mine, he just might make some money as well."

"A fool and his money are soon parted."

"Conventional wisdom is a fetter on consciousness."

"I can't afford any other kind. I'm economizing."

"Penny-wise, pound foolish."

She had forgotten this, too. He was smart. And now she remembered—a memory so surprising that it startled her, she who had for so long been accustomed to being ambushed by memory—she had once considered herself smart, too. It was another thing she had left behind in a room full of stainless steel drawers in Ely, Nevada, not even knowing she had left it. Now with a dim ache she remembered that until then, despite her lack of formal schooling, she had been something of a snob about her reading, her wit, her ability to move through debate with the same sort of clean-limbed strength she had once felt on the basketball court, thinking, hey, she could run the fast break, get out in front, take it to the hole. This strength had threatened Johnny Ray at first, so that she learned to keep it hidden. But in their last, best years at the Center, when he had grown to accept her more fully, she had been able to let it out again. Running the floor, always thinking two moves ahead. Others just couldn't keep up. Except Mongerson.

145

"We used to argue over dinner," Lily said.

"It was positively rabbinical," Mongerson said. "You were vicious. A native syllogist."

"You were a pain in the ass," Lily said.

Lily had to take a moment to focus, simply to *see* clearly this man before her. She wondered whether, and in wondering, knew, that he was there to seduce her. She was surprised to discover a slight thrill at the thought.

"Why did you send that stupid fax?"

"A rash impulse," he said.

"You've made money," she said. "What happened to voluntary poverty?"

"I'd like to tell you about it," Mongerson said, beaming. "It's my favorite subject."

"I'm working."

"Tomorrow."

"I'm working."

"I checked your schedule."

"You called Waldheim?"

"Your brother called him for me."

Lily just stared for a moment. The pores of his skin looked as though they had been cleaned individually with a special tool.

"So you really *are* the devil," she said.

Mongerson laughed. There was a keenness there, and calculation, surely. But he seemed to soften as he spoke to her.

"Sometimes I wish I was," he said.

"Why should I have anything to do with you?" Lily asked.

"I won't say 'for old times' sake.' I'd like a chance to explain myself. Is that too much to ask?"

"Everything is too much to ask," Lily said.

She could see his jaw muscles clench. His eyes narrowed the slightest bit and then, as though he caught her noticing, relaxed open again. What a bitch, he was probably thinking. Was that what she had become? One more sour-faced waitress with a sad story to tell?

"Maybe I should thank you for the fax machine," she said.

"I hope you've found it useful."

Lily blushed. Could Mongerson know about the faxes she'd been getting from her mother? Could he know she hadn't answered them?

"I'm afraid whatever ideas you may have about me are outdated," Lily said.

"If you think I'm here to dwell on the past, you don't know me."

"I don't know you in any case. But look—" She held up her hand as though stopping traffic. "Let's cut it out. What time tomorrow?"

"What did I do right all of a sudden?"

"You exhausted my patience. What time."

"I'll pick you up at eleven."

"Fine. You want to eat?" she asked, pad poised. "Mr. Lawrence Mongerson?"

But he didn't want to eat, and in a moment he was gone, so that Lily could at last let out the breath it felt as though she had been holding the whole time they had been speaking. Walking back to the kitchen, she tried to determine whether what she had done amounted to a betrayal. Somehow she had felt that by taking charge as she had at the last moment, not letting him talk her into

147

it, it was less of one. Besides, Kyle had not outright mentioned that he wanted to do anything tomorrow. She was within her rights. For if at times she had trouble feeling that she could ever be entirely her own woman, her soul having been mortgaged long ago, she could feel for a moment, now the fleet pleasure of being not entirely Kyle's, either.

Kathy was there at the kitchen door. "Who's the dude with the teeth?"

"A real estate developer."

"I was thinking tennis pro. Or animal trainer."

"He used to be an alfalfa farmer."

"Wow. He's so. So clean."

"I'll introduce you."

"No, you won't. You save all the good ones for yourself."

4

Facsimile for Lily Garnett:

Dear Lily,

What amazes me most is how silence unfolds into words, as though the clouds that drift across our sky were called forth by the unchanging blue beyond.

Please forgive your mother her precious ramblings. If you want more practical advice, here's something I heard on TV: Buy Johnson & Johnson, sell Ford.

Your mother

Wherein have I offended thee? What foul blast hath passed from my lips to poison the very air between us? By what outward marks hath my disfigured spirit made my visage hateful to thee?

It was the best Kyle could do, writing with a blunt carpenter's pencil on a bar napkin. He handed the note to Kathy, who gave him an annoyed look. She balanced a tray on one hand, and cleared his empties.

"You're not helping your case any, you know. Pestering her like this."

"What would you do?" Kyle asked, in what he wanted to think was the spirit of disinterested inquiry. He had switched from tonic water to beer two hours ago. "If you were a guy and your girlfriend had just told you she was using her one Saturday off in a

149

month to go out with somebody else."

"One thing, I wouldn't be in here drinking myself sorry-eyed right where she could see me. Two, I'd probably ask somebody else out. Get her attention. Me, for instance."

Kathy squinted as she read the note. "What is this, French?"

"I was in a Shakespeare play in high school once."

"She like this stuff? I prefer flowers, you want to know."

"Sometimes when we're, you know, in bed, she likes me to make up lines." Kyle felt a sudden rush of embarrassment. "Why am I telling you this?"

"'Cause you, like most guys, take one look at me and figure I've heard it all before. Problem is, I have."

"Poor Kath."

"I had a guy once wanted me to read the Bible to him while we did it. St. Paul on the subject of celibacy. Drove the man wild. Anyway, you want another drink, or are you going to get your ass out of here and get a life?"

"What are you doing after work?" Kyle asked.

"You don't mean that. And I'm sleeping. Alone. You want to see me, it's in daylight. Take me water-skiing."

"I don't have a boat," Kyle said.

"Well, *that's* a lame excuse," Kathy said, and was gone toward the kitchen, crumpling Kyle's note into the pocket of her apron.

Whether she gave the note to Lily, Kyle never knew, for Lily avoided the merest glance in the direction of his table as only a busy waitress can. And it was busy in there, the air hot and dense, people three deep at the bar shouting over the music. The foosball crowd formed a tight scrum around the table, grunting like hogs, high-fiving after each goal. Kyle knew some of them slightly: ex-

150

frat boys and jocks, guys whose college education seemed to have taught them only the manners and grooming required to sell expensive clothes to tourists and teach rich kids how to ski and play tennis.

In the meantime, he was too busy suffering. For I am an upright man, he wrote, trying now for a more biblical style, something Old Testament. Maybe Kathy would like it, at least. Show me where I have strayed from the paths of righteousness, and I will curse that place. For dark is the way before me, and my days are hateful unto me, and my nights are as the weight of a she-ass upon my back.

What, indeed, had he done? He had gotten there early, grabbed his corner table, hailed Lily with a hearty wave, greeted her with a tender yet tastefully brief—because public—kiss, at the same time tracing with one discrete fingertip the line of her hip, hoping to set up a vibration there for later.

"It's going to be a long night," Lily said. By which she meant, "No nookie."

"Fear not," Kyle said. "I am as patient as an ox. But I did hope we could at least talk."

"It's not a good night, Kyle."

"When *is* a good night?"

Lily had already turned to go, and when she looked back at him now, Kyle knew it was going to be tough sledding.

"Maybe not in this lifetime," Lily said.

"What's happened to us?" Kyle asked.

Lily set her tray on his table, leaned heavily on both palms, her head down.

"I don't know, I keep thinking I'm going to wake up from

151

this. That we'll both wake up and everything will be like it was."

"You're worn out, is all. We'll sleep in tomorrow, all day. I'll get take-out Chinese and pornographic videos."

"What you don't seem to get about me is that I'm prepared to live an unhappy life."

The words set Kyle back a moment. He had never known anyone who could be at once so morose and so beautiful.

"You could set your sights higher," he said. "How about 'guarded joy'? With spells of pleasant melancholy."

"You want me to think it's that easy."

"Easy as misery. More fun, too."

Lily drove a fingertip into the table, as though she had finally spotted the source of their argument, and pinned it there like a bug.

"It's this—this happy talk. Thing is, it's *not* that easy. You want to deny a certain part of me that's, well, not *pretty*. It's like, growing up in Shaftesbury, it was always 'There's Forrest Garnett's daughter,' and they've got some story about me, about my family. They want me to be a certain way. You come to feel you're a figment of other people's imaginations. I haven't turned out to be what people wanted. Not rich, not good at anything. I'm not *nice*."

"We'll play a round of miniature golf. We'll rent a kung fu movie."

Lily shook her head, smiling grimly. "You choose to be an ignoramus," she said.

"We'll do lunch at the mall. Shop for salad tongs."

"You don't want to hear me. You don't really want to be with me."

Kyle felt his humor run out, like tape off a spool.

"Not if you're going to keep feeling sorry for yourself," Kyle

152

said, feeling the small dark thrill of saying words he had often thought but never dared say.

Lily stared, as though she sensed what Kyle was feeling then. Kyle knew they had reached the end of something.

"I've got plans for tomorrow," Lily said.

"Plans?"

And then she told him about Mongerson, and then words passed between them swift and blunt as blows from rubber mallets.

He had not raised his voice, Kyle told himself later, after a dozen or so beers, and after spending the evening trying to get to Lily through Kathy. He had not blasphemed. Not one obscenity had passed his lips. Kyle now silently addressed the assembled multitudes, all those heavy with food, lips shining, flushed with cheer: Is there one among you who will say I am not a righteous man?

Water-skiing? Since his last exchange with Kathy, he had discovered lust in him like a 60-hertz hum, so steady he hadn't noticed it; but now that he had, he couldn't ignore it. He watched Kathy move now through the bar, one sturdy, graceful arm hoisting a full tray over her head. Kyle found himself lost among the weights and measures of her walk, assessing haunch and heft, wanting to trace the curve of her calf, probe with tender tongue the delicately furred porches of her ears.

But still it was Lily he watched most, her every move communicated to him as if by invisible wires tugging his flesh. Though she moved in darkness through the throng, he could still see what there was of her to be seen: a bare forearm hefting a tray, the sheen of her brow, the swift swinging of her limbs as she moved through that convulsive crowd the way a warrior moves among thieves. And so it was no accident that he caught it, as surely as a referee calls the one illegal hold amid the grapple and mayhem at the line of scrimmage. One of the onlookers at the foosball game had bumped her with a shoulder, slowing her up enough so that before she got out of reach, he could grab her just *there*. Lily's first move was to steady her tray with her free hand, and then attempt to disengage. Had she done it right away, she perhaps would have merely dismissed him with one hard stare and gotten on with her work. But she couldn't quite shake free soon enough, and Kyle saw the precise moment when instead of letting go, the man chose to grip down harder, trying, it seemed, to actually get some sort of handle on her nether parts, so that Lily moved beyond being startled, beyond angry, to registering on that uplifted face something like genuine pain, though by then Kyle was on his feet and charging, clearing a swath through the crowd as though through dry standing corn, thinking only: stop me, stop me before I break that man in half.

Yet even as he ran, he saw. In one smooth gesture, Lily dropped her tray, turned, and broke the man's nose with the heel of her hand. Then, neat as you please, she hit him in the throat and solar plexus and kicked him in the shins, giving one the impression that she was breaking him down like something to be shipped in a box, her moves swift and thoughtless and ordinary as folding a paper grocery bag. So that when Kyle arrived, the entire two-hundred-and-fifty-pound projectile of the offender was curled on the floor in what is known in yoga as the Baby Pose, thinking nothing, to be sure, but the sort of thoughts bruises have, while his buddies looked on with the wounded and slack-mouthed amazement one sees in news footage of tornado victims.

154

But it was too late to stop Kyle. With a last course correction, he steered himself into the center of mass of a man who was probably bending to help his fallen comrade but whose movements Kyle chose to interpret as a fresh assault on Lily. As Kyle would envision it later, it was at that moment that Waldheim, having heard the commotion from the kitchen, arrived to see Kyle, who had been a heavily recruited defensive lineman in high school, lower his shoulder into the ribs of one of Waldheim's regular patrons and drive him five yards back into the far wall. Kyle knowing, even as he did it, even as he felt the satisfying shock and heard at least one of the man's ribs break, knowing he was making a big mistake, hoping someone would hit him, knock him down, at least make it a fair fight. But not expecting it would be Lily who would pull him off, her voice hot in his ear, saying, "Out of here, Kyle, out of here right now," and before he had a chance to ask whether she was all right, before he had even a chance to turn and see her face, she had jerked his hand up behind his back and was marching him toward the door, Waldheim yelling: "Out of my bar, I run a clean restrunt here, I don't need ruffians," the foosball guys yelling for the police and already talking about lawyers, and Lily in his ear with "just stop and think, for once, for Christ's sake, this is where I *work*, can't you stop and think?" until he was out in the cold night and the air had turned suddenly cold and sharp and he was left with nothing but the echo of his father's words and the cold company of stars.

5

Facsimile for Lily Garnett:

Dear Lily,

Of course, I ask: could not God have managed his universe without cancer? Would it have inconvenienced him terribly to leave an old woman alone?

Job answers his complaining wife: "We have accepted good from his hands; wherefore should we not also accept evil?"

And, at his most righteous, at a place I am still trying to reach: "Though He slay me, yet shall I trust in Him."

God of darkness, God of light.

The Koran says: "There is nothing that is not from God." Meaning angel and devil, bread and shit, the green spurt of youth and the ravening of age, all beauties and all horrors, all of it is from God.

There are days when I curse God, and wish him dead.

I'm sending you a sweater. It may fit you. I've shrunk.

Your mother

By the time she reached her apartment and checked the mailbox (one letter, from a B. Rostow, which she stuffed absently into the pocket of her uniform), she had been breathing into her belly long enough to still the trembling and push aside all those men who could now be seen shouting silently—Kyle, Bud Grisham, Adam Townsend, Mongerson, her father, her brother, the guy who had grabbed her in the bar—mouths opening and closing like fish trying to breathe in the dense atmosphere there at the packed margins of her mind. With her first lapse in vigilance they would swarm the perimeter, overrun the bunkers, storm the command post, like that regiment of NVA in *Platoon*. And what, having conquered, would they possess? Lily chunked up the echoing stairwell, thinking that they had to want more than this footsore waitress's body, its bones weighty as leaded nightsticks, solid femurs and tibias hinged and cabled with a strength Kyle had always found surprising but which now seemed barely enough to get her up the stairs. Swinging open the heavy fire door, Lily looked down the dimly lit hallway.

No one but Lily knew how close she had come to killing a man that night. She had seen it coming: the sidelong glance, that flushed face blooming from the crowd, though all he had really done was cock his head at a certain angle, thrust one hip into her path. Her months of waitressing, never mind her years of Tae Kwon Do, should have told her simply to step aside, to make allowance for the coiled spring that the man's body plainly was. Let him spring on someone or something else. But something— Mongerson's perfect teeth? Kyle sulking in the corner?—had jammed her signals and sent her right into that man's grip. The open hand that broke his nose had stunned him, the blow to the throat had stilled him, and the punch to the gut had stopped his breath. That should have been enough, if it wasn't already far too much. The man hung before her, doubled up, his face down and away, showing her the whorl of his cowlick and a surprisingly slender nape. What chilled and shook her now was how calmly her next thought had come, if you can call what the body does at such moments thinking. The back of his neck had recently been shaved, the hollow between the tendons was somehow endearing, the bumps of the vertebrae like turtles sunning on a log. The thought had been loving, almost motherly: with a moment's work to rip the soul out of him like pulling a turnip, and in so doing, to set him free. What stopped her was his sweater. Red and white checked, its squares not perfectly aligned, its ugliness had struck her earlier in the evening, and she had used it as her visual marker for that party's tab. At that moment, looking down on it, she had seen that it was hand knit. And so, for the sake of that woman only—his girlfriend, more likely his mother—she had spared him. The last blow, a simple kick to the shin to set him on the floor, was pure theater.

Something was not right, though: down the hall the door to Lily's apartment was ajar, a sliver of yellow light leaking into the blue fluorescent of the hallway. An open toolbox lay just outside the door. Not even this, this small bubble of privacy she could only mockingly call home, could be counted on. After the fight, Kathy and Waldheim had surrounded her, held her. What did they see in her then? Even Waldheim was subdued and respectful. Kathy had offered to go home with her, knowing she couldn't, Waldheim couldn't let both of them leave. She could see Kathy think about offering her the keys to her place, and could see just as clearly the moment when Kathy decided, with a quick pursing of her lips, that all that had passed between them that night had made that impossible.

Lily pushed open the door to her apartment with one foot, then stepped back into the hallway and waited as the door continued its swing, pulled now from the inside, revealing Luke the maintenance man, grinning, squinting in the smoke from the cigarette that dangled foolishly from his lips.

"I was just going to shim the strike plate, firm her up."

"Not now," Lily said.

Luke held a screwdriver in one hand, a sliver of wood in the other. There are all kinds of truck driver bodies, but Luke's was the thin kind: long, noodle-y tattooed arms you could see working the big wheel, black Harley-Davidson T-shirt, oversized silver belt buckle, jeans, cowboy boots. Greased Dagwood hair, coal black eyes. A starved, Dustbowl-era face that told of some unmet need, the same lack, perhaps, that had put him here, moonlighting as a maintenance man, when he should have been someone you'd see only looking down at you, bouncing in the seat of his big rig as you pass, "Show Me Your Tits" scrawled in the dust of his door. Lily had not spoken more than a dozen words to the man, and had been surprised not to have gotten any trouble out of him so far.

"Take me a minute," Luke said.

Lily took a thorough breath, and though looking Luke in the eye, also registered fully the angle of his grip on the screwdriver, the hang of his right arm, the set of his hips and feet, which way the center of his mass might be taken and tipped.

"Not now, Luke. Please."

Luke was clearly not pleased. His face darkened.

"All I can say, he tells me to do a thing, you tell me not to."

"Who?"

"That big guy here."

159

"Kyle told you to fix the door."

"Get me coming and going. I'm all set up here to do a thing, he's been after me three months on it."

"It's after midnight," Lily said.

"That's when I'm working, missy. You, too, I thought."

"I'm home. You can do this another night."

"Sure, but what am I supposed to do now?"

"That's your business."

The smirk on Luke's face was probably his idea of boyish charm. "You want me to stick around a while?"

The sounds she made then were blunt and loud: she may have said simply "no" or "out," and she may have made the deep chesty grunt of a lion, but it was enough to make Luke pack up his tools and leave, muttering, eyes averted, something like a blush creeping over his face and neck.

"Ask me to do a job, waste of my time? Like you think I don't have a job to do. Eighty-eight dead bolts in the goddamn building, hollow core like nothing's there, jambs out of half-inch stock split every time you turn around there's another one and another one, guy on my case he doesn't even live here, none of my business, but just tell me when I'm supposed to do my goddamn job."

And finally, after he was out in the hall, and Lily had moved swiftly to occupy the door, he turned to meet her eyes. "Guy asks a simple question, you think I'm some kind of slimeball. You ever stop and think for a minute how you treat somebody?"

Lily was about to shut the door when she saw that Luke wasn't moving. He expected an answer. His figure sagged before her: another human being capable of nine degrees of woe.

"Yes, I do think," Lily said, so softly that Luke was briefly

160

startled. "What I think is that we all get treated far better than we deserve."

"I guess you can speak for yourself on that one," Luke said. "Nobody's done me any favors."

"And you've lived a pure and blameless life," Lily said.

"What if maybe I have?" Luke asked.

"Then you don't need anything from me."

The boyish smirk returned. "We all have needs, missy."

"What I need now is to be alone and get some sleep," Lily said, as frankly as she could.

"I hear you," Luke said. "You think I don't, but I do." He squared his shoulders and started to walk away. "Good night and sweet dreams, missy."

Lily shut the door then, threw the bolt, latched the chain, and listened to his footsteps fading down the hall.

This time, she had stayed in control.

Lily turned, breathed out, and walked to the refrigerator. She opened it and stared into the lighted space, though there was nothing there she wanted. She took comfort in the luxury of ignoring her mother's voice in her head, scolding her about standing there with the door open.

Lily felt the rustle of the letter in her pocket and decided to see what Mr. B. Rostow had to say. It was a brief note printed on thin computer paper, which she read in the refrigerator's yellow light:

> Dear Lily,
> I have been getting some advice about you from my Spirit Guides, who told me to send you these words from Akachu, a Shaman of the Jívaro

161

people in the Amazon:

"What is most important is that you must have no fear. If you see something frightening, you must not flee. You must run up and touch it. You must do that or one day soon you will die."

I'm not sure what this means in your case, but perhaps we should find out. The Guides are never wrong. Consider this a free introductory offer for a shamanic session. Stop by?

Cheers,

Bernie (down the hall)

Oh, Christ, Lily thought. Once at the Center they had had a visit from an anthropologist named Herbert Brenkman, who gave them a lecture on shamanism. A big, happy, round-faced man in sandals and shorts, for whom everything one had to say seemed to be of intense interest. He claimed that the world's shamanic rituals could be distilled into a few essential techniques that could be practiced by anyone. It turned out that Bernie had been Brenkman's student, and had been a field assistant on a number of his trips. Bernie had showed her his drums. The drumming took you to the spirit world, where you sought the guidance of your power animal. Lily had done crazier things, she supposed. The way things had been going lately, she was ready to try just about anything. Bernie seemed sincere enough, though of course it could all be another come-on.

She decided to take a yogurt, after all, and let the refrigerator door swing shut.

Slowly her life appeared to be coming off its hinges. Among

the crazier things she had done recently was agree to go out with Larry Mongerson on a day she had long ago planned to spend with Kyle. And now, seeing that two messages had scrolled out of the fax machine, her sense of foreboding returned. The first was in the hand-printed block letters she recognized as Fax Man's:

> Facsimile for Lily Garnett/June 16, 1989/4:15 PM:
> You have a talent for the extraordinary. Look for a red Mercedes. Shall we drive to the sea?
> —Lawrence "Fax Man" Mongerson

The second was from a different source:

> Dear Lily,
> In other words, we must seek, always, the angel of mercy. But we must come to know that death, too, is an angel.
>
> Your mother

Somehow Kyle had forgotten his parachute and could only aim the soles of his boots at the ground. Seeing that he would land on rocks, he waited to be swatted into darkness by the earth, which was rushing up at him. So he was surprised to feel only a hard wallop on his boot soles, then a series of lighter blows as he stumbled down the rocky slope, trying to check his speed.

"Get the fuck out of my car."

"Hey."

Kathy was beating on his boot soles with a lug wrench.

"I'm not in your car, am I?" Kyle spoke into darkness, vaguely aware now that he was lying on his stomach in a cramped space.

"The fuck you aren't. I almost called the police."

She walloped him again.

"Hey, quit it." Kyle unstuck his cheek from the vinyl. "I'm getting up."

Kyle got his elbows underneath him, then his knees, thinking: this is how babies learn to crawl.

"Hurry up, it's freezing out here," Kathy said.

Kyle was on all fours, crawling backwards out of the driver's side door of Kathy's car, a two-door Toyota sedan across whose bucket seats he had somehow draped himself, leaving the door open, his legs from knees down hanging out in the night air.

"I thought I was in my truck," Kyle said. He had gotten both feet on the pavement, and was pushing the rest of his bulk out after them, his hands numb from having slept on them. He finally turned to face her, rubbing his face to bring her into focus.

"I thought I was in my truck," he said again, not sure what sort of lie this was.

"You've got your basic body types," Kathy said. "Sedan, hatchback, station wagon, pickup truck. Should we review them?"

"What about waitress?" Kyle said.

"What about carpenter?" Kathy said. "I see two legs sticking out of my car door, what am I supposed to think?"

"That I've grown fond of you?" Kyle offered.

"I can think of other ways to show a girl."

"Let's discuss them," Kyle said.

The cold this June night had surprised them all, dipping well into the forties as air pushed down from Canada. Overhead the stars glittered hard. Kathy backed off one step, looking away toward the edge of the parking lot, at the ragged line of poplars there, leaves quivering.

"You really think there's any point?" she asked softly.

"Oh, Christ," Kyle said. "As much point as there ever is."

"Is that supposed to be encouraging?"

"Ink. A Dink." Kyle sang gruffly, did a slow shuffle step in the gravel. "Inka Dinka Do." He completed a turn, bowed. "There, I'm doing vaudeville in a parking lot at three in the morning. Are you encouraged?"

"That was the guy with the big nose, right?"

"Durante. My parents loved him."

When Kyle woke in Kathy's bed late the next morning, alone, he wasn't sure which mistake he had made: having come here at all or not having come here a long time ago. Outside, it was the sort of day that explained why butterflies and hummingbirds migrated thousands of miles each to be here every June. After the early greening of May, after daffodil and fiddlehead and lilac, the planet wheeling toward the solstice threw the land headlong into growth, maples deepening to full summer green, meadow grass up now about the knees, soil warmed through to the roots' reach. All this Kyle knew from his first waking breath of the sweet air that spilled over the sill onto the bed, and from the sun falling through gauze curtains that billowed and fell back soundlessly before billowing again.

Not since he left his parents' house had he slept in a room with curtains. Propping himself on his elbows, he could see most of the apartment from where he lay, and could fill in the impressions he had sketched upon their arrival in the early morning dark, when they had bustled into the bedroom, left a trail of clothing between the door and the bed, tumbled to the mattress, grappled, gained purchase on each other's essential parts. The result was that Kyle, though usually a considerate lover, found himself goaded into haste, and all too soon pitching forward into blackness and sleep. But not before discovering, with something of a shock, a whole new vocabulary of the flesh, ample and full to Lily's lean, round to her hard edge, as though the word "voluptuous" had at last found its incarnation. It was a difference so striking that just before love's small crisis, at that moment when a man's delusions are most fiercely held, Kyle was sure that in the smooth expanse of her inner thigh he had found the blank page on which he could write his life.

The task now was to square those recollections with the apartment he now found himself in. He had never before slept with anyone who thought in terms of bedroom "sets," but he saw

166

that the bed in which he lay had its cousins in a pair of bleached oak nightstands and a dresser, all the corners rounded and edges bullnosed in the style he supposed you'd find in the Contemporary Classics section of a furniture outlet store. The walls and fabrics (he had never slept with anyone who thought in terms of "fabrics") were in the mauves and pastels favored by mall designers, as was the oversized vase stuffed with cloth flowers. He was quite sure that no one in Shaftesbury had beige wall-to-wall carpeting. On the walls were an assortment of prints, landscapes mostly, in lacquered frames whose colors he supposed would have been touted as peach, cranberry, sunrise, lemon, snowdrift, sapphire.

Through the bedroom doorway he could see the refrigerator, on which magnets were arranged in rows, each holding precisely one grocery coupon.

Not that there was anything wrong with all this, but Kyle had some trouble seeing where he fit in, feeling as he lay there, bloated and sore from last night's ruckus. The Shaftesbury style that Kyle was most familiar with consisted of mismatched antiques and items scavenged from the dump, along with whatever furniture you could make yourself. Kyle had grown up in a 150-year-old farmhouse where antiques shrewdly acquired by his mother were buried beneath books and back issues of the two dozen magazines his parents subscribed to. Art work crammed the walls, mainly oils and watercolors done by Kyle's mother and her artist friends. It was a house with wide, worn floorboards covered here and there with threadbare antique Persian rugs, a house where a jumbled box of books could be plunked down in a corner and left there for twenty years, where the bathrobes of long forgotten houseguests hung in the closets, and where, in a locked trunk in the attic to

167

which only he had the key, Kyle knew he could still lay hands on his baseball card collection, his gyroscope, his Spiderman comic books, his moths delicately pinned to their trays, his barn owl stuffed and staring through yellow glass eyes.

Kathy had apparently gone out, but he could not look at these rooms without seeing her face, seeing now what he had not fully registered before: that the hint of powder on her cheeks, the rouge and eyeliner tastefully applied, were of a piece with that new car in the parking lot and the contents of this place, and together spoke of the sort of ambition Kyle had always found heartbreaking. When Kyle rose to stagger to the shower, he found that Kathy had laid out the full ensemble of towels in deep-napped royal blue, and found as well the expected basket of potpourri on the toilet tank, its spice not quite overcoming the odor of fret that hung over the whole apartment. What made Kyle most sheepish and sad, of course, was not the money and work and worry the place implied but that in the diligence of the entire performance he sensed the forced optimism of the truly lonely.

He had finished his shower, dressed, and decided to leave as quickly as he could when Kathy heaved through the door and plumped down a bag of groceries on the counter with a hearty, "Hi! Want breakfast?"

"Sure it won't be too much like working?" Kyle asked, trying not to sound disappointed.

"Believe it or not, I like feeding people."

Twenty minutes later, she thumped down plates of French toast, sausage, and eggs, mugs of espresso and hot milk, and Kyle found himself eating his way into warmth and good humor. He found that Kathy in T-shirt and jeans, the first outfit he had ever seen her in besides her waitress uniform, could set him at ease. He was reminded of what he had known all along: he liked Kathy a good deal.

"Wicked good," Kyle said, mouth stuffed.

"I like to cook," Kathy said. "Problem is, I like to eat, too."

"Nothing wrong with that. Feed the flesh."

"Ninety percent of your molecules are replaced every eight months," Kathy said.

"Every breath contains air breathed by Socrates," Kyle said.

"Problem is I ain't getting any thinner *or* wiser," Kathy said.

"Lily says—" Kyle blushed at the stupidity of the error, but decided to go on— "all that matters is that we grow toward God."

Kathy threw a quick, dark look at Kyle, and said evenly, "Yes, she might say that. I guess I'm growing every which way but up."

Kyle could not quite recover from his blunder. The small talk that followed was all conducted with a cheerful efficiency made more maddening by the fact that the more detached Kathy grew, the more attractive he found her. It was as though in dropping her hopeful fixation on him she settled more firmly into herself, filling out her skin with the confident ease of some sleek animal, a seal perhaps, sea-wet and shining, sunning itself on the rocks. So much so that when Kathy rose to clear the plates, Kyle did not bother to measure the precise mixture of sympathy and embarrassment and rekindled lust that made him follow her into the kitchenette so that he could rest the tips of his fingers on her hips as she stood at the sink. Kathy shivered, lowered the plates with a clatter, and pushed him toward the bedroom. Taking handfuls of her shirt to pull over her head, Kyle paused only for the barest heartbeat of reflection when, at that moment he held her captive, her arms raised and head shrouded by the shirt, he wondered just what he was taking into his hands.

In the hurly burly that followed, they explored geometries of the limbs Kyle had not before considered, busying themselves with a sequence of postures he could imagine pictured in manuals. He found himself moaning, huffing, crying out the names of goddesses, while Kathy panted, squealed, and during one languorous passage, hummed most of the national anthem. Still, when all was finished, Kyle couldn't help but feeling that they had worked a little too hard, that their ardent display of technique had been a bit too plainly just that. They had been too anxious to please.

Kyle lay cooling, drifting into sleep, Kathy's arm draped across his chest.

"You know what I think about?" Kathy asked softly.

"Hmmm?"

"Three billion people on the planet, right?"

"Uh-huh."

"Half of them men?"

"Right."

"Why I can't find just one who isn't bored with me after a half hour of rumpus."

Kyle stirred himself to look at her, her blue eyes six inches from his face.

"Who says I'm bored?"

"I know you. Your nipples are hard the second I walk in the room, but now you're lying there doing your taxes."

"That's the way men are built, Kathy. It's hormones."

"You love her?"

"What?"

"You know what I'm saying."

Kyle just sighed. "Guess that means you do," Kathy said.

"It's complicated," Kyle said.

"So's the tax code, honey. But I guess you'll figure it out."

Kathy withdrew her arm and sat up on the edge of the bed, speaking with her back to him. "You'll make out just fine," she said.

"You think I'm not serious, being here," Kyle said.

"Are you?"

"I guess, to be honest, I don't know."

"Men never do."

"I don't think that's fair," Kyle said. "I've been serious."

"With her."

"Yes—look, I didn't bring this up. Let's not talk about it. Let's go out, go for a ride somewhere, a day like this."

"I've got to work in an hour."

"Get the afternoon off?"

"It's Lily's," Kathy said with a certain grim satisfaction. "She's been wanting a Saturday for two months now."

"And she's off with this guy Mongerson."

"Drives a Mercedes. You better call her. Make sure she's okay." "Are you kidding?"

"Go ahead, babe, use my phone. Love works in wondrous ways. I'll be in the shower."

"I'd like to see you again, Kathy."

Kathy at last turned to face him, showing tears.

"You can if you want. Right now I've got to take a shower."

Kathy shut the bathroom door behind her, and Kyle soon

found himself dressed and dazzled by sunlight in the parking lot outside her apartment, remembering just now that his truck was back at the restaurant a mile down the road. He could have waited for a ride from Kathy, but he decided to walk.

Facsimile for Lily Garnett:
Dear Lily,
What is hardest to grasp: that we are dust and
ashes, and yet that we are gods.

Your mother

"It's the materiality of the land, the fact that we're talking
about dirt and rocks, that I can't get over. And I want all of it, sand
and gravel, subsoil and topsoil, root mat, ground cover, understory,
canopy, rights to the sun and wind, all things creeping and crawling,
birds of the air and fishes of the sea. You know what I'm talking
about? I would have liked to have been there, with Adam, for the
naming. And I'm not just talking woods, Lily. I want the cities,
too. I want the concrete, the asphalt, the pipe laid under the street.
I want that and the buildings and the people in them. Know how
many tons of copper wire are in these old buildings here?"

Mongerson waved at a row of brick tenements they were
passing. "To have all that, to take all that in your hands and steer it
toward some sort of destiny." He flashed a perfect smile. "That's
what I'm calling impact," he said.

During the hour's ride Lily had been listening to Mongerson
with a mixture of attraction and dread, fascinated as though by a
beautiful snake. She should have been simply disgusted by his self-
involvement, by his sunny insistence that all was right with the
world as long as he was making money in it. And yet he managed

to project an innocence that made him hard to dislike.

"What amazes me," Lily said, "is how you can be so smart and so clueless all at once."

"I don't intend to be perfect, my dear."

"But you do want to impress."

"And am I not succeeding?"

"Not in the way you think."

Though Lily had to admit she *was* impressed in many of the ways he wanted her to be. And despite everything she had gone through, she still had enough of the small town girl in her to be impressed by the car, the clothes, the easy talk of his successes in a world of high finance so remote that to her it might as well be the realms of angels: everywhere and invisible, tipping a butterfly's wing and guiding the paths of stars. But there was more, too: she had been struck, the day before in the restaurant, by his stillness, the way he hadn't moved when he greeted her. Now, after two hours with him, she felt the animal vigor in the man, filling his skin so completely that he didn't even have to move for it to be felt. And she was impressed, finally, that he was talking to *her*.

"I do like the car," she said.

It was a red Mercedes convertible. They had ridden with the top down at first, wind roaring and trees whipping overhead so that it made her dizzy to look up. Then he had put the top up to make it easier for her to hear him.

Mongerson did a rat-a-tat-tat on the steering wheel and gripped it hard. "Physicality," he said. "That's what I can't get over. That the creation is both spirit *and* matter. Right? Why not take joy in the mystery?"

"By owning things," Lily said, already feeling schoolmarmish

174

for saying it. And then, with what she felt was more like genuine insight: "You seem to want to be a caricature of yourself."

"Lily, my Lily," Mongerson said, looking her feelingly in the eye. "You don't have to live a sad life."

They drove into Portsmouth, an old seaport town that thrived on being an image of itself, the old brick buildings along Ceres Street fussily restored and presented as shops, restaurants, and taverns with decks at the back facing out on the Piscataqua River. It was one of these to which Mongerson took Lily, where they could sit and eat steamers and drink cold beer and look at the tugboats snug at their docks. They could have gone to the Blue Strawberry up the street, which had a chef Waldheim had said he would like to get if his place had more class. But Lily was glad, in a way, that Mongerson had picked a cheaper place. She didn't want to feel too indebted to him. Out the window she could see the tide coming in against the river, driving seawater up the harbor past Seavey Island, where submarines came into the naval shipyard for repairs. Gulls swarmed the harbor, and the moving water seemed hard and metallic in the lowering light, the broad mass moving landward, driving a wedge between the shores of New Hampshire and Maine.

"What you have to get is the thrill of it. Incorporation. Think of what that word means. You start with an idea, you pick up some land, a hundred acres of cornfield, say, somewhere northwest of Chicago. Access to a major transportation corridor, a shopping mall going in down the road. You've read the town's master plan, you know the action's headed your way, all you have to do is sit tight while one cornfield after another goes under, moving in your direction. You let somebody else pay the town to widen the roads, beef up the electric, lay pipe, pumping value into your land that's nothing but corn stubble and weeds. Sooner or later they're at your front door, and you're ready with the full package: you propose a gated community, a hundred- sixty homes on quarter acre lots, guardhouses and perimeter fence, articles of incorporation with all the thou shalls and shalt nots of garbage cans and lawn mowers and clotheslines, you've got cul-de-sacs and sidewalks, three-car garages and sodded lawns, hundreds of human lives contained, all neat as needles. The planning board squawks, but you know the town fathers are licking their lips: they want ponds, you give them bike paths, they want tennis courts, you give them a playground. You buy off the abutters with berms and plantings, re-route the access maybe, throw in a basketball court and a payout to the school system, and there it is, they're reaching toward you. You begin to actually see it: the whole network of town roads headed your way, a special branch of the gas pipeline just for you, electric, water and sewer all valved and piped—ever think of what the word 'conduit' means?—the entire infrastructure in its branchings and leafings, its manifold and glorious reach, stretching its fibers to join *your* development. And when it's done, and that subtle knot is knit, you stand back and behold the miracle. Incorporation. Your little development is now part of a town. Soon there are kids wobbling on bicycles and women kneeling in flowerbeds, and the garage doors are rising as the cars enter the driveways. You've created a place where teenagers can fall in love. And it all starts with an idea, the word made flesh. Amazing, isn't it?"

"An idea and lots of money," Lily said.

"What is money but the measure of the flow of ideas?"

"For me it's work," Lily said. "And putting up with a lot of crap."

"Exactly. And that's because you're not truly in the flow. Or you *are* in the flow—everybody is, can't help it, right?—but at a lower level. If you raised your level, it would be effortless."

"You and my brother must have a good time," Lily said. "Do you even have to speak, or do you just vibrate to one another?"

Mongerson tipped the last of his beer into his mouth, then waved the empty glass at the waitress. Lily had him pegged for the kind of customer who would be demanding, even obnoxious, but worth a good tip.

"I know you've got good reasons to be skeptical, Lily. You don't have to believe anything I say."

"Thanks, Larry, but I already knew that."

"Don't you prefer Lawrence?"

Lily giggled. "Lawrence sounds like a middle-aged man who wears his bathrobe all day and tapes reruns of *Star Trek*."

"What I wonder," Mongerson said, sipping his new beer, eyes narrowed, "is what you'd be like with the venom drained out of you."

"I don't care to be one of your projects," Lily said.

Mongerson smiled another perfect smile. "Keep the venom," he said. "It suits you."

"Sometimes I think it suits everyone," Lily said quietly.

"Yes," Mongerson said. "We're all both light and shadow,"

"I think—." Lily met his eyes, then looked away. "I think people try to deny their darker impulses."

Lily was embarrassed now, seeing Mongerson nod in agreement.

"It's what I've always felt," he said. "We have to own our

177

evil."

"Adam Townsend told me to let him know if I had any contact with you," Lily said.

"I suppose you had better do what he says."

"He told me I should stay away from you."

"Well, not everything he says," Mongerson said, smiling.

"I want to know about who you're involved with out west, Larry."

Mongerson's smile was guarded. "Why does it matter?"

Lily gave a short, grim laugh, wondering why in fact it did matter. "Maybe I'm fascinated by the criminal mind," she said.

"I'm not Johnny Ray Bushman," Mongerson said.

Lily was stunned. "That's not what I meant," she said. Though perhaps she *had* meant it. Perhaps Mongerson had seen more clearly than had Lily herself how much of her attraction to him had to do with another time and place and her unfinished business with Johnny Ray.

"I'm sorry," Mongerson said. "I didn't mean anything ... hurtful."

Lily tried her best to be businesslike. "I have a right to know who's buying into Rattlesnake Ridge."

"If you plan on joining the partnership, then you have a right," Mongerson said, a bit too sharply. "But even if I told you, I'm not sure it would help. We're talking corporations here. You've got to rethink your ideas of identity, of ownership. It's complicated, and not just because there are hierarchies involved. Finance today is more than the cat who ate the bird who ate the spider who caught the fly. Things are more fluid now — it's a question of interconnections, networks, flow. We're dealing with true globality."

"Why do men think bullshit is a turn-on?"

"Don't make the mistake of thinking I'm anything but a serious man."

"Adam heard something about criminal activity out there, that some of these companies you've been dealing with—"

"Don't you know that your ever-diligent Officer Townsend is just trying to dig up dirt for Bud Grisham? It's a small world, Lily. Sit down in an airplane, you're guaranteed that you know someone who knows someone who knows someone who knows the person sitting next to you. Any two people on the planet are only six steps removed. So just imagine Nevada, where the number of players in real estate is smaller than the congregation in the Shaftesbury church on Sunday. You go to meetings, you do deals, you rub elbows that have rubbed other elbows, it's unavoidable. And there are people out there operating at lower frequencies, Lily, I'm not going to kid you."

"Darkness and light," Lily said.

"It's all part of the process. One learns to see the shadows, to face them with... equanimity."

Then Mongerson broke off, as though feeling awkward. He touched a hand to his straw-colored hair and looked out over the water.

"Have you heard from your mother lately?" he asked.

The question was asked casually enough, but Lily felt herself stiffen.

"You monitor my fax traffic or something?"

"Look, Lily." Mongerson leaned forward and looked at her intently. She saw that there was a slight rift in his left eyebrow,

179

some childhood scar, perhaps. "I don't know what you expect from me. I'm, I'm—" He waved a hand as if to swat away some unseen object that was blocking him from communicating the blamelessness of his intentions. "Try honesty," Lily said. "Integrity. Try not smothering me with bullshit from the get-go."

"You expect too much from me, maybe." Mongerson's shoulders slumped, and he leaned back in his chair. "You think I'm slick, I know. Maybe I can't help it. But answer me this." He picked himself up again, looking at her intently but collegially, as though together they were working out a math problem. "What do you get out of being such a hard-ass with me?"

"We're talking fundamentals here," Lily said. "What most people on the planet understand, but I guess I've got to spell it out with you. I don't trust you, Larry. Not as far as I could throw your wing-tip loafers."

"What can I do to earn your trust?" He asked the question with such directness that Lily was once again struck with the force of his innocence. She had trouble imagining how this quality served him in business, except by making him impervious to insult.

"You could start by explaining what the hell you're doing here with me," Lily said. "And buy me another beer."

He picked up her empty glass and waved it in the air.

"I'm here because I thought I wanted to develop some property in Shaftesbury," he said.

"And now you don't?"

"Now I'm not sure. It's gotten complicated."

"You've bought my mother's land, and now you don't know what to do with it."

"Not exactly."

180

Mongerson's smile seemed condescending.

"Look, Lily, I'll tell you straight. I came here hoping to talk you into joining me and Howard in developing some property on Rattlesnake Ridge."

"You and Howard. You've made him a partner?"

"A limited partner, if you want technicalities. Why should that surprise you? We really have gotten to be friends. He's the one behind this thing. I'm really just here to help."

"Have you approached my father?"

"Your father is quite a character," Mongerson said with a short laugh. "Nothing definitive in that direction yet. We've been in touch."

"And you talked my mother into this?"

"This is what I was starting to say before. I respect your mother a great deal."

"More than I do, is what you're saying."

"I don't presume to understand your feelings for your mother."

"But you've become quite an expert on my family."

Mongerson's laugh was sincere, almost pleasant. "That would be the work of a lifetime, right? I try to stick to my own small sphere of expertise."

"And that sphere now includes Shaftesbury. Why do you need this?"

Mongerson pursed his lips, gazed steadily at her. "It's hardly a question of need. What does any of us need, after all? How much more than an animal? Enough food, shelter from the elements."

Lily eyed his gold watch, his linen jacket

"It would seem you need a whole lot more than that."

"You don't know me, Lily. I could lose all this tomorrow, and it wouldn't matter."

"Bodhisattva."

Mongerson laughed. "I'm no saint, no. No devil either. Just a man, Lily, with a man's share of foolishness. A man's needs." Mongerson's gaze became too intent, and Lily had to look away. She had expected all along some sort of come-on. What she hadn't expected was that she would be interested enough to be embarrassed. "Why do you need Jackson Island, then?" Lily said, hoping to cool him off. "For love, Lily. Because that's where we're different, isn't it? How much love does a cat need? A horse. That's where we're in deep shit, am I right?"

"We're talking about an island. I used to camp there as a kid. Good blueberries on the east end." She thought of Frank Creed, junior year in high school, the zippers of his leather jacket cold against her skin.

"I'm afraid you'll find me ridiculous," Mongerson said.

It was the first time she had seen him blush.

"I don't think I really understood what I was doing when I bought it," he said. "But now, seeing you, I do. I think in some way I bought that island for you."

Lily looked down at her legs, which were crossed, showing the muscle in her thighs beneath the hem of her shorts. She felt suddenly conscious that her arms were crossed, too, that she was holding it all in tight. She had always thought of herself as too tall, her bones too big, her hips too narrow and mannish. This morning she had experimented with rouge and mascara, and then, feeling foolish, cursing men, cursing herself, washed it off.

"I really wasn't planning on telling you that," Mongerson said.

182

"My little fantasy."

He looked out at the water, at the gulls wheeling overhead.

"When I first came here, the whole business with Rattlesnake Ridge was just a thought, you know, wanting to do something for Howard. Your mother wanted me to come." He stared at her intently for a moment, then broke off. "But it was Howard, really, who talked me into it. He was so insistent I see the place. And I was curious to see what had become of you. All these years you've been present to me as, well, unfinished business." Again the brief stare, too intense to be comfortable. "But once I got here, I had to admit it was more than that. You probably never knew how I felt about you back then, at the Center."

"I barely remember you, if you want the truth," Lily said.

"I didn't cut much of a figure then," Mongerson said.

"A lot of things I've just blanked out."

"I was flat out in love with you."

Now Lily stared back.

"You've really got no business bringing all that up now," she said grimly.

"Goddamn it, Lily." There was true heat in his voice for the first time. "It *is* my business. Yours, too."

Mongerson drew back again, aware that he had blundered. But Lily found herself amid scraps of memory from which she had been struggling to free herself ever since she had first heard his name mentioned, three months earlier: the feeling of a swelling life in her belly, the anticipation of a roundness there, a weight. She remembered how flushed she had been, the sense of energy brimming to her crown and beyond, spilling out of her, cocooning her in light. She had been hot in the night, kicking herself free of

183

the sheets, and spent mornings in bed fending off nausea only to rise and work hard in the garden, hoeing weeds, mending a stretch of fence to keep the deer out of the corn, picking a bushel of beans. Those days she felt that her every move, her every breath, was an outflow from, and a feeding back into, that small life wriggling in her womb. There were times, in the garden, when she could have buried her feet in the soil and rooted there, her trunk firm and strong, branches raised, her sap rising, her leaves gathering light, heaven and earth in her grasp.

Those were some of the best days, not only with Johnny Ray but with her mother, too. For her mother could be with her then with a wordlessness that for the first time in Lily's life felt right. Theirs had always been a relationship of silences: not of anger only, or rebuke—for her father's absence, Constance knowing that Lily blamed her for it—but of the sort of resignation and dull acceptance of pain with which generations of New Hampshire farmers had lived with drought and disease and stony soil.

But at that time, the bushel of beans on her hip, meeting her mother on her way into the Big House, where they would work side by side, washing and cooking and canning the beans for winter, Lily felt their silence to be once more that of two generations of New Hampshire farm women bound by the need, as common as breath, to spend the labor of their limbs and hearts in caring for those who were there to be cared for: the men and women and children of what seemed like one good place upon the earth, one place where work and love seemed to go well and where even a Lily Garnett might bring into the world with a measure of hope the grandchild of the woman whose gaze had at last found a gentleness for all the things it touched.

And then there were the few minutes spent in the room full of steel drawers, and weeks later, a bloody drive to the hospital in Ely, and all of that was finished. She left that place to return to the one that while perhaps not perfectly good, was at least perfectly hers: Rattlesnake Ridge. And now Lily realized, facing this man Mongerson, that she stood to lose that, too.

Maybe that was what she needed. The thought, barely a whisper up from some dark place, surprised her, sobered her, so that she looked at Mongerson now with a sort of detached wonder. *To lose everything.* This man seemed to be offering her a kind of surrender she had never before dared to consider. To lose the land, and so to lose this self she dragged after her like a heavy sack: might this not be the last freedom open to her?

"What are your plans?" Lily asked, surprised that Mongerson seemed not to sense the tremor in her voice. "Nothing definite. Howard has some ideas, and your mother's been supportive in a general way. There are problems with the parcel, from my point of view. You know, of course, that the only reasonable access is through your father's land. And through yours. We would like to bring your father into it, but I think he's cutting his own deal."

"He told you he's selling?"

"I think he may develop it himself."

"With Howard?"

"Lily, this is really your family's business. But I think your father wants to keep Howard out of it. I suspect your father might rather work with Bud Grisham than with us. Howard is rather upset."

Lily stared at him a long while, trying to decide what sort of devil he was. "You bastard," she told him. "Don't blame the

185

messenger," he said.

"But you got everybody started on this."

"That is exactly wrong," Mongerson said with a firmness just short of anger. "It was your brother's notion, encouraged by your mother."

"And you figured you'd buy me an island and try to sweet talk me into bringing my father into the deal. Or at least granting you a right of way across our properties."

"Forget about Jackson Island. That's—. Something else. Folly."

"You think you can buy me."

"I've thought about you for ten years, Lily. Don't be crude."

"Christ, I can't take this." Lily looked away over the railing. Thirty yards off, a man worked coiling rope on the deck of a tugboat, lost in the practiced, unconscious rhythm of the task. "Why do you men always have to include us in your pathetic little dramas?" she asked.

"If it pleases you to think of this as a battle of the sexes, then so be it. I prefer to think that we are all grown-ups here, and can make our own decisions."

"Why has neither of my parents spoken to me about this?"

Mongerson's small smile was enough to make Lily see the pointlessness of her question. He was right: they were grown-ups, and if neither her father nor her mother had chosen to tell her of their separate plans to plunder the family land, that was not something she could ask Mongerson to explain.

"Try to think of me as not entirely evil," Mongerson said.

"What are you proposing?" Lily asked. She returned to her chair opposite Mongerson, facing him resignedly.

"That you and your family come to some friendly understanding about the future of that property, that you allow me to be of some use to you in making that future possible, that in the meantime you find in yourself a certain susceptibility to my charms, and that one day soon you surrender yourself not only to the pleasures of material wealth but also to the bliss that our life could be together. That's the program. I could have it printed on a brochure, if you like."

Lily gave herself the small release of joining in Mongerson's laughter.

"You do please yourself, don't you?" she said.

"It's the one thing I can count on," he said.

By the time they finished lunch, the afternoon had grown hot. They walked through the streets, looking in shop windows at antiques and clothes and trinkets, Lily feeling sluggish with the heat and the beer. She was thankful that Mongerson was keeping his distance, speaking no more of what they had discussed at lunch. She was thankful, too, that he didn't offer to buy her any of the things they saw, though she couldn't help thinking that he could buy not only all of the whaling harpoons and scrimshaw and captain's chairs in the shop before them, but the building itself and all the others on this block. When he took her hand for a moment, casually, as they crossed the street, she felt thirteen again, embarrassed and giddy, surprised by the warmth and smoothness of this hand so much smaller than Kyle's. For the half dozen strides it took them to cross, she felt the possibility of some new life altogether. But when they stepped up on the far curb, she released his hand, feeling her old life return with a soft thud. She wondered where Kyle had gone last night, and where he might be now. She supposed that they might still have dinner together.

They drove home with the top down again, the roaring wind excusing them from further talk. Lily let herself lean her head back and drowse, until she picked her head up to find herself back in North Ridgeway, driving into the strip.

"Oh," she said, as though completing a thought: "What's with the Fax Man business?"

Mongerson gave her a twinkling smile. "A boyhood ambition of mine. I always wanted to be a superhero."

"Have you succeeded?"

"Beyond my shaggiest dreams."

"And Fax Man's super power is the ability to install fax machines in the homes of former acquaintances in order to harass them with unwanted messages?"

"Are the messages from your mother unwanted?" Mongerson asked.

"Those aren't the ones I mean," she said.

"Forgive me," Mongerson said gently. "If you want to know, the whole thing is just a promotion. I'm doing a fax newsletter for real estate investors, with Fax Man as the persona. We gave away some fax machines for publicity. Not a big deal really, but it has gotten us written up in the papers."

"Howard sure seemed taken with it."

"Your brother can be counted on for his enthusiasm."

"What can you be counted on for, Larry?"

They had pulled into the parking lot at Lily's apartment, and Lily scanned quickly for Kyle's truck.

"Dinner," Mongerson said. "At least."

Lily shook her head. "I think I've got plans."

Mongerson gave her a long look, as though testing the seriousness of that "I think."

"Count on this, then."

Mongerson bent his head toward hers. Their lips touched, and she felt the barest flick of his tongue, so that the kiss was soft and full, her eyes closing and what seemed like the stirring of leaves filling her head. Then she was out of the car, striding away, surprised, somehow, by the solidity of the earth that met her every step.

Chapter Four

1

It was the third week in June when Peregrine Weed, having at last had the proof of his own innocence forced upon him, collected his leather duds and horned headgear from his keepers at the state mental hospital and vamoosed for parts unknown. Forrest Garnett arrived in Shaftesbury on a Saturday night a few days later. Forrest had taken the late bus up from Boston, had Clarence meet him at Hal's Grocery in Wilton, where the bus stopped, and so arrived at last in Shaftesbury under what Forrest couldn't help but think of as "the cover of darkness." After a week at the IEEE convention, where he had spent more time on the tennis courts than in the meeting rooms, his enthusiasm for visiting Shaftesbury had chilled. Lily had wanted him here, and he had come, but he was not sure what his presence might accomplish other than to show the Garnett flag and perhaps foul things up even further. A town selectman had been killed on the property, and now that the madman who claimed to have done it had been cleared and released, the real murderer was presumed at large. The madman, who was convinced that he owned Rattlesnake Ridge, was now very likely roaming the Shaftesbury woods once more. His daughter was unhappy in love and much else. His son was in league with an apparent scoundrel eager to throw money at the locals. Forrest himself had received unwanted offers for the land. And last, there was the bear. Forrest would have liked to have thought it merely a dream he could leave behind in St. Louis, yet the bear seemed ever present, the steady drumbeat at the base of his skull to which he rose in the morning and lay down at night. It terrified him, yet to his most secret self he admitted that for now, at least, it was his best thrill.

Clarence told Forrest about Peregrine Weed as the old Ford pickup rattled down the Lake Road, a thin strip of pavement laid lightly over the land, heaving and bending over and around hills, then descending to follow the shore of the lake, which in the starless night was only a black emptiness stretching out to the west. Forrest could smell the dark water, feeling the pang of blood memory as he sifted pine and pollen and silt, blueberry and moss and stone, knowing deep in that reptilian part of the brain that he could be in no other place and time than Abenaki Lake in late June.

"I ask myself what I'm doing here," Forrest said.

Clarence's soft smile was lit by the green glow from the dash. "Most men would say they're going fishing."

"Men go fishing to get away from women," Forrest said. "I've got no women to get away from anymore."

"You'll figure out something to be getting away from."

"Looks to me like whatever it is, I'm headed smack into the teeth of it," Forrest said.

Clarence spoke without turning his head, softly but firmly: "Be brave, Cousin."

There was a hint of reproof in Clarence's voice, as though he could sympathize only so far with his cousin's self-pity. Clarence had said little about Howard's plans for the land, but Forrest knew

191

his cousin's frustration and all that lay behind it. Though they had been friends from childhood, their lives had followed different courses. Forrest had been sent to an expensive college in Massachusetts and then, after a stint in the navy, had gone on to a professional career. Clarence had gone into the navy right out of high school, and then had returned to Shaftesbury to stay. The years seemed only to separate the two men further. When his father died, Clarence came into Lakeside Farm, which he managed to hold together out of sheer cussedness. The dairy was gone, corn couldn't make a profit, there was no market for hay. There was no practical reason not to sell, so Clarence held on for impractical ones, bringing in enough as a handyman to keep food on the table and pay his taxes. Meanwhile, Clarence watched his brothers and sisters, who had been given parcels in other parts of town, either sell off all at once and move away, or sell off piecemeal and stay. Some of these Garnetts, Clarence's brothers and now his nephews, were loggers whom Forrest hired to work the woods on Rattlesnake Ridge. Pasture and woodlot sold to summer people, they held to their sagging farmhouses, penned within ever tighter perimeters. From there some moved into mobile homes parked in the back yard, leaving the old house leaky and rotting and stuffed to the eaves with junk, lace curtains in the windows like ghosts, at last handing the whole mess over to Bud Grisham and retreating to a slanting shack at the edge of a swamp. Through all of this they bore and raised children, so that Clarence's side of the family swelled and grew poorer, while Forrest's shrank and grew richer. With the deaths of Forrest's brother and sister, Rattlesnake Ridge had come to Forrest intact, and now Clarence could do nothing but stand by and watch him fumble it away. Forrest could imagine how he felt now, chauffeuring his out-of-town cousin who rode with a tennis racket at his feet.

Still, as they turned off onto the Old High Road and rumbled down the dirt track toward the lights of Lakeside Farm, Forrest felt his heart move in his chest and found himself saying out loud: "I've never really felt I was coming home here before now. Not like this, now."

"I always have," Clarence said. "Every day."

"You're lucky," Forrest said.

"Luckiest man in the world," Clarence said.

Forrest had a quiet supper with Clarence and Sylvia, thankful that she seemed willing to go easy on him, at least for now. She gave him only one sharp look, but held her tongue, when he told her he wouldn't be calling Lily that night. Early the next morning, he hiked in to the old fishing camp, carrying a bedroll and a canvas knapsack full of canned goods, coffee, and bread. He found the place still habitable despite little use in recent years. There was no electricity, a hand pump for water at the kitchen sink, propane for cooking and lighting, and an outhouse a hundred feet up the hill. There was a screened sleeping porch, two bedrooms partitioned by thin plank walls, and a large room with a rough pine table for eating and a few rocking chairs gathered by a blackened stone hearth. Forrest made coffee and spent the morning sweeping out dust and mouse droppings, hauling mattresses into the sun, cracking open windows to let in air. When he was done, he sat in his best rocking chair on the front porch, which looked down through a grove of tall white pines to the lake, where a stone-cribbed wooden dock tilted out over the water, some of its planks spongy with rot, some gone altogether. A shed by the water held a few old boats and the fishing gear, and Forrest would get to these later.

It felt good to be here, alone in the old place, and he could easily imagine letting the days drift on, summer ripening into fall. He could bring in a woodstove and tough out the winter. It took a certain perversity to love the Shaftesbury climate. The insects alone, Forrest knew, were enough to make a reasonable person see life here as a succession of plagues. By now the black flies had given way to mosquitoes and to deerflies that liked to burrow through sunwarmed hair and chew the scalp. After the fall's brief and bugless glory the leaves rattled down in cold rain, and one waited through a gray November for snow. Five frigid and dark months later, the thaw brought mud season, and soon after the mud left, the insects returned.

Between the climate and the stony soil it was little wonder that the people who had lived here, who had cleared and farmed this land now gone back to woods all around him, had gotten out as soon as they could. There was a town somewhere in Illinois named Shaftesbury, where a number of the families had settled in the 1850s. Forrest had heard there were Garnetts there, though he'd never met any of them. He had seen the town once, on a map. His people were the ones who stayed. By definition, he supposed, they were the ones who lacked imagination.

But there were more reasons than weather for Forrest to be uncomfortable here, the biggest being that Shaftesbury would never leave him alone. In St. Louis he was a consultant to the aerospace industry, and a member of a tennis club, and not much else. Here, he was Forrest Garnett, son of Caleb, grandson of William, and no matter how idyllic a getaway the fishing camp might appear, at any point within the one hundred square miles of this town he felt himself too well and thoroughly known. He would call Lily, perhaps tomorrow.

The drone of a small outboard announced that his solitude had already ended. Forrest made his way over the thick carpet of pine needles down to the dock. Coming around Deerpath Point in an old aluminum dingy were Clarence and, unexpectedly, a second person, who on closer approach appeared to be his smiling son, Howard.

"Howard helped me with the gas," Clarence said as he tied up. Forrest knew that Clarence said this to smooth Howard's way. A hundred pound propane tank lay in the boat like a bomb.

Howard sprung onto the dock and shook Forrest's hand, grinning beneath sunglasses.

"Dad. Amazing."

"You must be over thirty now," Forrest said.

"Incredible, isn't it?"

Forrest was relieved, for the moment, that they had the awkward business of lifting the propane tank out of the little boat and hauling it uphill toward the house. When they had done it, and hauled the empty one down to the boat, and carried up the bags of groceries Sylvia had sent, they made their way back to the porch for coffee.

"Where have you been staying?" Forrest asked, handing Howard a mug.

"Here and there," Howard said. "I'm not without friends. I suppose it's bad form to ask if there's any herbal tea?"

Forrest tried to settle more deeply into his rocking chair. He was aware of the tightness in his chest, and glad that Clarence would be here for this. He was thankful, just then, for Clarence's

195

kind and careworn face, for the easy way his big, calloused hands enfolded his coffee mug. And yet there was an alertness in Clarence's eyes, which were watching him and Howard keenly. Forrest felt the weight of his cousin's care and expectation.

Clarence sat beside him in a ladder-back cane-seat rocker, Howard sat on the steps, and they all looked out at the lake.

"I expect you haven't come here for the fishing, Howard. Or to hang out with the old man."

Forrest could see that, without wanting to, he had made Howard uncomfortable. Seeing him seated on the steps, in clean denim and loafers and a too-crisp polo shirt, Forrest remembered Howard's boyhood awkwardness. It wasn't a question of the basic skills. He could field a ground ball and make the throw to first, he could bait a hook and cast a line. It was awkwardness on a subtler level, in the way he sat in a chair or opened a door or looked you in the eye, a sense that the jambs and sills of being weren't square, the posts not plumb, something canted in the small gestures of living, the routine utterances askew, so that one sensed that for Howard the act of passing the salt or discussing the weather took on the freight of slanted intentions and bad posture, something brittle in the mind and sour in the bone. "Some good bass up in Harper Cove, I hear," Clarence said. "Haven't had time myself."

"I suppose I could remember how to fish," Howard said. "If I could remember the point."

"If you need to have a point," Clarence said, "don't fish."

"What Kant said about art," Howard said. "The Rishis, too. Pure Being. Pure Light."

"Indians conversed with the spirit of the fish," Clarence said.

"You should both go join this Weed fellow in the woods,"

Forrest said.

Forrest looked at his cousin, and all three men laughed. Yes, he was glad Clarence was there. But he was just as glad when Clarence excused himself with a wink and said he'd have a look in the boat shed.

"What are your plans, Howard?" Forrest asked as they both watched Clarence walk down toward the water.

"I'm trying to live more or less in the moment, Dad," Howard said.

"Do they publish newsletters with tips on how to annoy one's parents?"

"That wasn't my intention."

"Do you have intentions, or only 'moments'?"

"Let's, like, start this conversation again, okay?" Howard said.

"Take your best shot," Forrest said.

For a full minute father and son did the work of breathing and staring down through the pines to the lake. Clarence could be heard rummaging in the shed like a mouse inside a drum.

"I'd like you to meet a friend of mine," Howard said.

"You're getting married?" Forrest asked.

"I mean Mongerson. Surprise yourself, Dad. You may not hate him."

"This man fronted you money to buy land adjacent to our— to your mother's, am I right?"

"'Fronted' isn't the word, here. I'm a limited partner. Fascinating concept. There's a corporation. I used my own land and Mom's to buy in."

"Your mother deeded her property to you?"

"We've got some ideas. She's been supportive."

197

Forrest sighed. "That Thompson woman. I seem to have allowed her into my life for the sole purpose of tormenting me."

"From the perspective of my personal existence, I'm sort of glad you did," Howard said.

"Am I to take any comfort from knowing that the property is out of her hands?"

"Comfort can be a trap," Howard said. "I'm trying to accept the transitory nature of all things. Even real estate."

"I guess I've got my answer," Forrest said, for to call a piece of land "real estate" was already to have carved it up and sold it off, to have abstracted so many acres of root and rock and soil into a series of numbers in a bank account. "I suppose the most that's to be hoped for now is that your so-called real estate plans have nothing to do with me or your sister."

Seated on the top step, Howard leaned against a post, knees hugged to his chest, looking up at his father. Forrest saw the tightness of his jaw, sensed the anger in the taut spring of his body.

"Why are you so impatient with me?" Howard asked. "All I want is to be taken seriously."

"All right," Forrest said. "Let's do that. And let's start with access. You know you can't get into that property except on the Old High Road through my and Lily's land. And your deed restricts your right of way, so you can't use it for other than agricultural purposes."

"There are options here," Howard said.

"Such as?"

"Such as you amend the deed to grant us unrestricted use of that road."

"Doubtful."

"Such as just for once you listen to what I have to say."

Forrest took the measure of his son: more focused than he remembered seeing him. Angry, yet holding back. In a more impressive man it might be called forbearance.

"I'm listening," Forrest said. "Such as?"

"Such as you and Lily come in with us. Expand the program." Howard's eyes were bright now, jumping into this like a dog after a stick. "We're talking ten acre lots, Dad, stone wall boundaries, meadows, wildflowers, dirt roads lined with maple trees, dust in the air from a passing pickup truck, everything white clapboard, garages that look like barns, maybe even a town common with a schoolhouse and a church—strictly nondenominational—a community house for needlepoint demonstrations and reading groups and foreign films on Tuesday nights, maybe step aerobics and morning meditation. We're talking a life here, we're talking a place of pain and sweetness, fabulous lake views, waterfront marina with dock space for each property owner, all the sorrows and pleasures, we're talking about creating a world. We'll call it Garnett Farms."

Howard's flashing eyes, his face flushed with excitement, reminded Forrest of the boy who would run to him where he sat on this same porch, in this same chair, to show him whatever shining thing he had plucked from the world's bounty—a frog or a pebble of clear white quartz—offering it up to him for his approval, his blessing. All it took to please the boy was one charmed glance, the papal gesture of the lifted hand; a moment's attention settled on that upturned face. It was something Forrest's own father could never do. And now, seated on the porch of the cabin his father had built, seated in his father's own chair, Forrest

199

felt the old man's presence in the stiffness of his own spine. During the final months of his life, the old man had spent every night but his last sleeping upright in this chair to keep his lungs from filling with fluid.

"I wish I could be happy for you," Forrest said.

"Try it on, Dad."

"It's not exactly the Garnett way of thinking."

"We're talking a paradigm shift, I know. Opening whole new channels."

Forrest paced his words, knowing that what mattered most was to remain upright and breathe. "Have you talked to Lily about this?"

"Not in so many words, but Mongerson has. She's warming to the concept, I think. I gather she's getting more comfortable with the details, things like the permits and the planning board hearings. The Corporation has resources. We've got expertise. I've been busy these last few years, Dad, you'd be surprised: cash flow horizons, presale marketing, volume bidding. I know it all seems strange, but this is real, this is what's happening now. It's a question of putting yourself in the flow. It's the right time for us to be doing this. Time for the Garnetts to make a move."

"Garnetts don't make *moves*," Forrest said. "They cherish their squandered opportunities. It's our only morality."

They listened to the scrape and boom of Clarence dragging an aluminum boat out of the shed.

"I'm in a position where I've got to hope your attitude will adjust," Howard said, a slight tremor in his voice.

"You mentioned options before. You've got another option?" Forrest asked, wary now, wondering what sort of doom waited behind Howard's thin smile.

"That's what's unfortunate," Howard said. "And I've got to tell you it's not simple. The whole corporate environment right now, incredible. M and A people like sharks, companies eating others like the food chain. Bottom line is Mongerson's not entirely a free agent, finance-wise, which I admit I didn't fully understand the dimensions of. There's a Higher Corporation, in other words."

"You're telling me I'm going to like this option even less."

"There are levels of being in these things. Mongerson is higher than most, but lower than some. Which means he owes. There's a cash flow situation. In the area of nonperforming assets, this property is not a good position to hold right now. The complications are spectacular."

"Sounds simple to me," Forrest said. "You're in debt, you need cash, and the only way to get to it runs through property owned by me and your sister."

"But then there's the timber option," Howard said.

Forrest had to pause for a moment, knowing he was missing something. He had done a fair amount of selective cutting over the years throughout the property. Timber sales had paid for the college education that Howard had never finished. The right of way allowed for logging, and Howard knew it.

"You want to do some logging, that's your business," Forrest said. "Talk to Clarence. You've got cousins who could use the work."

"Here's where we have a problem. It's all economies of scale. What the Corporation wants is a clear cut. The whole parcel, and with the new additions that's almost a thousand acres. It's a scenario where aesthetics is not a high priority."

"I'll dynamite the road," Forrest said.

"Forget the road," Howard said. "We take it out by barge and offload at Wilton Bay onto the big rigs, drive it to the coast and ship it overseas. The Russians, the Japanese, they'll take hemlock, anything. Anything else we sell for pulp."

"Even a thousand acres isn't enough for that kind of operation to make a profit," Forrest said.

"The Corporation has holdings up north," Howard said. "Fantastic tracts of land. They own pulp mills, the works. We bundle ours with theirs, we've got enormous leverage."

"So either I go along with your plans to turn the place into some kind of Yankee theme park or you turn Rattlesnake Ridge into a stumped-over wasteland. Should I be thinking of this as extortion?"

"Some options are more attractive than others," Howard said.

"I suppose I should just take Bud Grisham's offer."

Forrest couldn't help but enjoy seeing the slight shock on Howard's face.

"Bud approached you?" Howard asked. He seemed to sag inwardly, as though sensing for the first time that the world did not run on the principles of fair play and honest dealing. "Why?"

"Same reason he gets up in the morning," Forrest said. "To make money. And he sees what you see: that without my property Rattlesnake Ridge isn't worth squat. He wants you to have to come begging to *him*." Forrest looked hard at his son, as though to say, "See how grown-ups play?"

"But you wouldn't sell," Howard said, with a small, sly smile. "Couldn't we count on that?"

Forrest shook his head, thinking the other thing he couldn't bring himself to say, not so much because it was cruel as because it revealed too much of his own calculation, thinking: don't you see that that's why I divided the land the way I did? To protect us all from your foolishness? And one heartbeat below that was the thought he did not want to admit, even to himself: that he had given Howard that bit of land to test him, to let him fail, to prove his son's unworthiness.

Forrest felt his heat rise, felt once more, without knowing he was feeling it, the presence of that old man in his stiff-backed chair.

"If you knew I wouldn't sell, then why have Mongerson write me that jackass letter? When you could have come to me like a grown man."

"I tried to talk about it that time I called," Howard said. "Guess I decided you might take it more seriously if it came from someone else."

"And this someone else, your pal Mongerson, is ready to sell us to the Japanese. I suppose I'd be wasting my time asking how you could get yourself into such a mess."

Howard's words came weakly: "Couldn't we see it as, like, an opportunity?"

They heard the cough and splutter of Clarence pulling the starter rope on an old outboard. Forrest found himself wondering how much fishing it would take, how many hours anchored in Harper Cove, casting and reeling in the shallows, for all this to go away.

"What I have to admit here," Howard said to his father, worrying the knot on his shoe, "is that I've done something brilliant or I may have fucked up in a big way."

There were three sharp explosions as the engine caught. Then

Clarence throttled it to a roar. A minute later, he was walking toward them up the path, a fishing rod in either hand.

"Got that old Evinrude going," Clarence said, holding up the fishing rods hopefully, one for himself and one for Forrest. Forrest gripped the sides of his chair and said to his son: "If I can help you, I will. Right now, you'd better get out of my sight." Forrest watched Howard's back as the boy made his way silently down the path to the dock, then he faced the question in his cousin's eyes.

"My son the entrepreneur."

"Some wild schemes he's got," Clarence said.

"He told you?"

"Sylvia got it out of him. She has a way."

"Ten acre lots?"

"Time and chance happeneth to all things. Can't say I like it, though. There'd be a hell of a time with drainage."

Forrest looked at the rods in Clarence's hands. He would have to clean and oil the reels, replace the line.

"Clarence, I forgot to ask you. In the past few months, have you seen any bear?"

On the eve of the summer solstice, three months after Orville Rogers's death, Adam got a call from Lieutenant Campo telling him that Peregrine Weed was being released. All along Weed's lawyer from the public defender's office had been screaming that Major Crimes had not come up with any physical evidence linking Weed to the homicide. And now, it seems, he had an alibi. An aunt had called in, from down in Portsmouth, saying he was with her for the entire week leading up to the murder. The story checked out, and now, though they had found Weed nuts enough to keep in the hospital beyond the initial thirty days' observation, they had no choice but to let him go.

"Why didn't the auntie call before?"

"Didn't know about it. Weed refused to call anybody, and we haven't been able to track down any relatives. Somebody read about him in the paper and finally called her. Weed's mad as hell, still telling everyone he's the perpetrator."

"He likes the attention," Adam said.

"He likes a bed and a shower and three meals a day," Campo said. "You've seen his camp."

Adam had seen it. He had shown the state investigators how to find it. An abandoned hunter's camp eight miles in from the Notch Road, in the national forest on the north side of Rattlesnake Ridge. Dirt floor, daylight through the roof, though he'd put some plastic sheeting over it and held the sheeting down with rocks. Chinks in the log walls stuffed with oakum and rags, lined on the inside with newspaper. A smell of wet ashes and woodsmoke, kerosene and sweat. Old iron woodstove, by the door an axe, felling saw, maul and wedges. Weed was a regular picker at the town dump, likely his source for the kerosene lamp, the one broke-back chair, a card table with a missing leg replaced by a stick, a few dented and blackened pots, the chipped plates and bent spoons. Also for the six toaster ovens neatly stacked, and the old books tucked in their open mouths. And also for the two lawn chairs and one pink flamingo that graced the scuffed yard. No doubt Campo thought the place some animal's fouled lair, but to Adam it had seemed workable and snug, a solitary man's reasonable last resort. His own father had not lived much better at the end.

One odd detail, though, a bit of madness leaking through: here and there around the yard—by the front door, beneath one window, near the woodpile—Weed had pushed sticks into the ground. Just a few inches high, close together like a little fence.

"I'll watch for him," Adam said. "Anything else I should do?"

"Enforce the law," Campo said. "Other than that, exactly nothing."

Which was typical. Campo had wanted Adam to sit on his hands through this whole thing. Problem was, the state hadn't produced. The whole time they had Weed locked up, the case had gone nowhere. Major Crimes investigators had interviewed a lot of people in town who dealt with Orville Rogers in one way or another, but they hadn't come up with much. Seemed that Orville had simply been checking out the property, anticipating a subdivision proposal to the planning board. But so far no proposal had been made. In fact, the surveying work had never been completed. Howard, who hadn't been around much lately, said only that they were still working out the details and that the surveyors would be back in there soon to finish up. As for that guy

Mongerson, he hadn't been seen at all. Maybe they had all been spooked by the killing.

Adam had gotten nothing more from Mansard in Nevada. As he expected. Adam could have asked for Campo's help, but he figured that would be a waste of time. He ended up calling a state cop in Concord. Neil Robling and Adam had gone through the academy together way back when, and since then they had done some hunting and fishing. Robling had contacts with various agencies in Nevada, and sure enough, a few weeks later a packet arrived with the Bushman case file. Like Mansard had said, it was thin, but Adam was at least able to see whom the investigators had interviewed. It was spooky to see Lily Garnett's name there, amid the ten-year-old scrawl. The interviewer had called her "unproductive."

Then, a few weeks ago, he had received a thicker envelope. The handwritten "C. Ringer" over the official return address had gotten his heart doing squat thrusts. God bless you, Cheryl. Inside, a file on John Harrington: sheets from NCIC, arrest record, copies of some illegible handwritten notes taken by the local investigators, and photos: mashed nose, part of one ear gone, the blockish head as though molded in concrete by a child. Ringer had also included a list of people she had served subpoenas to, people she thought were Mongerson's business associates. Adam had passed on copies to Campo, who didn't seem particularly interested. And maybe Campo was right, maybe Adam should quit playing detective. Mr. Plum in the hallway with the wrench. In the billiard room by Mrs. White.

After getting off the phone with Campo, Adam walked out to the barn. His truck was there in the yard, newly loaded with chicken manure. Adam would drive it over to his brother-in-law's, for his vegetable garden. He could hear Marilyn moving through the upper reaches of the barn, gathering eggs, the chickens astir. She had always moved briskly about the chore, getting in and out without ceremony. Ran the eggs through the sorter, an elaborate device of ramps and gates, the size of an upright piano. With the eggs sorted and boxed, she'd go back in the house and sit down on the sofa to watch her soaps. She had never acquired any fondness for the sound of the chickens, as had Adam, who found in the rumbling rustle and squawk of three hundred birds the sort of comfort he imagined men who grew up on the shore found in the sound of the sea.

Adam leaned on his truck and bent his knees slightly, feeling the pain there. Back when they were courting he had lifted Marilyn once, in a moment of horseplay. He turned the wrong way, and something popped, and that had been the end of his career in the lumber business.

Adam covered the heap of manure with a tarp, threw down a few old tires to hold the tarp in place, climbed into the truck, and started down the drive, thinking: what was the harm in imagining? Colonel Mustard in the drawing room with a knife. Chasing Miss Scarlet with a candlestick. He'd heard a talk once by those behavioral science guys from the FBI, out of Quantico, who developed profiles of serial killers. Spooky how accurate they could be. What a guy wears, what he eats, what movies he likes. Mr. Green with the ham sandwich and the string tie. Although if it had been an outsider, how would he have found Orville all the way in there on that land? Mr. Gray with a bad back in a rental car, looking for street signs in a town where there were none. A former

Boy Scout, maybe, with compass and topo map. X marks the spot.

Adam out on the blacktop road now, driving fast, leaving a fine dust of shit in his wake, imagined a man in his early forties in a rented Oldsmobile. Mr. Gray in a gray college sweatshirt, USC or Arizona, maybe, skin gray with bad diet, sour stomach rumbling, flipping Rolaids into his mouth. His first time in New Hampshire. The Granite State. The guy's thinking, a whole state named after a rock, what does that tell you? He's seen it on postcards, on calendar photos. Fall trees in circus colors. Men beating oxen with sticks. Live free or die. He's gotten instructions, maybe even seen pictures of the town, the Lake Road, Lakeside Farm. He's a professional, takes a certain pride. A man good with details. Neat. Tucks a napkin into his shirt when he eats, lines his shoes up on the closet floor before he sleeps. Never leaves the cap off the toothpaste. Leaves no fingerprints. And never gets lost. Mr. Gray hiding his car off the road somewhere, following Orville Rogers's tracks through the snow, snow getting in over the tops of his shoes, thinking what a godforsaken place; who'd ever want to live in here, anyway; can't see a thing for all these trees. Carrying a Glock 19 nine-millimeter handgun.

In the dream, the bear was covered with leaves, growling, just patches of fur visible beneath the mound of leaves, the growling steady. Forrest knew he should do something about it: cover the bear with more leaves, or uncover it to stop its growling, or maybe he should run away. But he couldn't move. He woke then, and heard the poorly muffled truck making the turn out on the Lake Road past Lakeside Farm. Though a mile away, sometimes they could startle you when the air was right. He waited for the sound to fade, but it kept growing. Not on the Lake Road at all. Forrest sat upright and swung his legs out of bed, feeling for his shoes with his bare feet. The noise kept coming, and he had a vision of a tank rattling down the path toward the fishing camp, about to bust through the wall. He wondered if he had time to grab his rifle, but when he looked where it usually was hanging, he remembered that he hadn't yet retrieved it from Clarence's house. He wasn't as awake as he had thought. He heard clanging metal, jouncing springs, the engine geared down and moving slowly along the rutted road. The sound gradually drew off to the west, a truck up on the Old High Road. Probably Howard's doing, though hadn't Howard said that the loggers would come by water? The chainsaws started before he had finished breakfast. He'd been planning on getting his rifle anyway; maybe now was a good time. But the rifle had been sitting a few years, and he'd be the better part of a day cleaning it. Forrest took his coffee out on the porch and thought about what he was going to do. People he didn't know had a truck and some saws up on Rattlesnake Ridge and probably had every right to be there. Though probably almost a mile from where he sat, the saws, two of them, were loud in the woods. He would have to go up there and see what they were doing. But he wouldn't go right away. Better to let the day develop. He would exercise that much self-control.

As it happened, Forrest had planned to do some cutting of his own that day. He had borrowed Clarence's saw to cut up the big maple that had blown down along the path from the High Road to the camp. After coffee he headed up the path and got to it, feeling himself wake fully with the work and the saw's pleasant jarring of his bones. It had a twenty-four inch bar, more saw than Forrest needed, but Clarence kept the chain sharp, and as the blade bit easily into the maple, releasing the wood's fresh smell in jets of white chaff, Forrest felt the returning pleasure of physical work. He worked steadily, building a rhythm, limbing the trunk and hauling the slash out of the way, then bucking up the stem into lengths. He would cut it into stove lengths, not thinking, for now, about the fact that he didn't have a stove. He would wheelbarrow the logs down to the cabin, where he would split them with maul and wedges, not thinking about much of anything except the steady rhythm of splitting logs, not thinking about what Howard had told him the day before or the chainsaws working up there on the ridge. Not thinking about Lily.

He had been at it an hour when Bud showed up. Over the saw's snarl Forrest didn't hear Bud coming, and he turned to see him all at once, bigger and balder than Forrest remembered. Always sneaking up on me, Forrest thought. His whole life, Bud Grisham had seemed to appear unexpectedly, stealing up on Forrest by degrees. "If there's nobody who would like to see you dead," Bud was saying, "then you probably haven't accomplished much in life."

The two men had upended logs to sit on. The sky was clear and deep blue above the sunlit green canopy. A light breeze in the treetops did not keep the mosquitoes from bearing in on the two men, who swatted and waved as they talked. Bud had the look of someone who had just showered and shaved after having been chased all night by hounds.

"Maybe you work too much," Forrest said.

"At my age, it's better than sex," Bud said. "I'm in the office, I've got a phone in each hand."

It was one of Bud's standard routines, and the sort of thing that had kept Forrest from ever liking Bud more than he did. For carving up the old places and selling them off to summer people and retirees up from Massachusetts, Forrest bore Bud no ill will. The man had made his moves and made his money, and that was that, as far as Forrest was concerned. And it wasn't simply that Bud made sure that others knew how hard he worked: Yankees had always found ways, quietly and not, to make their neighbors aware of their own industry and thrift. What rubbed Forrest raw was that Bud made it all seem like fun. He delighted even in his losses—his hair, his coronary arteries, three wives—as though perpetually charmed by the discovery of his own mortality. Come right down to it, Forrest was suspicious of any man who seemed to enjoy life as much as Bud did.

"I suppose you know all about that." Bud jerked a thumb in the direction of the saws at work up toward the ridge.

"Howard's project. I haven't been up there to look," Forrest said.

Bud cocked an eyebrow

"That's Randy Hodge and his boy. They're surveying those lots Howard's been talking about. Cutting so they can shoot their lines."

Forrest gave a small grunt of satisfaction. Randy Hodge was a distant cousin on his mother's side. Howard had played little league with Randy's son, Tim. At least Howard had the sense to hire local people.

"That what you come to see me about?" Forrest asked.

Bud sighed. "Forrest, I'm not sure anymore."

There was something boyish and pathetic in the way Bud looked at Forrest now. Bud's eyes were rimmed red. Forrest wondered if this was just more of Bud's salesman's routine. He nudged the chainsaw with the toe of his boot. "You didn't come out here for your health," Forrest said.

Bud crushed a mosquito against his forehead, then flicked the dead insect off his palm. The two men breathed evenly. For the moment the saws were quiet.

"I've never had a thing against you, Forrest. You know that."

"I suspect you have," Forrest said. "But not more than most people."

The two men listened as first one saw growled, then the second.

"You know that's not going to stop," Bud said.

"He can't get in there," Forrest said. "He's got no right of way."

"There have been cases like this before, where people have challenged the restrictions on a right of way. I happen to know that Howard's already had a lawyer looking into it."

This drew Forrest up. He stared at Bud: nothing boyish or pathetic in the man now.

"I've seen the deed you wrote," Bud said. "It's not airtight."

"Let me guess: you've got a plan."

Bud sighed, as though reluctant. "Think of what they're doing as a hostile takeover, only it's land instead of shares. Only way out is to buy off the raiders, which in this case is Mongerson and it looks like Constance. First we buy her out—I've got the cash to do that—then we bring Howard over to our side. Lily, too, if she wants. Put all that together with your land as collateral—maybe Clarence's too, if he's interested—we get a bank to lend us what we need to buy Mongerson out. We end up leveraged as hell, but at least the land's ours, and we can do anything we want with it. No outsiders involved."

"Whatever *we* want?" Forrest said, cynically. "And what if I want to do nothing at all?"

Bud smiled. "We'd be in debt, Forrest. This is what happens. We'll need a substantial development to get anything like positive cash flow. The bank will insist. But I won't object to calling it Garnett Farms."

Forrest sighed and swiped at the bugs on his neck, killing three with one pass.

"How can we buy Constance out when she's already sold to Howard?"

"Howard wants people to think that's what she did. The deed that's been registered names the Mongerson Corporation. But I happen to know that Constance has retained a share as a limited partner. She's only sold out partway."

"That woman was always smarter than she wanted people to

know," Forrest said. "And I suppose I shouldn't be surprised that you'd be sneaking around finding this out."

Bud stiffened. "I've got news for you, Forrest. The telephones reach all over the country now. I know what I know because I called her. Call that sneaking around, if you want. Something you might think about doing yourself."

"You assume that Constance would have anything to do with me."

"No. I just think it's worth a try. Maybe she could be persuaded that this is in her children's best interest, don't you think?"

"She's not in good health, Bud."

"All the more reason to act quickly." Bud allowed himself a careful smile. "She might even be persuaded to make a gift."

Forrest couldn't help but be impressed by the man's cool. He was a pro, after all. A man who had spent forty years reading the obituary pages, looking for leads.

"I'm trying to figure," Forrest said, "whether you're desperate or just have balls."

"I'm a businessman, Forrest. But I'll tell you, I got a call last week. Man doesn't say who he is, just says to stay away from Rattlesnake Ridge."

Forrest stood up, began kicking some slash off the path. "Why don't you listen to him?"

Forrest knew the answer: because where money was involved, Bud Grisham would never back down from a fight.

"There's going to be changes on this property, Forrest. I'd like to see they're the right kind of changes. As good as we can manage, anyway. And I don't have to tell you, people in town are concerned. This way, at least we keep local control."

Forrest snorted.

"Bud, you must own as much land in this town as I do, all put together. How much time do you spend worrying about what other people think you should do with it?"

"Maybe more than I ought to, Forrest."

Forrest tried his best to find Bud's pose of quiet dignity merely amusing. It was Bud, after all, who on the way to making millions had altered the face of Shaftesbury perhaps more than any single man in its history. He was a developer of course, and often downright greedy, buying low selling high. But, as he told Forest, he'd been selective. A few houses here, a few there. Because he said he also wanted to preserve the small town charm of Shaftesbury. It made economic sense: the quainter the territory the higher the land values. Rattlesnake ridge was prime territory. It had everything to warm a developer's heart – water front, lush woods, great views, privacy. Yet he made money. With a vengeance. Thumbing his nose at the planning board all the way to the bank.

Forrest was skeptical. "You'd have me believe you're acting philanthropically," Forrest said.

"I've tried to do right by this town," Bud said. "I know you have too, Forrest."

"Seems I've spent most of my life trying to escape other people's fantasies about me," Forrest said.

"We're not talking about fantasies. We're talking about land."

"I'm not sure they're all that different," Forrest said. He broke off to listen to a chipmunk rattle dry leaves. He found himself wondering about the precise nature of the animal's errand. And

216

then he thought for a moment that it was not simply any chipmunk he had heard, but *the* chipmunk, the one whose place this was, its territory as surely bounded as any farmer's, every twig and branch familiar, every rotted log and maggoty stump, every burrow and stone measured and marked.

"Tell me," Forrest said, "do you think that women get pleasure from tormenting men?"

Bud sighed, knowing that the interview had ended.

"Not sure I'm the one to ask," Bud said. "It takes me seven or eight years to figure out, with any particular wife, how to be the monster I'm capable of being. Once she wises up, she moves on."

"I'd like to keep Rattlesnake Ridge in the family," Forrest said.

"You think you can do it without me," Bud said.

Forrest informed him that he planned to try.

You are standing on a dock at dusk, watching swallows feed over the water. They twitter and tweet their cries part of a speech without speakers or listeners, a bright web of sound. Their wheeling flock flight stirs the bowl of light and air that rests on the calm waters of Abenaki Lake and brims to the dark crest of Rattlesnake Ridge. They take the slow bugs easily in the warm, wet air low over the water. Then all in a moment, with dusk deepening, the entire flock wheels and tumbles toward the forest, and is gone.

You stand with mosquitoes whining about your ears, brushing your cheek. Weathered gray and mottled green with mold, the dock runs so far out into Abenaki Lake that its end is barely visible in the gloom. You walk its creaking length over the still, black water. You keep your eyes on your feet, wary of rotted planks, smelling wet wood and the peaty water beneath. In this way you reach the end sooner than you expect, and not wanting to look out at the empty expanse of lake, you turn back toward shore. As you raise your head, you catch the odor of the wet, moldering leaves of the forest floor, spiced with balsam and white pine. The branches of tall white pines are black brush strokes against the lightening sky. Behind them the moon rises swiftly. The forest rustles with animal life. The breeze freshens, and wavelets now dapple the surface of the lake with silver.

The drumbeat is low, rapid, and steady, and you realize it has been there all along.

You do not see the bear leave the forest, but you are aware of its presence and breathe more carefully, sharing the air now with another set of lungs. You cannot see the bear, a congealed darkness moving toward you. The dock trembles with its weight. You rise on tiptoes and sniff a sour stink. Then it is as if you had been seeing it all along. It shambles toward you, head swinging side to side, shoulders rising and falling, now left, now right, the powerful mound between the shoulder blades, the great blunt head of Grizzly. *Ursus horribilis.* It eyes you casually, as part of the landscape. The dock sways. You risk a glance at the water, to see if there might be escape that way, but beneath the surface curls the body of a snake, milk-white and fat as a fire hose gorged on the hydrant's gush. Another swims beside it, and another, showing their fangs, twining their bodies together, and before you have taken your eyes off of them, you are turning, stepping, lunging toward the bear, which has already reared upright to stagger stiff-legged into your embrace. You clutch handfuls of warm fur and bury your face in its chest, choking on fishstink and bearsweat, and the tears gush out of you as you try to circle your arms around the massive chest, as if you're hugging a living, furred rock, choking now with sobs and your own bubbling snot, feeling your knees turn to warm water as you moan out loud that, yes, this is what you wanted, this is what you needed all along. At first you want to believe that the bear is holding you patiently, that it will go on holding you until you have spent your grief and gathered its strength into your limbs, but then deep within its chest you hear, like the shuffling of furniture in a distant room, the first percussive snorts and dragging rumbles of what you do not realize at first is a growl. Then you are staggered backward, thinking you will both topple into the water or crash through the planking of the dock, and you feel with a deep twinge that you have made a fatal and selfish error. What the bear wants, it seems, is for you to lean back and look up into its green eyes, what the bear wants is for you to stare into its teeth and feel the warm and fishy breath on your face, what the bear wants is to show you arms that can snap tree trunks and claws that can rip the doors off of cars, what the bear wants is for you to see how the fur on its neck glistens in the moonlight, what the bear wants is to be admired, what the bear wants is death, what the bear wants is to put its catcher's mitt paws on your shoulders and dance.

You grip handfuls of fur at its sides and dance, awkwardly, cowled in the bear's chuffing breath, staggering over the moldy planks in a waltz that any moment could pitch you into the lake, and then you realize that the warmth in your chest is your growl quieting to the contented chug of an idling diesel. Your paws rest on the fragile shoulders of a woman who barely interests you. She is pale and trembles, she needs your help, your power, and yet somehow you can't quite seem to focus on her, nor can you stand the thin smell of her sweat, and you swing your nose up to snuff the far more interesting forest: rabbit dung and deer dander, the muck of a beaver hut breathing its reek through the thatched top-hole. You smell worms turning up the soil, maggots roiling in the rotting stump, mushrooms blooming through leaf rot, the tangy underside of moss ripped up by raccoons, blueberry, huckleberry, raspberry, bitter sumac, sweet fern.

You dance with the bear, shuffling heavily to the drumbeat. But the bear seems oddly distracted, bored, its power withdrawn like an electric current slowly dimmed. And before you've had enough dancing, the bear has left you, backed off, waving its paws stiffly as though clearing cobwebs from the air. With a grunt it

220

thumps down to all fours and shambles off down the dock toward shore, and you realize too late that it has asked you to follow. The bear throws a last indifferent glance over its shoulder as you stand rooted to the dock, and then it flops away, hauling its gently swinging weight. Suddenly chilled, you watch helplessly as the bear fades into the forest, and you continue to stand with locked knees until the moon has passed overhead and fallen sizzling like a torch doused in the lake.

"I didn't call you back. I was still drumming."

"I couldn't go any further," Lily said. "I met the bear. We danced."

"The dance of transformation."

"I met the swallows."

"Two power animals. You're very fortunate."

"The bear wanted me to follow, but I—" Lily faltered, "I couldn't." She spoke these words into the dimness, the one candle guttering in the breeze from the open window, the flicker of shadows making the room seem small, close.

Lily startled when a hand took hold of one of hers.

"Here," Bernie said, "sit."

Moist, hot palm. A sure strength.

"Here. Easy, now."

Lily let herself be lowered to the floor. Slowly she allowed herself to recover her sense of where she was: seated on the floor of Bernie Rostow's apartment, a few doors down the hall from her own. She had been on her feet and dancing, she did not know for how long. In the flickering half light she saw once again the bookshelves to the ceiling on two walls, recalled that before they had begun, she had inspected their contents: not just books, but a great variety of vials, pouches, baskets, leather bags, ingenious wooden boxes with figured lids, pendants, wands, rattles, drums, masks, bracelets, anklets, rings. Bernie himself, seated cross-legged on the floor facing her, wore a blue track suit, a single amulet around his neck on a string, feathers held to his wrists with rubber bands. His bald head gleamed in the candlelight, yellow as the moon. He had set his drum on the floor beside him: it was broad and flat like a tambourine without the bangles, only wider, with a deeper sound. He had let her strike it with the mallet before they began, and she had been surprised at how springy it had been, how alive to the touch.

"I'll nuke some tea," Bernie said, springing up and hustling to the kitchenette.

The vision had left her trembling, and Lily wondered whether it would be best for her to leave. "No, please," she said, but softly, and too late.

"Take just a minute." Bernie was back, the microwave humming. He sat again, and she was thankful at least that he moved his cushion a little further away. It was his interest she feared: the way, when she had shown up at his door, he had looked at her a little too keenly, beamed too brightly at her every word. But now he sighed and flexed his right arm.

"Drumming really takes it out of you," he said. "What people don't understand."

Earlier she had studied his diplomas on the wall: a B.A. in history from NYU, Ph.D. in Anthropology from the New School for Social Research.

"What goes on a shaman's résumé?" she had asked.

He was a Jewish kid from the Bronx, he told her. He had

drunk the hallucinogenic *ayahuasca* with the Conibo Indians of the Ucayali River in Peru, been jolted off his bed and into startling visions by *guayusa* tea served by the Jívaro, in the Amazon, had flown through the air with shamans of the Pomo in California, chanted and danced with the Lakota Sioux in South Dakota, had drummed in the huts of hardscrabble Eskimos from northern Canada to Siberia. Most of this was with Brenkman, the man Lily had met once at the Center, who had been Bernie Rostow's doctoral thesis advisor at the New School. When he finished his degree, he did a three-year stint teaching comparative religion at St. Louis University, surrounded by Jesuits, sharp-witted men who told jokes in Latin. But the job market was bad, especially for anthropologists like him who had gone native and taken up the practices they were supposed to be studying. He had bounced around with temporary appointments, and now commuted between adjunct positions at the University of New Hampshire and the tiny College of the White Pines, settled for now in this small apartment with his drums and rattles, feathers, herbs, claws, tusks, and what all else she could only imagine: animal parts no one had ever heard of, dried organs of obscure reptiles ground to powder and sewn into leather pouches, rabbit's fur matted with wren spittle, an entire library of root and blossom, sinew and gland, all the dung and dust of his trade. He was trying to build up a private practice, he said.

The tea was hot and bitter. Lily was afraid to ask what was in it.

"A dance with the bear," Bernie said. "Intense, right?"

The keenness had returned to his eyes, along with a throaty pleasure in his voice. He was attractive enough, for a bald man. A thin face, bright blue eyes, something trim and catlike about him, with a cat's primness and physical ease. He could sit down cross-legged on the floor in one fluid motion, then tuck his legs in a neat half-lotus. He had spent years in places where people don't have chairs, sitting patiently in smoky hovels to win the confidence of cagey old men and women, waiting for them to open their secrets, their magic.

"I might be enjoying this," Lily said, "if you didn't seem so damned interested."

"You don't have to tell me about it," Bernie said.

Though casually spoken, she figured that this, too, was the professional's line, for she imagined he knew everything about laconic sorts, was ready always to be put off and put down, not to mention outright lied to, ears aquiver for all the blarney and blooey spoken to the white guy from out of town.

And in the end she did tell him about it, her journey to the lower world, calmly and thoroughly, if only so that she could fix it in her own mind, like writing down a dream so you'll remember. The swallows, the dock, the lake, the bear, the snakes, the dance. Watching the bear leave, knowing she was being left behind.

"Weird stuff, isn't it?" Bernie said.

"No weirder than my life," Lily said.

"What do you think it means?" Bernie asked, managing to sound as though he had never heard of such things before.

"You're the witch doctor," Lily said.

"People think I can wave a magic wand," Bernie said, smiling. "What color were the bear's teeth?"

Lily was surprised to discover that she knew.

"Yellow. Pink gums with some brown mottling."

"Great detail. You really have a gift. And he'd been eating fish?"

"Fish."

"Stinks, doesn't it? But a bear who's eating fish is feeling generous, my Athabascan friends say. A bear on berries you want to avoid."

Lily found herself trying not to make too much of the fact that she was on the floor of a candlelit apartment with a man she barely knew. "How much do you charge your clients?" she asked. "When you do charge."

"More than a bartender. Less than a shrink."

Bernie seemed harmless enough, but in the end, how harmless were any of them? He had told her, before, that he was going to have his apartment painted a more soothing shade. He needed a place to stay while the men were working, and she had not been sure just what he'd been proposing.

"I'm not sure how far I want to get into this," Lily said.

"It only gets weirder. But I'll tell you," he said, seriously now, as though moving in on her, crowding her somehow, though he remained immobile as a yogi in his half-lotus. "You won't get away from it," he said.

"From what?"

"From the bear. From whatever it is you're dancing with. We could work on it. There are techniques, practices. You've got to be willing to risk."

"I'm just not sure I can deal with it right now," Lily said.

Bernie's kind smile masked what she assumed was disapproval, his mild acceptance making her all the more ashamed of her gutlessness, her underachiever's habit of selling herself short.

225

"All I can say, from my experience," Bernie said, "is that if you don't deal with it, it will deal with you instead."

"Is this a sales pitch?"

"Don't be silly. This isn't tango lessons. Why do people think soul work is extra-curricular?"

"Time for me to go."

Bernie shrugged and smiled. "Do what you want." Then he rested a hand on hers, for just a moment, a gesture that could have been simply friendly. "You could stay a while. Nuke some popcorn, catch the end of the Sox game?"

And now the keenness was gone, making her think that it had been just professional interest before, a professional observer's routine acuity, like the orthopedist alert to posture, the neurologist noting every twitch. What, she wondered, had he seen? And now, making all the motions of leaving, she regretted not having had the nerve to ask him, to have pressed him further, before, when he was still in his professional's crouch. What did he know? She wondered whether he had been avoiding her as deftly as she had been avoiding him. That crack about the magic wand: had he glimpsed some secret? No point in asking now, for the keenness, the interest was gone, replaced by something else more supple, more furtive and unpredictable. His lips were suddenly slack and moist. It was this Bernie, not the other, who would come on to her.

But at the door, as she was taking her leave, he recovered his professional manner: "Reflect on it, the next couple days. The bear. It may come to you. And why you didn't follow him. You want to talk more about it, let me know."

"They say grizzlies used to live on Rattlesnake Ridge," Lily said suddenly.

"Great," said Bernie. He had halfway closed the door. "That's very good."

Lily saw that he didn't know what Rattlesnake Ridge was. She thanked him quickly and padded down the hall.

It was a Monday night, Lily's night off, and not yet ten o'clock. She didn't really want to sit alone in her apartment, but she couldn't think of anywhere she wanted to go, either. Over a week had passed since that mess at the bar with Kyle and her drive with Mongerson. She had expected her father to be here by now, but he hadn't called. She had begun to wonder whether he would once again vanish, avoiding her, avoiding Shaftesbury, everything. Mongerson had phoned a couple of times, out of town on business, and had managed to be breezy and chatty, just calling to say hello. He made no further propositions, which made Lily feel both relieved and let down. A girl does like to be asked. At work Lily and Kathy barely spoke. She had seen Kathy and Kyle together in the bar that night, and the bartender had called her the next morning asking when Kyle would be coming by to get his truck, which he had left in the parking lot. When she had gone in that Sunday, one look at Kathy told her the rest. For ten days she had seen and heard nothing of Kyle at all, and she felt his absence like a pain in her side.

The big news lately had been Peregrine Weed getting out of jail. Lily knew him. He used to visit Shaftesbury during summers when they were kids. He had been sane enough then. Once, when they were thirteen or fourteen years old, they were in the same weeklong canoe camp together on Abenaki Lake. She remembered that one day they paired off in a canoe and argued over who would take the stern, Lily, of course, furious when he assumed a girl wouldn't want the harder job. She got her way, and then had to spend the day staring at his back, watching his strong, smooth stroke. Arrogant or not, he knew how to handle a paddle. But so did Lily, and they ended the week friends. She had seen him only rarely after that, though. Recently she had driven by him a few times in Shaftesbury, where he seemed to spend all his time walking the roads in that mountain man outfit of his. Poor kid. To end up such a screwball.

Then again, she wasn't sure she was all that much better off—shuffling down a low-rent hallway in her sweatpants. She was thirty-five years old, half of her biblical allotment of three score and ten. She felt year by year the thickening of her thighs, the growing roundness of her belly, her weight pulling her more firmly to the earth. The way of all flesh. If she was going to have children, she had better get with the program.

How did one do it, this business of living? She remembered once asking her father—she had caught him at the point of mounting the stairs in the old Thompson farmhouse, a sheaf of papers in his hand, busy with his thoughts—asking him—she must have been twelve or thirteen, it would have been after she had gotten her first period, an age at which she had begun to feel time's tricks and the body's small rebellions, learning that there were larger rebellions, too, for now she remembered: her Aunt Margaret, her father's sister, had died of cancer that year, so she must have been twelve—asking him—with her newfound sense that the fates could be insulting, that grace descended willy-nilly, hoisting some into the spheres of light, like her cousin Edwina, who married a millionaire, and leaving others, like her Uncle Bernard, the alcoholic, in the pouches of fire—asking him—with that sense still with her from two years previous, when she had been needled by auras and could pass her hand through solid objects as though through a swarm of bees, the sense, though now fading like an echo down a hall, that life could be extraordinary, fading, so that what followed after seemed flat by comparison, the future dull at best and at worst a cruel joke—asking him—and he would have been in his mid-forties then, his hair still dark and full, still a relatively young man, she realized now, with a man's full strength—asking him: "Dad? Like, what happens if things don't work out?"

Seeing him stop, one foot on the bottom step, one hand on the whorled newel post, bending close as though he hadn't heard.

"What?"

"I mean, what if when I grow up, things just don't work out? What do I do?"

"What do you mean?"

"Like if nobody ever likes me and I can't get married and don't have any money, what do I do? Or if I get in some horrible accident so I can't walk? Or what if I just keep growing until I'm seven feet tall and no one will dance with me? What if I never learn to drive a car or fill out all the forms the government sends you where if you don't fill them out, they put you in jail? What am I supposed to do then?"

"None of that's going to happen."

"What if a tornado wrecks my house?"

"It won't."

"But what if it does?"

Releasing his hand from the newel post and placing it on her shoulder, squeezing just a bit too hard, his face down now close to hers, his eyes bright, kind, but commanding: "You hold on. That's what you do. You hold on."

He smiled then and patted her shoulder gently, a bit embarrassed, she now supposed, at the inadequacy of his response, and lurched up the creaking stairs.

By then he had been keeping a separate apartment in Boston for twelve years.

And now Lily did not know whether she could hold on, grip the bear's fur, stare into those teeth, hold on even as they danced into darkness. Perhaps the greater wisdom was in letting go.

Back in her apartment the fax machine blinked. Another missive from the West:

> Dear Lily,
> The body is the rock that our words break
> upon.
>
> Your mother

Lily allowed herself a wan smile. Perhaps her mother was plugged in somehow, attuned to her daughter's nighttime thoughts. There are no coincidences, Ananda had told them. Lily tore the paper off and placed it in the drawer with the others that had been arriving, every week or so, since soon after the fax machine had been installed. She had not answered any of them.

But then Lily pulled them out, clutched the whole awkward sliding mess of curled fax papers to her chest and took it with her to the wicker chair. Okay, Mom, she was thinking. Okay. As though this night's stray energies demanded at least this much of her. Whatever Bernie thought of her, she would not, after all, run away.

She kicked off her canvas flats and curled into the chair with the papers in her lap. The night air through the open window behind her was cool and pleasant. If Shaftesbury was a habit of mind, then in this chair Lily could enter it and feel the town's evening stillness the way one feels an easing of the breath, as though she stood for a moment in the town's center, seeing the white clapboard houses clustered around the one blinking traffic light, the dour spire of the church somehow softened and made vital by the dark haze of new growth in the trees and the sweetness of new grass, while overhead the north star held its constant place.

She placed the faxes in order, smoothing each curled sheet against her thigh, and read through them once again, imagining as she did so her mother writing them in her room in the Bunkhouse, with its walls of limestone block and its barrel-vaulted roof. Lily now realized that she had all along been picturing her mother in the room that Lily herself had occupied at the end, that nun's cell, a crucifix and a picture of Ananda on the wall with his white hair and his intent but kindly stare. She saw her mother hunched at the desk in her nightgown, pecking at the typewriter, and then—what? Had Mongerson installed the fax machine for her, right there in the room? On the desk, or perhaps on the little table by the bed? Her mother tapping in the number, then feeding the sheet through, becoming suddenly this angel of the wires, leaping to satellites, falling again brightly to earth, singing in her daughter's ears like blood.

The body is the rock that our words break upon.

231

Two feelings tugged Lily opposite ways: that her mother had grown up to be someone Lily didn't necessarily like; and that her mother was sick and alone and needed her. Right now the first feeling was winning. It wasn't that her mother's words were strange. They were the sort of thing Lily imagined had always crouched behind her mother's slow smile, behind the joyless competence with which she had run their household. Nor was it strange that she was speaking them now. Lily had seen this change come upon other women of a certain age, women finally rid of husbands and children, free to bristle with inconvenient passions. Other women got advanced degrees in poetry writing or traveled alone in Africa or took lovers half their age.

Lily found the pad of paper hidden under the pile of magazines on the coffee table, and fished out the pen with it.

> Dear Mom,
>
> Dad once said to me, once when I asked him why so much of the time he didn't talk (I was probably only nine or ten): "Communication is overrated." I have ever since taken that to be the perfect motto for our family. It's hard, perhaps cruel of me to say this, but because I may not have another chance, I will: I have never felt that you were mine. You were always certainly yours, always consumed with fighting your own demons (maybe that demon was simply your husband). And perhaps I have followed your example. That's why I've never been able truly to give myself to another—except once, and we both know how that turned out.

What does it mean, to surrender oneself?

I wish for you grace, and strength, and peace.
I should learn how to pray, but to be honest I'm
not sure I'm up to it.

Your daughter

Tuesday afternoon Adam was in the office catching up on paperwork when he got the call saying that Bud Grisham was dead. He heard Campo's siren before he had even gotten off the phone. Bud's latest wife had just returned from playing tennis and found him in the vegetable garden. Part of his head blown away. A bunch of radishes clutched in one fist.

Bud lived up on Coombs Road, in a big white federal style house on a hill with a view northward all the way to Mt. Washington. Adam got there just after Campo and just before the county sheriff. Bud's wife, hysterical, was being led into the house by a neighbor. In the garden more neighbors stood around, staring. Campo was on the radio, and yelling at everyone to stay back. Adam heard more sirens on the way.

Campo caught Adam's eye. "Shaftesbury," he said. "Murder capital of the Granite State."

Adam led the neighbors gently away from the scene. Then he drove his cruiser back down to the driveway entrance and sat there with the lights flashing. More cars began pulling up, and he waved them away. But people parked along the side of the road and started climbing over the stone wall into the field, mounting the hill toward the garden in waves like some kind of Revolutionary War reenactment. Adam knew he should be doing something to keep them back, but it seemed that his body had decided to remain in the car. He felt hot and tingly and realized he was going to faint. This seemed okay. It seemed like the thing he should be doing. Some sort of black bubbly pool and he was going down into it.

Over his head.

"Adam."

Marilyn had opened the car door and leaned in to shake him where he had slumped over on the seat.

"Adam. I heard it on the scanner. Listen, come on."

She had him out of the car, sitting in the weed stubble of the road bank, his feet in the ditch. Adam felt life returning, blood returning to his veins. For a while it was enough to breathe the cool, dry air. Marilyn crouched beside him, fanning mosquitoes from his face.

He remembered reaching his arms around her, gathering her flesh to himself. He was young then, a lumberman, strong enough to lift the world. And he had done it, he had gotten her up off the ground, arching his back and lifting her so that she squealed and kicked her feet. If only he hadn't turned, taken that step. Then his knees had given way, and that was the end of it. And the beginning of something else, this new dependence, this need. Or maybe not. Maybe he had been a weak man all along.

Adam stood, Marilyn holding one arm, and looked up the hill toward the house. They had gotten the sawhorses up, the orange tape everywhere, state cruisers with lights flashing, a crowd of men in uniform. The men seemed small on that hill. It all seemed high and far away. Adam doubted he could ever make it up that drive, wasn't sure he wanted to. He would rather stay here by his wife, feeling her warmth against his side.

Back in the office he had left a pile of papers, cases he was prosecuting, all of it motor vehicle work, mostly speeding, a few DWI's. Public defender discovery requests. Papers to be sent down to court, t's crossed, i's dotted. It was work for which he had no particular talent. Interesting as mucking out a cow stall.

"Why did we think I should be a cop?" he asked his wife.

"It was a steady job, hon," she said.

Adam looked up the hill, thinking about the birdhouse set on a pole up there by the garden. He could see it now against the sky. It was a replica of the famous Mt. Washington Hotel, complete with red-roofed towers, balconies, flagpoles. A giant construction with a hundred rooms, one of Orville Rogers's finest creations, it must have taken him a month. And Bud had paid him for it. Maybe they hadn't been such enemies, after all.

Adam thought about his Mr. Gray as he must have walked up that hill just a short time ago, up the drive and into the field toward the garden, up into all that light and air, the mountains stretched out on the horizon, blue and silent. Seeing Bud Grisham straighten and turn, the freshly pulled radishes in one hand, first of the season. A moment's work, and then he's looking down at Bud Grisham there in his garden, among the radishes bulging from the soil and all else in sprout: corn now just above the ankles, feathery carrots, stout squash, lettuce like rows of rabbit's ears. Mr. Gray looking down at a man who never thought there would be a day like this in his life and thinking: why do people think they're so special?

By now he would be back in his rented car, out on some highway far from here, observing the speed limit, careful to use his turn signal when changing lanes. Was his job finished?

Kyle had not shaved for two weeks, and his face was now covered with impenetrable thatch, his lips had vanished, the movements of his cheeks were masked so that you couldn't see his smile coming, flashing out at you unexpectedly, strangely out of place, like teeth in peat moss. He had stopped shaving after that night in the bar, he was not sure why. He had stopped doing laundry, too, and each morning rummaged through his hamper to recycle underwear, unearth a shirt not too badly soured and stained.

For several days the town had been roiling with the news of Bud Grisham's murder. Adam Townsend and the state police were being tight-lipped about the whole thing. A few people claimed to have sighted Peregrine Weed in the area, and at first most people assumed that Weed had struck again, which was irrational, seeing as he had been cleared of the first one. The more interesting rumors tried to connect Shaftesbury to that wide and wicked world most local folks only heard about on television or saw in the tabloids in the supermarket checkout line. Louise Morgan at the selectmen's office wondered out loud whether Bud had become addicted to crack cocaine. Martha Bingham at the post office offered the solemn opinion that he had quarreled with his homosexual lover, whom she claimed was an insurance agent from Laconia. Tommy Townsend at the store was working on the theory that it was all tied in with the savings and loan scandal.

But the identity of the killer was only part of what people had to talk about. This was Shaftesbury, after all, and hard after the question of who had done it followed another one: what would happen to Bud's land? Bud's son and daughter both lived out of state, and had shown no interest in the business of watching over the nearly two thousand acres Bud owned, scattered about town in dozens of parcels. The thought of all that land dumped on the market, sold off willy-nilly by some disinterested executor from out of town, scared some people more than the thought of a killer on the loose.

Kyle had his own problems. He was driving to North Ridgeway on a perfectly good Friday morning, the last day of June, when, if he wasn't working, he could at least be fishing or lying on his back beneath his truck. For that matter, he *could* be working: there was that window replacement for the Grimsbys and the new roof for Mrs. Thayer's garage. But apparently he figured it was better to be driving northward while he still had a feeling of choice about it, like the alcoholic who takes just one drink to prove his self-control. For he wasn't going to see Lily. He was just driving in her general direction.

She would apologize for what she had said to him.

Who was he kidding? She would spit on his shirt.

Maybe he really wasn't going there to see Lily. There was, after all, a second waitress, in a second apartment complex slightly more upscale than Lily's, in another part of town. But even at his most fondly deluded Kyle could not imagine that a flushed and expectant Kathy was at home fluffing up her pillows for him. He had called her once, the day after their morning after, called not so much out of renewed desire as out of politeness—for he *was* polite, he *was* that good kid his parents had raised.

But he had to admit it was more than just politeness. He had never been a Don Juan type, but couldn't escape the small thrill of having now made love to the entire dirndled waitress staff of DooHickey's. It put a little swagger in his step. Then again, maybe he had called Kathy simply because he liked her. It seemed, these days, as though he had fewer and fewer people to talk to. Or maybe there was a worse reason yet—and this was the thought that made him grind his teeth in his sleep, the one that made his feet sweat, the one that kept his gaze from meeting what was before it, so that even now he was in danger of driving into the soft shoulder off of Route 35—the thought that he called Kathy simply because he wasn't yet through with hurting Lily.

Whatever his motives, Kyle called her, and they spent two or three dreadfully cheery minutes being polite to one another, until the time came for Kyle to end the conversation. But somehow he couldn't bring himself around to a proper sign-off, and at last they sputtered into silence.

"Kyle," Kathy said, after a pause whose length was just short of cruel, "for a basically decent person, I don't see why you're being such a shit right now."

"Is that the way you see it?" Kyle asked.

"You don't need to be calling me up."

"What if I haven't made up my mind about things?"

"And what if I *have?*" Kathy said.

"Is that where we're at now?" Kyle asked, trying not to sound too pathetic. "You're giving me the heave-ho."

"I believe in telling where the bear sat in the buckwheat," Kathy said.

"I just thought we might see each other again," Kyle said, not fully aware until the moment he said it that it was a lie.

Kathy paused long enough for Kyle to wonder whether she

had hung up.

"I didn't figure on such a normal-seeming guy as you being such a piece of work. But why should I be surprised?"

Kyle could hear a note of self-pity in her voice and imagined her gaze would be turning inward now, softening as she held the receiver casually a foot from her mouth, speaking to the invisible audience beyond the footlights.

"What I figure, based on my experience with the male species, is that what you're really after is a knee to cry on about Lily. And if you can't get that, you'll settle for some whoopee with the nearest waitress that's got all her bodily parts in the right places. If you think that's mean of me to say, wait a minute, 'cause I'm just getting warmed up."

"You don't think it's possible for me to desire you for your own self?" Kyle asked.

"Christ, tell me about 'desire,'" Kathy said. "That's the word exactly. You want to measure me out by the pound?"

"I didn't mean it that way," Kyle said, backtracking, knowing that he *did* mean it that way, or at least a hefty portion of what he felt for her was felt that way. "And even if I did," Kyle said, conceding the point, scrambling for advantage, "what's so wrong with that? You're an attractive woman, Kathy."

At which point, she really did hang up.

So that now, over a week later, Kyle drove northward thinking about how it was that women were always after men to express their feelings. Fact was, men expressed their feelings all the time, only the feelings they expressed didn't happen to be ones that women wanted to hear about. Kyle made a note to reprimand himself later for being righteous on this subject. For now, though, he figured he owed himself a dose of self-pity, enough to cruise up the North Ridgeway strip and take the turnoff for Village Square. He wasn't going to see Lily. He just happened to be driving by. Maybe he would buy some socks.

He was better-looking than most single men over thirty. He came from a stable family. He washed his whites and darks separately. She would see him from her window, throw open the sash, and call out that she found him as beautiful as an Andalusian stallion. Or she would throw his toothbrush at him.

He wasn't going to see her. He told himself it was merely habit that made him pull into the apartment residents' gravel lot instead of the paved one much nearer to the Socks 'n' Stuff Factory Outlet Store he might have imagined himself going to. Habit, too, that had him see, with a pang, Lily's car parked there: the dented and rusting Subaru wagon that Kyle could not help but associate with Lily's own humble and resilient self, her low-gear, four-wheel grip on the world. Though not habit so much as the jilted man's fine-tuned antenna that had him notice the red Mercedes convertible parked there, too, as out of place in this lot full of cast-offs as a pearl in a bag of nails. Its license plate was "SHANTI," which Kyle knew from the yoga class Lily had made him go to once was the Sanskrit word for "peace." The top was down. Was it possible for a car to be parked smugly? The sight of it should have been enough to make Kyle leave, until he reminded himself that he hadn't come there to see Lily, anyway, so the fact that she had a visitor shouldn't make him change his plans. But just what were his plans? The question left Kyle sitting in his truck, morose and muddled, wondering after several minutes if what he was doing was what it looked like: was he *stalking* her, for Christ's sake?

241

He had loved her by his best lights, he thought. When she first returned to Shaftesbury, it had taken Kyle years, until he turned thirty, for it not to matter anymore that she was three years older, his childhood friend's big sister, out of his league. It happened at a dance in the Shaftesbury Grange Hall, Kyle playing mandolin with the band while the folks stomped and whirled through contradances and squares. It was a hot summer night, and though they had all the windows open, the old hall was hot, the dancers glowing and slick with sweat. He had seen Lily new then, the pleasantly horsey sweep to her nose, the delicate flaring of the nostrils, her long hair whipping as she turned, something equine, too, about her high-hipped, long-legged gait. He found himself watching her, his playing effortless, feeling the music move through him as she swung her body through the dance. And found, by the end of the night, that she was giving back his gaze. That was all, that was enough—a hot summer night, a country dance, afterwards the dancers and players sipping lemonade and eating cookies, nothing happening in that old hall, in those hearts and limbs and the reverberant air, that could not have happened a hundred or a thousand years ago.

What had become of them? Sometimes it seemed as though he had simply been squeezed out, as though she was too busy with her old troubles to take time for the new and delicious trouble that he promised to be to her. Kyle knew her past, he had heard all the stories. But somehow he kept hoping that she'd be able to break clean of it all, step out of the history she seemed to carry around with herself like a shell. But maybe people didn't change. Maybe life was both more ordinary and more complicated than he had imagined. Nothing so simple, surely, as that night when they had left the Grange together and walked across the road and out behind the school to where, in the center of the baseball diamond, they stood and held hands and looked up at a sky stuffed with stars.

Kyle turned the key in his ignition and started the truck with a bit more of a roar than he intended. He wouldn't go barging in on Lily with Mongerson there. He would call first. Anything else wouldn't be polite.

But before he could back out of his space, he found himself waiting as a familiar figure approached his open driver's side window.

"Going up to see missy?"

"Not today," Kyle said. "Buying socks."

Luke's face was edged like a hatchet blade, his dark eyes welling up out of deep sockets like some old bad dream. He gave Kyle a smirk that was probably his version of a man-to-man smile. "You seen the car, I guess."

Kyle kept his poker face, glad now to have a beard to hide behind.

"Guy sits there and the one thing he wants to know is how long that fancy-ass car's been there, am I right? Think I haven't sat outside in a girl's parking lot before? Every man in America's done it at least once, doesn't make you some kind of slimeball. What do they think, they can just change the locks on us any time they want?"

"She changed her locks?" Kyle asked.

"I'm not saying she wasn't planning on giving you the new key. Who knows, maybe some other nut's been bothering her."

"Have there been other people around here?"

"What I'm saying, this is a free country, people want to come

243

around a girl's place that's not invited, that's their business, not saying I haven't done as much myself a few times, doesn't make me some kind of degenerate. But we've got a good news–bad news situation here so far."

Luke's smile might have been just a squint from his cigarette smoke, but Kyle could see that the man was enjoying this.

"Give me the good news first," Kyle said.

"Which is that the red car, Mr. Candy Man, only got here an hour ago, and as far as I know it's the first time he's ever been in there, so you can holster your pistol a while yet if that's what you're thinking."

"Should I feel good about your keeping such a close eye on my girlfriend?" Kyle asked, not fully realizing, until he saw Luke take a step back, showing Kyle his raised palms, just how much threat had been behind the words. We are beasts, after all, Kyle thought, hiding his small smile. We should have horns to butt with.

"Hey, man," Luke was saying, on his face the wide-open honest look of the veteran liar, "Far be it from me, all I'm doing is passing on what I figure a guy in your position wants to know. You want to go heaping suspicions, that's your business, and I'll just shut my trap and be on my way, think I don't have enough sense to stay out of another man's business."

Luke was doing his best to look wounded, so that Kyle had to shake his head, wave it off, saying, "No, no, no, it's all right."

"Because don't think I haven't been thrown from a few horses in my time," Luke said, regaining his confidence, his squinting smile. "And if I keep an eye out, doesn't make me some kind of pervert, I know where to draw the line and besides she's one lady I wouldn't, don't mind me saying this, touch with fire tongs, but that's your business, and all I'm saying is it's sure not me or Mr. Candy Man in there with his grocery bag you've got to be worrying about because you don't know some of the things I've seen." Luke dragged on his cigarette emphatically, arching an eyebrow as he fixed a stare on Kyle that seemed to want to say, "See? See what I'm talking about?" Which Kyle didn't, or at least not entirely, and he wasn't sure he really wanted to.

"The bad news situation," Kyle said.

"Exactly," Luke said.

"There's been someone else, not the guy with the red car."

"Answer me one thing, Mr. Cooper."

Kyle was surprised Luke knew his name.

"You ever done anything nasty?"

Kyle realized that his engine was still idling. It would be simple enough to put the truck in gear and back away. "I'm not sure what you mean," Kyle said slowly.

"What I'm saying is, if you've been there, you know. The things a man gets into in this country, it doesn't take a whole lot of effort to put blood on the back seat of a car. Doesn't mean you're a hardened criminal, just saying you know your way around a certain mentality. So when a guy comes around here a week ago and he could be a dozen guys I've seen in the joint, he's going to do you a big favor or bust you in the head with a shovel, and he doesn't care which."

"Who is it?" Kyle asked. "Who's been here?"

"Not like he leaves me his calling card. You see a guy like that around, you're watching your back. Wide as a house, dark hair like a Marine, one ear chewed."

245

It wasn't Adam Townsend, nor Bud Grisham, nor anyone else Kyle could think of.

"What did he want?"

"Asked if I'd seen a man in a red Mercedes, which at the time I hadn't. Asked me which apartment Lily Garnett was in."

"And you told him."

"Right there on the mailboxes anyway. Figure the dumb fuck can read."

"Did he go in?"

"Gives me a twenty and walks out of here. He's got a rental car in the lot. Buick."

Kyle felt a sudden weariness. He draped his arms over the steering wheel and rested his head against them. .

"You want it to go away, it ain't going to," Luke said.

"Why are you telling me?" Kyle said.

"Hey," Luke said sharply, so that Kyle would pull his head up and face him. "I told you I keep an eye out. I don't owe Miss Lily Garnett one thing, doesn't mean I'm going to let an animal like that around here and not say a word."

"You call the police?" Kyle asked.

"We're not on speaking terms," Luke said. "Plus the guy hasn't done anything yet."

"I'm wondering if you aren't a pretty good guy after all, Luke."

"What I'm wondering is why the hell you haven't been around."

"I will be," Kyle said. "I'll be back." Kyle put the truck into gear, but Luke stopped him with a hand on the door.

"One thing I'm going to do here." He held up a brass key and placed it in Kyle's hand.

246

"I don't owe you nothing," Luke said.

7

"You could sell anything," Lily said.

"Only when I believe in the product."

Mongerson had removed his white linen jacket and draped it over the back of the kitchenette chair he was now sitting in. He folded his hands in his lap, the table top before him invisible beneath newspapers, junk mail, dirty socks, wadded Kleenex, panty hose like shed skin.

"Howard is rather pleased with the way things are lining up," Mongerson said.

"You're eager to give Howard the credit," Lily said.

"I also happen to think it's a good idea."

"Garnett Farms. Ten acre lots."

"All that land." Mongerson smiled. "Think of it as an opportunity to share."

"I'm surprised Howard thinks there are enough flatland suckers out there to sell it to." "We've run some profiles, there's a marketing concept. But what about breakfast?" Mongerson peered into the grocery bag at his feet. "I finally found some decent croissants. And melon. You have any eggs?"

Mongerson had called a little while ago from his car phone, getting Lily out of bed, asking if he could come up. She didn't see any reason why he couldn't, and found herself pulling on her tightest jeans and looking for a decent blouse.

He arrived looking breathless, as though he had run up the stairs, though she knew he hadn't. There was something hurried about his presence, so that even though he appeared at ease in her kitchen pitching his and Howard's plans for Rattlesnake Ridge, he seemed to be working hard to sit still.

It was an edginess that Lily hadn't seen in him before, and it made her happy for the chance to shovel the contents of her kitchen table into an empty cardboard box and set about the comforting business of making eggs and boiling coffee. The thought occurred to her that she would rather be doing this with Kyle. She then felt surprise, and a twinge of guilt, at how easily she set the thought aside. There was something here for her to do, and she would do it, follow this business to its necessary end.

The breakfast made and set upon the table, Lily sat across from Mongerson and spread a napkin in her lap. She passed the platter of eggs, thinking yes, she had even put out napkins, thinking the flatware almost matched, the coffee mugs were clean. She found herself wondering if it was possible for her to live some semblance of a life. She looked at Mongerson with a measure of genuine surprise.

"We're having breakfast, and you didn't even sleep here," she said.

"There is a certain thrill to it," he said.

"Maybe I shouldn't get used to it."

"Ananda said that gratitude for the present moment is the chalice in which we receive grace."

"Receive grace, then," Lily said. "And eat your eggs before they're cold."

They did eat, Lily finding that in fact she *was* grateful for what seemed like the first true meal she'd had in days. Since her experience with Bernie earlier in the week, and with the business in Shaftesbury about Bud Grisham, she had been too distracted to

249

cook, too distracted even to take the meals she could have gotten free at the restaurant, and now she felt the simple fullness of the warm food, charmed somehow by the mere sight of the buttery brown croissants and the steam rising from her coffee. "Do you practice all that now?" Mongerson asked.

"What?"

"The teachings. Ananda. You were into it pretty deep back then."

Lily blushed slightly. She rarely spoke of her spiritual life now, or of what remained of it after the events of ten years ago. She knew that what she had pursued at the Center seemed to most people just some hippie foolishness, something cultish and of the 1970s and best forgotten, and sometimes even she felt that way about it. But in her most sober and lucid moments Lily knew that the spiritual work she had done there was not, and never would be, mere foolishness.

"The easy thing to say would be that I just can't seem to find the time," Lily said. "But to be honest, I just don't think I can deal with it any more."

"I never got to tell you—really tell you," Mongerson said, "how sorry I was for you about Johnny Ray, about—everything."

Lily found it hard to meet Mongerson's eyes, not sure she was ready for this sort of intimacy. It could have been simple kindness, but she still held the shred of a doubt that everything Mongerson said was in some way calculated.

"You've heard from your mother?" Mongerson asked, shifting ground only slightly, it seemed.

"She's been sending me these—faxes."

"I know," he said, then added quickly: "No, I haven't read

them. She told me she was writing."

"You've seen her?"

"Last week. I have business out there, so I stop in."

Lily faltered a moment, then nerved herself to ask: "How is she?"

Mongerson gazed levelly at her now, and Lily wondered how it was that this man had managed to insinuate himself so thoroughly into her family. He was everywhere, it seemed, filling all the gaps between them.

"For someone who will be leaving her body soon," Mongerson said, with no apparent irony, "she's doing very well."

Frowning, Lily got up to pour more coffee, wanting suddenly for breakfast to be over, feeling a twinge of guilt, angry at herself that she had had to ask him about her mother. "What about you?" she asked him suddenly. "Do you still practice? Are you up at five A.M.?" She had meant the question as a jab at him and was surprised by the seriousness of his response.

"I should, more than I do." There were furrows in his perfect brow. "I could use the help now."

"Don't tell me, you have troubles," Lily said, taking sudden pleasure in her callousness. She really was mad at him for the business about her mother. "Mr. Real Estate Mogul."

She had succeeded. Mongerson faced her with a look of sodden pain.

"I'm going to be unprofessional right now," he told her, his voice sullen and firm, setting her on guard. "Sometimes you do seem to think you're the only one with worries in this world, Lily. As though that land on Rattlesnake Ridge was the center of the universe. You don't know the levels I'm dealing with, the kinds of

251

commitments I've made. There are people who depend on me for a certain... *efficiency*. People you've never met who have come to care very deeply about your little postage stamp of native soil. I'll spare you the details, but I've got to tell you that it's very important to both Howard and me that we work out a deal."

"And what if we don't?" Lily asked.

"There's no need to discuss unpleasant consequences. But you should know that the people I'm involved with lack a certain subtlety."

"Darkness and light," Lily said.

"I'm not going to kid you."

Lily set the coffee pot back on the counter, then turned to place both palms flat on the table and face him. "You wouldn't be threatening me, would you?" She leaned close enough to Mongerson to breathe on his face.

Mongerson sat still, unblinking. "I need your help, Lily. It's not you that's in danger, now."

"Do you know who killed Bud Grisham?"

"No."

"Let's try again: Do you know someone who knows who killed Bud Grisham?"

"There are situations where knowledge alone isn't enough. The potential for human folly is unlimited, Lily. Certain elements here are beyond my control; it's a question of looking at what *can* be controlled and taking some action. If I could just have your commitment to consider a deal, and to talk to your father about it, that might be enough to stop this from getting worse than it is."

Lily straightened, breathed out.

"You got my brother into this."

"He makes his own decisions. And besides I've—" Mongerson hesitated. "I've protected him from anything … unseemly."

"Why shouldn't I call the police right now?" she asked.

"Because it wouldn't do any good," Mongerson said. And after a pause, he added: "And because you don't want to."

Lily could not quite account for the change she sensed in Mongerson now. He seemed quieter, smaller, more dangerous. And then she saw it: he was afraid.

"You need this deal," Lily said.

"I think you do, too," Mongerson said.

Once again, she felt the thrill of considering that he might be right. His words seemed strangely sensible, spoken in her kitchen, the remains of a decent breakfast on the table. Lily sensed, as she heard them, that a door had opened somewhere and she was about to step through it.

"What's in it for me?" she asked.

"Anything you want." Mongerson seemed to read her thoughts. His skin seemed to glow, and his eyes sought hers more boldly.

"You have a theory about me," Lily said.

"It's about anger, Lily. Call it a working hypothesis."

"And you, like everyone else, think I should stop carrying the past around with me. I'm not interested in another lecture."

"Then stop pitying yourself. Your anger defines you. You've earned it, it's your life. Stop battling your demons, because there's nothing demons find more entertaining than a fight. You need to own them, welcome them, give them a home. Then they won't own *you*."

Mongerson looked away now, as though embarrassed by his own intensity. Then he said quietly: "I can help you do that, Lily."

Lily let out a bitter laugh. "You'd lock me in a castle tower on Jackson Island. Let me beat against the walls, talk to ravens, mix poisons in a bubbling vat."

"If that's what you want."

"I take it you're offering me more than money for my land on Rattlesnake Ridge."

"The potential for human folly, Lily. I'm offering you my life. Nothing is ever going to give you back what you had with Johnny Ray. But maybe I could give you some part of what you had."

"No island is going to do that."

"It could be anywhere. A world apart. Imagine a life without constraint."

"You *do* think you can buy me."

"Don't be limited by fear."

"I think it's time for you to leave."

"I will come back."

"Out," Lily said.

Mongerson flashed her his most boyish, mischievous, charming smile. "May I see you again?" He stood and put his jacket on, ready to leave.

"Oh, Christ," Lily said, knowing that she had to get him out of there before she said yes.

"I'll take that as a maybe." . "We need a meeting, at least. You, Howard, your father, and I. You need to talk to them, Lily. Let's reach some understanding."

"I don't know where my father is," Lily said.

Mongerson seemed almost startled.

"I thought you knew. He's at the fishing camp. Howard saw him last weekend."

"But Uncle Clarence said—" Lily's anger choked off the sentence. "You go to some lengths to close a deal," she said.

Mongerson had a hand on the door. "I wish I could get you to understand," he said. Was his lip trembling? "I really do care about you. It isn't about land, is it? You reach a place where all that—" the wave of his hand seemed to take in Rattlesnake Ridge, Shaftesbury, perhaps the whole state of New Hampshire, perhaps more: the whole language of grant, deed, legacy, and trust that separated the landed from the landless as into separate orders of being, creating the illusion of ownership, the sense of a stonewalled and surveyed self that was in fact riddled with rights of way, encroached by abutters, threatened with subdivision and seizure by eminent domain, and finally emptied of substance by the very notion of real estate, which made everything one wanted to think one knew—houses, barns, fields, hills, forests—into something else, endlessly transferable, the property of ghosts, all the solid who, what, and where of a place made to vanish into air. "—where all that doesn't matter," Mongerson said. "We must learn the discipline of emptiness."

When he was gone, Lily threw the new bolt in her newly reinforced door.

8

Neither Luke nor Kyle saw the man in the white linen jacket leave the building. Luke had gone, and Kyle was backing out of his space when he noticed that Mongerson's car was moving. Not knowing just what he intended, Kyle swung his truck around and backed up to block the red Mercedes from leaving. The driver of the car, sandy-haired, clean-shaven, wearing sunglasses, looked over his shoulder at Kyle, waiting.

Kyle leaned out of his window.

"You Larry Mongerson?"

The man hunched down for a moment as though placing something on the floor, then turned back to stare at Kyle from out of the open convertible, right arm thrown over the back of the seat.

"I'm Kyle Cooper."

The man pulled the car back into its space, then got out and walked toward Kyle's truck.

The man has balls, Kyle was thinking. I'll give him that. Kyle observed with a certain bemused respect the man's firm stride, the shoulders thrown slightly forward as though expecting impact. We should be bellowing, Kyle thought. We should be horned and hoofed.

"Lawrence Mongerson," the man said, holding out his hand.

Kyle waited a beat, then shook it, struck by how small and smooth and womanish a hand it seemed. When they unclasped, Kyle left his own hand in place, calloused and creased, cuts and scrapes scabbed over. He held it between them as a momentary wonder.

"Which one of us has been working?" Kyle said, letting out a short laugh.

Mongerson smiled without blinking.

"I'm sure you work very hard."

"When I can," Kyle said.

Mongerson understood the reference; he made a slight bow of apology. "The Jackson Island project. Sorry about that mix-up. I still hope to be able to work with you on that."

Kyle was wary of the man's glibness. He would have been wary of this man in any case: the white jacket, the soft white leather shoes, the whole scrubbed and pressed performance. A man who couldn't be imagined cutting his own fingernails.

"You weren't here to talk about Jackson Island," Kyle said.

"She's there," Mongerson said. "If you're going up."

Kyle was tiring of hearing about Lily from other men. And he was thinking about a man with a Marine haircut. About Bud Grisham. "Thanks for the info," he said with a thin smile. "Is this the part where I say you better be out of town before sundown?"

"What I'm sensing here is a certain hostility," Mongerson said.

"You don't want me to get out of this truck, do you?"

"Hardly. Though there would be a certain thrill in the spectacle, I'm sure."

"I imagine," Kyle said, "that you get great pleasure out of the use of your mouth."

"I make my living with it," Mongerson said.

"And what kind of a living is that?"

"A life of peace, my friend. What are you afraid of?"

Kyle faced Mongerson with a sort of weary confusion, wondering if Lily could possibly care that he was out here in a parking lot facing down this man on her behalf. He wondered if he could encircle Mongerson's neck with the thumb and forefinger of one hand. He wondered if his life was going to change. He felt himself grow stupider by the minute.

Just then Mongerson swatted a mosquito away from his ear, and Kyle saw the handgun tucked in the waistband of his chinos.

"Christ," Kyle said, startled. "The man of peace. Christ."

He shifted the truck into gear, gave it a little gas, foot ready to engage the clutch. He needed to know whether Lily was all right.

Mongerson didn't seem to understand, and Kyle wasn't sure exactly what was happening. Had Mongerson not meant for him to see it? Or had the movement been deliberate? The situation had taken a step toward an ugliness he had not thought possible.

"Let's not make this a big deal," Kyle said, thinking only of getting away from here, getting to Lily. But maybe Lily didn't want to be gotten to. Maybe Kyle was simply a failure at everything.

Then Mongerson seemed to realize that Kyle had seen the gun. He placed a hand there where the gun was. "Oh, that," he said, a slight flush coming to his face. "I didn't mean—that wasn't for you."

"That cheers me right up," Kyle said. He started rolling the truck forward, watching Mongerson, thinking: better to roll or sit still? Run from a dog, it sees prey.

"Wait," Mongerson said. "You don't understand." He put a hand on the window frame. "Just wait a minute."

Kyle shifted back to neutral, took his foot off the clutch.

"Don't misjudge me," Mongerson said.

"What am I supposed to think?" Kyle said.

"That I'm not a fool," Mongerson said. "It's a dangerous

world."

"Seems it is, all of a sudden," Kyle said. "And I don't suppose you know anything about why that's so."

Mongerson gave him a level stare. "How can I help you, Mr. Cooper?"

"Look," Kyle said, sighing. "I don't know shit about you. All I know is my life's been less pleasant since you've been on the scene. I don't like what's happened down in Shaftesbury, and I'm not real happy about concealed firearms in the vicinity of my girlfriend."

"I didn't bring it in with me. I had it in the car."

Kyle remembered now how Mongerson had hunched toward the floor of his car when Kyle had called his name. Getting the gun. Maybe this much at least wasn't a lie. "I also don't like hearing about ugly people coming around Lily's place asking for you."

Mongerson was suddenly alert. "Where did you hear that?"

"Janitor told me. Said it was a big guy, Marine haircut, something funny about one ear. Sometime last week."

Flustered as Mongerson had been a moment before, Kyle was now once again impressed with the man's cool.

"I'll look into it," he said, his gaze giving nothing away. Still, Kyle saw for the first time the lines beneath his eyes, a tiredness there. Soon he would no longer look young for his age.

"Maybe you should stay away from Lily," Kyle said.

"I imagine Lily is capable of making her own decisions about what company she keeps."

"I don't care," Kyle said. "Right now most people in my situation would be getting pissed off in a big way."

"Be extraordinary," Mongerson said. "You're blocking my

car. I'm late for an appointment."

Kyle put it in gear and roared out of the parking lot, tires spitting gravel. Before he got too far, he found he was hyperventilating, and he had to pull over before he blacked out. He spent untold minutes with his forehead on the wheel, breathing into his hands. By the time he had circled the complex and returned to check on Lily, Mongerson's car was gone.

9

About a half mile up the Old High Road, well before the Weed homestead and the place where they had found the body, a track to the left led down to the Garnett fishing camp. Adam had been down there a few times for drinking parties Howard had thrown as a teenager. Adam had been in his mid-twenties then, about five years older than Howard and Kyle and their buddies. He was working as a logger and not yet married, and he remembered standing awkwardly with his can of beer as a bunch of kids—guys and girls together—stripped to go skinny-dipping off the end of the dock. The night was cloudy but still moonbright, and their bodies glowed white in the dark, then vanished with the sound of splashing and drunken laughter, dark heads bobbing. He had clutched his beer so that the can buckled, watching from up on the porch with one or two others too embarrassed or drunk to go in, feeling then a bit of a loner, a bit jaded, lacking the spirit needed to fling his body off a dock into dark water. Feeling also, in the looks some of the girls had been giving him that night, that he was somehow too, well, *experienced* for any nakedness of his to be entirely welcome.

But then again, Adam thought now, walking in along the path to the old fishing camp, when had any of it been innocent? What were they doing out there, in the lake's cold velvet, if not thrilling to the full sense of their own skins? Adam felt his own juices stirring now with the memory. For he remembered also that as he stood there listening to the plunging and lashing of water, the boys' guffaws and the girls' shrieks made more intimate by the unhurried

261

fullness of sound carried over water at night—he remembered how he had enjoyed his sense of difference then, how those girls had looked at him through hooded eyes. Open and easy with the younger boys, their flirtations with him were more guarded, curbed by that same delicious sense of danger that dropped their voices to husky whispers when they spoke close to his ear. He was a man, they knew.

He wondered now, with a start, whether Lily had been among them. But she would have been out west by then. And once Marilyn was in the picture, he would have stopped going to those parties. God, thought Adam. The pleasure that had stirred in his trousers had faded, quelled by the pain in his knees as he hiked down the last steep pitch to the shore. God, how he missed the way his wife used to be, before she had turned cold. From the back the place hardly looked occupied, though Adam saw that one propane tank had been replaced since the time of Orville's murder, when Adam had come down to check the cabin out. But rounding the corner of the cabin, he saw socks and a shirt on a line, and called out hello to let Forrest know he was here. He had an image, as he came around to the front of the cabin, of Forrest Garnett up there in a rocker on the porch, cradling a shotgun, ready to take the head off of anyone fool enough to bother him. Marilyn had made him buy a bulletproof vest for occasions like this, but he had left it in the car.

Forrest wasn't on the porch, but when Adam stood down at the bottom of the porch steps and called out—he was afraid, somehow, to go up there and knock—he heard shuffling inside, and then the door swung open with a curious slowness, as if whoever was doing the opening wasn't entirely sure he wanted the world to get a look at him.

"Mr. Garnett," Adam said again.

"Oh," a voice said, softly, as though to itself. "Hello, Adam."

When Forrest Garnett stepped full into the frame of the door and looked down at him, Adam could see that he had not shaved for the week he had been in there. His beard looked more grizzled for the fact that his hair was almost pure white. He wore faded green work pants with the suspenders down and dangling around his knees, and though it was now the end of June and would be a hot day, he wore a flannel shirt over what looked like long johns. What struck Adam was not the oddness of the man's appearance, but its familiarity. There were a couple dozen like him in the town, lonesome old cats sealed up in their own funk in houses with the paint long gone and the fields grown up around them. Or in mobile homes behind houses boarded up or fallen in a heap. Always the same shuffling within, the door opening with the same creeping caution. The man looking down at him now could have been his own father, who had quit logging to pursue alcohol full time until he died alone in his late fifties in a shack with cloudy plastic stapled over the windows and blue tarps on the roof held down with tires.

Could have been. Except that the gleam in these eyes was not put there by alcohol. And the man had spoken Adam's name with a softness and subtlety that would have cost his father too much effort.

"You going to tell me something I don't want to hear?" Forrest asked, not leaving the doorway.

"That's what cops do, I guess," Adam said.

He wondered if Forrest Garnett was going to leave him

263

standing down there in the dirt, but then with a surprising quickness Garnett stepped out onto the porch and, gesturing to Adam to come up, installed himself in the better of the two rocking chairs. Watching him move, Adam could see that the man's body was lean and hard. No wobbly old coot, after all. He sat not out of need but out of a sense of decorum, taking his chair with an easy air of command.

"You saw Bud last week," Adam said. "Day before he was killed."

"You've got a theory?" Forrest asked.

"I figure I'm not a theoretical guy," Adam said.

"You've got questions, then," Forrest said.

A bit blunt, Adam thought. But that was always his way. His daughter just the same.

"Bud say anything you think I should know about?"

"Said a lot of things you probably already know about, even though you shouldn't."

Adam couldn't quite tell whether Forrest was joking. "He seem worried about anything?" Adam asked.

"Said he got a phone call, didn't know who from, told him to stay away from Rattlesnake Ridge."

Adam made a note to find out more about that phone call. "He mention anything about this fellow Mongerson?"

Forrest's jaw clenched, then released. A man not used to repeating his private conversations. Adam watched Forrest consider how much he wanted to say.

"Bud wanted to help me buy him off."

Forrest spoke as if each word cost money. "You should be talking to Mongerson, I think."

"We're looking for him," Adam said. "People at Major Crimes down in Concord would like a whole lot to know where he is."

Forrest gave a grim smile, as if to say, "Why are you asking *me*?" "People would also like to know where Howard is."

Adam hadn't thought it was possible for Forrest to sit any more upright in that chair.

"Tell you truth, Mr. Garnett," Adam said, "I'm a little worried. I got some information from the authorities out in Nevada. He's getting mixed up with people I wouldn't want to share a toothbrush with."

"I've long ago relinquished any interest in his hygiene."

As Adam told him what he had heard from Cheryl Ringer about Mongerson's business associates, he felt himself talking into a gathering silence. What he chose not to tell, for it seemed more in the nature of superstition than fact, were his thoughts about the Bushman case. Adam had spent some time parsing bad handwriting on bad photocopies, and he found that some of the people interviewed in the Bushman case matched the names on the list of Mongerson's business associates that Cheryl Ringer had given him. This was something Adam had not even told Campo.

Adam couldn't be sure, at first, whether Garnett was simply uninterested or whether he didn't want to be hearing any news from Adam. There was a third possibility, of course: that Garnett already knew about Mongerson, or at least suspected something. Whatever the case, Forrest Garnett had a way about him, a certain jut to his jaw, his gaze fixed on a distant spot, that gave Adam as he talked a growing sense of his own irrelevance, as though beneath Garnett's indifferent eye the strivings of men such as Adam—after

265

Truth? Justice?—were as significant as what ants do, as substantial as a breeze.

"You know what I mean," Adam said. "If you were thinking of having any dealings with these people."

"Which is what you're really here to find out about."

"I don't follow you."

"You'd like to know what's happening with Rattlesnake Ridge."

"If you think that's all I care about—," Adam sputtered. "There's a man been killed here—." He stopped himself. Angry now, he looked down through the pines to where the lake shone beneath the hazy sun. It would be a hot day. Adam had already missed the better part of the fishing season. He was in over his head and wasting his time. The others would get to Forrest soon enough. Campo. The real cops.

"I wish I was smart enough to know exactly what I *was* here to find out about," Adam said quietly.

"You're under the mistaken impression that I can help you."

Adam gathered himself up. One more effort. "It's no secret Bud was interested in your property."

Garnett sighed. "So have a lot of people been for a lot of years." He then turned to give Adam an odd smile. "Including me."

"I don't mean to go into your private affairs—."

"Yes, you do," Forrest said, the smile broadening.

Adam met the man's stare. "I've known your family a long time, Mr. Garnett. I wouldn't want to see anything happen to Howard."

"But you'd be happy to see him in jail, if the law required it."

"I'm not sure that would make me happy, Mr. Garnett."

Forrest Garnett turned away to stare down toward the water, leaning back in his rocker.

"For the information about my son, I'm grateful. I don't quite know what I'm to do about it, though. People seem to think I've got some special pull over the course of events. I don't. Not even sure I wish that I did."

He looked at Adam quizzically a moment, then continued his study of the grove of pines before him. It occurred to Adam that here was a man who probably was used to thinking several things at once. He probably *was* studying those pine trees, thinking about fungi and beetles, counting dead limbs, guessing which were likely to go in the next big storm.

"You're waiting for me to say something that will help you link my son to Bud Grisham's murder."

"I'm not sure that's what I'm doing," Adam said. "I just figure you'd like to have this mess cleared and done with."

"You have sons of your own now, right?"

"Two boys."

"I've found that to survive as a father, you have to cultivate a certain ignorance. Spies and politicians call it 'plausible denial.'"

"You have something you want to deny?"

"What I want to deny is that I have anything to deny," Forrest said with a wry smile. "You see, I really am ignorant. All I know is some fools have been pestering me about the land. I believe you know as much as I do about that. But you do understand, don't you, that I'd never do anything to harm my son?"

"All I want, Mr. Garnett, is to help put an end to this thing. If you learn anything that might help me do that, will you let me know?"

Garnett continued to stare down toward the water until Adam began to stare down there, too. Both men rocked slightly in their chairs. There was still no wind, and the water was a dull white sheet in the sun.

"I knew your father," Forrest said. "Took life hard. Did you know he taught me how to set a trap line?"

"No, I didn't know that," Adam said.

When Forrest faced him, the odd smile had returned. "I do appreciate the visit, Adam. I suppose the next time you come, you'd better have a warrant."

It didn't take Adam very much of the walk back to his truck to decide he had had enough of this family. So much thanks for his pains, he figured. Though perhaps Forrest had been right in sensing that his motives were not entirely pure. He had wanted to warn Forrest that Howard might be getting into trouble, but he had also hoped to turn up another lead. And there had been more than that, too, but it took Garnett's sensing it to make him realize that: Garnett had caught him in the unprofessional act of nosing about the Garnetts doings, looking for a good story for the folks in Tommy's store, the way any resident of Shaftesbury would. That's what the smile had been about, and that's what had made the whole visit so aggravating: Forrest Garnett gave you the feeling he knew more about you than you did about yourself.

So screw him, Adam thought. Screw the whole business. Let the real cops handle it from here.

10

Kyle took the stairs two at a time, his hand hot where it tugged at the railing, creasing the flesh. He needed to calm himself, he knew. Foolish, this rushing up to her apartment, to what? Certain humiliation. He felt like the breathless schoolboy, rushing to ask a girl to the dance, knowing somebody else has beaten him to it. He checked his stride down the hallway, where the nap of the carpet was already slick with wear.

He was a damn good carpenter. He subscribed to *Smithsonian* magazine. He could recite St. Anselm's argument for the existence of God. He made a killer eggplant parmesan.

Kyle took a breath, knocked not too loudly, three times. "Lily, it's me."

"I'm not at home."

They spoke through the closed door.

"What does that mean?"

"It's an expression. Means I'm not receiving guests at the moment."

"I'm not guests, I'm Kyle."

"Don't force me to be more blunt."

"Lily, did you know that Mongerson guy carries a gun?"

There was a pause long enough for Kyle to think that Lily had gone into the bedroom.

"What do you want, Kyle?"

The door from the stairwell swung open, sucking air from the hall. Luke appeared, squinting. Seeing Kyle, he stopped where he was, leaned against the wall, smoking, watching, flicking ashes on the carpet.

Kyle leaned his forehead against Lily's door. "I want you, Lily." He swiveled his head for a glance at Luke, who gave him a thumbs up.

"Are you okay?" Lily asked. "I mean, you're not sick or anything."

"I'm standing in a hallway reminds me of a subway tunnel," Kyle said. "Don't know how this lighting meets code."

"You've been on a subway?"

"I've seen the elephant, Lily. Let me in."

"It's better this way. I'm getting comfortable. I've got a chair from the kitchen."

Kyle thrust his hands in the pockets of his bluejeans. In the left were scraps of paper bearing phone numbers, credit card receipts, a four-penny nail, three washers, the keys to his truck, two wood screws, the stub of a pencil, a half roll of lifesavers, one half of a latch to a kitchen cabinet. In the right pocket was a single brass key.

"Give me a reason why I shouldn't walk out of here right now," Kyle said.

"Let me think," Lily said.

"Look, Lily, I'm worried about you. This thing with Bud, and Peregrine Weed on the loose. And your janitor says some guy's been coming around here, asking about you and Mongerson."

Kyle again looked at Luke, who gave him a nod of encouragement.

"What are you going to do about all that, Kyle?"

"I'll sit out here all night."

"When I call, I'll ask the police not to be rough with you."

"Is it too much to ask—that I want to protect you?"

"From what, other men?"

"From—." Kyle extended an arm, pointing down the hall toward Luke, and beyond, to a world of mayhem and carnage that seemed to be circling like some new bypass of the Interstate they've suddenly routed through your town, the wash and grumble of its trucks always in your ear. "From what's out there."

"Do you really think that's possible? What's out there is only a more solid version of what's in here."

"You don't really believe that," Kyle said. "We're talking about men with guns. Shaftesbury's in a panic. They've got teams combing the woods."

"We cast our own shadows, and mistake them for living beings."

"Adam Townsend is going around in a bulletproof vest."

Lily giggled. "He must be excited."

"Lily, I'm here to ask you to forgive me."

"I'm thinking maybe forgiveness is overrated."

"I was out of my head, Lily. All that with Kathy meant nothing."

"Are you reading this off index cards?"

"Doesn't honesty get me anywhere?"

"Maybe you should cultivate some secrets."

"In first grade I stole Ross Findlay's space helmet out of his locker at school. I've never told anyone that."

Kyle heard the scrape of a chair, then nothing, then a low choking sound that could have been Lily laughing. Except that she was crying.

"Lily, can I come in there?"

271

Kyle fingered the key in his pocket.

"It would only confuse things," she said.

"Are you okay?"

"Fit as fiddleheads."

"Lily, I don't know this guy Mongerson. I think he wears cologne. But I'm in no position to tell you what to do. All I can tell you is that you've got nobody in the world who loves you like I do. The only thing I want is for us to be together. My heart hurts too much when we're apart like this, when we're separate. I can't offer you a perfect life, Lily, I think you know that. But I can offer you a life. Shaftesbury is only a town, land is only land. When all this mess is over, I want us to build a house together. Post and beam with twelve foot bays. I want to put in radiant floor heat and lots of low-e glass. I want us to spend weekends shopping for plumbing fixtures, lie in bed at night reading furniture catalogs. I want you to circle what you like and let me build it for you. I want to build your tables and chairs, your sofas and sidebars, your cabinets and counters and bookshelves and coffee tables. I want to make your dressers and beds and nightstands.

"Lily, I want to make a crib and a cradle, and then I want us to make the children to go in them, a boy named Laredo-Who-Holds-the-Sky-Up and a girl named Marzipan-of-the-Shining-Water, and we'll eat fishheads and drink skunk cabbage tea and invent a new language without words for the things that hurt us and with hundreds of synonyms for the things we like, and I'll learn to lasso groundhogs on our groundhog ranch, and you can make a telescope out of birch bark, and invent new numbers, and decorate walls with pomegranate seeds, and I'll build a barn for our stuffed orchid collection and another for goose-drawn sleighs and another

272

for painted mussel shells, and we'll grow cucumbers the size of dachshunds and watermelons like whales...."

Kyle did not notice the point during his speech when he had slid to his hands and knees and begun mumbling through the crack under her door, and he didn't know at what point the door opened and he found himself looking at Lily's scuffed slippers, grasping her ankles, sensing the rest of her rising there like some magic beanstalk whose seeds he was not aware of having planted. He hauled himself upward more with hope than fear, climbing by calf and thigh and hip toward what heights he could not imagine, hoisting himself onto the shelf of those shoulders, reaching at last that chin, those lips, those quivering fluted nostrils, those red, puffed lids opening to reveal brown and emerald eyes that told him at once he had gained the entrance to a soul not yet prepared to make him welcome.

"I'm here," Kyle said.

"I wanted to make sure you were real," Lily said. She grasped his upper arms as though testing their solidity, though for now going no further, not yet quite taking him into her embrace.

"I've missed you," Kyle said.

"I know."

"You're okay?"

Lily nodded. She leaned her forehead against his chin, and the smell of her shampoo almost made him weep.

"When can I come back?" Kyle asked.

"Soon, I think," Lily said. "Just not now. Soon."

"All right," Kyle said.

He released her then, and turned, and as he walked down the hall, Lily Garnett watched his retreating back, thinking: I'll get back to him, I will find my way. And then thinking: I have other things to do first.

11

Lily retreated to her bed, where she gave herself the release of tears and then sleep, dreaming of fur. She woke with the smell of fur, and scattered memories of fur's warm dark, of the urge to burrow into some dank embrace, warmed by fishbreath, her cheek scoured by a hot tongue. She seemed to remember drawing the furred flesh around her, as though zipping herself into a suit, letting herself be packed there among the blood-hot organs and slabbed muscle, afraid at first of suffocating until she found the nose holes that allowed her to breathe, sucking in the cold damp, stuffing her lungs with the air of wet woods, feeling her pulse steady and slow, letting her arms stretch and fill the arms of the beast, letting her palms be padded with small loaves of flesh, her nails be claws.

There was a knocking on her door, and, still under the sway of dream, she walked toward the sound. *You must have no fear. If you see something frightening, you must not flee.* She opened the door without hesitation, expecting Kyle, expecting a fanged serpent or a hundred-eyed beast, expecting anything, nothing.

What she got was Mongerson, in a white suit, holding roses.

"Permit me to look ridiculous," he said.

"You're not. You don't." The small flutter in her breast surprised her. Say what you will, a girl likes flowers.

And when she invited him in, and when they were seated at her kitchen table, pretending to converse as she pretended to make tea, it was as though she could not hear her own voice for the drumming of blood in her ears. So that they didn't even make it all the way to the bedroom, but came to ground someplace short of it, on the welter of their own shed clothing, all as easy as sliding downhill, Lily remembering the nights she used to go sledding in the moonlight, the snow frozen to a glittering crust that grown-ups would plunge through but which bore the weight of children and dogs, out in the crashing dark on plastic sleds that sped down the icy slope with a sound like zippers, spinning down toward the waiting maw of the woods, where cold branches clacked in the wind, wind biting her cheeks, Lily with her arms outspread on the ice, hands locked with his, staring down into this man's eyes, sensing speed, the thrill of traveling too fast in the dark.

And when she slept again, she dreamed she was running on all fours, a growl in her throat, the taste of iron in her mouth, plunging into the thicket at the forest fringe, through alder and bramble, raspberry and willow, over the stone wall and on into forest, thumping through snowdrifts, on through the deeryards, under the hemlocks, startling rabbits, flushing the grouse, nothing to fear in woods ever deepening. She ran until the joy of it ebbed, and her limbs grew heavy, and then she stopped, and breathed, and let the night air slow the hot muscle of her heart.

Lily Garnett woke on her living room floor, finding a blanket thrown over her, finding herself alone. Moonlight struck through the window to illuminate a dozen roses slumped out of a coffee thermos. She wrapped the blanket around herself and got to her feet, feeling winter in her knees, wondering whether that was all, that was it, whether Mongerson had gotten everything he wanted.

Chapter Five

1

The next morning Forrest was up and out in the cool air of dawn, happy simply to be breathing with the sun still below the trees and not yet burning the mist off the water. The day had such a sense of rightness to it that Forrest wasn't surprised to find the puddle on the stone step at the base of the porch stairs. It had not rained. He bent to dip a finger in it, and confirmed the smell. Then as he straightened, he saw the mud smeared on the railing, and looking back up toward the front door, saw what he hadn't seen upon leaving it: mud wiped on the screen and to either side of the door as high as a man could reach. He stepped back up to the porch to study it, seeing now the black hairs stuck to the weathered shingles where the mud was. In one place four parallel grooves scored brightly through the wood. About time, Forrest thought.

Soon Clarence's boat could be heard rounding the point, and Forrest walked down to the dock to wait for his cousin. Soon Clarence pulled up, Forrest climbed aboard, and they motored out of the cove, not speaking, the bow tearing gently through the still water, out into the mist as if into a dream. Sitting in the bow, Forrest hugged himself in his old sweater, feeling the cool, damp morning air slide past him, the boat now bumping slightly as they came out into the open water of the lake. There was no need for speech, the great stillness of the lake both lulling and commanding,

277

surrounding the noise of the motor with a deeper silence. Clarence, good old Clarence, had remembered to bring sandwiches and a thermos of coffee. They would make a day of it. Clarence wore a rough wool shirt over his flannel one. He steered with one arm thrown back to grip the throttle, guiding them now surely past the buoys that marked the rocks around Maddox Island.

Forrest could only steal glances at his cousin, who when steering boats wore the casual yet serious expression of a man who had spent his life in and out of them and yet still viewed the lake with a farmer's indifference. He wondered, sometimes, at his cousin's calm. At sixty-five, Clarence was a master of skills outdated long before either of them had been born. Clarence could build a stone wall using oxen. He could build a log cabin entirely with hand tools. He knew how to tap maple trees and sluice the sap downhill using troughs fashioned from hemlock logs. He knew how to build an Indian sweat lodge, and what to do inside of one. He could trap, shoot, and skin a bear. He could find water with a dowsing rod. Clarence somehow managed to face his own irrelevance without bitterness. He was quick to remind those nostalgic for the old days that if farming these bony hills had really been any decent way to live, more people would still be doing it.

Clarence's great advantage, Forrest figured, was to have been lucky in love. Married over forty years, he and Sylvia still held hands in public. They had had no children. Forrest and Constance had held hands one entire teenage Shaftesbury summer and were too foolish to know that they should have left it at that.

Harper Cove was a long, crooked finger from whose farthest end you couldn't see the open water of the lake. To reach it, you passed through a throat only a dozen yards wide, threading your way between rocks in a channel marked by buoys. Once you were through, the cove widened out but was never more than two hundred yards across. It was weedy at the farthest end, where a stream wound into the lake through a swamp. By the time they neared the swampy area, the mist had lifted, but the low sun still struck shadow across most of the cove. Clarence cut the engine and they drifted, casting spinners in toward shore.

One advantage of fishing was that you could talk without looking at the man you were talking to.

"Bear rubbed its backside against the cabin door last night," Forrest said. His voice felt creaky, unused. One loses the habit of speech, he thought.

"Maybe."

They drifted silently, Forrest fished a number three Mepps, casting toward the place where a hemlock slanted out over the water, soon—in next autumn's storms, perhaps—to lose its hold on the bank and plunge in. There was nothing hitting, but he liked the vibration of the lure in the water like a small electric current. When it cleared the water near the boat, he whipped it neatly overhead to cast it out again.

Forrest knew Clarence was angry with him for not seeing Lily. And perhaps for more than that. Clarence had said little about the land, and Forrest wasn't sure what that meant. In a family suspicious of speech, one learned the elaborate variations of silence, all its shapes and textures and hefts. But Forrest couldn't fool himself, this time, into thinking he knew all that lay behind this one. And there was Bud Grisham to think about.

"Bud told me people in town were worried about Rattlesnake

Ridge," Forrest said.

"Are *you* worried?" Clarence asked.

"Some days it seems mostly I'm just *tired*," Forrest said. He glanced sidelong at his cousin, hunched over his rod, lined face studying the water. Clarence was always studying something: the way a tree would fall in the next big wind, the way a barn had settled and racked, and what might be done to square it, how a field lay to the sun, where the soil would drain and what could be grown there. Always reading the book of the world.

"I can imagine what you're thinking about it," Forrest said.

The remark pulled Clarence up, and the two men looked at one another for an uncomfortable moment.

"Hardly much matters what I'm thinking," Clarence said, with surprising bitterness. He snapped his next cast sharply out over the water.

There it was: despite their lifelong friendship, Clarence would always be the poorer cousin. But he had no heirs, Forrest thought to himself, no sons to hatch schemes of plunder and pillage. They had never discussed what would become of Lakeside Farm when Clarence and Sylvia were gone.

"You can't like Howard's plan. Whatever you might say about time and chance."

"No, I don't like it. But I do think we fool ourselves into thinking there's some kind of permanence in this life."

"Look at that," Forrest said. The boat had drifted so that now above the trees on the far shore they could see the entire sweep of Rattlesnake Ridge, early summer green on the lower slopes giving way to the dark boreal green of spruce higher up and the granite ledges gleaming on the knuckled crest. "Tell me that's not permanent."

Clarence shook his head, smiling softly, sadly.

"Cousin," he said. "I'd like to believe you."

Forrest sighed. "I don't see any way out of this mess Howard's in."

"There may not be any," Clarence said. "Without a whole lot of money."

"That's where Bud thought he had me."

Forrest had told Clarence about Bud's scheme to buy off the out-of-towners. Now the silence between the two men thickened, and Forrest imagined they were both thinking the same thoughts: Orville Rogers and Bud Grisham were dead, and somehow Rattlesnake Ridge was the cause.

"Hard to figure somebody wanting the land that bad."

"Unless it was you," Forrest said, with a short laugh. "Or me."

"I've got a pretty tight alibi: mowing all day in the village, in plain view."

"Could have sneaked away a half hour," Forrest said, smiling.

"What about you? Been oiling up that rifle, I know."

Forrest sighed, serious once more. "People assume that I'm a better person than I am, Clarence."

"They want to believe all that land comes with a certain virtue attached."

Forrest felt a tug on his line, but then it pulled free: weeds. He reeled in, pulled the dripping green from the hook, and cast again, reeling faster now to keep the lure from going too deep. He said, "You can't understand why I haven't seen Lily."

"I guess that's your business," Clarence said, his words clipped short. And then, after an uncomfortable pause, "You know I was always a sucker for that girl."

"Has she called?"

"Once, a week ago. Told her you were still in Boston. Told her you'd call as soon as you got here. Sylvia near took my head off."

"I've lived a coward's life," Forrest said.

The boat continued to drift toward the swamp inlet, and Clarence continued to cast and reel. They would be in the weeds soon.

Forrest lifted his lure out of the water. He watched the shoreline, the granite boulders there, the exposed roots of pine. The blueberry bushes were done flowering now, but their smell was on the water, their bunched green fruit hard as gravel.

"People who say everything works out for the best haven't considered the evidence," Forrest said. Past the furze of blueberry at the shoreline he could see the ferns unfurled in full summer leaf, green against the black trunks of pines. He wondered whose land this was, and whether the man had sons. "Pete was the favorite, you know," Forrest said. "When he was killed, my father didn't speak for almost a year. And then, when Margaret died and I saw the whole thing was coming to me, I was scared, more than anything. That I wouldn't handle it right."

"Who's to say there's a right or wrong in the matter."

Forrest looked at his cousin sharply. "Try telling my father that."

Clarence's short laugh echoed back from the woods. "He's not here, Forrest."

Forrest's vision blurred, his eyes gone wet, the woods now a mottled band of green over black water. "I feel it getting away from me, is all."

"The man who hasn't known fear can't be truly brave," Clarence said softly. "And you haven't lost it yet."

Forrest pulled himself upright. "You're telling me to get off my ass."

"I'm telling you at least talk to your daughter before I have to bust you one."

"Soon as I catch something worth bringing home," Forrest said, flinging his lure out over open water.

2

She didn't realize what she was doing at first. She just got dressed and started packing. Her first thought had been simply to drive down and see her father. Then she figured she might want to stay the night, which meant deciding whether she would want to stay there with him at the fishing camp, or in her tent up on her own land. She found her tent and sleeping bag at the back of her closet. She would carry them in her old Kelty frame pack. In the pack she found her mess kit, stove, water bottles, all pretty much untouched since she had last used them, which she realized was probably ten years ago, out west. She imagined all the gear was coated with Nevada dust. Then she found herself stuffing clothes into the pack, more than she needed for one night. It was not until she had it all strapped and zipped that she remembered she was supposed to work at DooHickey's that night.

In the kitchen she found paper and wrote a note to Bernie, asking him to keep an eye on her place. He was welcome to stay there while he had his apartment painted, if he liked. Please eat whatever was in the refrigerator. She put the letter and a spare key in an envelope, which she would slip under his door on her way out.

The last things she packed were the faxes from her mother, including the one that had arrived that morning. It read as follows:

> Dear Lily,
> Not to suffer gusts of emotion is the snail's
> advantage. One imagines that a toad has no pride

284

to wound. What one strives for is to be altogether as anxious as moss, imperturbable as stone.

I have tried, Lily, not to flutter with delight at receiving your letter. I have tried with even less success not to be wounded by your portrait of me. I would have hoped to arrive at this stage of life less vulnerable to such jostling than I am. Not that I care to argue, I'm sure your perceptions are valid as far as they go.

There is just one point on which I will quibble: that we won't have another chance to say what needs to be said. Here, now, is that chance. But what is there to tell? Not great truths, surely. As I imagine the next world to be an abstract place, what I clutch at in leaving this one are precisely those things that can be clutched. I would knead bread dough with you, if I could. I'd have you feel with my hands just once that moment when you've got enough water into it. I'd have you with me to rub one cheek against a white birch's powdery skin, and bend low for blueberries among the high granite ledges. Oh, quick, before I forget: use tapioca in berry pies only, not in apple.

Love,

Your mother

Having stuffed the faxes into a zipper pocket, Lily had everything stowed and strapped when there came a knock at the door.

"Lily Garnett?" A smile like piano keys. Desert tan. A head that looked as though it had been rolled down a mountain. "I'm Randolph Tucker. I'm an old friend of Larry Mongerson's. May I come in?"

"No, I don't think so." Lily felt the man's aura, which was like a bow wave, wanting to drive her back into the room.

You must have no fear.

"I won't take up much of your time."

"I'm just leaving," Lily said. She stood firm, and the man gave a slight bow and stepped back half a pace. Wide shoulders, close cropped hair. Despite his upright posture and his balanced stance, Lily sensed a lack of symmetry about him. Perhaps an athlete. He was dressed casually in gray sweatpants and shirt.

"I'm just a little confused, Miss Garnett, because Larry said I could find him here."

"He told you that? He gave you my address?"

Now she saw it: he was missing part of one ear.

"Pardon me." That smile. "I don't mean to intrude into your personal business. I'm here in connection with the Rattlesnake Ridge project." He was broad-chested but thin-hipped, and there was something prim about the calves and ankles. Agile. A big man who could move, with the body of a discus thrower. The kind of guy who spends his whole life in sweatpants. Lily stood on the balls of her feet.

"I'm surprised that Larry hasn't mentioned me. Would you know where I can find him?"

Lily shook her head.

"Miss Garnett, I'm not a pretty sight, I know. Been this way

286

since birth."

"How can I help you."

"Maybe not at all. Could I find him in Shaftesbury, on the property, maybe?"

"Property? You mean our land."

Smile. "Yes. Beautiful place. We're very happy to be working with you on this."

"Not sure I *am* working with you. Mister…"

"Tucker. Gosh, I'm surprised he hasn't mentioned my name."

"Larry doesn't discuss his business associates with me."

"Ah." Pursed lips, considering. "Just as well, I guess. Though Larry and I go way back. Doesn't he talk about old times?"

"I don't know what old times you mean."

"Seems to me I remember him telling me that you used to live at the Center up there. You must talk about those days?"

"As little as possible."

"Just as well, I guess. Let the past be the past." That smile again.

"I really was just leaving," Lily said.

Again the polite half-bow. He left with a hint of saunter in his stride. Lily watched his retreating back, the broad muscular shoulders were menacing. What sort of creature was this? Mongerson, and now this man: the feeling that she had descended another level in the chain of being.

She waited a few minutes to be sure the man had left the building, then hoisted her pack. At the bottom of the stairs she could not help checking her mail. All bills and junk except for one letter, addressed in a flowing hand. Shaftesbury postmark. She stood in the airless vestibule to read it:

> Dear Lily Garnett,
> VIGILANCE IS CALLED FOR.
> I have chosen to offer you my protection, to set straight what is now awry. While a foreign enemy stalks among us, our quarrels must be set aside. Only the WATCHFUL and the RIGHTEOUS will survive the storm.
> My sword is swift, my eye keen.
> I am at your service.
> Peregrine Weed

Lily stood with the pack heavy on her shoulders, thinking: she should show this to Adam Townsend. Then thinking: no, leave poor, crazed Weed alone. Clarence and Forrest were still fishing that afternoon when Lily parked at Lakeside Farm, shouldered her pack, cinched the belt, and started down the Old High Road. The day had grown hot, the air was still, the sky an unblinking blue, though at the horizon an encroaching haze hinted at thunderstorms by day's end. Lily moved fast to keep the mosquitoes off. She had the impulse to run, as she often had as a girl, but now it was not just the weight of the pack that made her feel heavy and slow, clunking down a hill whose rain-washed ruts made her worry about turning an ankle. She felt the flesh jiggle at the back of her thighs, and thought of how embarrassed she had been as a teenager at the beach, seeing her mother's own curdled flesh there, her calves like bags of pudding. All the old ladies in their rubber caps, tottering into the water, their nubbled backsides bruised and hanging. She had thought then that having children did that to you.

At the bottom of the hill the road picked up the stream, and in among the hemlocks the air was damp and heavily scented with a smell Lily had found nowhere else in the world: an earthy sweetness that seemed compounded of time and loss, of the artery's pulse measured against the slow life of trees and the stillness of windswept granite knobs along Rattlesnake Ridge.

She found the path down to the fishing camp, and soon came to the place where her father had sawn up the fallen maple. Her pulse quickened at the sight of the confetti-strewn ground, the tangle of branches heaped in the woods, cut ends still bright as coins. There was life in the old man yet. Down by the cabin she saw where he had tumbled the logs in a pile. Socks, shorts, and a shirt hung on the clothesline. Needed bleach, she thought. But she refused to pity her father.

Lily called out as she rounded the corner to the front of the cabin, then mounted the steps to the creaking porch and knocked at the plank door whose wood had weathered to caramel and burnt sugar, raised ridges of the grain flowing around the knots like a windstream. The door latch rattled when she knocked. Lily wasn't sure she wanted an answer.

In the empty cabin she found dirty plates scattered on the table, a tennis racket leaning in the corner, the odor of wet ashes, used coffee grounds, tar. And yet, settled over all this as lightly and surely as dust: peace. Lily had always thought, once she was old enough to think it, that her father must have lived in Boston so he could carry on with other women. It now seemed more likely that for all those years it wasn't other women's company he craved, but his own.

Back on the Old High Road, she thought only of getting up to the higher ground, eager to get the tent up before the rain. But as she walked, she found herself thinking of Peregrine Weed, holed up in that cabin on the other side of the ridge. Or was he here, somehow, watching? His presence seemed to her part of the sky's haze, the poplar's nervous trembling. She sensed that he belonged here, to this place, its resident ghost. Not entirely a bad feeling.

Not like that other one. Tucker. He was real enough. His UNLV sweatshirt, sunglasses on a string around his neck. A piece of Nevada made flesh. Had she dragged all this after her when she came east? She moved quickly, trying to keep a step ahead of the mosquitoes, pinching the deerflies that tangled in her hair. From the porch of the fishing camp she had seen the thunderheads piling up in the southwest.

She would avoid the Weed homestead today, taking a path to the right that angled uphill toward the ridge. She was headed to the place her family had always called simply "the clearing," a small meadow on a level shoulder of land just below the last ascent to the ridge top. Howard and Lily had camped there with their father as kids, and considered it their special place. When the land was divided, the clearing had been included in Lily's portion, and she liked to think that if she were ever to build a house somewhere, it would be there. She and Kyle had hiked up there a number of times. They had made love in the sunwarmed grass and fantasized about a house there, Lily laughing as Kyle stalked through the meadow, pacing off the foundation.

Kyle, as strong as a house. She had told him once that he

290

worked wonders with his tongue; he had blushed for a week. She thought of his thighs between hers, wanting him, and then she thought about Mongerson last night, how she had wanted him, too. So much pleasure and sadness in the world.

Following the path through her father's land, she traveled through mixed hardwoods. The ground was drier now away from the stream, the rustle in the treetops promising some relief from the bugs once she got higher up. Lily's boundary came just before the clearing, and then the path continued on westward into what was now Howard's land. The division of the property had been a queer sort of topographical exercise of her father's. Lily and her brother's parcels, a hundred acres each, lay side by side, squeezed between 1,600 acres owned by their father to the east, and eight hundred acres to the west that had been deeded to their mother as part of the divorce settlement. But Lily's and Howard's uppermost boundaries were just below the last ledges, so that the crest of the ridge itself remained in her father's name. Seen on a map, the arrangement appeared as though her father had thrown an arm over Lily and her brother, stretching along the ridge to touch with his fingertips his former wife.

The meadow looked weedier than Lily had remembered it, patches of moss and blueberry having replaced the grass, with buckthorn, willow, and birch crowding the edges. Mid-afternoon and a week past the solstice, the sun had just slid off the day's and the year's height, but Lily now felt the warmth on her crown. She stood with her eyes closed, her arms outstretched, trying to feel the light fill her brain, charge the length of her spine, press downward through her thighs, her calves, at last through her toes draining back into the earth. Then she laughed, remembering something

Kathy had said last winter about sunlight entering the brain through the skull. Poor Kath, stranded at DooHickey's. Lily hadn't even bothered to call in. She allowed herself a twinge of vengeful pleasure. Near the center of the clearing was an outcropping of ledge among whose scoops and hollows the family had each had their traditional seat: the largest and best formed had been their father's "armchair," two shallower bowls served for Howard and Lily. Lily made her way toward the spot, and even as she gasped, there was a part of her that was not surprised to see one of the places occupied. "You should be armed," Howard said.

Lily realized there was a part of her, too, that was happy to see him. "Can't get any privacy around here," she said.

"Forgive me my trespasses," Howard said.

"You wanted this place to be yours, I know," Lily said.

"I'm learning to live with disappointment."

"My poor brother."

"My girl scout sister. You running away from home?"

Lily unslung her pack and slumped it to the ground. "I guess I am home," she said. "You're in Dad's chair."

Howard shrugged and stood, brushed off khakis that didn't need brushing, sighed deeply, then settled into his own place on the rock. In rugby shirt and loafers, sockless despite the bugs, handsome and boyish face tipped toward the sun, legs tucked into a half lotus, he could have been posing for a Zen version of the Williams College alumni magazine.

"You tried to find Dad, of course. He's fishing with Uncle Clarence. Pretending they're boys."

"Have you seen him?"

"He did grant me an audience." Howard sighed. "Do you

think it's true that we choose the parents we're born to?"

"He's mad at you, is what you're saying."

"He's been mad at me since I was born," Howard said. "He thought Mom got pregnant to try and convince him to stay with her."

"It didn't work, did it."

Lily dug a box of raisins out of her pack, then took her own seat on the rock. They both faced south, passing the raisins between them, looking out over the treetops toward Abenaki Lake.

"I suppose I should be mad at you, too," Lily said. "But I don't know if I have the energy for it."

"Should I come back tomorrow?" Howard asked. "Might do me good to see my sister in a snit."

"Just keep talking," Lily said. "It won't take long."

"I'm happier now, Lil. More than in years. I'm learning to put myself in the flow of money."

"That's what I'm afraid of."

"You and Dad can't accept the fact that I might be a success at something."

"Selling off our land."

"I'm not even talking about the land. Where do you think I've been these last three months? Nobody even asks."

"You missed mud season."

"Fax Man has been a big hit, over ten thousand subscribers. I've been handling the distribution. Working with our people in Denver."

"You've been waiting a lifetime to use phrases like 'our people in Denver.'"

"It brings a certain satisfaction."

"Our friend Mongerson has been good to you."

"You may find Lawrence hard to understand," Howard said.

Lily wondered what Howard knew—about Bud Grisham, about last night. "He has a certain force," she said, looking away, hoping her cheeks wouldn't flush.

"He's operating on the higher planes."

She realized then that if she trusted her instincts, the very fact of her embarrassment was a strike against Mongerson. And if she had made a mistake in letting him get close to her, then her brother was making one, too. She was not sure she cared for her own sake, but her brother was a different matter. "One of those planes includes some criminal types, according to Adam Townsend," Lily said.

There was a slight hitch before Howard spoke.

"The fantasies of a provincial mind," Howard said coolly. "Lawrence is large. He includes people. That doesn't mean he's done anything unsanitary."

"What I can't get over," Lily said, "is what a grown-up jerk you've become."

"Awareness is the first step toward acceptance," Howard said.

"And how naive."

"Is there something you want to tell me?"

Lily looked into her brother's face, seeing there an openness he had had as a boy. She had been wrong, before, in seeing Mongerson as the innocent. The true innocent was before her.

"I met one of 'your people' this morning. Tucker. A real beauty."

"Tucker?"

Lily described him, but it was clear that Howard didn't know the man. She wondered just how much "unseemliness" Mongerson had protected him from.

On some level it was always there: the memory of one thing she had never told her brother. That one summer when he was seven years old, while his back was turned, she had passed her hands through his body as though through a swarm of bees. It had been an intimate moment, too intimate, really, to be spoken about. She realized now that the experience had always given her a sense of responsibility for him, as if for that one moment, and somehow ever since, she had held his life in her hands. The old memory was present to her now: her tingling hands cowled in what looked like blue flame. She was responsible for his life.

"Be careful, Howard," Lily said.

Howard met her gaze, and now beside the innocence she saw something else, too: the lines at the corners of his eyes, the pouch of flesh beneath his chin. They were getting old.

"You be careful, too, Sis," her brother said.

Lily looked out over the treetops to where she could see just a sliver of the lake. She would have to clear downslope a ways to get a full view. "I'm going to build a house here," she said. The words came through her as if spoken by someone else, and once she heard them, she knew they were true. Somehow a decision had been made.

She faced her wondering brother.

"That's terrific, Lil. I'm happy for you." And then, laughing: "Don't let Peregrine Weed find out."

"Do you think he's out here? I got a letter from him." She dug it out of her pack and showed it to Howard.

"I think he's mostly harmless," Howard said when he handed

it back.

"Then who killed Bud Grisham?"

Lily watched her brother carefully, relieved to see that he didn't flinch. Maybe he really didn't know.

"Plenty could have," he said. "He's screwed enough people. The negative energies accumulate."

"I suppose we really shouldn't be out here," Lily said.

Howard smiled, stretched out his legs, lounged back on one elbow, a Garnett at home. "Where else would we go?"

Lily sighed. "I just want out of all this. This business with the land."

"Then get out," Howard said.

Lily could hardly bear her brother's words. She thought of all Mongerson had said about offering her an escape: fantastic, impossible words, the mutterings of some dark dream. "Do you ever plan to actually live anywhere, Howard?"

"The whole concept of permanent residence," Howard said, looking nervously away. "We make a fetish of physical location."

"It's all some of us have."

"And here you are with your tent and your freeze-dried pasta primavera."

Lily gave a short, grim laugh. "I suppose it looks silly."

It occurred to her that coming up here had been a bad idea. The sky was darkening. There was already rain on the far reaches of the lake, a gray blur beneath the clouds. But Howard was right: where else would she go? She couldn't go to Kyle's, not after last night. Or could she? The thought was painful.

"Why are you up here, today?" she asked.

"Poking around. Call it nostalgia."

"You're really going to do this thing, this Garnett Farms."

"It's on rails."

Lily supposed he wasn't *trying* to be cruel. "You really do seem happy," she said softly.

"Alarming, isn't it? I'm learning to grasp the impermanence of all things."

"Isn't it possible to learn that lesson without bulldozers?"

"You and Dad. We can't go on denying the simple fact that we've changed. The world has changed. Our relationship to the land has changed."

"Changed into what?" Lily felt herself growing small and petulant, her belly tightening, the breath choked off. She was not prepared, she realized, for her brother's confidence. Nor for the look he gave her then: soft, alert, *seeing* her as no one had for months.

"Why such a sad sister?"

Lily hopped down from the rock and tugged the tent from her pack. "I'm in no mood to tell you," she said.

"You want a hand with that tent?"

She let him help, though she could have done it faster herself, in total darkness if she had to. They slipped the segmented aluminum poles through the sleeves, staked the corners, fastened and staked the fly. Lily unzipped the door and shoved her pack inside. Then she stood back, admiring her little green home.

"Kyle going to join you later?"

Lily felt as though she'd been punched.

"What's the matter?" Howard asked.

"Don't you know he's been chasing after Kathy?"

Lily knew this wasn't exactly true. But the truth was harder to

297

admit: she had sent Kyle away.

"I saw Kathy yesterday," Howard said. "Asked her out, you want to know. Said she was seeing some guy now, a ski instructor."

"She was just saying that."

"He showed up while I was there. Thighs like tree trunks."

"You sure he was her boyfriend?"

"He had a proprietary air. Placed hands on her in my presence. They talked about skiing in Chile."

"Where does this leave me?" Lily wondered out loud.

The thrashing of trees announced the approach of rain.

"In a tent," Howard said. "Unless you want to get wet."

The first big drops fell, splotching the tent fly. Crouching, Lily backed into the tent and held the door open for Howard.

"You don't want me in there," he said. "I've got to get going anyway."

"You'll be soaked," Lily said.

"Out in the elements," Howard said, backing away, spreading his arms. "Positively cathartic."

"Howard." Lily had to shout now through downpour.

Suddenly he was there, crouching at the door.

"Oh, Lily," he said. "I spoke to Mom this morning. Glad you've been in touch. Gave her quite a boost."

He was as quickly gone again, walking across the meadow, so that Lily had to shout to make him turn.

"We need to talk. All of us. You, Dad, me, and Mongerson."

Grinning, Howard made the okay sign.

"I'll set it up," he yelled, and was gone through rain.

Lily lay back and listened to the rain pummel the tent, the air driving through the open door in wet gusts. If she had wanted him, Kyle would have been here, now, in this tent, listening to the rain, holding her, saying only words she wanted to hear.

She wished it could be that simple.

Lily waited out the storm, then crawled out to make dinner. She would want to eat and be back in her tent before dusk, when the mosquitoes would become intolerable. The clouds had blown over, leaving the ground damp, the grass matted, the leaves spangled wetly in the sun, the air rinsed clean and clear so that the swifts wheeling up above the ridge seemed sharply drawn against the blue. Lily had brought one water bottle, and she emptied it into a pot for rice. When she got her little stove humming, its flame pale in the bright light, she took the empty bottle and followed a track that led from the edge of the clearing to the spring. She descended into a shaded gully, into a patch of the boreal forest that grew at the higher elevations, all spruce and moss and fern. At the bottom of the gully, water trickled from beneath a mossy boulder the size of a one-car garage, forming a sandy-bottomed pool just a few feet across. Carefully straddling the pool so as not to disturb the silt, she dipped her bottle in, not noticing until it was almost full the row of sticks, less than a foot tall, that someone had apparently stuck into the sand along one edge of the pool, like a miniature palisade.

Lily capped the bottle and then crouched for a closer look at the sticks. She resisted the urge to look over her shoulder and see if anyone was watching. She would have heard—well, she would have *known*. The sticks had not been sharpened, simply broken off and driven into the sand, in what could have been a minute's idle work. She wanted to believe Howard had done it. He knew about

299

the spring, and might have visited it during his nostalgic ramble. Hunters knew about the spring, too, but they wouldn't have been here for many months. Clarence and her father also knew, but she couldn't imagine them doing such a thing.

That Peregrine Weed could actually be on the property was not something Lily wanted to think too much about. It had been one thing to consider it merely as a possibility, as she had done before, but this was different. She didn't want to think of him as a man with his own smell and set to his shoulders, his own way of holding his hands when he spoke, his own queer notions of duty and love. The man she had glimpsed during the past year, striding along the roadside with the fixed gaze of the monomaniac, little resembled the earnest teenager she remembered paddling a canoe. Lily moved swiftly up the path to the clearing, the low sun slanting golden through the forest. She tried not to wonder what the night would bring.

At first it brought very little. She cooked, ate, used the second bottle of water to wash up and make tea, then retreated to her tent for relief from the bugs. After the afternoon showers the air was drier and cooler, but the night would be still and pleasantly warm. Lily wore a long-sleeved shirt and lay in her bag, listening to the patter of insects against her tent.

Then she heard a sound that could have been a footstep. After the second, then the third, there was no doubt. She hoped for a bear. A bear she could handle. Bang pots and yell while it snuffled at her food and then ran off.

She shifted to peer out of the tent and held her breath. What she saw was the silhouette of a familiar-looking figure entering the clearing, a tall man carrying a rifle. She took three deep breaths into her belly before she spoke. "Dad." "Lily."

"How did you find me?"

"Howard left a note at the cabin. I — ." She could see her father's awkwardness. "I came right up."

"It's a little late for visiting."

"You shouldn't be out here."

"I guess I know that," Lily said.

"Anybody could be out here now."

"Including old men with rifles."

Her father shuffled his feet in the grass. "I'm not that old," he said quietly.

"Dad." Lily crawled out of her tent and stood. She embraced him quickly but then stood back, remembering her anger. "You've been here a week," she said.

Her father hadn't shaved. He wore a flannel shirt buttoned to the neck against the bugs, and a floppy wide-brimmed felt hat he'd sprinkled with Woodsman's Fly Dope, with its pungent smell of tar and citronella. She had written, asking him to come, but he had seemed more powerful in the abstract. Now he stood before her, grizzled and unwashed, in the ineffectual flesh, an ordinary man on a fishing trip.

"I imagine you disapprove of my behavior," her father said.

"Not my place to disapprove, is it?"

"The dutiful daughter."

"Dilatory Dad."

They both laughed, but neither moved, her father merely shifting nervously from one foot to the other. The moon had just begun to tickle the treetops. Its light, together with the residual glow of day was just strong enough to allow her to see her father's

301

sad smile.

He shifted his stance again, cradling the rifle in both arms. "There was a time I thought I was going to *do* something in this life," he said. "As though I was chosen for something special."

"When did that end?" Lily asked.

"Into my early twenties, I think." Her father spoke crisply now, as though repeating the facts of a story he'd gone over many times. "Not long after your mother and I married."

"Could she have been so terrible?"

"Terrible?" He seemed amused by the thought. "Hardly. Hardly that. Individually, I suppose she and I were representative of the species: no more cruel, no less decent. It was only together that we were terrible."

"What happened?"

He looked at her suddenly, snapping out of his reverie. He laughed then, returned to his aloof self, her distant dad, that planet circling on the far side of the sun. He walked off a few steps, stood looking into the trees. "I imagine you're going to stay out here, ignoring your father's advice."

"I imagine so."

They listened to night sounds: the drip of rain from the leaves still wet from the afternoon storm, small stirrings on the forest floor, and from downhill in the swamp the creak of frogs finding their summer voices. The moon now lit the far edge of the meadow, though Lily and her father were still in shadow.

"You've spoken to Howard," her father said. "You know what he and this Mongerson fellow are planning."

Lily was relieved that her father didn't seem to know she had met Mongerson.

"I imagine you like it even less than I do," he said.

"You can't know what I feel about it," Lily said.

"Can't I?"

Lily felt her churlishness rising, thick in her throat. "Whatever you think you know about me, you've made up."

"I *did* make you up. That's what fathers do."

"I'm making my own self up, now."

"Fine. Then by tomorrow you better make up what you want to do about this land. Howard's note said that he was going to set up a meeting. With us and this Mongerson. Right here."

"Will it make any difference? I heard you were going to develop the land yourself, anyway."

"Who told you that?"

"Adam Townsend, who heard it from Bud."

Her father sighed through clenched teeth. "It's bad form to speak ill of the dead," he said. "Yet one is sorely tempted."

"It's not true?"

"No. I think Bud was dreaming about something he knew was never going to happen."

"Is it never going to happen, Dad?"

"We'll find out tomorrow. Will you be here?"

"I'm not going anywhere."

"Okay, then."

Her father began to walk off.

"I'm going to build a house here," Lily shouted out suddenly. She wasn't sure why she had to tell him this. But she had said it twice now, so it must be true. Her father turned, looking her way for several moments, standing in the moonlit sliver of meadow with his face in the shadow of his hat brim, his shoulders silvered

303

and his pale hands holding the rifle at his waist, the barrel a dull gleam.

"That's fine," he said evenly. She could not see his mouth. "That's fine."

He moved off into the woods, with his deerstalker's glide, not so much walking as merging into the trees. "Be careful out here," he called back. And then he was gone.

Lily dove back into her tent, zipped the bug netting quickly closed, burrowed into her bag, hoping for sleep. She lay on her back; the tent walls glowed faintly from the moon. A mosquito had slipped into the tent with her. She listened to its whine, knowing from long experience that she would not sleep until she had killed it. In a way it was a relief, having this small thing to do. She felt it brush her ears and nose, and then it stopped, resting silhouetted on the wall of the tent. Lily knew she would get her chance; it was a discipline she had learned in childhood. The whine started again, and soon she felt the insect land on her forehead. She waited while it sank its needle-like proboscis into her skin, and then, with the insect anchored in her flesh, she killed it with a clap. She wished sleep could be accomplished so easily.

She rolled on her side, snugged the bag up around her shoulders, and was met suddenly with an image of her father as a younger man. Her father's face, lively and laughing. He was showing her something. A magazine, one of his scientific journals. He was still on the rise then, still making his mark. It was all about antennas, things she barely understood, satellites in space bouncing signals from here to someplace else. There was a war in Vietnam, and somehow his prosperity was connected with that. He read to her out loud, knowing she couldn't understand, though she remembered some of the words, and for years would repeat them to herself like a ritual chant: sidelobes, beam width, gain. Her father had published an article proving something, there had been letters in reply, more letters, a controversy, it went on for months. The articles he showed her were full of equations with Greek letters and funny squiggles. She recalled his excitement, and most of all how he pulled her close to him—she must have been in her early teens, he was sitting in the big wicker chair on the porch of the Thompson farmhouse—pointing to his own name in a column of print, saying, "There I am." Laughing, "Look here, it says: 'Garnett argues—.' It says, 'Garnett's derivation neglects the edge-effects at distances less than dee squared over lambda.' That's your old man he's talking about," he said, laughing some more. "Me, this fellow named 'Garnett.'" She had been proud of him, she supposed, happy that he mattered in some realm beyond her senses and that he seemed pleased by this. Prouder still to be held by him, to feel his hand tightening on her waist, the heat of his breath on her face, to be the prize he clutched in victory.

When she woke several hours later, she had slipped down into her sleeping bag, her own breath heavy and close, her heart pounding. She tugged the bag down and sat upright, gulping cool air. As her pulse slowed, she found herself gradually aware that she was not alone. And yet it seemed something she had known all along, accepting this watchful presence in her sleep as a matter of course. She leaned forward close to the door of the tent, her view of the meadow made fuzzy by netting. The moon was now nearly overhead, setting everything aglow. He had taken his place on the rock. He sat upright, still as stone, shoulders stooped only slightly with age. His hat brim shadowed his face, and his rifle was propped against his knees, barrel toward the sky.

Lily lay back to feel sleep take her like a warm wave. When she woke to birdsong and sunlight, her father had gone.

Kyle reached in past the shower curtain and yanked the lever to cold. He grabbed the thin man by the neck and pulled him from the shower, gasping, then pressed him up against the tile wall of Lily's bathroom The man, he was shocked to discover, was bald.

"Who the fuck are you?" Kyle said.

"K-Kyle," Bernie managed to choke out.

"You're that guy Bernie, aren't you? Christ." Kyle released his hold.

Bernie stood breathing, looking grateful, , naked and dripping in the cold air that was coming through the open door. .

When he had seen the man's clothes on the bed and the shower going, Kyle expected to find Mongerson. Wring the fucker's neck. But now this. Bald Bernie. Kyle looked through the bathroom door at the rumpled sheets on the bed. He kicked the door shut to blot out the sight, rage filling him with a sort of reckless joy. They were together in the tight, damp space of the bathroom.

"You live here now?" Kyle asked.

"I just spent the night," Bernie said, reaching for a towel.

"You want me to feel happy for you?"

"Wait—."

But Kyle didn't wait. He'd been wondering how hard it would be to punch his fist through the hollow-core bathroom door.

It wasn't hard. He threw the punch and suddenly felt a little silly, standing there with his hand sticking through the door, flexing his fingers in the cooler, drier air of the bedroom.

"Does anyone need my help?" someone called from outside the bathroom.

Kyle extracted his hand, scraping his wrist on the splintered veneer. He opened the door to find Mongerson in a white linen suit, holding a bouquet of flowers.

Bernie wrapped the towel quickly around himself.

"Perhaps I should come back later," Mongerson said.

What Kyle intended was simply to get past Mongerson and out of there before he did something truly gruesome. But in the cramped bedroom, Mongerson must have misunderstood, for he reached under the linen jacket.

It was more than Kyle could stand. "I've had enough!" With an open paw he swiped the flowers from Mongerson's left hand and then yanked the right up into the air, the pistol pointing toward the ceiling. It seemed important to get Mongerson away from Lily's bed, so Kyle dragged Mongerson out to the living room, where he pinned him to the floor with a knee in his back, arms twisted up behind him, and extracted the gun from his right fist. Kyle held Mongerson's wrists in one hand, the gun in the other.

"Easy on the suit," Mongerson said.

"Is this loaded?" Kyle asked.

"I suppose if I said no, we might have an accident."

"You didn't leave town by sundown," Kyle said.

"In fact, I'm on my way. Leaving the entire state for a while. I stopped to say goodbye."

"Where's Lily?" Kyle asked.

Mongerson did his best to smile with one cheek pressed to the floor. "Am I supposed to guess?" he said.

"Down in Shaftesbury for a couple of days," Bernie said.

"Here—." He crossed the room quickly, ripped a fax out of the machine. "Must have come in while I was in the shower." He held it up for Kyle to read, trying to keep from shaking, hoping that if he humored these people, they might go away.

> Dearest Lil—
>
> Not sure where you are, but the meeting is on for noon today. We'll meet at the Clearing, which I thought appropriately dramatic and Kipling-esque, the wolves gathering at the Council Rock, or some such. Mongerson will be there, Dad and Uncle Clarence, too.
>
> Cheers,
>
> Howard

"Thought you were leaving the state," Kyle said.

Mongerson's face flushed, and Kyle pressed his knee a little harder into the man's back, wrenching the arms up until Mongerson gasped.

"I could learn to enjoy this," Kyle said. Then he eased up, letting Mongerson breathe.

"I've changed my plans," Mongerson said. "I'm not needed there anymore."

Kyle jacked up the arm again until Mongerson winced. He could play this man like a trombone.

"I have reason to believe," Mongerson panted, "that Rattlesnake Ridge will be a hazardous environment for the next several hours."

"Is Lily in danger?"

"No." Mongerson groaned. "I don't think so. I think it's just me they want."

"You *think?* You aren't sure?" Kyle asked.

"I can't be sure of anything now."

"So you were just going to skip out," Kyle said.

"Howard is fully empowered to represent me," Mongerson said.

"Or take a bullet for you? Who is it?" Kyle pulled Mongerson to his feet now, moving him on tiptoes toward the kitchen. "Who else is going to that meeting?"

"It would be in your best interests not to know," Mongerson said.

Kyle grabbed Mongerson's right arm and pulled it into a hammerlock. Then he yanked hard, and Mongerson moaned. Kyle reached out with his other hand and set the gun down on the counter, and opened a drawer where he found the roll of duct tape he kept there. He was tired of hearing Mongerson.

"I feel as though I should call the police," Bernie said. He stood with towel tucked around his waist, hands folded before him, hovering like a hostess. "Which one of you should I recommend they arrest?"

Kyle had Mongerson bent over and his mouth out of commission. He was working on the hands when the apartment door swung open.

"Heard the ruckus, tell myself either I get up here now or I end up with a mess later."

Luke leaned around the door, took in the scene, and then stepped fully into the room. He stood relaxed, smoking his cigarette. "Guys know how to party," he said.

310

"Christ, Luke," Kyle said, "how many keys to this place you give away?"

"Admit the guy you're gift-wrapping there I let in myself, thought nobody home, no harm. He wants to drop me a twenty and go in there sniff her panties, that's none of my business. Not like he's going to rip her off, guy in that suit, with the flowers. Anybody'll tell you I'm a sucker for romance, doesn't make me some kind of pimp I pull in a coupla sawbucks from a fella now and then. Bad news is, if Mr. Witchdoctor here got a key it's one Missy gave out herself."

Kyle finished and jerked Mongerson up straight. "How does he look?" Kyle asked.

"You'll want to do his legs, too," Luke said.

Howard was edgy on the phone. "Never thought I'd find myself asking for a police presence," he said.

"It's a sign of middle age," Adam said.

After hanging up with Howard, Adam called Campo and agreed to meet him at Lakeside Farm. It was their one chance to get all the Garnetts together in one place, and Mongerson, too. Walking in along the Old High Road, Adam couldn't help but feel a twinge of pleasure at seeing Campo look nervous. Been up here all these years and still mostly a city boy. A good enough cop out on the highway, Adam figured. In here he's thinking he should have brought mosquito repellent. He's worrying about the shine on his state trooper boots.

They had seen Howard and Lily's cars out at the farm. Clarence's truck, too. They would all be in there ahead of them, Adam figured. And who else? No sign of his Mr. Gray. Maybe Gray was coming by boat or helicopter, like some goddamn James Bond. Jet pack. Of course it was all something Adam had made up, a kind of entertainment. Fantasy of the small town cop. Adam had started to tell Campo about Nevada, about his theories of the case, but Campo told him to be quiet. Keep his eyes open. That was a joke. Adam saw more in these woods in a half hour walk than Campo would in a lifetime. The walls and the cellar holes, the old roads branching to left and right, fields he had known as a kid now grown up in trees. Campo was seeing none of this.

5

What Forrest remembers is the pleasure of striking a man down.

What Kyle remembers is taking Lily in his arms.

What Lily remembers is her mother, shrouded, rising toward her through the woods.

Adam remembers thinking: this is the end of it. These woods won't survive this family.

The way Lieutenant John Campo wanted to tell it, it should have been funny. Every time he tried, though, something caught him, thickening his voice, something that made him always want to be looking over his shoulder. Let me tell you what New Hampshire's like, he'd say. And before he could get it rolling, get the laughs coming, it would be there again, creeping up. Let me tell you about a day in the woods. Guys around the table thinking this is going to be good, Johnny's got a good one, fucking Yankees up there with their deer rifles, their moose on the highways, guys in love with their wood piles. But then their smiles would hang frozen, waiting.

Let me tell you.

John Campo had spent most of his childhood in Woburn, Massachusetts, in St. Barbara's Parish, then moved north to Nashua as a teenager when his father took a job up there. He had always wanted to think of southern New Hampshire as an extension of the Boston area. Less than an hour's drive returned him to his friends in Woburn. Southern New Hampshire was sandy plains of white pine. The sons and daughters of mill workers and machinists. Scruffy, blue collar, southward- and seaward-looking. Not much different from Woburn, only more space. The whole northern half of the state, with its granite hills and queer local accent, was a mystery to him.

After two years of college he started on the local force, then studied part-time to finish the degree before joining the state police. He had served the state twelve years, the last six up at Troop N in Pinkham County. It was his first northward posting, and he had never felt comfortable there. The highway duty was all right, he brought in his ten tickets a day, kept everyone happy. It was the local work that never seemed to come off right. In the little towns people wouldn't bother to introduce themselves; they expected you to know who they were. Married women assumed you knew their maiden names. People referred to houses not by their current occupants, but by the names of people who had lived there thirty or a hundred years ago. They referred to roads by names other than the ones on maps. In the woods their landmarks were roads, fields, and buildings that no longer existed. Most of the buildings that did exist used to be something else: go up past the farm used to be Bob Lyman's, they'd say. Turn left at the little place used to be a schoolhouse, go down past the barn where Ketchum used to have his dances. Every statement seemed to have a meaning just around the corner from the obvious one. He was made to feel clumsy and unnecessary and kept out. This was why he couldn't stand Adam Townsend. The guy was a slob, but he was one of them, and the people in Shaftesbury liked him. He seemed to be what the town wanted.

Even before the Shaftesbury case he'd been thinking: enough. He had his pension coming, and if the state didn't screw him

314

somehow, he'd be doing all right. Only forty-five, he had plans. Get out while you're still in good shape, he told his friends. Enjoy yourself. He had a place picked out back down in Nashua where he wanted to open a diner, a little breakfast and lunch place. He had already made an offer. His aunt had run a diner for a while in Woburn, he had helped out there as a kid, knew the ropes. Breakfast and lunch, play golf in the afternoons. Sit by the pool.

Maybe he could tell it then, maybe then it would be far enough behind him, a few friends over, burgers on the grill, kids doing back flips off the board. Then he could make it funny. Not like the time he tried to tell it down in Georgia, where he went for Missing and Exploited Children. Or like the time he told it again at Ritualistic Crimes out in Vegas, some of the same guys around the table helping him out with the story this time. They wanted it to be funny. He would tell it after a day spent in and out of conference rooms, breaks in the hallways with danish and Styrofoam coffee, a bunch of guys at last unbuttoned around a table in the casino bar, gambling floor spreading out all around them like some kind of electronic forest, slot machines chiming, flashing lights, thinking a couple of drinks before they get dinner at one of the buffets, then maybe head for a tittie bar. But right now Johnny's got a good one. Johnny's going to tell us all about New Hamp-sheer.

Let me tell you, he would say, laughing.

Then it would creep up on him. Those woods. Months had passed, but it was just the same. And he had never even fired a round.

What he couldn't get over was the sense of people coming out of the woods. It had started out okay, even if it was an unconventional set up. They want to meet out in the woods, he figures that's their style. He was dealing with Garnetts, and he had learned to make allowances. These old families with their peculiar customs. Townsend had set it up. Tipped off by the brother. Supposed to be the daughter, her brother, her father, and this guy Mongerson he'd never been able to track down. It was Mongerson he was most interested in.

Thinking: If it hadn't been in the woods, it all would have gone differently.

Saying: I meet Townsend at the gate and we start down the old road.

A couple of the guys who've heard it before pitching in:

—He's the local.

—The chicken farmer.

Right. The local. No love lost between us, but he's the one knows the way, and I thank him to keep his mouth shut. A half mile in along this old road, mosquitoes on you like fur, then another half a mile up a footpath, almost to the ridge. Of course Townsend can't help himself, every ten minutes points into the woods and says there used to be a house there, a barn there. Damn people with their "used to be's." At last there they are, the daughter and her brother sitting on a rock in a meadow a little bigger than a basketball court, the brother with sets of plans rolled up in a tube under his arm and a smile that's got chainsaws to back it up.

Campo now looking at the men around the table, thinking: *they should be laughing now; if it weren't for all those woods, this would be funny,* saying: Keep in mind we've got a homicide just a week before all this. A Mr. Bud Grisham.

—The real estate guy.

And selectman. Townsend's boss.

—Plus the other one three months earlier.

—And the second one was your lead suspect for the first.

Was. After we cleared Weed, the lunatic.

—And now you've got a perpetrator at large, you're walking a mile into the woods with one sheep-dipper cop for backup.

You're getting the picture.

—Fucking New Hampshire.

That's what I'm trying to tell you.

—Feel like you're crashing the wrong party.

Because everyone there except me walked around in those woods like it was their living room. Townsend pointing out where fields had been thirty years ago, old skid roads I can't even see. The daughter's got a tent there, the brother lounging on the rock might as well be in bathrobe and slippers.

—And the old men.

Out of the woods. Here's where it should be funny.

The father and another guy, turns out it's his cousin, come out of the woods with deer rifles. Not like they use the path, nobody hears them coming, it's like they grew there, two old men with rifles at the edge of the clearing. Faces like concrete. They nod to Townsend, but it's like I'm not there.

—What's their word for it, when you're not from around there?

Flatlander. Twelve years of service, six in their own county, they don't care. I've had enough, I'll tell you. Get out while you're still young. *Too far in. Shouldn't have let them get me in there.*

The daughter looks uneasy about the guns, and I'm thinking at least there's one other person here not happy with the level of armament. She asks them to put the guns down, but they don't bother, and I'm looking at Townsend like watch my back, you stupid son of a bitch, bringing me out here with the Hatfields and the McCoys. The son's smiling like he's got the Hope diamond up his ass, says Mongerson will be along, but let's start, and he spreads his plans out on the rock, everybody hunches over, and I'm thinking about what we have going here, Mongerson's a no show and either I'm about to get my ass shot off or I'm just wasting my time.

—Then you hear the first shot.

No, that comes later. First, the boyfriend shows up.

—The boyfriend. The daughter's boyfriend.

These two we can hear. Coming up the path, this guy Mongerson in front, his mouth taped, hands behind his back, the boyfriend marching him along. Boyfriend's built like a truck and got a handgun tucked in his belt, I'm thinking just dandy, thinking time to hose down the lot of them. Now the boyfriend I know, he's a local builder and normally I wouldn't expect trouble from him, but now he's got this look, I'm thinking methamphetamine. Thinking: *It's the girl, the daughter, he's in love with the daughter, love can make a man look like that.* I'm cutting Mongerson loose with the boyfriend in my ear about this is the guy behind everything, Townsend trying to keep the boyfriend off but telling me maybe get the tape off but put the cuffs on. I say cuff that one there, meaning the boyfriend, which I shouldn't have, because the boyfriend's now getting hot, and I'm thinking time to lie the whole bunch of them down and get a lid on this. Then we hear the first shot.

—The lunatic.

Sounded like a handgun, so I think the pro got in the first one.

318

—Then the rifle.

The rifle once, and somebody's screaming. Up above us on the ridge. Townsend and I both draw and we're looking up into the woods. Then another. I think it's the handgun and now there are two guys screaming, then the rifle again, and the screaming stops. We're all looking into the woods, the old men with their rifles up. Next thing Mongerson's got a gun to the daughter's head, and he's walking off, talking in her ear, looks like he grabbed the gun from Cooper's belt.

—You've got a hostage situation.

Yeah, but what I can't figure is she's talking to the guy got an arm around her throat, and he's talking back, and she doesn't look too concerned about it all, like we're having our own private conversation and could you please excuse us? Both backing away, they could be practicing some dance step.

Then the old man's charging.

—The father.

—Guy's got a gun to his daughter's head.

He's charging Mongerson like if he had a bayonet he's going to run the guy through. Mongerson takes the gun off the girl's head, points it at the old man.

—He keeps charging.

Like the battle of Shiloh.

—Nobody's got a shot at Mongerson.

He's got the girl in front of him. I'm looking for an opening, yelling to Townsend to keep an eye on that situation up in the woods.

All coming out of the woods at once. This should be funnier than it is.

The old man's running at him, and looks like Mongerson's going to kill the guy, shoot him point-blank, but before he fires, he raises his arm a little. I see it: he lifts his arm, he aims high. He fires twice, sends two bullets over the man's head, but the old man keeps coming, reverses his rifle like a basic training drill, takes Mongerson down with a rifle butt to the head. They both go down, and the boyfriend grabs the girl like he's ready to carry her off to his cave, and there's the cousin, the other old man, standing over Mongerson with a rifle pointed at his heart, saying he assumes Mongerson doesn't want to die. Like that: "I assume you don't want to die." The daughter is screaming about her father, she doesn't know that Mongerson didn't aim to hit him, the brother is helping the old man sit up, and of course he's okay.

—Then the lunatic.

Townsend is yelling into the woods.

—Daniel Boone.

Guy named Peregrine Weed, thinks he's a pioneer.

—I can see why you love this place.

Standing there with a bloody leg, rifle at his hip, dressed like an Indian. Says we're all trespassing and could we come help him because he's just killed a man.

—You sure know how to have fun up there.

I get my pension, I'm done.

Because it was this family, finally, that he couldn't get over. As a cop he had learned to feel at home in other people's problems. Welcome, even, the way a sore tooth might welcome the probing tongue. After years of highway carnage, the routine villainy of drunken men with their bruised women and stolen cars, the runaway girls whose bodies end up in trash bags near the on ramps, he had learned to enter into the scene of calamity the way you'd check into a motel room belonging to a familiar chain, knowing where the extra blankets will be, where they keep the TV remote, whether they'll have shampoo in the shower. He could always tell when he was in the room and when he was out of it. He checked in, and when he had done what needed to be done there, he checked out. It was how he kept himself sane. But in the woods that day, it seemed he couldn't find the door. People coming out of the woods bearing old griefs, trouble pouring out at him like out of a dark hole, these people with secret faces and buried hearts, expecting him to know their names. He felt at home in none of it. So that when they had gotten Mongerson secured and then followed Weed to the dead man, Weed with his story about how his family had lived there since before the Revolutionary War, showing them the man lying twisted in the bloody ferns and lecturing them about property rights, he was thinking enough, this is all and this is enough, I have been too far north for too long.

—So the guy the lunatic killed was the perpetrator of the first two.

—Served up on a bed of ferns.

My lucky day. The daughter looks down at him and says Tucker, the guy's name is Tucker.

Townsend looks down at him and says his name is John Harrington.

—The guy from Nevada.

Marine haircut, one ear half gone.

This should be funnier. But all I want now is to get a lid on and get out of there. I'm on the radio for backup, and Townsend, the one good thing he's done all day, he asks Weed for his rifle. And

Weed's got a smirk like something's funny, says, "I gave it to you once, already."

"It wasn't loaded, then," Townsend says.

"I bought some bullets," Weed says.

But then he hands it over, and I get the cuffs on him, and I figure it's done. We leave the dead man there and hike Weed back to the clearing, limping on that bloody leg, and I'm thinking how to lead this parade out of here, when here come the two old women up the path.

—The mother.

—The old woman turned into a hippie.

Coming up at you out of the woods.

One turns out to be the cousin's wife, and she's got her arm around the other wrapped up in a blanket looks like a Muslim. The mother. The father's ex-wife. *Who are these people.* It's just bones moving underneath that blanket, *or not even that, the way you pop an old cocoon sometimes there's nothing but air.* Mongerson's cuffed and on his face, the cousin's got that rifle poked in Mongerson's back, the mother says "Hello, Clarence," like she's come for tea, then sees who it is on the ground and says to Mongerson, "Aren't *you* a disappointment?" The brother and his father sitting on the grass like they've taken a few too many rides on the merry-go-round, she looks down at both of them: "I hope you two can stop your foolishness." Then the daughter is in her arms, and I'm thinking who else, who else is coming?

—It's all right, Johnny. Yeah, Johnny, it's funny. It's all right. It should have been funnier.

—Everything came out all right.

Who are these people.

322

It should have been funnier than it was.

Adam remembers thinking: this is the end of Rattlesnake Ridge, for sure. They'll hand it all over to the flatlanders, now.

Peregrine Weed remembers thinking: I am the land, yet they know me not.

Kyle remembers wanting to hold Lily in his arms forever.

Forrest remembers charging, his heart on fire, running toward death, fierce with joy.

Lily remembers Mongerson's arm at her throat, his voice at her ear saying, "Lily, Lily, forgive me, just walk with me now and forgive me."

And she did walk with him, a step backward, then another, Mongerson saying, "I need to tell you everything." And Lily saying, "Tell me," and then seeing her father tear after them like a beast.

And then the shock—no other word for it—the shock of her mother rising toward her out of the woods, Lily folding her in her arms, feeling the frail bones, the failing flesh, knowing that her mother had brought the little of herself that was left.

And Kyle's arms, yes, Kyle's arms.

Her father tottering toward her now, gripping her, so that she is enveloped by his sour old man smell. For a moment she is staggered back in his embrace, her ear against his chest hearing the growling there, surprised by her own words:

"You're the bear, aren't you."

As though not spoken by the mouth but formed out of some buried part of her, out of her cartilage and bone, muscle and gut.

"You're the bear."

Her father saying, "Yes," first in a fierce whisper, and then, holding her tighter, saying, "Yes" in a voice deep in his chest that she had never heard before but imagined she had always known.

Constance, her daughter in her arms, thinking: why do we waste the better part of our lives on men?

Peregrine Weed lay on his back, his bleeding leg propped on a rock, handcuffs fastened in front. A bullet had apparently passed through his right calf muscle. Lily found a bandage in her backpack and wrapped the wound tightly.

"Thank you," Peregrine Weed said.

"Shouldn't I be thanking you?" she asked him.

His gaze came at her out of some deep, wounded place, but whatever was down there bubbled to the surface in the form of a smile.

"You could," he said. "That would be welcome."

"Then thanks, I guess." Lily offered him a box of raisins, which he accepted.

Kyle had gone for water at the spring, and passed around a plastic bottle.

Lieutenant Campo had Mongerson on his feet now, cuffed hands behind his back, Campo holding him by the arm as he talked rapidly into the radio. He had already read Mongerson and Weed their rights, and told them all to sit tight.

"I suppose you should lock us all up," Lily's father offered from his seat on the rock. "Might do everybody some good." He sat peeling an orange, which he shared with Howard and Clarence, who were sitting on the rock beside him.

"Hush," Sylvia said. "Let the man do his job."

Lily now stood away from Mongerson, staring at him intently, her hands at her sides balled into fists. "You wanted to tell me everything," she said. "Tell me."

"I'll want you to tell *me*," Campo said, ready to step between them. "And we'll do that privately, and to do that, we'll have to have some help." He glanced over the group of them there.

"Christ, there's a lot of them," he said to Adam, who stood with his gun still drawn, looking shaken.

"Officer," Constance said to Campo. "This man has something to tell my daughter." Constance sat cross-legged on the sleeping bag Lily had spread on the ground. She wore a blanket wrapped around her body and cowling her head, and her voice spoke out of that hooded space with surprising force. "Tell her, Lawrence."

Mongerson straightened his shoulders. Lily wondered at the intimacy between her mother and this man. They didn't have to look at one another to speak. Mongerson addressed himself to the two policeman:

"Gentleman. That man lying up there"— he nodded up the slope to where the man lay dead in the ferns— "is, or was, a Mr. John Harrington. A contract murderer, a thug. I will spare the present company the sorry details, but he is the one who murdered both Mr. Rogers and Mr. Grisham."

"Did you bring him here?" Lily crowded him closer now, and Campo placed a hand on her breast bone, though she didn't seem to feel it.

Mongerson returned her gaze, their faces a foot apart. "Yes, I suppose I did. He came here today with the intent of murdering me."

"Tell her, Lawrence," said her mother.

Lily was vaguely aware that Adam had his hands on her shoulders, but now she felt lifted out of herself, as though she had simply brimmed full and bubbled out, subtleized into a hovering thing, a mist above their heads, so that she looked down at them all gathered there in the clearing, the whole place now full of sunlight, and saw not bodies there so much as the forms that bodies fill, buzzing like bees.

And then Adam Townsend was pulling her away, saying, "There's something else here, something you ought to know."

Lily found herself looking into Adam's concerned face.

"That man, Harrington," Adam said. "He's the one who killed Johnny Ray Bushman, too."

Lily sought Mongerson's eyes, noticing now the bruised cheekbones, the scraped forehead, and yet beneath it all that strange inertia, like that day he first came into DooHickey's, sitting still as a mannequin while his voice jumped out at her.

"That's what I wanted to tell you," Mongerson said.

"How do you know?" Lily heard herself ask.

"I know him, Lily. I know his employers. They did business with Johnny Ray."

"But how——." Lily felt her voice growing weaker, thinner somehow, as if it, too, had become a winged thing, fluttering like a moth. "How did they find us?"

"I told them where you were."

She could only stare at him now.

"I've made mistakes, Lily. It's taken me ten years to tell you. These people, they loaned me money, got me started in real estate. Before they did that, I did them a favor. They wanted Johnny Ray, I didn't know what for. I told them where he was."

"You son of a bitch," Lily said, though her words were fainter now, softening, for even as Mongerson spoke, she felt him growing

328

smaller, his hold on her diminishing. There was no edge to his voice now, he was sober but not sullen, almost happy, as though for the first time in years.

"I wanted to tell you, but I lost my courage," Mongerson said. "I saw you that first day in the restaurant, I saw—from the first moment—that I still had feelings for you. And I froze."

She recalled again his odd stillness as she approached his table. How he had not risen from his chair. That had been the look of a man falling in love.

"I couldn't tell you," he said. "Because I knew you would hate me for it."

Chapter Six

1

It wasn't until a year later, when the trials were at last over in Nevada, that Adam had anything like the whole story. He got the call from Mansard one afternoon at the office, telling him of the convictions, and that evening he shared the news with Marilyn at supper.

"Racketeering, narcotics, conspiracy to commit murder, they got three of the big guys." Adam was buoyant. "There's more coming, and there's connections over to Los Angeles County. They'll be at this for years."

Marilyn listened with one eye on the boys, who had gone into the next room to watch TV. The boys had been scrapping all afternoon. "Sit separate, now," she called in to them. "Hands off your brother. And what about him?" she said now to Adam. "Mongerson."

"He's into witness protection. He's gone. He's history."

"That's too bad," Marilyn said. "Knock it off in there," she yelled into the other room.

"Why do you say that?" He couldn't tell, sometimes, whether she said a thing because she really meant it, or whether she wasn't paying attention and said it just to say something.

"Seemed to me like he was trying to do the right thing," she said.

"He was a sleazeball," Adam said. "He should have been a politician."

"Not all politicians are sleazy," she said. Marilyn voted, while Adam didn't bother, and this was an old disagreement between them.

But Adam wasn't going to let anything dampen his spirits that night. Later, when Marilyn had installed herself between the two boys on the sofa, Adam found himself whistling as he washed the dishes in the kitchen. He had taken a shower before dinner, and he had even shaved again. Marilyn had been more lively than usual lately. There had been a few nights when, after the boys had gone to bed, and after she had watched her shows, she had taken him by the hand and led him upstairs.

Adam scrubbed the countertop and thought with satisfaction about the whole Mongerson business. It felt good to know now about the convictions, that it had all come to something. That was all satisfying, from a law enforcement perspective. But most of what really mattered, from a local point of view, he had learned that first afternoon, sitting around the kitchen table at Lakeside Farm. They had carried Constance back there on a stretcher, despite her desire to walk. Campo had wanted her taken to the hospital and questioned there, but Adam had held him off. It was his one victory that day. That and the fact that Howard had called him about the meeting on the land. Howard had sensed something wrong about the whole business, and had finally come to his senses. Afterwards, Major Crimes had clamped a lid on everything, sealed the area, hustled everyone out of there for separate interrogations, including Forrest, Clarence, Howard, and Kyle.

Adam would never get near Mongerson, in fact would never see him again; his last glimpse was of Mongerson ducking his head into the back of a state cruiser. Campo's one concession to local jurisdiction had been to allow Constance to remain with Adam, on account of her frail condition. Campo, the bastard. Adam had whooped with joy when he heard he had retired and moved back down to Nashua.

Sylvia had made up a bed in a guest room, but Constance refused to get in it. Instead they sat drinking iced tea in the kitchen. The window sashes were thrown up, and a breeze off the lake swept over the field and through the old farmhouse, cooling them where they sat around the table. The day had warmed, the haze from earlier having burned off. It was turning into one of the first truly hot days of summer, a day when people left work early and headed to Abenaki Lake. The season's last holdouts, even some of those older men who wore long sleeves well into July, would be seen peeling down to shorts and plunging their pale bodies into the cold water.

"He was a boy who had gotten ahead of himself," Constance was saying. "He set things into motion he couldn't properly harness."

Adam had gotten out a yellow lined pad to take notes, but then set it aside. It was enough, for now, to take tea in the company of these two pleasant old women.

"Constance, you're too trusting in people sometimes," Sylvia said.

Adam held off from reminding Sylvia that she had gone around town, a few months before, describing Mongerson as "a nice young man."

"I thought he could be saved," Constance said.

"You thought he could be *used*," Adam said.

Constance fixed her gaze on him. Her soft brown eyes were wide; they seemed too large for her head. The flesh was taut on her face, though loose beneath, hanging in wattles from her throat and neck.

"You're right, aren't you, Adam."

Her familiarity pleased him. She spoke to him as to someone who had known Lily and Howard as children. Adam was tired, right now, of being a cop.

"I did think I could use him," she said. "I thought I could use him to do some good. I suppose even that was wrong of me."

Constance said she had learned, years before, about Mongerson's knowledge of the Bushman murder. At the time she felt it better to leave the business alone. But she continued to worry that Lily had never gotten over the trauma. When she became ill and felt time running out, she decided to act. Mongerson had become almost like a son to her. Constance persuaded him, for his own sake and for Lily's, to seek Lily out and explain to her what had happened. She had also encouraged his dealings with Howard, believing, perhaps foolishly, that everything could be set right.

"He had good intentions," Constance explained. "He knew he had to clear his karma. But I confess I wasn't aware of how much he cared for Lily."

"That was what ruined him," Adam said.

"No," Constance said evenly. "What ruined him was fear."

Adam considered her words now, a year later, staring into the open refrigerator. Were men more fearful than women? Is that where this craving came from? Adam got down on his knees and began hauling the contents of the refrigerator out onto the kitchen floor. When they had bought it a month ago, Marilyn had made a special note of the glass shelves, of the fact that they could be cleaned, and Adam hadn't appreciated this until now.

The rest he had pieced together from Mansard, and from what he heard from Major Crimes, and from Howard. They confirmed that John Harrington had killed both Orville Rogers and Bud Grisham. Harrington had caught wind of Mongerson's plans for some deal in New Hampshire, and when he heard it involved the Garnetts, he got nervous. Mongerson, after all, knew that it was Harrington who had killed Johnny Ray Bushman, to avenge a drug rip-off. For his own reasons, then, Harrington didn't like the idea of Mongerson having any dealings with Bushman's former girlfriend. At the same time, Harrington's employers, who were now also Mongerson's business partners, badly needed the Garnett land deal to go through. Real estate ventures had been failing all over, taking a lot of savings and loans with them, They had committed a lot of cash to this project, brutally eliminating anyone who got in the way. Harrington had -convinced his employers, exaggerating to suit his own purposes, that Orville Rogers and Bud Grisham were obstacles to the deal. By taking them out, he also hoped to scare Mongerson into keeping his mouth shut about Bushman. He shot Orville Rogers where he did, and left the body there, knowing Mongerson would get the message. But all he succeeded in doing was to scare Mongerson away for a few months. When it seemed that the deal wasn't going to work out anyway and Mongerson was getting too cozy with Lily Garnett, Harrington went after Mongerson directly. But not before checking out Lily Garnett to see what she knew. Lily could not have known, that morning when Harrington showed up at her door, using the name Tucker, what kind of danger she was in. Harrington had seen, apparently, that she still didn't know about Bushman, and had left her alone.

After scrubbing the first shelf clean by reaching in there with a sponge, Adam discovered that the shelves were removable. He had thought that was only so that you could adjust the height, but then he realized that, hey, you could take these guys right out of here and work them over in the sink.

One of the ironies of the whole affair was that the land deal had ended up going through after all. Forrest and Howard went into business together. Constance turned over her shares in the Mongerson Corporation's holdings to Howard and Lily, and then Howard and Forrest were able to get financing from a local bank to buy out the rest. Even Clarence had joined the venture. They had gotten purchase commitments for three lots already, enough to keep the bank happy. In the end it had worked out much the way Bud Grisham had proposed, only it turned out that Grisham's money wasn't needed. The development would be more modest: ten lots of twenty acres each, just enough to pay off the debt. Most of the land would be preserved, locked in by conservation easements that allowed selective timbering and public access. Lily had scraped up enough savings to start building a house, using her shares in the project as collateral for a loan. Howard had pulled in a trailer which he used as a business office, and in which he slept on a cot. It was only temporary, he said. He had no plans beyond that. Forrest had settled into that fishing camp, surrounded by a hundred acres he had kept for himself. He and Clarence had put in a woodstove and spent last fall insulating the place. They would get electricity in there this year. Forrest was even talking about indoor plumbing.

Adam felt the warm water running over his hands and decided that it couldn't all be about fear. That was just too depressing a way of looking at things. From where he stood at the sink, he could see through the doorway to where his wife sat on the sofa. The boys had gone up, so she sat alone on the middle cushion, her face flickering in the changing TV light. She had slipped on her housedress and removed her bra. Adam sniffed under his arms. He had carefully trimmed his nails, even gone over them with the file. As soon as this was done, he would go in there. He would sit beside her and feel himself tipped into the crater she made in the sofa, feel himself drawn toward her warm weight. He would take her hand. And later, if it came to that, upstairs with the lights out, he would settle between her thighs like settling into a canoe: gently rocking, then steadying, finding his seat. He wouldn't hurry, he wouldn't move at all at first, but only lie there, holding her and floating, feeling himself floating in the dark over what he loved.

What had Constance really wanted, all these years, but some vision of her own? She had always loved magic. From her earliest youth she had gone pop-eyed over anything that bloomed from under silk handkerchiefs. She had always wanted to believe that the transformations offered with such flourish—pigeon to vase of flowers, elephant to acrobat—had actually occurred on a plane beyond sense. She had suffered a keen disappointment on learning about the mirrors, false bottoms, and cleverly stitched pockets into which disappeared not only sequined ladies, quivering bunnies, and colored balls, but also the better part of her hopes for an extraordinary life.

She had married a man who told her, while they were courting, that he had once heard a voice from the sky. She had a daughter who could see auras. Constance had eventually followed that daughter to Nevada to study the teachings of a man who had spent days at a time in the company of the "elder brothers," beings whom Constance imagined as white-robed and hovering at shoulder height, burning like thousand-watt bulbs.

But when she got there, and especially after Lily lost the baby and left, Constance found only what she had known all along during her disappointing marriage, after she had returned to her mother's house and to the daily discipline of work and prayer. In Nevada, as in Shaftesbury, she cooked and canned and milked and butchered and got in the firewood, finding nothing more extraordinary than the maul's swinging weight, her own hardened muscles, the log upended on the stump, the dark circle of heartwood at which she aimed her blade.

And after she took ill, there was only prayer.

She prayed for another day and for rest at the end of it. She gave thanks for her pain, which burned in her bones like a forest fire gone underground, ravaging the roots. When spitting on her dress to rub out a stain, she gave thanks for both the spittle and the stain. She prayed for breath, and for an end to breathing.

In the end this came to be enough. Constance never had her vision, but in the end that didn't matter. It mattered more to have her daughter back. She wrote to Lily after the Mongerson business, after she had returned from her trip to Shaftesbury:

> Dear Lily,
>
> I've lost my taste for berries, so what remains to me now are the colors: June's pale pink of the strawberry not yet ripe, July's raspberry red, August blueberry's dusty blue. Shaftesbury's summer spectrum.
>
> You were right, before, to accuse me of selfishness. And so this is the last release: to say good-bye to our precious *selves*. God loves us, but it isn't because we are good. God doesn't need *reasons*. We face God, finally, not with a mask of our making but with the face He has given us. And that is a face terrifyingly without qualities, at least not mortal ones.
>
> When you come, take any of the books and clothes you care for. There's a green vest that might pick up the color of your eyes. Give the

rest away. Please spread my ashes among the bristlecones.

Love,

Your mother

Forrest Garnett peered into the open top of the toilet tank, jiggled the flush lever, observed the ball cock, listened for the leaky flapper valve to seat itself properly, thinking: "I am not yet done with this life." He had salvaged the toilet from the dump and installed it himself, saving a couple hundred dollars after he had already spent several thousand on a new septic system. The town had forced all this on him when he subdivided the land. Orville Rogers may have gone, but his beloved planning board still laid down the law. Forrest looked out the small window—also taken from the dump—in the new bathroom he had had Kyle Cooper build onto the back of the cabin. He could see up the hill to where the mounded leaching field stood in a clearing like a small Mayan temple. Something fitting in all this, Forrest thought. You know where your shit's buried.

He supposed he would have to stop calling it a cabin. With insulation, plumbing, and electricity, it had become a house. His house. Oddly enough, the first house he had ever owned. He felt a certain giddiness about it all. It was midsummer, a year since the killings, and Forrest had made a clean break. Left St. Louis, left his consulting work. Semi-retired. When he filed his income taxes that year, he would list "real estate developer" as his profession, relishing the irony. He had even allowed Howard to install a fax machine.

"Gone over to the other side," Clarence had kidded him recently. "Son's supposed to become like the father, not the other way around." "Not sure there are sides to this thing anymore,"

Forrest had said.

"You even talk like a developer," Clarence said.

"If I ever start sounding like Howard, shoot me."

The two men had laughed. In the course of a year Forrest had come to regard his son sometimes as a grinning incarnation of the devil, sometimes as a reflection of his own worst self, but mostly as a more or less ordinary young man, likable and annoying in the usual proportions. They were able, at least, to do business together. Father and son had spent weeks tromping through the woods scouting out new lot lines, leaving orange flags of surveyor's tape hanging from branches behind them. Leaving Howard to handle the paperwork, Forrest himself spent a great deal of time standing with arms crossed beside pickup trucks, worrying the ground with the toe of a boot or staring off into the woods in the company of other men who did likewise. They talked road gravel and culverts, ditching and grading, they talked clearing and chipping and pulp and timber, they talked power lines and pole placement, they talked septic system locations, they talked boat ramps and parking. Forrest knew some of these men, including some who were his cousins. He let Howard talk to lawyers about deeds and covenants and rights of way and easements. Forrest preferred the company of men with trucks full of tools, men versed in hydraulics and all things geared and bladed, men who spoke sawtooth and flail, bucket and scoop, men who owned the things that mashed and tore and tumbled the good earth, who changed the course of rivers, who made swamps disappear, who turned forests into lawns.

He had fallen into the work easily, almost greedily. Forrest worked ten-hour days, slept like a stump, ate in quantity and with pleasure, and had bowel movements that left him feeling like an

Olympic athlete. He woke some mornings surprised to be holding a hard-on. "Not done with this life," he told himself.

He had kept an eye out all year for bear, expecting always the black tumbling shape in the corner of his eye. He had seen plenty of scat, and tracks by the stream, and once a black rump scampering away through the brush. But on the morning he received Lily's fax he had not yet met up with one face to face.

> Dad:
>
> When I got out here Mom was almost gone, but I was able to be with her at the end. That seemed to make a difference. I'd like to tell you that there was no pain, but that wouldn't be true. Still, she seemed peaceful, and was able to die in her own bed. There's nothing here but some books and things. She gave all her money away. The only thing she kept was the land, and now she's given that away, too. She wanted her ashes spread up in the mountains near some old trees, so I'll do it. She asked me to send you her regards.
>
> Love,
>
> Lily

Forrest took the sheet of paper onto the porch and lowered himself into his rocking chair. He had not had any communication with Constance since she visited Shaftesbury the year before. Their conversation then had been brief and cordial: She had offered to

342

make certain arrangements about the land, and he had thanked her. It was only recently that he had found that he missed her. Not keenly, not even with any sense of lost opportunity, for he was beyond all that, but simply and without guilt, as one misses an old friend passing from the earth.

Up toward the ridge a dozer growled and snorted in the woods. He and Howard had sold three of the lots already, and there was interest in more. Forrest had seen one of the buyers driving in to look things over: a family up from Massachusetts, the husband in Madras shorts and baseball cap, trim wife in tennis whites, a minivan stuffed with big-toothed children. In time, if all went well, ten such families would each own a piece of Rattlesnake Ridge. Forrest was content, he supposed, to be giving them a place in which to find their own ways to what small joys this life afforded. Perhaps they would fare better than he and Constance. He wished them well.

When the bear came, it shambled towards the cabin up the path from the dock, unhurried, an ordinary black bear of average size, its coat sleek and shining, muscled girth filling out with summer fat. It stopped twenty feet from Forrest's rocker. Unconcerned, it nosed the air. Forrest gripped the sheet of fax paper in his hand and looked down at the animal in his yard. He'd been on the lookout for a bear, but now he hardly cared. He hardly knew what to make of things anymore.

"I'm cultivating ignorance," he had told Clarence, later.

"That's a good place to start," Clarence said.

The bear sniffed. Forrest imagined it was making a choice. To continue up the path meant getting closer to the man on the porch, and it found that distasteful. There were good smells from the

343

house behind the man but the man himself smelled bad and would make problems. I'm letting go of the meanings of things, Forrest told himself, watching the bear and speaking now to Clarence in his head. Signs and symbols. Voices from the sky. I'm letting it all go. What have I proved, after all, but a talent for the ordinary?

Forest saw his future. He would rise in the morning. Go to sleep at night. Gather wood against the winter's cold. Gather his children to his breast.

The bear turned off the path, cast one indifferent glance Forrest's way, and beat it out of sight around the cabin.

Lily drove the rented car up through pines, snaking up switchbacks, the narrow road winding to a gravel parking lot at nine thousand feet. Then on foot, knapsack slung across her back, up the dusty path three miles through scrub pine and over the last bare ridge to the lip of the cirque. The bristlecones grew at the edge of the mile-wide bowl, which had been scooped by ancient glaciers between the shoulders of Small's Peak, the tallest in the Baker Range. It was a place of wind and snow and stone. Sheer rock walls rose a thousand feet above her to the jagged crest, crevices veined with ice. Though this was July, snow slumped at the shadowed base of the cliffs. Nothing grew here but these twisted trees, appearing mostly dead, bark blasted off their gray weathered trunks except for one thin lifeline that snaked up to feed the bottlebrush needles. Grotesque, they pushed up through limestone rubble with their delicate offering of green. They were the oldest living things on earth.

Lily slung her knapsack to the ground and turned away from the trees and the cliffs to look out over the open miles of sagebrush valley to where the next range of peaks glittered. She had come here years before, sometimes alone, sometimes with Johnny Ray. She had sat beneath the trees, meditated with her back against a five-thousand-year-old trunk. She remembered that once she had found a sticky golden drop of bristlecone sap, had placed it solemnly on her tongue, wishing for long life, for wisdom. She felt no pull toward wisdom now. Perhaps that was for the better. Nearing death, Constance- had quoted Meister Eckhart, the medieval mystic, saying that to be one with God required surrendering the will, being without even the will to do the will of God. Or perhaps that was what Lily felt now, this emptying. Perhaps she was only tired and ready to get home. She hadn't understood all that her mother said at the end, but it didn't matter. She had been there, had held her mother's hand.

Perhaps Mongerson understood her mother better than any of them. Lily had heard from Adam Townsend that he was going into witness protection, that he had proved extremely useful. Lily herself had heard nothing from him since that day on Rattlesnake Ridge, and that had been just as well. As it turned out, she received his last message standing in her mother's room, the fax machine humming by Constance's bed.

> Dear Constance,
> After this transmission I will cease to be. Many would see this as a loss, as the ultimate sacrifice. But consider this great gift: to obliterate a self, wipe an identity clean from the books, and thus to face in the mirror a blank, a hollow form.
> How better to learn emptiness?

Right now, such questions wearied her. Wind tugged at her hair, cooled the sweat on her back. Lily bent, unzipped the knapsack, pulled out the water bottle, tilted her face to the sun, let the warm water pour down her throat. Then she lifted out the brass urn and unscrewed the heavy lid. She knew she had dreamed this once, long ago. The ashes were gritty. She held some in her hand, let them sift through her fingers. She put a pinch on her tongue. They tasted like nothing. She flung handfuls on the wind. Having shaken the last grains from the urn, she sensed it was time to be headed down. She wanted only to be with Kyle, now. She would catch a flight out of Salt Lake that night, back to New Hampshire. She hoped Kyle would be there to meet her plane.

She had not said yes, she had not said no.

Balanced on floor joists, the balls of his feet precisely sixteen inches apart, Kyle peered down through the empty space between them into the crawl space below. No basement: they had run into ledge right away, not much of a surprise, and Lily hadn't wanted to blast. So they had tied their footings into the ledge and gone up from there. They would lay the plywood subfloor over these joists tomorrow. They'd have the walls up inside of a week. From the second floor you would see most of Abenaki Lake.

The rest of the crew had gone for the day, Kyle staying on just to check a few things. Mostly he liked having some time there alone. Lily would be flying the red-eye back, arriving down in Manchester in the morning. They'd be dancing on the first floor deck by the afternoon.

Her deck. Their deck. She had not said no.

She had not objected to seven-foot doorways, high enough for him to walk through without ducking. She had not objected to his-and-her sinks in the master bath. She had not argued with his suggestion of where the bed should go, where to put the window so you could see the lake without taking your head off the pillow.

His head, her head.

She had wanted three bedrooms, saying matter-of-factly: "Maybe I'll have children."

She had not let him co-sign the loan.

Lily had moved out of her apartment in North Ridgeway and was staying with Clarence and Sylvia while the house was built. She spent most of her nights at Kyle's. He had put a skylight in his bedroom so that she would feel less confined. Some mornings he woke to find her on her back and staring up through it. Together they watched wind shake sunlit leaves against the tattered blue.

"I dreamed I'd been made president of a small country, someplace hot and flat, no trees, the people mean and sweaty. They made baseball bats and rubbed them with Vaseline. I told them I couldn't be president because I had to be a grandmother. Just like that. I wasn't even a mother yet, but I knew I had to be a grandmother, and then there they were, all these kids, penned in with chicken wire in the yard, hundreds of them, crawling on all fours and wagging their tails like hairless dogs. I had to feed them out of fifty pound dog food bags, which I knew was terrible, but it was all I could manage. The food was spilling out on the ground."

"You'll make a fine grandmother," Kyle said.

"Kids will hate me. I'll growl and poke them with broom handles."

"They'll learn to avoid you on your off days," Kyle said.

Lily then rolled on her side to face him.

"Kyle, be honest now." Her eyes wide with urgency. "Do you really think an eight over twelve roof isn't too boring?"

He assured her that eight over twelve was a fine roof pitch, the finest he knew.

"And we agree that shed dormers are tacky?"

He reaffirmed his view that gabled dormers were the only way to go.

"And if I ever marry somebody, he won't spend years learning to hate my eyebrows, or the sound of me blowing my nose, or the way I hold my spoon, and decide that these are precisely the things

349

he promised himself from a young age that he would never have to endure?"

Kyle assured her that for the man lucky enough to marry her, these things would not be a problem.

Then he asked her a yes or no question. She did not say yes, and she did not say no.

The house was sited at the edge of the forest, leaving as much of the clearing undisturbed as possible. They had cleared downslope enough for the leaching field, but she would want to do more later, for the view. When he suggested that someday she might want to build a small barn, with a woodshop such as a carpenter might need, she had simply nodded, as though this was only reasonable. Her flight came in at six the next morning.

Kyle bent and banged with his framing hammer at the joist he stood upon, knocking the board true. He could rise at four and meet the plane. He could shave with a new blade. He could clean his fingernails. Walking out to his truck, he could pick that bunch of daisies growing by the drive. He would ask her one more time.

About the Author

Philip Simmons, writer and teacher, started working on this book, his first novel, while still a professor at Lake Forest College in Illinois. Early drafts were read to friends and colleagues, and they loved it. But in 1993, Simmons was diagnosed with ALS, Lou Gehrig's Disease, a degenerative neuromuscular condition, always fatal. Simmons was warned that he would live only 2 - 4 years. Suddenly, all his attention focused on coping, on moving the family to a familiar place, to his beloved woods of New Hampshire. He had little time. This book was put on a back burner.

He beat those odds, and lived nearly 10 years. In that time he devoted himself to his writing. He wrote a book of essays, *Learning to Fall: The Blessings of an Imperfect Life*; he founded a community arts group, the Yeoman's Fund, in his hometown of Center Sandwich, NH; he wrote essays and poems, still unpublished; he gave speeches at Universities, Colleges and church, did radio interviews nationally and locally, and managed somehow to squeeze time in to complete *Rattlesnake Ridge*. *Rattlesnake Ridge* was finished but never edited nor published.

Simmons was born in Washington, DC, and grew up in Winchester, MA, spending summers among the hills and lakes of central New Hampshire that became the setting for *Rattlesnake Ridge*. He earned degrees in English and physics from Amherst College, a Master of Fine Arts from Washington University in St. Louis and a Ph.D. in English from the University of Michigan. He published both short fiction and criticism, including *Deep Surfaces*, a

351

work praised by the distinguished critic, William Pritchard, as an example of someone who really cared about literature and wanted to share it with others.

Simmons died on July 27, 2002 at the age of 45. His wife, artist Kathryn Field, picked up *Rattlesnake Ridge* and decided to get it published. It was finished but unedited. That's where David Reich came in. He polished the text with great skill and good humor. Reich, a former editor at *UU World,* the national magazine of the Unitarian Universalist Association, had been editing Simmons's work since the middle 1990s. In fact, many of the essays from *Learning to Fall* were published in the UU *World* first, and when it came time to put the collection together, Reich edited that, too. An admirer not only of Simmons's writing but also of the courage with which he lived and died, Reich says, "I am thankful to have had the chance to edit Phil's last work."